D0436707

ALSO BY DIANA RENN

Tokyo Heist
Latitude Zero

WITHDRAWN

Blue Voyage

DIANA RENN

VIKING

VIKING
An Imprint of Penguin Random House LLC
375 Hudson Street
New York, New York 10014

First published in the United States of America by Viking,
an imprint of Penguin Random House LLC, 2015

Copyright © 2015 by Diana Renn

Penguin supports copyright. Copyright fuels creativity, encourages diverse voices,
promotes free speech, and creates a vibrant culture. Thank you for buying an authorized
edition of this book and for complying with copyright laws by not reproducing, scanning,
or distributing any part of it in any form without permission. You are supporting writers
and allowing Penguin to continue to publish books for every reader.

LIBRARY OF CONGRESS CATALOGING-IN-PUBLICATION DATA
Renn, Diana.
Blue voyage / by Diana Renn.
pages cm
Summary: "Adrenaline junkie Zan finds herself in the crosshairs of an antiquities
smuggling ring while on vacation with her mother. She must help them find the ancient
treasure they seek in order to keep her family safe!" —Provided by publisher.
ISBN 978-0-670-01559-7 (hardcover)
[1. Smuggling—Fiction. 2. Turkey—Antiquities—Fiction. 3. Mystery and detective stories.]
I. Title.
PZ7.R2895Bl 2015
[Fic]—dc23
2015013011

Printed in U.S.A.

1   3   5   7   9   10   8   6   4   2

Set in Scherzo Std   Designed by Kate Renner

FOR all my parents:
Jan and Max Stiefel,
John and Sally Renn

Blue Voyage

PART ONE

The Turkish Riviera

1

Looking up from the Lonely Planet guide at the rocky hills all around us, I spoke for the first time in seventeen hours. "You know that sign we saw back at the roadblock?"

"What about it?" Mom asked.

"I'm pretty sure it said 'detour.'" When I pointed to the word in the "Useful Phrases" section of my guidebook, she tore her eyes off the desolate road to look. "We should have seen more of those signs if we were on the right track."

Mom gripped the steering wheel tighter. "Well. That's good to know, Zan."

I snapped the book shut and pressed my lips together.

"Does this mean you're officially breaking your vow of silence?" Mom asked.

I sunk low into the passenger seat, my arms folded across my chest. Until this moment, Mom and I hadn't exchanged words for the entire flight from Boston, Massachusetts, to the coastal town of Bodrum, Turkey, including airport transfers in Munich and Istanbul. But now it was hard to sit back and say nothing. After veering off the main road to Marmaris, Mom had been looping through the landscape on bumpy roads for almost two hours. There was no sign of the harbor town where we were supposed to meet Aunt Jackie for our Blue Voyage cruise. Our map from the car rental agency had flown out the window miles ago. Asking directions at a village restaurant had resulted in only more confusion, with men pointing us in three different directions.

The little Fiat shuddered as Mom shifted gears. "We'll get there," she said. "Remember our family motto? 'Things could always be worse.'"

Now that I'd started talking again, I couldn't hold back. "I thought it was 'Things are even worse than they seem.'" Though maybe Mom's backwardly optimistic motto made sense. After all, things *could* be a lot worse for me. Instead of being in forced exile in the Turkish Riviera at the moment, I could be doing court-ordered community service. I could be in juvie.

A police car zoomed up behind us, lights flashing. Instinctively, I tensed and ducked farther down in my seat. Which was ridiculous, since we'd been in Turkey for only a few hours and I hadn't broken any laws.

"That's the third police car we've seen!" Mom exclaimed as it passed.

"A good sign, right?" I said. "There must be some kind of civilization ahead. I mean, they have to be going somewhere."

"Maybe." Mom sounded doubtful. Then she sighed and chewed her lip. "God, what was I thinking, renting a car in Turkey?"

"Adventure," I reminded her. "Life experience. Fresh perspective."

"Right." Mom tucked a lock of her bobbed hair behind one ear. "Still, if we'd gone with that nice man at the airport transfer service, I wouldn't have gotten mixed up at the roadblock."

"What happened to doing stuff without men?" I asked. "Sisters are doing it for themselves. Standing on their own two feet. Remember?" I hummed a few bars of the song Mom had blasted over and over after Dad had moved out of the house last month.

She smiled and hummed along with me. So I stopped humming, since I'd only meant to remind her of her mission—I wasn't staging some mother-daughter bonding moment. Sure, we used to sing together, and laugh together. But now we were miles away from all that.

Mom stopped mid-hum. "Zan! Hold on!" she cried out, throwing her right arm in front of me. She hit the brakes. Hard.

I grabbed the handle above the window and squeezed my eyes shut. I heard weirdly inhuman wails outside the car, sounds in no language I knew.

Mom took her safety-latch arm off me, and I slowly opened my eyes. A group of goats clopped by, baring their teeth and bleating at us as they crossed the road. Then they trotted up a hill bristling with pine trees.

Mom sighed, and I released my death grip on the door handle. Then, seeing a blue stripe in the distance, I sat up straight. "Hey. Isn't that water? Could that be Marmaris down there?"

"I think so," said Mom. When we saw a sign for Marmaris a moment later, she sped up as fast as the Fiat would let her. The road wound downhill, spiraling toward the harbor like a nautilus seashell.

I kept my eyes trained on that blue stripe of water, afraid that if I looked away we'd veer off course again. Whenever I'd thought of Turkey in the past, my images were based on things I'd heard from my expat aunt Jackie and her Turkish husband, Berk. The storybooks and presents they'd given me over the years had led me to imagine a land of soaring minarets and domed mosques, belly dancers and samovars, djinns and flying carpets. But on the road for the past couple of hours, my senses had felt dulled by the crumbling landscape—the dirt, the dust, the rocks, broken up only occasionally by an olive grove, a forest, or a village. Sometimes women working in fields—they were always women, for some reason—stared at our passing car.

Now, finally, we were heading toward color, toward something interesting. The blue stripe grew in size and intensity as we neared. It practically vibrated.

I switched on the car radio. After flipping through scratchy stations, I found some electronica that sounded vaguely Turkish: stringed instruments I didn't recognize wailing against a pulsing dance beat. It was kind of cool. I cranked it up.

Mom switched off the radio.

I glared at her. "What? It's not enough you took my phone, now I can't even listen to music?"

"I need to focus. This is extremely stressful driving." The road had widened, and traffic suddenly picked up, merging from unseen roads. Cars and huge trucks sped by, passing us on both sides, horns blaring. Mom sat rigid, eyes unblinking.

We rounded the next bend in the road, the white, crumbling hills and scrubby trees offering up a fresh view. I sucked in my breath sharply at the sight of masts of countless boats swaying in a crescent-shaped harbor. The sun danced across the turquoise water, making it shimmer. As we descended to the Port of Marmaris, I couldn't stop staring at the glittering harbor, at the Mediterranean Sea, at that rich, impossible blue.

◇◇◇◇◇

Up close, the harbor reminded me of a carousel. Only instead of horses it was filled with wooden yachts—called *gulets*, according to Lonely Planet—bobbing merrily up and down in their moorings. Most of them had blue, green, or red stripes painted across their gleaming wood hulls. The sails were rolled up and covered. Turkish flags flapped from the masts: red with a white crescent moon and a star.

With a pang, I realized my dad would have loved this view too. When I was little, my family had a small sailboat—*The Whisper*—that we kept moored in Hingham. Dad had sold it eventually, admitting that he wasn't a very good sailor. Mom was never that into the boat and all the labor it involved. They used to argue about it: *You just want the boat for show. You don't want to do the actual work that having a boat requires,* Mom had seethed at him once, on the dock, as she blasted a sail with a pressure-washer. Still, I had a few happy memories of helping Dad steer around Hingham harbor, and going to the Boston boat show with him. His eyes would always light up as he imagined taking the helm of a new boat.

But all that was ancient history now. I dropped those happy memories into a little stone well deep inside me and sealed them up tight.

After we returned the rental car, Mom and I ran along the harbor, up and down one long dock after another, looking for our boat. Our suitcase wheels thumped on the boards and scraped across the asphalt. Our bags bashed into each other like misbehaving dogs.

There was so much to see, I kept getting distracted. The late-afternoon sun was beginning to lower, casting our surroundings in gold. The narrow boardwalk was clogged with people: tourists, boat crews, and salespeople from travel agencies waving tickets and flyers. Men outside the restaurants and cafés across the street waved menus and called out to us. Girls and women strolled past, arm in arm, some of them dressed in head scarves and chic yet conservative outfits—blazers and long, tailored skirts. A group of British girls looked like an exotic school of fish in comparison, wearing bright tank tops and tight skirts, revealing so much skin. They brushed past me as if I were not there as they hurried across the street to a souvenir shop.

I instinctively reached into my pants pocket, thinking I'd snap a picture and share it with my friends. Then I remembered my phone wouldn't work in Turkey. And then I remembered I had no phone. That buzzing I felt on my leg was like the presence of a phantom limb, the phone not in my pocket. I'd lost phone privileges in May, after what was now known in my family as the "Athleta incident." And *then* I remembered that none of that even mattered anymore because I'd also lost my friends. Even if I could take pictures of my every move, who the hell would care?

So instead I just took mental snapshots of this mix of people. Which eventually wasn't such a mix of people. Mostly what we saw as we continued along were men, seemingly appearing out of nowhere. Men leaped into our path and followed us at every turn.

"Ladies! Ladies! Let me show you my boat!"

"My cousin, he own carpet shop, not far. You have time to look for carpets, yes?"

"I have boat. I can get you good deal."

"I have leather shop, not far. I have jackets, they look beautiful on you."

It was kind of fun at first, getting all that attention. Usually Mom was the one who turned heads, not me. Her Pilates regimen kept her fit; with her monthly facials, crisp preppy outfits, and expensive highlights, she was prettier and younger-looking than most of my former friends' moms. Then again, those moms didn't have to look pretty for the cover of *Boston* magazine or TV interviews.

But now I was getting just as much attention, even though I wasn't dressed to look twice at. I was wearing my usual long-sleeved running shirt and loose-fitting cargos. Most likely these men were staring at my mom because she was pretty, and at me because I was a freak. It was entirely possible I'd sweated off my foundation in that hot car ride.

At a kiosk where we paused to buy water and ask for help finding our boat, I glanced at my reflection. My long brown bangs were pulled forward so they covered most of my face in case of Catastrophic Makeup Failure, and the brim of my pink Red Sox cap was pulled down low over my eyes. I pulled my hair back and performed a quick inspection. I always wore heavy foundation on my left cheek, under my nose, and

on my forehead, to cover up lost pigment caused by my vitiligo. Without the makeup, the patches were really noticeable.
Fortunately the makeup seemed intact; no white splotches
showed through.

"Zan, let's go!" Mom called, an edge to her voice, and I hurried to catch up.

The directions the kiosk salesclerk had given us to our boat
didn't make sense, nor did directions three other people gave
us, pointing us in different directions. Once again, we were
lost. As the shadows lengthened across the docks, some turned
into more men, with more offers: boat rides, fresh fish, plastic-
wrapped socks. The attention wasn't fun anymore. It was
exhausting.

"Ignore the hustlers," Mom muttered when I opened my
mouth to hurl back a retort at a guy who kept waving nightclub
flyers in my face. "Avoid eye contact."

"At least there are police here," I said, noticing a couple of
parked white cars with the now-familiar POLIS sign on them.
"Maybe they can give us reliable directions." Normally I steered
clear of police. I always felt as if they could see right through
me, even when I hadn't done anything wrong. But right now
I'd have taken help from anyone just to stop running around
in the heat and the crowds.

"I don't know," said Mom, frowning. "They look a little
preoccupied."

I followed her gaze. Two officers wearing pale blue shirts
and navy blue pants and caps walked briskly up and down
the docks, speaking into walkie-talkies. Four others talked
in a huddle, with serious faces. Mom tried approaching them
anyway, holding out our boat reservation ticket, but they just
looked annoyed and waved her aside.

Finally we found a female tour operator. She looked at our
tickets and said we'd been misreading the dock number. She
sent us to the correct dock, and we spotted our boat at last, our
home for the next three nights: a gleaming brown yacht with

the words *"Gulet Yasemin"* in white letters on the side. The boat had two masts, with the sails rolled up and covered in blue canvas. A blue awning stretched across the stern, providing shade on the deck. Another wide deck up at the bow offered more space, plastic chairs, and no shelter from the sun. That's the part of the yacht I'd be avoiding.

Then I spotted Aunt Jackie pacing on the dock beside it, her gauzy white tunic and blue palazzo pants fluttering in the breeze. I pointed her out to Mom, and we both broke into a run. My throat felt tight. I'd never been so glad to see her. How weird it was to think we had actual *family* here, in such a foreign place.

2

"Jackie! We made it! We're here!" Mom called out, waving frantically.

Aunt Jackie turned toward us, beaming. She set down a large canvas tote bag she was carrying and hugged me first. I could feel her bones through her clothes. "Zanny! Or should I call you Alexandra now?" She pulled back and looked at me. "You're all grown-up since the last time I saw you."

"You can call me Zan," I said. "I usually go by that." I studied her face, noting the fine lines etched around her eyes and the dark shadows beneath them. She was sporting a new haircut, her once-long blonde hair now cut short and spiky. But instead of looking cheerful and hip, it looked limp. Actually, all of Aunt Jackie looked wilted.

Aunt Jackie and Mom hugged gingerly and briefly, more like strangers than sisters.

"So what's with all the men here?" Mom asked. "It's been such a trial, just getting around. Do I have a sign on my back that says 'I'm a tourist, rip me off'?"

"Oh, not all the men here are like that," said Aunt Jackie. "You know that Berk wasn't. It's just Marmaris. It's a scene here, isn't it? Anyway, I'm *so* glad you got here in time. I was getting worried. I kept calling your cell, but you didn't pick up!"

"I thought I'd set it up for roaming charges, but it didn't work. My phone's dead," said Mom.

"Well, I was desperate to reach you. I wasn't sure if you'd be able to get through. The police around here are setting up roadblocks."

Mom raised her eyebrows. "There's more than one roadblock?"

"Lots. Police are working with Interpol to close in on a criminal network. There's been a rash of robberies all along the coast."

"So that's why we keep seeing police!" I exclaimed.

"What's being robbed?" Mom asked.

"Museums, mostly," said Aunt Jackie. "A few mosques. Turkish artifacts and Islamic art objects are being taken from storage facilities."

Mom frowned. "That's horrible."

"I know. They're not only blocking off roads, they're inspecting all the boats here at the docks."

"For stolen art?" I asked.

"Yes, and they're looking at passenger manifests and passports, too," said Aunt Jackie. "In case the thieves are looking to use the water as an escape route. We were just told to disembark for about ten minutes during the inspection." She gestured toward the boat, which had three policemen and a coast guard official in it. One of the officers was talking to the captain, while another flipped through papers on a clipboard. I took a step backward and hid behind Mom. That old reflex again: *See police. Hide.*

"So I was trying to call and tell you to have your driver seek alternate routes," Aunt Jackie went on. "Gosh, I wish you'd flown into Dalaman like I told you to. It's *much* easier to get to Marmaris from that airport. Did the taxi driver from Bodrum rip you off?"

"Nope, I rented my own car," said Mom, holding her head a little higher.

"Wait. You *drove*? Kitsie! I'm so impressed! Driving in Turkey's not easy."

"Thank you," Mom said with a smile. "But enough about me. I want to know how you're doing."

Aunt Jackie shrugged. "Dealing. Trying, anyway," she added. She took a deep, shuddery breath and blew it out long. Ginger-flavored, I noticed, as she'd been sucking on some kind of candy. Then she pressed her hands to her eyes and stood still, swaying slightly.

That's when it really hit me: Aunt Jackie had lost her husband. Widows weren't just creepy old ladies in fairy tales. *She* was a widow now. And the wound must still be fresh for her. It had only been six weeks since Uncle Berk had lost his footing while hiking in the Cappadocia region of Turkey. He'd gone off a marked trail, slipped on an eroded patch of ground on a cliff, and plummeted to his death. It was ruled a tragic accident, though Mom said Aunt Jackie was convinced there was foul play behind it.

That was actually one of the reasons Mom had dragged me here for the summer: she was sure her sister was losing it. I'd recently overheard her discussing the situation with Grandma and Grandpa. "The police investigation *clearly* showed that there was only one set of footprints there, and they belonged to Berk. They matched his shoes, right up to the place where the ground gave way. There was no sign of a scuffle. She's having a terrible time accepting the truth."

"Bring her home, Kitsie," Grandma had said. "I'd go get her myself, if I were strong enough to travel that far."

Watching Aunt Jackie brush tears from her eyes now, and Mom's face twisting in sympathy, I probably should have felt more emotional about the whole thing. But the sharp twinge I felt was guilt, not sadness. Maybe I felt guilty about not feeling sad. The fact is, I never knew Uncle Berk that well. He was a quiet man, kind of intense, his nose usually buried in an archaeological journal or some paper he was editing. He always seemed to be working.

I actually didn't know my aunt that well, either. She and Uncle Berk had met when they were both in grad school at Boston University. They'd gotten engaged on a trip to Turkey, married in Boston, and moved to Turkey permanently soon after, when Uncle Berk got a job at the Archaeological Museum in Istanbul. Aunt Jackie got hired to teach English at a high school. They visited us and my grandparents only once a year. For some reason, my family had never gone to Turkey to visit them. Until now, thanks to Aunt Jackie's obsession with murder and cover-ups, my sudden notoriety in Boston, and Mom's frantic need to get us out of the spotlight.

Mom patted Aunt Jackie on the back. "Hey. It will be okay. We'll help you."

Aunt Jackie shot her a skeptical look. I couldn't blame her. How could Mom and my grandparents have left Aunt Jackie all alone to deal with her loss? No one in our family had flown out to Istanbul to attend the funeral, even though Aunt Jackie and Uncle Berk owned a boutique hotel and we could have stayed for free. How lame was that?

"We're here now," Mom reminded her, more firmly, as if reading my thoughts.

"I know. And I'm really glad you came," Aunt Jackie said. "But I'm starting to feel like going on a Blue Voyage cruise at this time was a really bad idea."

"No, Jackie. It's a *good* idea. You convinced me of it," Mom said. "Look, I know it's a busy time to leave your hotel for a few days, but you have a capable staff. And you're going to finally have some closure, going on the archaeological cruise Berk was to lecture on, and revisiting the site where you two got engaged."

Aunt Jackie nodded. "I know. You're right," she said, unconvincingly.

"And besides, it's all been paid for," Mom went on. "You were supposed to go with him anyway. He'd *insist* that you go."

Aunt Jackie smiled sadly. "You're probably right." Then she glanced back at the *Gulet Yasemin.* "Here's the thing, though. Everyone's so disappointed that Berk isn't giving the lecture."

Mom raised her eyebrows. "I thought they replaced him with another guest speaker."

"They did. Right away. But that replacement went to the hospital last night. Appendicitis. They couldn't get anyone else on short notice. And it was Berk the guests really wanted to hear." Aunt Jackie sighed. "The Lycian Society sent a representative over to explain the situation and go through the itinerary for shore excursions with local guides, but it hasn't gone over very well so far with the other passengers."

I remembered that the Lycian Society was some kind of historical society. Mom had told me they also had an educational tourism office offering chartered archaeological boat tours of ancient sites in the Mediterranean.

"What do you mean it hasn't gone over very well?" Mom asked. "Are they rioting?"

Aunt Jackie looked pained. "They're drinking. They got into the wine right after they found out who I was. Erdem Tabak— that's the tour office representative—had to insist, three times, that I wasn't Berk's replacement. Can you imagine? I'm not even an archaeologist."

"Couldn't you do some version of Uncle Berk's lecture?" I asked. "From notes or something?"

She smiled wryly. "I'm afraid not. He never used lecture notes. He knew his subjects thoroughly. Besides, I'm an English teacher. I know remarkably little about his field. Anyway, the other passengers are nice enough to me, but their disappointment is obvious. This one Australian man keeps shooting me looks, and muttering to his wife about being gypped. Like it's my fault or something." She gave a sharp, strangled laugh. "I mean, I'm disappointed, too, right? Doesn't he get that? I was supposed to be on this romantic cruise with my husband, watching him in his element, talking about topics that were close to his heart. I never dreamed he'd get killed."

"Jackie. Berk *fell*. Careful what you say," Mom whispered. "You don't want to mislead people."

Aunt Jackie's eyes blazed. "He *was* killed, Kitsie. He was. We've talked about this."

"Wait, how do you know?" I couldn't help asking.

Aunt Jackie turned to me with an odd, eager look on her face, as if grateful to have a potential supporter. Mom pressed her hands to her temples and began rubbing them in slow circles. "You were pretty young," said Aunt Jackie, "but do you remember when Berk broke his leg hiking five years ago?"

I nodded. They'd cancelled a Christmas visit to Boston because of that accident.

"Well, right after that he promised me—from his hospital bed—that he'd never hike alone again. *Especially* if he were going off the beaten path. So I'm *positive* he didn't go on his own to the edge of that bluff where he fell. He had to have been *coerced* into going there."

"By whom?" I asked.

"That's the great mystery," she said. "But I have theories. I think—"

"Jackie. Men break their promises all the time," Mom interrupted. "I should know."

"Berk's not like that. He's always been a man of his word. And he died in an area where other hikers and mountain bikers have been robbed, assaulted, and, yes, even killed." Aunt Jackie's eyes grew wide. "This week, I dug up news reports of *five* suspicious deaths that have happened there in the past year."

"The cave-ins, right?" Mom asked. "That made international news. Some of those old caves out there got damaged in last year's earthquake, and some are beyond repair. I heard about some hikers getting buried alive."

"That's true," said Aunt Jackie, tapping her foot. "And tragic. But I'm talking about deaths that weren't accidental. There have been cases that get superficially investigated and then dropped. Why?" She looked at me, as if I could possibly know the answer, and I shrugged. "Because someone's *paying some-one off* to cover up the crimes out there. They need the tourist business."

I watched Aunt Jackie carefully. She had a wild look in her eyes. Dad always referred to her as "the crazy one." But was it crazy to think criminal cases could get buried by people with money?

Aunt Jackie was talking a mile a minute now, almost babbling. "There are warning signs about crimes in every parking lot in every national park in Cappadocia," she said. "And *still* the police want to call this an accident. You really want to help me out, Kitsie? Help me find the monster who took my husband's life. Help me convince the government that the investigation should not have closed after only two weeks. They're putting in all this effort to find robbers on the coast, but meanwhile innocent people are getting *killed* in Cappadocia!"

Several passersby turned to look at us. One woman ushered her small children away.

"Jackie." Mom laid a hand gently on Aunt Jackie's arm. "I'm happy to listen to anything you want to say. But I think now isn't the time or place."

The policemen came down the gangway of our boat, glancing at us and then—to my relief—moving on. The captain waved us on board. Six other people came up the dock, pushed past us, and boarded, followed by an anxious-looking man in a blue polo shirt with a Lycian Tours logo on the pocket.

"So." Mom flashed a tight smile and went into her work-mode voice, chirpy and efficient. "Looks like we've got the all-clear. Shall we get on this vessel before it sails?"

Aunt Jackie took the handles of our suitcases, which we'd set down on the dock, and managed a small smile. "Of course.

I'm sorry. You two must be exhausted, running around with those bags in this heat." And even though she looked so fragile, she dragged both our suitcases up the gangway and onto the boat, when two men dressed in khaki shorts and white polo shirts rushed forward to collect them from her.

On board, a smiling, gray-haired gentleman named Captain Mehmet took our tickets and apologized for the inconvenience of the police inspection. He introduced his small crew, just two other men: his first mate, Selim, and the galley cook, Orhan. Then we met the other six passengers. They were lounging on the gleaming teak deck beneath the blue awning, sitting on bolsters and wicker-backed chairs. They were drinking wine and sampling appetizers, which they told us were called meze. The meze—stuffed grape leaves, hummus, yogurt, cold cuts, white cheese, and stuffed vegetables—were spread out in a tempting array on the table. My stomach rumbled appreciatively.

Friendly and tipsy, the passengers introduced themselves in a variety of accents: British, Australian, Norwegian. There was no one else from Massachusetts, thank God. No one who knew our pathetic story.

As for people my age? Zero. The first mate, Selim, a skinny guy with close-cropped hair and acne scars, was the youngest of the crew. But he looked to be in his late twenties and was definitely not hot. The next up in age was the galley cook, Orhan. He was easier on the eyes, with olive skin, thick but shapely eyebrows, and dark, wavy hair. He wore tight black jeans and a fitted polo shirt that accentuated his muscles. He looked more like a fitness trainer than a cook, and acted like one, too—from all the banging around we could hear in the kitchen, and the way he set everything down a little too hard on the table, he seemed too big for the space. Too big for the boat, even. But he also looked to be in his mid-thirties. Ancient.

This was the geezer cruise. I hadn't talked to someone my age in so long, it would have been nice if there were just *one* person on this boat I could hang with. But no.

We all gathered around the long table and sampled the meze, except for Aunt Jackie, who said she wasn't hungry, though I saw her pop open a little tin from her canvas bag and eat a couple more ginger-scented candies. Captain Mehmet and first mate Selim went over basic safety rules on the boat. Some of the passengers weren't listening, though. Mom, Aunt Jackie, and I sat down on some cushioned seats at starboard. I could see passengers shooting dark looks at Erdem Tabak, the tense-looking tour representative, while he filled out meal vouchers for restaurants at our ports of call. I could hear two of the passengers near us, an Australian couple, muttering about how disappointing the cruise was going to be.

"Mind you, we mean no offense," the Australian man, Milton, whispered to Aunt Jackie.

"And we're very sorry for your loss," his wife, Maeve, added, more kindly. "We just want to get our money's worth. We've come from the other side of the world to see this, you know. And Milton's not sure that the local guides at the ports of call will give the detailed explanations we'd expect from a Lycian Tours guest speaker."

"I understand perfectly," said Aunt Jackie. "I wish there was something I could do for you all."

Orhan, the cook, came out of the kitchen carrying two fresh bottles of wine. While Orhan uncorked the wine bottles, the Lycian Tours rep stood up and passed out the restaurant vouchers. "Please enjoy some complimentary meals at your ports of call," he said. "And know that you will not be lacking in any experiences or information on your Blue Voyage. We have a network of excellent local guides ready to give you the best Turkish experience possible. Your smooth transfers at all shore excursions are taken care of for you. You should have no worries."

Milton cleared his throat. "What about the police presence around here?" he asked. "Shouldn't we be worried about that?"

Erdem Tabak smiled. "Not at all," he said. "This is only a

standard safety precaution. Let me also assure you that Lycian Tours partners with the very best cruise operators in this region. You are in very good hands on this boat."

"What about a partial reimbursement?" demanded an older British woman. "Meal vouchers and buses are nice, but we paid for a speaker on board that we're not getting now."

"Right. Yes. Of course." Erdem Tabak stroked his thick mustache and looked almost longingly toward the boat's railing, as if he'd like to leap overboard. "I have put in a request at the head office, and am waiting for authorization. I will check in with you again at Fethiye, which is your final port of call, and I will let you know the result."

The passengers continued to grumble and whisper among themselves.

"Meanwhile, will you happily enjoy some more wine?" he said, a note of desperation creeping into his voice.

These magic words stopped the grumbling. The old folks lined up with their glasses, and Orhan cheerfully filled them. He even filled an extra one and handed it to me.

I reached for it, but Mom practically knocked the glass out of his hand with the look she shot him. Then she took the glass for herself. "My daughter is only sixteen," she said. "No wine for her." As Orhan slunk off toward the kitchen, she whispered, "Remember, your party days are over. Alcohol flows freely on cruises, but not for you. You are drying out. And I am watching you."

My cheeks burned. I could feel the curious stares of some of the other passengers as we sat down across from each other at the end of the table.

"Why don't you just lock me in a room below deck, then," I muttered. "Might as well. Since I have no freedom."

"You think eating appetizers on a yacht on the Turkish Riviera is no freedom?" Mom snapped. "How about sitting in a four-by-six cell in juvie? Because that's where you could be!"

I looked down at my feet, shifting, feeling the strangers' stares glance off my skin.

"I need to know where you are at all times," Mom continued, "thanks to your record of extremely poor decision-making. So guess what? I don't have freedom, either."

I met her eyes again. My breath came fast as we sat there glaring at each other. "Dad's the criminal here," I said. "We wouldn't even be here if it weren't for what he'd done."

"Don't offload all the blame on him," she snapped. "You're old enough to be responsible for your behavior. And face it. The only reason you don't have more of a record is because he intervened. Bargaining with those stores, cutting deals, just to protect your name."

"He didn't do it to protect my name. He did it to protect himself! And why are you suddenly defending him? Why are you on his side now?"

"It's not about sides. I know you're angry at him right now, but he's still your father. And your situation could be a hell of a lot worse if—" Mom bit her lip and fell silent as Orhan cautiously approached us again, this time with a basket of pita bread.

"Perhaps you would enjoy some pita?" he asked, a note of concern in his voice.

Mom took a slice. "How did you guess. Thank you."

Orhan held the basket out to me. "You'll have to ask my mother," I said. "She makes all my decisions for me now."

Orhan looked at Mom questioningly.

Mom sighed, reached into the basket, and handed me a pita.

We chewed in silence for a moment. The pita was probably the best I had ever tasted, incredibly light and soft. But it failed to smooth out the tension between me and Mom.

"What do you want from me, Zan?" Mom asked as Orhan moved away.

"Just stop treating me like a criminal."

"Happy to. When you stop acting like one. Even before the shoplifting, you were sneaking out and partying with your friends. You want my trust? Earn it back."

"Well, lucky for you, I lost all my friends. You must be thrilled."

"I'm not thrilled. And if you lost them so easily, maybe they weren't really your friends."

"You never liked anyone I hung out with," I complained.

"Okay, now you're just picking a fight. And you're pissing me off," she said, struggling to keep her voice lowered. "And could you maybe think about someone else besides yourself for two seconds? We're here for Aunt Jackie. To provide moral support. We can't do that if we're at each other's throats. Do I make myself clear?"

"Oh, sure. You want us to just fake it, right? Act like everything's perfect and we have a perfect little life. Even though there's no one here to interview us."

Now Selim approached. He reached between us for our suitcases—gingerly, as if he were sticking his hand into a bee's nest—and took them by the handles. He offered to take Mom and me below deck and show us our room.

Selim led us down the stairs to a hallway with gleaming wooden walls, and Aunt Jackie followed. He opened the door to a room that was just across from Aunt Jackie's. But the room was so small that she had to wait outside while Mom and I moved our luggage in.

"I thought I was getting my own room," I said, surveying the tiny space in dismay.

Mom glared at me. "Hey. These cabins are not cheap. Do you know how lucky we are to be on this cruise? Aunt Jackie had a free ticket, since Berk was supposed to lecture, but for us to come, I had to buy two."

I backed away, as much as I could in a room that was only six feet wide. "Okay, okay. I just thought, you know, when we all traveled before, like to Mexico and stuff, I always had my own room, so . . ."

"Well, these are not those times. This is now. This is different. Everything is different!" Mom yelled.

Selim, who had been standing at the foot of our bed with a frozen smile, backed into the narrow bathroom and pretended to fix a hinge on the door.

Mom rubbed her temples. "It's been a long day for both of us. Can we call a truce?"

I didn't answer. Forget the vow of silence; I was all out of words. Nothing I could say would please my mom. I opened my suitcase and took out a fresh, lighter-weight shirt to change into as soon as Selim left our cabin. It was cooling off a little up on deck, but down here, it was sticky hot.

"Always lock your suitcase," Mom warned as I half-zipped it again. "You never know who's inclined to steal something," she added with a long look.

That remark could only be aimed at me. Her criticism, my God. It never ended. I zipped my bag all the way closed and flipped the lock with a dramatic gesture, just to get her off my back.

"An Academy Award-worthy performance," said Mom, watching me.

"Thank you," I said, bowing. Then I sank gratefully onto the crisp, white sheets of my berth and gazed out a porthole window, while Selim explained the bathroom fixtures to Mom. Suddenly my eyelids felt so heavy. I couldn't process what Selim was saying in his broken English about how to transform the sink in our closet-sized bathroom into a makeshift shower, or where the life jackets were, or what time breakfast was served, or the name of our first port of call.

"Zan?" said Mom, after Selim had left our cabin. "Don't you want to come up and have something more to eat? Get to know our traveling companions?" Her voice sounded far away, as if she were underwater.

"Not hungry," I murmured, closing my eyes as the boat gently rocked. The meze and pita bread had filled me up.

The door clicked behind her as she left to join Aunt Jackie in the hall. "Sorry. She's being her difficult self," I heard Mom murmur.

My mom's and aunt's voices trailed off. I was already slipping away, into sleep, letting the boat lull me into the sense that everything would somehow be okay. I still wasn't forgiving Mom for dragging me into a summer of exile. And it was totally unfair that *I* was being punished for my dad's stupid decisions. But as far as places for exile went, Turkey wasn't the worst. Spending the whole summer here wouldn't kill me. Right?

3

Most people have pretty simple stories about how they ended up in a foreign country. They wanted to go on vacation. They bought an airplane ticket. They went. End of story.

Mine's a little more complicated.

Once upon a time, my dad, the Massachusetts attorney general, decided to run for governor. His approval ratings were sky-high because of how he'd handled a corruption case.

Or maybe they were high because he had great hair. The media always liked to comment on how he had just the right touch of dignified gray at the temples, never a single hair out of place. What they didn't know was that Dad's personal hairdresser came to our house every week to touch it up. He spent more on his hair than Mom did.

Things were good from the end of my freshman year, when he announced his plans to run, and all summer long, and even into the start of my sophomore year. Mom quit her job and put all her event-planning energy on fund-raisers for Dad's campaign. Celebrities with ties to Massachusetts turned out to show their support. My friends and I got to meet all the local royalty. Ben Affleck and Jennifer Garner. Steven Tyler. Chris

Cooper. Tom Brady and Gisele. A steady parade of Red Sox and Bruins.

My own approval ratings at Cabot High School skyrocketed, too. I had tickets to all the hot Boston events. I suspected, deep down, that people were more interested in me because of the perks of being friends with the potential governor's daughter than because of any desire to get to know the real me. There were times I had no idea who my real friends were anymore. And sometimes being photographed was exhausting, or having to dress and act a certain way, or darting into bathrooms to make sure my makeup was okay. To make sure *I* was okay. I felt that if I stopped and let down my guard, I'd explode into a million pieces.

But I liked the challenge of juggling social plans, deciding whom to invite to things and whose invitations I should accept. I liked seeing my picture in magazines and newspapers and on social media, knowing I'd pulled it off. People had fallen for my costume, my makeup, my entire act. On some level I knew that playing only a version of myself was deceitful, but it was fun, too, almost like a game, and I was good at it.

Then one day my dad's gubernatorial opponent launched a bomb: a video of my dad kissing a woman in the Boston Public Gardens. They were under a willow tree, surrounded by bags of takeout from Fresh City Wrap. Oh, did I mention this woman was *not* my mom?

The video made me sick to my stomach. I couldn't even watch the whole thing. And it got replayed all over the news, with headlines like "Attorney General Glazer Gets Fresh." Then, of course, there were all the joke headlines: "Close Shave for Glazer" and "Glazer's Sharp-Tongued Mistress." Because as it turned out, the woman was Victoria Windham, divorced heiress of the Boston-based Windham Shaving Company, which manufactured razors.

At the campaign manager's urging, my family met with a crisis management expert. Mom kept sputtering about how embarrassing it was: her life was now made-for-TV material. "It's bad enough you had to run around behind my back, but with *Victoria Windham,* of all people?" she shouted at Dad at that first meeting, before the crisis expert even had a chance to begin.

Victoria Windham was old Boston money, a philanthropist whose main job seemed to be doling out money to museums, foundations, and charities. She lived in a four-story townhouse on Beacon Hill, with her two greyhounds and a cat with no tail, and high-ceilinged rooms stuffed with art and antiques. I knew this because she'd hosted one of the key fund-raising parties for Dad's campaign—a party that *Mom* had organized.

Mom figured Victoria's generous campaign donations had to be the reason Dad was drawn to her. What other reason could there be? She was like the opposite of Mom, more dramatic-looking than pretty, and too skinny, with skeletal cheekbones and intense green eyes buried in deep sockets. She wore her long auburn hair halfway down her back like she probably had since high school. Usually she dressed all in black and smelled of strange perfume, which she told Mom and me she was learning to mix herself; she'd actually traveled to Thailand to take a perfume class. Rich people—I mean, *mega*-rich people—could be weird that way, pursuing eccentric interests and yakking about them to anyone who'd listen. I'd met enough to know.

At that meeting with the crisis management expert, Mom couldn't stop ranting about Victoria. "At least it wasn't an intern. I should be grateful, right?" Mom laughed bitterly.

Dad looked down and twirled one of those fancy pens he collects, an astronaut pen that they say can write upside down and even in outer space, which is probably where he wished he was at that very moment.

I shrank into the leather couch and pulled at my running-shirt sleeves, which had somehow crept up my wrists to reveal the constellations of white spots on my hands. I couldn't shake the thought that I could have prevented this mess. I'd seen clues for weeks. Texts coming in to my dad's phone, with messages like, *Can you get away for an hour?* Or *Desperately missing you.* I'd heard him end calls when Mom or I came into the room. That, of course, was when he was actually home, which was next to never. Long hours at work, longer hours on the campaign trail.

Then there was the big clue, in Victoria's bedroom. Where, yes, okay, fine, I had been snooping while my mom was helping set up that big fund-raising party in February. Why was I snooping? I don't really know. I just did that sometimes. My shrink said it was from growing up in a political household, around people who were always trying to stay a step ahead of someone else. *You were raised in an atmosphere of mistrust.*

So during the party setup at Victoria's house, after using one of her bathrooms, instead of heading back to the living room, I turned and walked down a corridor to her bedroom. I looked at all her bottles of odd-smelling Thai perfume, and eventually found myself standing before her closet. I opened the French doors. And nearly fell over. One whole section was filled with button-down men's shirts. Pinstripes and pastels. My dad's initials monogrammed on the cuffs. *MDG,* for Marcus David Glazer. I stared at the shirts, then bolted from the room.

I arranged my face so my panic wouldn't betray me. I watched Dad and Victoria from afar and told myself lies to explain everything. The shirts? Extras, in case he spilled. Victoria's pat on my dad's arm? She was just being supportive. His smile at her from across the room? Meant to signal, "Great turnout tonight!" I had a whole alternate script by the end of the evening that I honestly tried to believe.

Maybe I could have talked to my dad, and convinced him to ditch Victoria, before it hit the news. I could have warned my mom. Then the whole thing could have been handled privately.

But I didn't say anything. I was too scared they'd blame me, somehow, for snooping. Or maybe I was scared that once I voiced my suspicion, it would become all too real.

The crisis management expert gently took over and got my mom off her Victoria Windham rant. A plan was formulated: My dad would sever all ties with Victoria and return her campaign donations. He would issue a public apology at a press conference. Mom and I would come along. We were given a script: *We are working as a family to get past this bump in the road. We are pulling together. We are all on board.*

"Voters will be moved by your resilience as a family," the expert explained. "Americans tend to be quite forgiving of sex scandals," she added, looking at Mom. Mom was staring ahead with a sharp glint in her eyes I'd never seen before.

Sex scandal. Because of course that's what it was. The video was just the tip of the iceberg. Dad and Victoria had been together since January, and now it was late May. Still, those words shocked me. I couldn't even look at him. All during my sophomore year, as his campaign for governor ramped up, he'd lectured me about how our family was in the spotlight, how I couldn't get in trouble, how everything we did would get magnified in the media and reflect back on him. How I should hang out with "quality people."

Then he had gone and done this.

Soon after the meeting, I found myself with Mom at Neiman Marcus shopping for conservative matchy-matchy dresses. The morning of the press conference, we both got our hair blown out, our makeup professionally done. It was almost like a party. Except I couldn't fight the feeling of dread inside me. The voters of Massachusetts would be watching us. As would my friends—or now, my ex-friends. Because as soon as the scandal broke, people stopped texting and calling, and the party invitations dried up. All those people who wanted stuff from me when the campaign was in full swing went out of their way now to avoid me. I was radioactive. All because of Dad. I tried to shrug it off, but it hurt to be dropped so fast, and to realize how shallow all my school friends were.

After our blowouts, I drank a couple of beers I'd stashed in my closet from one of my mom's parties. I grabbed my sports bag and told Mom I was taking the bus to the climbing gym. Burlington Boulders was my sanctuary, the one place where I felt as if I wasn't in the spotlight. On the wall, nobody cared who I was.

"Are you insane? Zan, you are so not climbing two hours before the press conference," Mom said, blocking the door. "You'll sweat and mess up your makeup."

"Ah, the makeup. We wouldn't want my real face emerging on TV, right?" I shot back.

"That's not what I meant. Come back here. You are not leaving this house!"

I pushed past her and walked out the door.

And kept walking. I took a bus to Burlington, but I didn't go to the rock gym for some reason. I went to the mall, and headed straight to the Athleta store, as if propelled by invisible forces. Everything felt underwater and unreal.

But what was real was this: though I'd left my parents to face the cameras at the press conference without me, I got caught on camera in the end—a security camera—stuffing three hundred dollars' worth of merchandise into my bag. A pair of leggings, a sports bra, and two of those long-sleeved tops I like, with the thumb hooks so the sleeves never ride up your arms. Which is about all you can get for three hundred bucks at Athleta. I was spluttering something about their criminal prices when mall security arrived.

I sobered up fast while I waited for Mom to show up. The security officers said she had sixty minutes to collect me before they called the police. Things only got worse when I saw that it wasn't Mom picking me up after the press conference; it was Dad.

I couldn't look at him. The last time I'd gotten caught, taking nail polish at a CVS, he'd said he couldn't keep springing me like this. That he was worried I'd "graduate" from lipsticks to pricier items. That's what the visits to the shrink's office were meant to combat.

We just sat in the car while he talked at me, his eyes blazing, not even driving for a long time. "Dammit." Dad slapped the steering wheel with his palm. "I had a chance of salvaging this campaign."

I shot him a skeptical look.

"My own daughter bolting from a press conference, and then breaking the *law*?" he continued. "You had to put the final nail in my coffin, didn't you? If this leaks out to the press, it could be the end of the road for the campaign."

"Are you kidding me?" I shot back. "Do you remember why we were having the stupid press conference in the first place? And by the way, your timing could use work, too."

"Look. I'm sorry you had to hear about Victoria and me the way you did," he said, taking his voice down a notch as he started up the car and pulled out of the parking lot. "But adult lives are complicated. We were both lost for a while, Victoria and I, and we found—"

I put up a hand. "Spare me the details."

"I just meant to say, things haven't been so easy for your mom and me for a while now. And every story has two sides. But *your* job, right now, is to stay the course. Go to school, join the temple youth group again, get your work done. Eye on the prize, Zan. You can't just be a reactor and live your life in meltdown mode. And you can't be acting out like this. Three hundred dollars of merchandise! That's serious. This just isn't you."

"Thanks for the motivational speech."

"Hey, I just *saved* you. *Again.* Do you have any idea how much worse this could have been? How lucky you are they aren't pressing charges? This is a major-league screw-up!"

"Learned from the best," I said. And as my dad stopped at a red light, I opened the door and got out of the car. On Route 3 North, cars swerved to avoid me.

"Zan! Zan! Get back in the car! Right now!"

I made it three long blocks, at a fast run, before I lost him and managed to call my mom to come get me at a McDonald's.

After that, the real fun began. My incident did hit the news, thanks to a video shot by a shopper, showing mall security dumping out the contents of my bag and hauling me away. The video got posted on YouTube and showed up right under my dad's in search results; "Glazer Kid Gets Rap Sheet" trended on Twitter, even though I avoided a formal arrest. Then *that* ended up being even more media fodder, with headlines like: "Preferential Treatment for Attorney General's Daughter?"

So much for presenting a unified front to the American family. Mom and Dad couldn't seem to agree on how to handle the fallout from the Athleta incident, so instead they just fell apart. Dad moved into a one-bedroom condo in Cambridge, in a building that seemed filled with separated and divorced men. He slipped further behind in the polls, and struggled to pick up the pieces of his campaign, granting interviews and giving speeches.

My shrink appointments ramped up to twice a week. I had nothing to say to her, though. All through those last drawn-out weeks of school, I heard about the sex scandal and the Athleta incident. My dad's crime and my crime were forever hooked together. And even when Mom announced that we were going for a long-overdue trip to see Aunt Jackie in Turkey and offer her our moral support, I knew it wasn't going to solve our problems. I could go thousands of miles away, but still our crimes would always be there, awaiting our return.

4

The purr of a motor leaked into my dreams. I sat up and looked through the porthole, blinking stupidly at the glare of sunlight glancing off the turquoise water. The boat was motoring slowly, hugging a rugged coastline. I sat up straighter. Where were we? How long had I slept? I saw no sign of Marmaris. I saw no other boats. This was my world now, stripped down to basics: boat, water, pine trees, hills.

Glancing at Mom's sleeping form on the other bed, I decided not to wake her up. On a ninety-two-foot boat with nine passengers and a crew of three, personal space was hard enough to come by.

I rinsed off one limb at a time in the tiny bathroom sink. I slathered on my high-SPF sunscreen and dressed in a long-sleeved top and a lightweight pair of cargo pants. I applied heavy foundation strategically over the white blotches on my hands and face. This turned out to be really hard to do in the dim bathroom light, on a rocking boat, with the medicine cabinet door banging in my face. I did the best I could, then threw on my Red Sox cap and lowered the brim to hide any mistakes.

At the last moment, I went to my suitcase and took out my

journal—an extravagant hardcover thing with heavy cream paper, a bon voyage gift from Dad at our pathetic pre-trip "let's pretend everything's normal" ice cream outing. "Think of me when you use it," he'd said. "Write down all your adventures, and then you can tell me all about them when you get back."

Of course, this was a far cry from the conversation I'd overhead him and Mom having at our front door. "So now we reward her behavior with a fancy vacation?" he'd burst out. "What kind of values are we teaching? You shoplift, no problem, Mom'll take you on a cruise!"

"It's not a reward, Marcus," Mom had countered. "It's about our daughter's emotional health. We need to get her away from the constant media attention. Which *you* brought on us!"

"How about more hours with the psychologist? How about working on an organic farm? Or Camp Feinman. She used to like going there. Did you even think of that?"

"What, *now* you've decided to step up and be a father and offer up some opinions?"

"I *am* a father. And I have a legal right to see my daughter this summer. You cannot take her away. I could actually press charges against you, you know."

It had taken Mom twenty minutes to persuade Dad that the six-week trip was really about getting us both away from the media glare, as well as helping her grieving sister get her grip on reality again. The sister argument had done it; he'd finally backed off. Tickets were purchased, suitcases packed.

But I didn't want to think about Dad right now. I tossed the journal back in my luggage and grabbed the Lonely Planet guide instead. The Lycian Tours representative had made it clear we were on our own until he hooked us up with a local guide at our first shore excursion, so any information I got about where we were would have to come from this book. At the last minute, I remembered Mom getting on me about locking my suitcase. I zipped it, then locked it, if only to not start the day with her yelling at me, and tiptoed out of the room.

I looked both ways down the cabin's narrow hallway. The lantern-shaped wall sconces were turned off, but sunlight leaked down from the stairway to the upper deck, making the wood on either side of the thick Oriental runners gleam. All six cabin doors were closed, everyone apparently still asleep. At the end of the hall, I climbed the steep steps hand-over-hand until I came to the sundeck. There I stood for a moment, squinting in the strong sun and taking deep breaths of fresh air.

The sails were still wrapped in their blue canvas covers— Aunt Jackie had told us most *gulets* weren't actually rigged to sail—and we were motoring at a good clip. We glided past brown rocks jutting out of the water, and the occasional village clinging to a hillside. Now I could see other *gulets* dotted throughout the bay, and a long three-masted yacht with a shiny wooden hull cruising just behind us. While our boat bobbed up and down like a toy, the bigger boat moved steadily ahead, slicing waves out of its way.

Wincing as my bare feet seared on the sun-baked deck, I made a beeline for the shade of a blue awning at starboard and curled up among the fat bolsters on a cushioned seat. I was overdressed and already beginning to sweat.

Minutes later, our boat slowed and turned, approaching a cove. There were no buildings—just rocks, water, and trees, and the occasional goat grazing on stubbly grass on the hills. The boulders on the hillsides called out to me, though. I did bouldering and top-rope climbing at my gym but had never tackled real rocks. If ever there was a great place for a first outdoor climb, this would be it.

If only I could get some climbing in, I could survive this trip. Though they'd grounded me after the Athleta incident, even taking my phone, my parents had let me keep my membership at Burlington Boulders. I guess even prisoners are allowed exercise. So in the few weeks after the school year ended and before leaving for Turkey, I'd spent all my spare time climbing.

Away from the social climbers at my school, I met a few people—mostly college kids—whom I took turns belaying with, but they ultimately saw me as a kid and didn't really want to hang out much. So mostly I just bouldered on my own or used one of the auto belays. I'd found a kind of peace when I climbed. Climbers are focused on looking for the next handhold or foothold and, you know, the whole business of not falling. They give you your space. Before Mom bought our airline tickets, I'd thought I could spend the rest of my summer like that.

"Good morning," Orhan said, coming out of the kitchen. He passed me, carrying a bucket, then sloshed water beneath the wooden table nearby. I drew my feet up onto the cushioned seat as a small river trickled my way. "You should be wearing your swimsuit," he pretend-scolded. "It is beautiful morning to swim," he added when I raised an eyebrow at him.

I pulled at my sleeves and hooked my thumbs in the thumbholes. "I'm not that big a swimmer."

"You do not know how?"

"I do. I just don't really like to."

He paused mid-slosh and looked at me with real concern. "But you will be too hot, yes? The sun here, it is very strong now. It will become stronger."

"I'm all right."

Orhan shrugged and returned inside with the bucket. He came back with silverware, which he proceeded to lay out on the table. He glanced at me a few more times, but I buried my nose in the Lonely Planet guide, reading about the Mediterranean coast.

◇◇◇◇◇

Stirrings below deck interrupted my thoughts. A door banging, a toilet flushing. I heard pots and pans in the kitchen, and smelled something delicious frying. But not even the breakfast smells, the perfect surroundings, or the Lonely Planet guide could distract me from Orhan's comment about the sun. Would the awning offer enough protection? How exposed was I going to be on this cruise?

I hadn't done a geography lesson for a long time. I pushed my shirtsleeves up to my elbows and dared myself to look, really look, for signs my skin disorder was progressing.

The stark white patches on my right elbow looked about the same. But the ones on the left had shifted. My Australia patch looked as if it had detached and was traveling toward the top of my forearm like a continental drift—definitely on the move. At first glance, the archipelago of eight spots that I'd dubbed Hawaii appeared unchanged. But then I realized the diameter of one of the minor islands surrounding it had widened. And Molokai had morphed, too, the right side bulging in a new way. I lowered my sleeves and rolled my pants up to the knees. The patches and speckles looked pretty much the same, except that Greenland almost covered my left kneecap now, and on my right shin, Patagonia had extended its reach farther.

I rolled my pant legs back down and hugged my knees. Dr. Shaw had always cautioned that vitiligo could be stable for years, or it could spread slowly. It affected people differently, at different times in their lives. She'd also warned that stress could cause it to flare up and lead to more loss of pigment.

Stress. The gift that keeps on giving. Thank you, Mom and Dad.

The most stressful thing about having vitiligo was dealing with people's reactions to it. So I always tried to cover up. I hadn't been to a pool party or a camp with swimming since sixth grade, when some kids saw the blotches and teased me. Those same kids recoiled from me in the lunch line, afraid they'd get whatever it was they thought I had, even though it's impossible. That was the end of Camp Feinman for me. Not knowing how fast the disease would spread or where it would progress next on my body was another annoyance. And now my skin felt more vulnerable than ever, under stress levels that were increasing by the hour and the intense Turkish sun. I'd been told to avoid the sun because tanning my regular skin would make the contrasting white patches more noticeable. I'd be slathering on sunscreen constantly on this cruise.

The boat stopped a few yards from the cove, and I looked up. It was a quiet place compared to Marmaris. No bustling docks, no busy boat traffic. No police lights, either. I wondered about that big search yesterday, and if they'd caught the robbers.

Captain Mehmet and Selim lowered the anchor. One of the Australians, Milton, emerged from the cabins wearing a tight Speedo. He stretched his scrawny arms, which were already burned lobster red. He patted his paunch and grinned at me. "Hell, isn't it?"

"What?"

He gestured toward the sea, the rocky beach, the sun-dappled hills enclosing the cove. A black goat, bleating loudly, skittered up a hill, nibbling on tufts of scrub grass. "This. Everything. Ha. I'm joking. This is heaven on earth! Got your swimsuit? Care to join me for a pre-breakfast dip?"

"Oh. No, thanks. Looks a little cold."

"Right, then. Toodle-oo."

Captain Mehmet and Selim lowered the swim ladder over the side of the boat, but Milton ignored it. He took a running jump and swan-dived over the side, his body surprisingly agile as it sliced the blue water like a neat blade.

Great. Now I was trapped on this cruise, with geezers in Speedos, unable to sit out in a swimsuit. And the rocks in this cove were not big enough to climb. Feeling sorrier for myself by the second, I watched Milton knife through the water, take two laps around the boat, and strike out in the direction of the super-fancy yacht. Soon I lost sight of him. I stood up, suddenly worried he'd drowned, but then saw his snow-white hair coming around from the back of the yacht. He was doing laps around both boats.

I wished my grandparents could see Milton and take a

lesson. They'd been against our trip here. They thought Turkey was dangerous, and showed us an article in *Travel and Leisure* magazine about crime being on the rise. Maybe it was—we'd seen enough police yesterday—but museums seemed to be the targets, not tourists. And now this old guy was here, swimming, having the time of his life.

The sounds of breakfast intensified. More passengers came up on deck and reintroduced themselves to me. There was Maeve, Milton's wife, who was just as sunburned as her husband; Nils and Ingrid, the slim, athletic-looking Norwegian retirees; and Fiona and Alice, a mother-daughter pair from England who were celebrating their fiftieth and seventy-fifth milestone birthdays together on this cruise. One by one, everyone dove into the sea for a swim. All of them urged me to jump in, and shook their heads like they thought I was crazy when I politely refused.

I retreated downstairs to the cabin. Mom came out of our room, dressed in her new blue-and-white-striped maxi dress. She plucked at the billowing fabric, as if she weren't sure what to do with all the freedom; most of her outfits were tailored. She looked up and smiled when she saw me. "Hey there! We missed you last night, sleepyhead. Where are you off to now?"

"Room. Bed."

"I see we've moved from the vow of silence up to one-word utterances."

I sighed. "I'm going to go lie down. Read or something."

"What's everyone else doing?"

"Swimming. Snorkeling. It's apparently what one does on a cruise. Fun in the sun."

"You can swim, Zan," Mom said. "Dr. Shaw never said you couldn't. Besides, we bought you all those cute cover-ups and SPF-coated swimwear. And the swim tights and long-sleeved rash guard. What about those?"

"No one here is wearing those things. Everyone will ask me questions."

"Just say you have sensitive skin. Lots of people do. Look at those sunburned Australians! They'll turn green with envy when they see all your protective gear."

"Mom, I just want to be out of the sun. I checked, and the patches are getting worse."

"I'm sure that's not true. It doesn't happen so fast. And you brought plenty of makeup."

"It takes forever to put on. And I don't want to swim if it's just going to wash off and need reapplying. Go have fun with Aunt Jackie. I'll find something to do."

"I'm not so sure 'fun' is what Jackie's up for," Mom said in a hushed voice, glancing toward her sister's closed door. "She's totally stressed."

"About Uncle Berk?"

"About Uncle Berk, yes. The 'murder,'" said Mom, with air quotes.

I was starting to really hate how Mom acted like Aunt Jackie was crazy, or lying. I knew that tone too well. It was like when I insisted I wasn't going to shoplift again after the Athleta incident, and Mom refused to believe me. Or when she checked out my Google search history—which had a long list of athletic-wear stores—and accused me of plotting more elaborate shoplifting sprees, when honestly, I was just checking out new styles. "What if Aunt Jackie's actually right?" I said, feeling a strong urge to take my aunt's side now, if only to get under Mom's skin. "What if he really was killed? I thought they found him with no cash in his wallet."

"Right. That's mostly why she thinks he was killed by some hoodlum. She's sure maybe he did something risky like refuse to hand over his wallet. Or maybe he fought back, and paid with his life."

"That all sounds totally possible to me."

"But, Zan, the facts are the facts. I saw the English translation of the coroner's report. Berk fell from a significant height and broke his neck."

"Yeah, but couldn't he have been pushed?"

"Of course. But there was a thorough investigation. The only footprints found up there were his. He'd gone off the marked trail. He made a bad decision."

"But what if—"

"Honey, Aunt Jackie is really struggling emotionally. She's at the denial stage of the grieving process, and looking for somewhere to place blame. Our job is to ride it out for a while and then try to help her move on."

"Okay."

"Anyway, it's not just Berk that stresses her out. She spent most of dinner last night texting her guest relations manager."

"How come?"

"I guess the hotel's having real problems. Staff is quitting. Scathing reviews went up on TripAdvisor. But we shouldn't be discussing all her problems in the hall."

I felt a sharp twinge of sympathy. Aunt Jackie didn't deserve all this stress and grief at once. And the fact that Mom didn't believe her theory made it that much worse. *I* believed Aunt Jackie. I didn't think she was so emotionally off-balance. I decided I would do all I could to support her. And if that happened to piss off my mom, well, that would be an added bonus.

We both turned to look as the door lock of a cabin clicked. But it wasn't Aunt Jackie's door. It was the last room at the end of the hall. I expected to see one of the Geezers.

I blinked. A girl stepped out. A girl around my own age. She was so tall she had to duck her head slightly to avoid grazing the ceiling. Her curly red hair was pulled back into a messy bun held with a plastic clip, and she wore a pair of aviator sunglasses propped on her head. Her green halter bikini top with white polka dots and a matching swim skirt looked not only stylish but expensive, too. She had a heart-shaped face, broad shoulders and arms sprinkled with freckles, and a bit of a muffin top going on at her waist, but she wore her outfit with so much confidence, she looked like a swimsuit model from a sportswear catalogue. She clutched two books to her chest and nodded a brief greeting to us as she headed for the steps to the upper deck.

"Who's that?" I asked, watching her climb up into the sun.

"Her name's Sage," said Mom. "She's from Oregon."

"That's weird. How did I not meet her yesterday?"

"You went to bed really early and practically passed out from jet lag."

"Oh yeah."

"And she came running down the dock at the last possible moment. Almost missed the boat. It was a very dramatic way to start a cruise. Her plane from Istanbul had been delayed."

"Is she here with her family?"

"No, she's traveling solo. Can you believe it? She's barely nineteen years old. She said she's been in Turkey for a year as an exchange student. This Blue Voyage is her farewell trip. Anyway, now you have someone close to your age here. Isn't that nice?"

It would have been nice if the girl hadn't seemed so completely disinterested in us, almost rude, as she pushed past us in the hallway. "I don't know, Mom. You didn't love most of my friends back when I actually had them. So you tell me—is she a quality person?"

Mom took me by the shoulders and steered me back to the steps. "Let's go find out." But when we got to the deck, Sage was already in the water, swimming with firm, confident strokes. She swam a couple of laps around the sleek, three-masted yacht anchored near us. I noticed the boat's name, *Gulet Anilar,* painted on the stern in scrolling black and white letters. I also saw a tanned blond couple eating breakfast on the sundeck, gazing at each other while feeding each other fruit. They reminded me of my parents on family vacations in happier times. I winced and turned away.

Mom was gazing at them, too. "Selim said that's a private charter. Those two people booked an entire luxury boat. Must have cost a small fortune."

I shrugged. It did seem extravagant to have a huge yacht with empty cabins, just for two people. But they were probably just eccentric rich people, like Victoria Windham. If you had enough money, you could buy all the privacy you wanted.

Then my gaze shifted, distracted by a new person coming into view on the *Anilar*: a tanned younger guy wearing khaki shorts and a white polo shirt that showed off his strong biceps. He had a mop of dark hair, ruffled by the wind. He looked Turkish, though at this distance it was hard to tell. He was definitely unrelated to the couple. Maybe he was their first mate, their version of Selim. He began tying up lines on the back deck.

"Why don't you put on your suit and dive in," Mom urged as Sage abruptly changed course away from the *Anilar* and began swimming toward the beach.

"God, Mom, give it a rest! I just don't feel like swimming!" I burst out.

We sat opposite each other at the table, silently steaming. Mom rubbed regular sunscreen on her arms, vigorously. I scooted my chair back a few inches, then leaned over toward the cushioned seats to check out Sage's books. You can learn a lot about a person by what they read, Dad always said.

I hadn't heard of either of the books. One was a dog-eared biography called *Passionate Nomad*. The other was called *The Lycian Shore: A Turkish Odyssey* by Freya Stark. Both were warped, as though they'd been out in damp air a long time. A hefty biography and a dense travel memoir about archaeological sites. Not exactly light beach reads.

Anyway, it was no wonder Mom was pushing me to talk to this girl. Exchange student. Bookworm. Independent traveler. Athlete—probably a champion swimmer, judging by her perfect form. I wouldn't have been at all surprised if Mom had actually hired her to make her good values rub off on me.

Orhan approached and set out two steaming glasses of black tea, fussing over the tiny spoons and bowl of sugar cubes.

"You don't have any coffee, do you?" Mom asked. "I'm a little jet-lagged. Tea isn't really going to do it for me, I'm afraid."

Orhan looked surprised, and I flinched. Sometimes both my parents got attitudes in restaurants, like they were royalty or something, asking to sit at a different table or sending their food back. I always hated that. And this wasn't a restaurant. This was a family-owned and -operated boat. The food and drinks came from somebody's kitchen.

But Orhan nodded and said, "Of course." He returned to the kitchen and came back minutes later with a cup of dark sludge for Mom. "Turkish coffee," he explained when she stared at it. "But some Americans, they find it too strong. Maybe you will, too?"

Mom seemed speechless, inspecting the glass of thick coffee, and suddenly I felt bad. Orhan had been trying to be nice to us since the moment we'd boarded the boat, offering things, asking us if we were okay. So I said thank you and then pointed to one of the phrases I'd found in Lonely Planet. *Teşekkür ederim.* I had no idea how to pronounce it in Turkish, but I stumbled through.

Orhan smiled. "You can say like this: tea sugar and a dream."

"Tea sugar and a dream," I recited.

"Tea sugar and a dream," Mom echoed, as if suddenly waking up. She manufactured a smile. "And thank you for your cooking, too. The dinner you served last night was amazing."

Orhan beamed at her. "You enjoyed?"

"Oh, yes."

"It was *imam bayildi.* This means 'fainting imam.' Baked eggplant. I have many fine dishes planned for this Blue Voyage." Orhan leaned against the table, suddenly in no hurry to leave, or to get back to whatever breakfast foods were sizzling in the kitchen. "I am only a student in culinary school, but I am nearly finished with my course. After this cruise, I return to the school in Dalaman and take my final exams."

"And then you'll come back and work on this boat again?" Mom asked.

He shrugged. "The boat is temporary job. I like it, but I want to cook bigger." He made a grand gesture. "I hope to work for very nice restaurant, and someday have my own."

Mom finally smiled an authentic smile. She liked ambitious people. "Well, that's wonderful, Orhan. Good luck with all that. I'm sure you'll ace your exams."

He smiled wider, displaying white, even teeth. "Thank you. If I do, perhaps you will celebrate with me, yes? I can meet you in Fethiye. There are nice restaurants there."

"Oh!" Mom looked startled. "Thank you. But no. We're going to Fethiye and then back to Marmaris. Round-trip."

"Ah. Fethiye," said Orhan. "This place is beautiful. But the Blue Voyage stop will not give you so much time there. You should extend your journey and see more of it."

"It's a lovely idea," said Mom. "But I'm afraid we're completely inflexible. We're on my sister's schedule."

"She has to get back to work in Istanbul," I added. "My aunt runs the Hotel Mavi Konak, and— *What?*" I hissed, as Mom shot me a sharp look.

Orhan's face fell. "Then I must try to make my best meals first."

"Is something burning on the stove?" Mom asked, sniffing.

"Oh! Excuse me!" Orhan hurried away, frowning.

Mom gave me a long look. "First lesson of travel, Zan. We do not tell strange men details about our itinerary. Okay?"

"But he's not a strange man, he's the cook on this boat. And all I said was—"

"I'm serious. We're women traveling alone in a foreign country. You saw what happened at the docks yesterday. We're man-magnets. We look like rich American tourists. Which we kind of are. So there's no reason for Orhan to know we're going to Istanbul later. Got it?"

Now I was the one to give Mom a long look. "Wow. Paranoid much?"

"Not paranoid. Just cautious. It never hurts to be cautious."

Orhan grinned at us from the galley kitchen window and gave us a thumbs-up. "All okay!" he called out. "Nothing burned! Not to worry! I will not disappoint!" He winked at Mom.

"I think Orhan has the hots for you," I whispered when he turned away.

"Oh, Zan. Please. He must be ten years younger than me."

But she smoothed her hair and smiled, just a little. And suddenly our eyes met and we burst into laughter. Loud, snorting guffaws. I couldn't remember the last time we'd really laughed together like that. It actually felt pretty good. For a moment.

Then I remembered all the stuff she'd said about how I had to earn back her trust. And the way she was micromanaging every moment of my life here. And how she didn't even believe her own sister. This trip was an endurance event, not a pleasure cruise. I put on my scowling mask and tied it on tight.

5

Orhan's breakfast temporarily took the edge off my mood. The sizzling on the stove had been something called *sucuk,* he told us: a Turkish sausage made of ground beef and spices like cumin. He stepped back and watched our faces carefully to gauge our reactions.

"Wow. The *sucuk* is a*mazing,*" gushed the alien who had replaced my mother. Mom normally logged her calories on an app. Now she was practically inhaling this sausage, and looking at Orhan with an expression of rapture.

"*Sucuk* doesn't suck," I agreed, reaching for seconds.

"You like it? You really like it? I am so glad!" Orhan exclaimed.

Orhan also served up fresh bread, halvah, eggs, olives, and the richest yogurt and honey I'd ever had. It was a weird breakfast because it seemed more like lunch, but he said it was very traditional. Everyone feasted, having seconds and thirds. Except Aunt Jackie, who only drank tea and picked at a hardboiled egg. "I get a little seasick on boats," she explained.

Mom frowned. "Jackie, you skipped dinner last night. You really should eat more."

Aunt Jackie took another sip of tea. "Later. Takes my stomach a while to wake up."

Sage returned from her swim at the end of the meal, when Orhan was clearing the dishes. She threw on a cover-up tunic and followed him to the kitchen. Through the window, I saw her loading up a plate with food. For some reason, my eyes kept drifting her way. Maybe it was because she was pretty, with that long red hair—I'd always wanted hair like that. Or maybe it was the way she took up space with her body, as if she had every right to be there, in that kitchen, helping herself to food. I felt like such a timid traveler in comparison.

"Bit of a loner, that girl," said Alice, the older of the two British women, with a sniff. "You'd think she'd be glad for our company. But she seems to prefer her own, doesn't she."

Alice's daughter Fiona whispered something about Sage being a "sad case, adrift and alone," but I couldn't hear it all because suddenly people were pushing back chairs and getting up from the table. Everyone shifted to stake out their territory with beach towels, bottles, and books. The Norwegian retirees sat on the sundeck up front, sharing a pair of binoculars to scan for birds around the cove. The Australian Lobsters sat at starboard. Milton muttered a steady stream of snarky remarks about the "rich bastards over there on the *Anilar*."

"What are you on about now, Milton?" his wife, Maeve, complained.

"We've got ten bloody people over here, on twenty-eight meters of an un-air-conditioned vessel that we paid far too much for. Those two over there have got *forty* meters all to themselves! And eight empty rooms!"

"How do you even know that?" Maeve demanded.

"I went on board. I was out for my constitutional swim. The couple—Americans, nice folks actually—saw me and invited me up. I say the Lycian Society ought to contract with *that* boat. Then they could move some of us over there to the *Anilar*, let us have more breathing room, and some air-conditioning. And satellite television. I'll be telling Mr. Tabak that when we see him next. They *owe* us!" He shook his fist.

"Oh, give it a rest, Milton. Honestly." Maeve pursed her lips and returned to her book.

Fiona and Alice played cards at one end of the breakfast table, and I had a sudden vision of a nightmarish future in which I spent every summer for the rest of my life taking vacations with Mom.

Sage emerged from the kitchen. She retreated with her plate of food and her books to a plastic chair on the port side of the boat, even though there was room on the cushions where Mom, Aunt Jackie, and I had set up camp. She had to be aware that she and I were the only young people on the boat, and that we should be allies. But obviously she'd rather sit and read than get to know me. Fine. I didn't need to get to know her, either.

I curled up on the cushion under the awning, next to Mom and Aunt Jackie, who silently gave me the most shade from the sun. They were draped over wicker chairs, reading self-help books Mom had brought. *Conversations with Difficult Men* for Mom, *Getting Past Grief* for Aunt Jackie. Good times.

I leafed through the Lonely Planet guide, past the Turkish Riviera section and on to the section about Cappadocia. Even though we weren't going there at all, I was curious about where Uncle Berk had lost his life. Aunt Jackie had said he had gone for a job interview with the Ministry of Tourism, and gone hiking right after the interview.

I learned that Cappadocia was about an hour east of Istanbul by plane. The photos showed a wild and almost lunar landscape made up of canyons and hills. It was considered a paradise for hikers, balloonists—and rock climbers, I noted with a pang. Also, according to the guidebook, archaeologists flocked there, and archaeological treasures were still being excavated all the time. Caves and tunnels threaded through the region, and some of the caves went down eight stories deep! It sounded like the perfect place for my uncle. I looked at pictures of weird rock formations called fairy chimneys, and mesas and cliffs, morbidly wondering which one he might have fallen from.

Well, that was totally depressing. So I flipped back to the Turkish Riviera section, hunting for activities we could do off the boat, in case Mom ever granted me shore leave from this floating prison. I found a pen on the deck and underlined places of interest. I flipped to the Notes section in the back of the book to make a list of the top attractions. Writing took so much effort on a yacht bobbing in the Mediterranean sunshine. I yawned. My list deteriorated into doodles.

Every now and then I looked up and toward the fancier yacht, hoping to catch sight of that hot first mate on the *Gulet Anilar.* There he was, polishing a railing. Maybe he'd look my way again, which would at least be some form of entertainment. I stretched out my legs and reclined on the bolster. Then I realized there was absolutely nothing alluring about someone covered head to toe on the back of a boat. If he looked at anyone on this cruise, it would be Sage, who was in the sun, wearing a swimsuit that showed off her curves. So I tried sketching him instead, from afar, even though I've never been a great artist. My hand ached for my phone, and for friends to share the view with.

Aunt Jackie tossed her book aside. It hit the deck, startling me.

"Read on," Mom urged. "It's got great advice. It helped me when Marcus's parents died."

"Wow. You're really comparing your in-laws to the love of my life?"

Mom sighed and closed her book. "Hey," she said in her cheery changing-the-subject voice. "The captain said we might see cliff tombs when we move to a new cove this afternoon."

I looked up. Presumably cliff tombs were found on cliffs. And that sounded interesting. Maybe I could climb! I didn't have ropes, of course, but I could do a little free bouldering, not so high off the ground.

"This area feels familiar to me. I think we are getting close," said Aunt Jackie. "Let me show you what I brought for the ceremony." She fished in her bag and extracted a small, elaborately carved urn. It was about eight inches high, with a handle on either side that reminded me of a woman with her hands on her hips. There was a lid on top, with a little knob. The gold was dull, but even so the urn seemed to glow, as if it might feel warm to the touch.

"What an unusual urn!" Mom exclaimed.

"Was it Uncle Berk's?" I asked, leaning forward to see.

Aunt Jackie nodded. "It was a teaching tool he used for his lectures. He collected replicas like this one so people could really get a feel for the motifs and styles of ancient artifacts. Some he had specially commissioned for his talks, when he ran the education programs at the museum. He thought slides put people to sleep, but if they could touch or hold an object similar to what artisans made centuries ago, history would feel more alive to them. Would you like to hold it?"

"Of course." Mom reached out to take the urn from Aunt Jackie. She turned it carefully in her hands, admiring the details. "Exquisite craftsmanship," she said. "Real gold?"

"Gold plate," said Aunt Jackie. "Metal underneath. It would be too expensive to use solid gold objects just for educational purposes."

"Can I see it?" I asked, and Mom passed it to me.

The urn was surprisingly heavy, considering how delicate it looked. Filigree, loops, and whorls encircled the base and top. The handles were shaped like seahorses, and you could even see little scales. The seahorses had wings, and mouths that almost appeared to be smiling. The knob on top of the lid resembled an acorn. Maybe it was all the talk about Uncle Berk, but suddenly the urn seemed to radiate energy, to feel alive. Or was that the sun heating it up?

Then a memory jolted me. I was in first grade, playing at a friend's house. There was an urn, plain and white but about the same size as the one I was holding, on the mantel. My friend and I climbed a chair and got it down. For an hour we played with the fine whitish powder inside, dumping it on the floor and setting our Barbies up in a beach scene, until my friend's extremely freaked-out mother ran into the room and made us stop for reasons she didn't explain. We found out several years later that we'd been playing with the cremated remains of my friend's grandpa.

Shuddering, I handed the urn back to Aunt Jackie. "Is it, um, what I think it is?"

"Oh, no. They don't do cremation in Turkey. He was buried in the traditional way. In a Muslim ceremony." She lifted the lid. "See?"

I looked inside and saw a piece of folded paper.

"That's just a certificate saying it's a replica of an antique," Aunt Jackie explained. She lifted it to show withered pieces of flower petals. "And these are dried rose petals from a bouquet Berk gave me the day he proposed. I'll be scattering them as a symbolic gesture."

"Where?" I asked.

"At the cliff tombs in Fethiye. Berk loved that area. His doctoral thesis was on Ancient Lycian art motifs. And that's where he proposed to me, on a Blue Voyage ten years ago. It's the perfect place to hold a memorial."

"Can you climb the cliffs there?" I immediately felt a twinge of guilt for asking. We'd been talking about Uncle Berk, and his soul, and I was asking about rock climbing. Aunt Jackie probably thought I was shallow and selfish, and Mom shot me a sharp look.

But Aunt Jackie had no big reaction. "There are some trails, but they're pretty steep," she said. "Mostly they're sheer rock cliffs. The Lycians built many of their tombs into them, and styled entryways and windows to look like houses."

"Why?" I asked.

"They believed a winged spirit would come to pick up the souls of their deceased loved ones and carry them to the next world. I'd take that over a traditional funeral any day." She sighed. "Berk's funeral was arranged by his parents and siblings. They didn't really involve me. And I didn't feel very connected to it. I wanted to do something more personal."

Mom patted Aunt Jackie's arm. "It's healthy. I think this simple ceremony will bring you some sense of closure. And it will let us participate, too."

A vein pulsed at Aunt Jackie's temple. "It's nice you're here, Kitsie, but it doesn't make up for your not coming to the funeral. I have to tell you, that really hurt."

Aunt Jackie's voice was calm and even, but Mom instantly sat up straight, her eyes blazing. "I told you, I *wanted* to come. But we were having a family crisis at the exact same time. The whole month of May was a nightmare."

"I wasn't living a nightmare here?"

"It's complicated, Jackie. I had to deal with Marcus's scandal. And the other stuff. You don't have a teenager. You don't know what it's like." She looked at me, biting her lip.

"Don't even," I interjected. "Don't blame me. Dad and I both told you to go to the funeral. Remember?"

"How could I leave?" Mom burst out. "Every time I turned around, you were sneaking out! Or swiping stuff! Your dad was AWOL. I couldn't put that burden on your grandparents."

"Oh, great, so I'm a burden?" I said.

I glanced in Sage's direction, suddenly wondering if she was witnessing all this. She had set her book down and was draping a gauzy blue scarf over her shoulders as a makeshift cover-up. She didn't look our way, but she must have heard us. My cheeks burned. Not even in Turkey could I escape my crazy, drama-filled family and the unwanted attention they brought me.

Orhan came up to us with bottled water and a nervous grin. "Everyone is enjoying themselves, yes?"

I took the bottles and gave him a thumbs-up sign while my mom and aunt glowered at each other. "We're doing awesome," I said.

"Then I am glad," Orhan said, though he cast a doubtful look at Mom and Aunt Jackie before hurrying back to the kitchen.

Sage yawned and stretched, then stood up and let the blue scarf slide off her shoulders. She padded over to the side of the boat and climbed down the swim ladder.

Mom stood up. "Sage has a good idea. I'm going for a swim too. I think I need to cool off. I did not pay all this money to bicker on the Turkish Riviera. Are either of you joining me?"

"I'm good," said Aunt Jackie, putting the urn back into her tote bag and picking up her book once more.

"Me too," I said, reaching for my Lonely Planet and my pen.

"Fine. Great." Mom peeled off her maxi dress and stood in her matching blue bathing suit for a moment, hands on her hips, glaring at us. "You two are about as fun as a car full of clowns," she said. "Remind me not to invite either of you to Disney World." She turned on her heel and disappeared over the swim ladder.

"She gets like that," I said to Aunt Jackie. "She's super sensitive lately."

"You don't have to apologize for her, Zan," said Aunt Jackie, watching Mom breaststroke slowly toward the beach. "Don't ever apologize for other people. It's not worth it. The fact is, your mom's a little broken right now. I mean, life as she's known it has ended."

"What do you mean?"

"Think about it. She's been publicly embarrassed. She's lost her power position as the wife of a man in high office, and all the perks that brought her. She would have made a great governor's wife, and she knows it. Believe it or not, that's a job. It's the end of an era for her."

"She could get her old job back, doing corporate event

planning," I said. "She's really good at that. She just gave up that job to focus on Dad's campaign."

"Maybe she'll go back to that. Maybe not. Either way, she's still going to have to figure out who she is and what the next part of her life looks like. Same as me," added Aunt Jackie with a wry smile. "I suppose I'm a little broken, too. So I'm trying to be patient with her. We're all a little broken. I forget that sometimes."

So here we were, then. Three chipped shards from some lost era, floating on the Mediterranean Sea. Three broken shards that did not fit together at all. We didn't even seem as if we were from the same family.

I didn't want to be all emotional about it, though. I flipped back to the Notes section of Lonely Planet and tried to look like I was busy. I didn't know what to write, so I scribbled a "You Are Here" entry. It was a trick my English teacher had taught us when we had to keep journals for a class and we didn't know what to write. "Just write about where you are now," she'd said. "Look up. Look around you. Capture the moment. It might seem boring to you at the time, but you might look back again later and find that it was actually interesting."

The pen felt heavy in my hand, but I wrote:

> I am here. On a boat where I fit in nowhere. Sun, blazing hot. Mom, blazing mad, is following Sage's lead and cooling off with a swim. Aunt Jackie is eating ginger candy and reading her book.

As soon as I wrote those last words, Aunt Jackie glanced at Mom, who was swimming laps around the boat. She set down her book, reached into her bag once more, pulled out a small stack of newspaper articles, and riffled through them. Some were in Turkish, others in English. I caught one headline: "Crime on the Rise in Cappadocia." Then she took out a bright orange pen, lowered her sunglasses, and began to read, high-lighting just about every sentence.

The rocking movement of the boat made me start to nod off after a while. I startled as Aunt Jackie patted my arm. "I'm sorry, by the way," she said. "I forgot to say that. You've had a loss, too. All that stuff with your dad. It's the end of an era for you as well."

"I'll live."

"Your mom said your friends weren't really there for you, when it all went down. That must have felt awful. Do you want to talk about it? I mean, I know we don't know each other all that well, but I'm a pretty good listener."

"That's okay. I'm fine." I really *didn't* want to talk about it. Talking about it made me feel like crying. Talking about it made my stomach seize. And I did not like mushy heart-to-heart talks, on principle, with anyone.

Aunt Jackie raised her sunglasses and looked at me. "You're fine?"

I lifted my chin and nodded.

"Well, good then," she said. "I'm so glad you're fine."

6

After lunch, Captain Mehmet motored the *gulet* away from the cove, striking out for new waters. We all gathered at the stern, in the shade of the awning and around the table, seeking relief from the sun.

As we ventured farther out into the bay, away from land, the wind whipped up. Hard. It tossed Maeve's paperback overboard, and scattered Fiona and Alice's playing cards all over the deck. For a few minutes, we all worked together to try to collect the swirling cards. Then we stumbled into seats as the waves became choppier. The red Turkish flag snapped and hissed on its pole. Halyards and winch handles clattered and banged.

Sitting on a wicker chair, I squeezed my knees up to my chest, wrapping my arms around myself. My stomach sloshed.

"Watch the horizon line if you're queasy," advised Nils.

I tried to lock my gaze on the retreating horizon. But glancing at the other passengers, I saw they all looked uncomfortable too. Sage sat across from me on a cushioned seat, perched on her books to keep the pages from flapping, and tied her hair back more securely in a bun. Then she wrapped the pretty blue scarf with white stars over her head, tying it under her chin to keep her hair from whipping around. Clearly she wasn't immune to the boat's movements either, because she kept her gaze held fast to that horizon line.

She caught my eye at one point, and flashed me the barest of smiles—signaling sympathy or misery, I couldn't tell which. But the smile was friendly. I managed a startled smile back just before she turned away. Then I noticed a spray of brown freckles on her pale face, and all up and down her arms. She was like the opposite of me, in a way. I felt something shift inside me and connect to her.

Maybe I was so starved for friends I was just looking for an excuse to break down her snobbishness, and my shyness, and talk to her.

Or maybe I was just incredibly bored.

"Where do you suppose the captain is taking us?" Alice, the older British lady, wondered aloud. "Seems we're getting a bit far from shore. I'd hate to miss the ruins."

"We're trusting the crew to follow the archaeological itinerary, even without our guide," said Ingrid, "but I've heard routes can change, depending on the weather." Then, as if realizing what she'd just said about our lack of a guide, she glanced worriedly at Aunt Jackie and pressed her lips together. Aunt Jackie frowned but said nothing.

"Routes can change depending on the captain's whims, too," added Fiona, Alice's daughter. "I read these cabin charter itineraries aren't as fixed as they promise."

"The captain is making a special stop to a quiet inlet near Dalyan," announced Orhan, poking his head out of the galley kitchen window. "Lycian Tours has arranged for a shore excursion to Dalyan and a guide there. You may also be lucky enough to see loggerhead turtles resting on the beach. I think you will enjoy this place. It is very beautiful." His eyes lingered on Mom a moment longer before he ducked back into the kitchen.

"Well, well. Somebody fancies you," Maeve teased her.

Mom shook her head. "He's just friendly," she insisted. But I noticed her cheeks were no longer as pale, and I caught her smoothing her maxi dress.

Dalyan. I liked the sound of that. What kind of place was it? I took out my Lonely Planet and scanned the index. It was hard to read, or even hold the book steady, as the boat bounced over the waves, but eventually I found the page and read about the Lycian rock tombs that were visible on the eastern cliffs.

Cliffs! My heart beat a little faster. Maybe I could climb *something.* Whenever I felt totally out of control, climbing reset everything for me. The feeling of rock beneath my hands— even the fake rock of a gym wall—anchored me.

"Excuse me, everyone," said Aunt Jackie, rising unsteadily to her feet. "This chop is really getting to me. I think I'd better head below." She headed below deck and the rest of us could hear her retching.

"Poor dear," murmured Alice. "She's got no stomach for the sea."

Minutes later, Captain Mehmet turned the boat back toward land. Golden pine-studded hills that reminded me of brown sugar came into sight again. The waves calmed, the wind lessened, and the sun beat down once more. About thirty yards away from an inlet beach, Selim and Mehmet cranked the winch and lowered the anchor with a splash.

I sucked in my breath as I looked from the starboard side to the port side. A large yacht was moored there, about twenty yards away from us. It was the fancy boat with the couple on it: the *Gulet Anilar.*

"There they are," I heard Milton mutter as he too noticed the boat. "The lovebirds. Rich bastards. Hope they're enjoying all that space."

The tanned, fit-looking couple radiated joy, even from a distance. They stood close together at the prow, taking in the landscape together. The man stroked the woman's blonde hair.

"They seem happy, don't they," said Mom, sounding a

little wistful. Or bitter, I couldn't tell. "This setting is made for romance. No wonder Berk proposed to Jackie around here."

My eyes scanned for the hot first mate on the *Anilar*. It was a fun coincidence that our boats had ended up in the same place, even though we'd taken different paths. Maybe I'd dare myself to catch his eye. Back when I had friends, we used to hang out at local cafés and "fish" for boys, trying to get them to look at us without ever going up to them or saying a word. We tried to exert some kind of magnetic pull, willing them to turn around, and gave ourselves points if they noticed us within a certain amount of time.

But suddenly what caught my eye were rocks. Large, carved brown rocks, rounded at the top and perfectly smooth, jutted out here and there around the inlet,.

"Doesn't it make you want to go in?" Mom nudged me and gave me a knowing look.

I ran down to our cabin and quickly changed into my swim tights and long-sleeved rash guard. From down the hall I could hear puking sounds. After I changed and locked up my suitcase, I paused at Aunt Jackie's door and knocked softly.

She opened it, looking pale and drawn, her hair a mess.

"Can I get you anything?" I asked her. "Water, maybe?"

She shook her head. "No thanks. I'm fine. I'll be up in a bit."

"Should I get my mom? You don't look so good."

"No need," she said. "Your mom's a worrier. Really, I'm fine."

She seemed anxious to be alone, closing the door midsentence, so I ran back upstairs and lowered myself down the ladder into the clear, cold water. Then I let go. In a second, the water had warmed to the temperature of a cool bath. I breaststroked to the nearest rock, taking care not to let my head go underwater and wash my makeup off. Just in case the hot first mate from the *Anilar* happened to look my way. The makeup was supposed to be waterproof, but past experience had taught me that the packaging lied.

I reached out and put my hand on the rock. It felt as smooth as sand.

"Hey," said a girl's voice.

I started and turned around to see Sage treading water right behind me.

Her curly red hair had come out of its bun and now spread out around her on the water.

"Quite a ride over here, huh?" she asked, grinning.

It took me a moment to find my words. I couldn't figure out why I was so nervous around her, but I was grateful she'd decided I was worth talking to after all. "Oh, yeah, choppy water. I thought I was going to yurk."

"Me too," she said. "Anyway, I'm surprised to see you in the water. Everyone's been saying you can't swim."

I'm surprised to see you in the water, too, talking to me, I wanted to say, but I stopped myself. It was incredible to be talking to someone near my own age at last; I didn't want to blow it. "No, I can swim. I just usually choose not to. I have, um . . . highly sensitive skin."

"Well, then let's not waste any time! Come on. Let's check out those rocks over there." She flipped underwater and pushed off with her feet on the base of the rock. She glided several yards away before coming up for air.

I swam after her, keeping my head up to avoid Catastrophic Makeup Failure. The next rock we found had a large base and a ledge jutting out that was just wide enough for two people to perch on. Sage pulled herself onto it.

I glanced at the *Anilar,* where that hot first mate was oiling the deck. I hoped he didn't see me. Sage looked like a voluptuous mermaid, her legs tucked up beneath her, hair tumbling over one shoulder. I looked more like a harbor seal. Or a drowned rat.

"Look." Sage pointed to some cliffs. High up, they were honeycombed with windows and doorways. Some had columns sculpted on either sides of the doors. "The Lycian rock tombs."

"Can we swim to the beach and climb them?" I asked eagerly.

Sage shook her head. "They're fenced off. But there's

supposed to be more in Fethiye, and those tombs you can actually hike to."

"Seems kind of wrong, doesn't it, to hike around people's graves?" I said as I clambered up beside her. It's funny, I usually felt entitled to go anywhere—even stores after hours, or into locked rooms—but the tombs seemed different, despite the open doorways. The tombs seemed like they actually belonged to *people.* Which was almost funny, because it's not like the people who occupied them could protest my being there.

Sage shrugged. "No different from a stroll through a cemetery. It's just life moving on, right? Besides, any time you walk anywhere in Turkey, you're walking on graves. There are centuries of buried civilizations here, layers and layers of them. Hittites, Greeks, Persians, Romans, Byzantines, and more. One of my teachers at my international school liked to say that we're always walking over the dead in Turkey." She gave me a small smile, as if embarrassed by what she'd just said. "I'm so sorry, by the way."

"For what?"

"About your uncle."

"Oh. Thanks."

"How'd he die?"

"Hiking accident." I was tempted to share Aunt Jackie's theory, but I didn't want rumors to fly around the boat. I knew what it was like to have people whisper behind your back. So I gave Sage the official story. "About six weeks ago, he went out to Cappadocia for a job interview. And he went hiking. Alone. He missed a sign that said a trail was closed for erosion. Lost his footing and fell forty feet. Broke his neck."

Sage listened, then looked down, quiet for a few moments. "Jesus, that's horrible," she said. "I had an older brother who died," she added, in a quieter but matter-of-fact voice.

"Wow, really? What happened?"

"Drug overdose."

"Oh my God."

"Yeah. It was pretty much a nightmare," she said, after an awkward pause. "I was only in sixth grade. He was in high school. My parents kind of freaked out. For two years my mom spent every evening sitting in his room. She kept it the way it was, like he might come back any day. My dad spent more and time out of the house. When he was home, it was like he was gone anyway. You'd talk to him and he wouldn't hear you."

"Wow." I nodded, taking in her painful story, unsure of how to show sympathy or how she might take it. "So was your brother into drugs for a long time?"

Sage shrugged. "Who knows. I think he was in pain for a long time. Depressed or something. He spent a lot of time in his room, I remember, starting around freshman year. I think drugs became his bigger escape at some point."

I hugged my knees close to my chest. I may have drunk a lot, and smoked a little weed on occasion, but I'd always stopped short of doing any serious drugs, even though they sometimes showed up at parties. I had enough escape hatches when my life got to be too much to handle. Or did I? Maybe ending up like Sage's brother could happen faster than you thought.

Sage looked toward another cluster of rocks. "Race you?"

I felt something like emotional whiplash, trying to keep up with such a personal confession followed by a sudden retreat. "Uh, sure," I mumbled, as she slid into the water.

We raced, sort of. She won by a huge margin, since I could only do a modified breaststroke to keep my face out of the water, and I'd never been much of a swimmer. That was fine by me. I was just happy not to be alone for once.

I wanted to ask her more about her brother. What he was like, what exactly happened. It was awkward because I didn't know her. She'd told me this really intense, personal thing. Getting personal information from someone felt kind of like receiving a gift. But if I asked for more details, would I look interested, or just nosy? I didn't want to screw things up. This was the closest I'd come to hanging out with a friend in two months, and I was desperate for company. The rules of friendship suddenly felt unfamiliar to me, the words that new friends typically say to each other like a foreign language.

As we climbed up the base of the next rock, Sage was still burying her confession by piling on questions about me. "It's nice you and your mom came all this way to be with your aunt. Do you come to Turkey a lot to see her?"

"No. It's our first time."

She looked surprised. "Really? You didn't come to your uncle's funeral?"

I shook my head.

"Why not?"

I dipped a toe in the water and swirled it around, uncertain of how much to reveal about my weird family. Still, I felt I owed her something. "We were kind of busy. My dad was having some really bad, um, work problems. And then my parents sort of . . . separated." There was talk of divorce; I just couldn't bring myself to say it yet. I glanced at Sage's face. She was listening intently, even sympathetically, but she didn't seem to know what I was talking about. So maybe the news about the scandal hadn't made it this far. And if she were from Oregon, she probably didn't follow news in Massachusetts. I could still be anonymous here.

Sage made a sympathetic face. Then she shook her head, as if in disbelief. "But wait. You *never* came to see your family in Turkey? I heard your aunt runs a boutique hotel in Istanbul!"

"They only opened the hotel two years ago, when my uncle lost his museum job and he inherited the building from his parents. But no, we've never visited them. It's just—I don't know. The timing never worked out right. And my mom's seven years older than my aunt. They weren't that close growing up. Mom always said they were like two only children whose lives overlapped for a few years." I didn't confess what I thought was the real reason we'd never made it to Turkey before: Dad. He'd never liked my aunt and uncle very much. Once, I'd overheard him saying something to Mom about her "freaky hippie sister and that moody guy she married." And then he'd go on about how she had to be crazy to live in Turkey, citing crime statistics, Kurdish militia groups, wars in nearby Syria and Iraq, terrorist cells.

"So where to next?" Sage asked.

"Istanbul," I said. "We'll stay with my aunt for almost six weeks."

"That's cool. But I meant, where should we swim to next? Another rock or the beach?"

A warm feeling spread through me. She wanted to keep hanging out. I felt like I'd passed some kind of test. I pointed to the narrow spit of beach about ten yards away; people from nearby boats were already headed in that direction. She nodded and dove into the water headfirst.

"I noticed your books," I said when we sat on the beach to dry off in the sun. "Who's Freya Stark?"

Sage decorated a sandcastle she was building with a pattern of tiny pebbles. "She was a famous British explorer. One of the first woman explorers to travel around the Middle East alone. She died in 1993, close to her one hundredth birthday."

"A 'passionate nomad,'" I guessed, thinking of one of the book titles.

"Yeah. She also traveled through Turkey alone, and wrote a lot about it. I adore her travel writing. 'To awaken quite alone in a strange town is one of the pleasantest sensations in the world. You are surrounded by adventure.'"

"That's cool. Freya Stark said that?"

"Yeah. Those words are like my personal motto."

"I wish I had a motto." My own motto, not my mom's fake-optimistic family motto. I'd never thought much about what kind of life approach I wanted. It hadn't ever been up to me to decide.

"You'll find one. I'll loan you one of her books, if you want," said Sage.

"Sure. I'll read it. Hey, how'd you end up traveling alone?"

"My family was going to come join me here, to celebrate the end of my exchange program. But my mom's been in and out of the hospital. Nothing too serious," she added quickly, when I started to express concern. "But travel would be hard on her right now. So they paid for the Blue Voyage and said to take a friend. I like traveling by myself, so I came alone."

"I can't believe they don't mind that you're on a cruise all by yourself!"

"They don't exactly know that part. I mean, parents don't really have to know *everything*. Right?" She glanced at the hot first mate on the *Anilar,* who waved at us. Sage waved back, and, emboldened, I did too.

Oh, yeah. We exchanged a knowing smile. Parents could definitely remain in the dark.

◇◇◇◇◇

Back on the *Gulet Yasemin,* I ran down to my room, reapplied my sunscreen and makeup, and changed into fresh clothes: a long skirt and a button-down long-sleeved blouse. I caught my reflection in the full-length mirror on the back of our door and made a face. I felt like freaking Laura Ingalls Wilder. But I wasn't risking exposure in the midday sun.

When I went back to the upper deck to hang my swimming clothes to dry, I saw that besides the *Anilar,* three more boats were now moored in our inlet. All the passengers from our boat were either snorkeling or lounging at the stern. Then a *put-put-put* sound made me turn and look toward the front of the boat.

A motorboat had come right up alongside us. Whoever was steering it tossed up a line, and Sage caught it neatly and tied it in a perfect knot around the railing. A guy stood up on the motorboat and started talking to her. He was curly-haired, maybe our age, and more deeply tanned than the first mate on the *Anilar*. He wasn't as hot as the *Anilar* guy, but he was still kind of cute. He held up a big silver tray and grinned at Sage.

Seeing me, Sage waved me over. "Baklava!" she said. "Want some? My treat."

Baklava? In the middle of the water? She had to be kidding, right? But no. When I got there, I saw a tray with rows and rows of triangular pastries, phyllo slathered in honey and sprinkled with the greenest crumbled pistachios. There were also cheesy pastries, and powdered cubes of Turkish delight candy.

I took my time picking out pastries for myself, as well as for my aunt and my mom, and Sage did too, sampling some, licking honey off her fingers, and glancing slyly at Baklava Guy.

Sage bought baklava for everyone and asked me to distribute the treats to the rest of the passengers. "You're buying for *everyone*?" I asked in disbelief.

"Consider it a gift from my parents," she said.

I loaded up napkins with pastries and delivered the goods. When I walked back toward the prow, licking honey and sugar off my fingers, Baklava Guy and Sage were still talking.

Then Sage reached over for something on the guy's tray. Something that flashed as she slipped it into her black canvas knapsack. It didn't look like baklava.

Spotting Nils and Ingrid's binoculars on a nearby table, I picked them up and put them to my eyes, my fingers fumbling to adjust the fit and the focus.

Sage reached for another item and put it in her bag. Then another. I didn't know what she was buying now, but I was sure it wasn't pastry.

There was no honey in the world that could shine like pure gold.

7

My heart thudding, I watched Sage transfer things from the tray to her knapsack. I zoomed in with the binoculars and saw what they were. Small gold figurines. They looked like little Oscar Awards. Each figurine was slightly taller than Sage's hand; the head and the legs stuck out when she gripped one in her fist. I watched her take four of them from Baklava Guy and put them in her knapsack. Then she handed the guy a large stack of bills. I zoomed in as far as I could, just in time to see that they weren't Turkish lira or Euros. They were American dollars, but I couldn't make out the numbers on them. I wondered how much she was spending.

"Spot any beauties?" said a man's voice behind me.

I spun around to find Nils, one of the Norwegians, pointing to my binoculars—no, *his* binoculars. My face warmed. I handed them over, not wanting him to think I was swiping them. "Sorry. I was just borrowing them."

"It's all right. Please, enjoy them." The lines around his bright blue eyes crinkled as he smiled. "I take it you are interested in ornithology?"

"Orni-what?" Maybe that was Norwegian for *spying on people.*

"Ornithology. Bird-watching. Perhaps you can help Ingrid and me to find the elusive Smyrna kingfisher." Nils stooped and picked up a thick bird guide he'd left on the deck. "Or, if not the kingfisher, then any of the fifty bird species we are hoping to identify on this voyage." He unfolded a checklist from the back of the guide and pointed to the Smyrna kingfisher's mug shot. It was a beautiful bird with blue feathers, a chestnut head, white throat, and bright red beak. "After that we can look for the Dalmatian pelican. Some make their nests in rivers and deltas such as this one. It is the largest of the pelicans, and has quite distinctive curly nape feathers. You see?" He showed me the picture.

"I'll keep my eyes peeled," I said, jogging toward the front of the boat to join Sage.

The line tethering the motorboat to the *Gulet Yasemin* slipped off as Baklava Guy zoomed back toward the rocky cove, heading for the mouth of the Dalyan River.

"How did everyone like the pastries?" Sage asked when she saw me.

I coughed from the motorboat's gasoline fumes. "What were you buying just now? From Baklava Guy?"

"Baklava."

"After that. It didn't look like food."

"Oh! Gifts for my family. I just didn't want the crew to see how much cash I was carrying. I like everyone on the boat, but you just never know who to trust."

I got that. I didn't trust people easily either. And I knew Mom had divided up her cash and hidden it throughout our luggage; she was obsessive about checking to make sure our suitcases were always locked. Still, it surprised me that you could buy jewelry and souvenirs without even going to shore. "I didn't know he had other stuff for sale," I said.

"Most people have other stuff for sale," said Sage. "If you ask them. Anyway, jewelry and knickknacks are way cheaper here on the coast than in Istanbul. Want to see what I bought?"

I did. Sage reached into her knapsack and took out her scarf. She set it to the side, then took out a small box. In it was a pair of teardrop-shaped gold earrings, with cobalt blue stones set inside, ringed with smaller turquoise stones, as blue as the water around us. "Those are so pretty," I said. My hands twitched with the urge to touch them.

"Aren't they? I love them. I'd wear them myself, but they're for my mom." She held them up to the light, letting them sparkle and dance. "And I also got these." She took out the four small statuettes I'd seen through the binoculars.

"Interesting," I said, picking one up. It was surprisingly heavy. The little figurine had no clear facial features, and the gold was bright yellow and gleaming.

"Just little statues. Gold-plated replicas of stuff from ancient civilizations," said Sage. "They make great souvenirs. My dad's a History Channel addict. He'll love them."

I thought of Aunt Jackie's urn, the gold-plated replica she'd brought for the ceremony.

"The gold on these earrings is real, though," said Sage. "Eighteen karat. Too flashy?" She frowned, holding the teardrops up to the sun. "Turkish gold is so yellow. More yellow than most Americans are used to."

"I'm sure she'll love them. It's a great gift," I said. "And I'm sure your mom'll be excited to see you again. How long have you been in Turkey?"

"Ten months. Not nearly long enough," Sage added, putting the earrings back in the box.

"Really? I can't even imagine being away for so long."

"I'm not ready to go back. I *love* it here. I love *travel*. I don't want to stop. *Ever*," she added with unexpected fierceness.

"But don't you think your parents miss you?"

She shrugged and slipped the box into her knapsack, then packed the scarf around everything. "My parents always said you have to travel while you're young. Like, for graduation last year? They gave me a compass and a suitcase. And they said two words: *Just go.* I can't think of a better gift than a suit-case. Anyway, these are the gifts. I'm done shopping. This stuff cleaned out the rest of my cash." She swung her knapsack over her shoulder and stood up. "Hey, Selim said the Lycian Society arranged for a guide to row us down the Dalyan River if we want to see the village and the ruins down there. Do you want to come?"

"Sure!"

"Great!" She grinned.

"I just need to grab something from my room."

My mood was improving by the second. I ran to the back of the boat, toward the stairs that led down to the cabins.

Mom was just coming up. "We're going on the ruins excursion. The guide is waiting for us in the tender."

"I'm coming. I just need to grab some stuff first. Is Aunt Jackie going?"

"She said she's not in the mood. I couldn't convince her." Mom sighed. "Maybe all the stuff about ruins hits too close to home for her. This was Berk's great passion. Anyway, hurry up. We don't want to keep everyone waiting." She smiled at me. "Hey. I'm glad you and Sage are hitting it off. It's good to see you hang out with someone so nice."

"Nice?" My rising mood went down a few notches.

"Nicer than some of the kids back home."

"Ah. Is that what made her pass quality control?" I asked.

Mom sighed. "Oh, Zan. Do you have to twist everything around to the negative? Honestly, it's exhausting."

"What's exhausting is every compliment from you is actu-ally a backhanded criticism," I said.

"What's exhausting is fighting with you every minute of the day."

Thanks to Mom, my enthusiasm for this shore excursion was rapidly dwindling. I ran down to our cabin and threw into my backpack everything I'd need to ward off Catastrophic Makeup Failure: sunscreen, cover-up, a compact mirror, a floppy hat.

On my way back down the hall, I noticed Aunt Jackie's door was open a crack. I peeked inside and looked around the room at her clothes draped across the end of the bed and at her suitcase. Her bathroom door was closed, and I heard her rustling around in there. I should have left, or called out to her. But I didn't. I opened the lid of her suitcase—and waited, wondering what to do next. I sifted through a layer of clothes. I didn't know what I was looking for, but my instinct for snooping took over.

Usually I snooped or stole stuff when I felt like things in my own life were out of control. At least, that was my therapist's theory. And I'd usually get this weird, light-headed feeling, kind of a rush. But now I was in my *aunt's* cabin, poking around. It didn't feel so good.

I was backing away from the suitcase, toward the door, when something in the trash caught my eye. One of those candy tins Aunt Jackie was always opening. I kneeled down to inspect it. The candies were made by some British company; the price tag showed both British pounds and Turkish lira. I read the label: *Ginger Preggo Pops. Take as needed for morning sickness.*

I backed away as if I'd just found a loaded gun. Was Aunt Jackie *pregnant*? Then I heard retching coming from the bathroom. The toilet flushed.

"Aunt Jackie?" I tapped on the door. "Are you okay?"

"I'm fine," she said between sniffs. "Don't worry about me, Zan. You don't want to miss that shore excursion."

I left her cabin, my stomach twisting. Should I leave Aunt Jackie alone, when she felt so sick and miserable? Or run off with the others—with Sage—and have an adventure?

I remembered too well what it felt like to have no one to count on. Everyone bailed on me when I needed them most. So I called up to Mom to tell her I had changed my mind, and I went back down to Aunt Jackie's cabin. As I sat on her bed to wait for her, I noticed spreadsheets strewn on the floor.

I was about to reach for one when Aunt Jackie emerged from

the bathroom, red-eyed and pale. She looked startled to see me. "What? You didn't go?"

I shrugged. "It's hot out. And I kind of hate the sun."

She smiled. "It *is* hot. And you know what? I kind of hate the water. So we're a good pair, you and me." She winked. "I've always been prone to seasickness," she went on, taking a seat beside me on the bed and tucking her legs up beneath her. "Ever since I was little." She passed me a tin of gingers. "Want one? I should have passed them out to everyone when we hit that chop this morning, but I'm hoarding them. My stomach's so sensitive lately."

"Sure. Right." Seasickness. So probably that's all it was. But still, I had to ask. "Aunt Jackie . . . I know it's none of my business, but . . . you're not pregnant, are you?" I whispered, even though no one was around to hear.

She hesitated, then grinned.

"Oh my God!" I squealed. "You're pregnant! I can't believe it!"

She put her finger to her lips. "Top-secret for now, okay, Zan?"

"What? You have to tell my mom! She said you couldn't get pregnant. She said—"

"I know. Berk and I didn't think we could. We'd had trouble; I had five miscarriages. It's made me superstitious, so I didn't want to say anything to anyone until I was past the first trimester. But I'm about there. I'm just waiting for the right time, the right moment, to tell your mom. Preferably not when we're arguing. So can I ask you to keep it secret for just a little bit longer?"

"Of course," I agreed. Suddenly I felt something like real happiness for the first time in ages. I liked knowing something Mom didn't know yet. And I felt honored that Aunt Jackie had told me first.

"So what can I do for you? Are you comfortable?" I got up and fluffed her pillows. "Do you want your window open? Something to drink?" I spun around helplessly, looking for something to serve or clean or fix.

She laughed. "No need to fuss over me. But if you want to help pick up those papers that fell off the bed during the chop, that'd be great."

"No problem." I kneeled down on the floor to gather the spreadsheets, trying to look at them without being obvious. Could they be part of Aunt Jackie's research on crime in Cappadocia? "What are these for, anyway?" I finally asked, unable to figure out the numbers.

"Financial reports." She made a face. "That's the part of running a hotel that Berk and I were never very good at. But when we inherited the hotel, it was already in bad shape. I have to somehow make these numbers look better soon, or I'm going to lose the hotel."

"Really? How could you lose the hotel?"

"Berk's brother, Serhan, and his sister, Ayla, legally have claims on it. Even though they've had no involvement in running the place."

"That doesn't sound fair."

"No. But it's the way Turkish inheritance law works. The surviving spouse gets a percentage of the estate, and the rest gets divided up among siblings. When Berk's parents died years ago, Serhan and Ayla weren't interested in the Mavi Konak. But now the neighborhood's a hot real estate market. If I can't get us back in the black, they're going to start the process of selling the place."

I handed her the stack of papers. "And you don't want to sell?"

"No." Aunt Jackie pressed her lips together, thought a moment, then continued. "Which is strange, considering hotel management wasn't a first-choice career for either Berk or me. But when Berk lost his job, and when he couldn't get steady employment in his field, it was a logical move for us, and I had the better English skills we needed for marketing. Now more than ever I want to finish what we started together and see it succeed. But I guess I'm a bit distracted these days."

I frowned. "They should be nicer to you. I mean, you just

lost your husband. How could your own in-laws sell the hotel out from under you?"

"They have the right to do so. And I guess they see me as this American interloper. We were never close. Serhan and Ayla are both busy professionals, married, with two children each. I never really bonded with them. And Berk was so different from them, especially after spending so many years in the US. There was a vast family divide we just couldn't seem to cross."

I nodded. I knew a lot about family divides, having grown up in the widening chasm between my own parents.

Aunt Jackie sighed and shoved the spreadsheets into a file folder. "They didn't express any interest in the hotel—or us— until after Berk was gone. Now they're coming around all the time. The more they can learn about what kind of shape the building is in, financially, the more ammunition they'll have to get it shut down. But you don't want to hear about my financial woes. Let's talk about you instead."

"Me? There's nothing to talk about."

"Nothing?"

I hesitated. I didn't like talking about myself. But Aunt Jackie, like Sage, had shared something personal. So I told her a little about some of my ex-friends, and even an almost-boyfriend I'd had before the whole scandal, and how I'd lost everyone pretty much overnight. "They only liked me because I had access to celebrities and parties and stuff," I admitted. "Once all that went away, and once my dad became this public embarrassment, they were out of there. I guess they weren't my real friends."

"No"—Aunt Jackie reached over to pat my shoulder—"they weren't. And you know something? They did you a favor, painful as it was. You don't need people like that in your life. You'll find new friends," she added. "Close friends. Give it time."

"I'm not sure I want close friends anymore. When people know too much about you, stuff gets out. This is the second time I've been burned."

"What happened the first time?"

"Camp Feinman. Sixth grade. I told my bunkmate I had vitiligo."

Aunt Jackie nodded. "That must have been scary, to confide in someone new."

"It was. Because then she told everyone else, and then everybody started acting like I had a contagious skin disease, and teasing me about it, and basically avoiding me."

"Oh, Zan."

"My dad thinks I loved that camp, and he still thinks I should go back and be a counselor."

"I get it," said Aunt Jackie. "Now you have trouble telling which people are real friend material and which aren't. You can't trust people."

"Exactly."

"Well," she said, "I don't have the answers. I'm no oracle. But I can pass on a little wisdom from your uncle Berk. You probably don't know this, but one of the more interesting parts of his job was that he sometimes did side work with the TNP, the Turkish National Police."

"As an archaeologist?"

"Yes. The police department calls in authenticators when they find art objects or antiquities. They need people to appraise things and say whether they're real or have value. Berk was so good at this. He always had a gut reaction first."

"What do you mean?"

"He could hold an art object and feel a connection to its maker. Even though he was an intellectual, a scholar, he trusted his instincts. That emotional sense never betrayed him. About objects, anyway. I just wish he'd had the same sense for people." She looked down and twisted the sleeves of her tunic. "Because that's what it came down to in the end. His instinct was off. And he was deceived."

"By whoever mugged him and pushed him off the cliff?"

"Exactly. I think he trusted someone enough to get pulled into the wrong conversation."

I sat up straighter. An idea hit me. "Aunt Jackie, what if it *wasn't* a random crime? What if someone *set out* to kill him? What if they followed him there—or even made him go there? Did any of his colleagues not like him?"

"I've had that thought," she said. "Believe me, I've gone to all kinds of dark places in my mind. But he got along with *every-one* he worked with. He was diplomatic, and would walk miles out of his way to avoid a controversy. It's probably why he was one of the first to go when the museum had its budget cuts. He might have been seen as too passive. Too agreeable. Berk just never made waves."

I leaned forward, resting my chin in my hands, thinking. "What kind of job was he interviewing for in Cappadocia?"

"A tour guide job. It was beneath him. He'd have been hired to lead tours of the rock caves during high season. But he agreed to go out and interview for it anyway, to see if it might lead to something else. He didn't like to close doors to opportunities. He didn't think we could afford to."

Now I felt bad that I hadn't known my uncle well. It made me mad that someone had probably offed him. Why did so many bad things happen to our family? It didn't seem fair.

And now that I knew Aunt Jackie's secret, it seemed really wrong that she should be on her own to figure out why her husband had died so tragically. Not even her own sister was on her side. I knew what it felt like to be left alone. Maybe I could spare someone else from feeling that pain.

"I want to help you," I said.

"With what?"

"I know Mom doesn't believe your theory, but I do. And I want to do something. I want to help you prove that Uncle Berk's fall wasn't an accident. I'm a good researcher," I insisted, when she started to object. "I can help you find articles online. Or organize them for you."

"Thank you, Zan. I appreciate the offer. But I can't involve you in this. Your mother would be furious."

"We don't have to tell her."

"No, one secret's enough. I'll keep plugging away, and when the time's right, when I have enough evidence of violent muggings, then I'll go to my lawyer. But your moral support means a lot to me. Truly." She shifted off of the bed and stood up. "Anyway, I'm worried I'm dragging you down in all this. You're supposed to be having the time of your life on a cruise. Come to the upper deck with me and hang out. I'm suddenly starving. Let's ask Orhan to fix us something delicious to eat."

I followed Aunt Jackie to the upper deck. Orhan was fishing for dinner but immediately jumped up to get us some snacks from the galley kitchen. As he did, I fixed my gaze on a stand of pine trees near the water's edge at the cove. Branches rustled and a bird flapped out, soaring over my head and displaying its colorful feathers and tufts—white, blue, brown, and red. I nudged Aunt Jackie and pointed. We watched it together, mouths open in awe, before it swooped, turned, and flew away.

The Smyrna kingfisher, from Nils and Ingrid's bird book. I was pretty sure—no, I *knew,* in my gut—I'd just glimpsed something real and rare.

8

I had trouble getting to sleep that night. I couldn't stop thinking about Sage's purchases earlier in the day. Three or four more small yachts had discovered our secluded cove that evening, and I'd seen two more baklava vendors going up to all the boats and holding up silver trays after dinner. One had come up to our boat, offering pastries for dessert, which Orhan politely declined. It wasn't the same vendor Sage had bought from, though—this guy was much older, and his motorboat didn't have the same blue tarp in the back. Part of what kept me awake was wondering if all the baklava sellers really had other things for sale or if Sage had just gotten lucky.

When I eventually dozed off and lapsed into half-dreams, I pictured ancient Lycian women carving tombs into cliffs. I dreamed of winged spirits taking dead bodies away, cradling corpses in their arms, including a baby's corpse. I peeled back a white blanket to see the face of my unborn baby cousin. I woke up, heart pounding, dry-mouthed.

Mom was snoring away. I tossed and turned, then sat up straight when I heard the click of a door opening down the hall. Footsteps followed, climbing the stairs, thudding quietly on the upper deck. Could that be Sage? Maybe she'd want to hang out. I could use a distraction. Or a friend.

I got out of bed and yanked my Burlington Boulders hoodie on over my tank top and pulled lightweight sweats on over my shorts. Then I slipped out of the room.

On deck, the table under the awning was cleared, the floor washed, all traces of our dinner gone. Then I heard clinking sounds in the kitchen. I went to the doorway and saw Sage, wearing a bathing suit and a cover-up tunic, leaning against the small countertop and drinking a glass of milk.

I shrank back into the shadows. The sight of the water faucet suddenly reminded me that I'd washed my face before bed. I'd have to run back downstairs and try to put on makeup in the dark.

Too late. Sage saw me. "Ah! A fellow night owl? Quick, where's Nils's bird-watching guide? We should check you off the list!"

"I can't sleep," I admitted, covering my left cheek with my hand and hoping my bangs would cover my forehead. "Guess I'm still jet-lagged. What's your excuse?"

"Insomnia," said Sage. "Chronic. I almost never sleep at night."

"That sucks."

"I'm pretty used to it by now. It started after my brother died. My doctor gave me pills last year, but I don't like to take them. That's okay. Night on a boat is beautiful. Night on the Lycian Way? Magical." She set her glass down in the sink. "Did you see all those stars out there?"

I shook my head.

"Come outside. I'll show you. Hey, what's wrong with your face?"

I swallowed hard. "My face?"

"Yeah. Why are you holding it?"

"Toothache. I just, um, came up for water, so I could take an ibuprofen."

"I have something way better. Lion's milk." She got me an empty glass from the cabinet.

"They have lions in turkey?"

"No. But this drink I'm going to make for you is called *aslan sütü*. It means 'lion's milk.'" She reached for a bottle from a small bar above the sink. *Yeni Raki,* the label read. She filled a glass with water, then poured clear liquid from the bottle into it. When she handed me the glass, the liquid turned cloudy white. When I sniffed it, it smelled like licorice. I held the glass, still keeping my left cheek covered up with my hand.

"Raki," she informed me. "It's kind of like ouzo. Or sambuca. It's the national drink of Turkey. I like it best with chilled water. Cheers." She raised her glass and clinked it with mine.

I sipped slowly, letting the liquid burn my tongue and throat.

Sage watched me, an amused smile playing at her lips. "Like it?"

I didn't. But I nodded and managed a smile instead of making a face. Even if I didn't like the drink, it felt so *normal* to hang with someone and drink in the dark, almost like being home with my ex-friends. Like when my friends and I would raid our parents' liquor cabinets at sleepovers. I felt like this bottle of raki had unleashed genies: memories of happier times, flitting all around me.

Shadowed by memory-djinns, glass in hand, I followed Sage outside, to the cushions at the back of the boat. I was grateful for the cover of darkness, but still wary of the moonlight. I positioned myself so she'd only see my right side. But Sage was looking at the sky, not at me.

"Look at the stars," she said. I did, and the sight took my breath away. The sky was full of them, way more than you could ever see in our driveway in Cabot, Massachusetts. We looked for constellations, and made up crazy names for the ones we didn't know, naming them after the other passengers on the boat.

"There's the Bird-watcher, known for its binoculars shape," said Sage, tracing a pattern with her finger while the waves gently lapped against our boat.

"And there are the Lobsters," I said, tracing two lobster claws in the dark and pretend-sipping my raki to show Sage I liked it.

"The Lobsters? That's a great name. Who are they?" Sage asked. "Wait. Let me guess. The grumpy, sunburned Aussies?"

"Yeah. Milton and Maeve."

"Okay, guess this, starting from that bright star." Sage traced a rounded shape in the air.

"No idea."

"The Urn. Otherwise known as your aunt."

"Why do you think of her as an urn?"

"Because she's just like that urn she brought with her."

I shook my head. I didn't get it.

"I'll explain. But first: refills."

I quickly tipped my glass and poured my drink over the side of the boat so she wouldn't know I'd been fake-sipping. Sage darted off to the kitchen with our empty glasses. I debated running downstairs for the makeup, but there wasn't time. She was already coming out of the kitchen, bottle of raki in hand.

"You'd think she'd be empty," Sage said, sitting back down and pouring the drink, "because she's this grieving widow, right? But she's really so full of life."

I clinked my glass with Sage's again, and this time I drank a full swallow. Then another. My throat burned and my eyes watered, and finally I couldn't hold back my cough.

"Raki's a little strong," said Sage. "Maybe too strong for you?"

"I'm fine." I lifted my chin. "It's just, what you said startled me. That's why I coughed. My aunt *is* full of life."

"What do you mean?"

I'd said too much. But I couldn't go back. "She's pregnant. But she's not ready to announce it yet. My mom doesn't even know. You can't tell anyone, okay?"

"I won't. I promise." Sage grinned. "That's awesome news! I bet your aunt and uncle conceived right before he went to

Cappadocia. And you're going to have a little baby cousin in a few months. Cheers to that." Sage raised her glass and we drank to the good news. This time I went back to pretend-drinking.

"I'm jealous," Sage added, when she'd drained her glass. "You'll probably be spending a lot more time in Turkey."

"What makes you say that?"

"Your mom will want to help her sister and dote on her niece."

"Nah. They're not that close."

"A baby is a game-changer."

"Maybe my aunt and her baby will just move back to Massachusetts," I said. "There's nothing keeping her in Turkey now that my uncle's gone."

Sage shook her head fiercely, making her curly ponytail shake. "Nope. She'll want the baby to know its home country and your uncle's family. She can't rip the baby away from all that family history and your uncle Berk's roots."

"She might want a change of scene. Uncle Berk was depressed the past couple of years."

"Really? How come?" She shifted on the bolster, leaning forward.

"He lost his job at the archaeological museum after government budget cuts. He took it really hard."

As I spoke, I remembered a Thanksgiving dinner at my grandparents' house two years ago, right after Uncle Berk was laid off. Aunt Jackie and Uncle Berk were in town visiting. Uncle Berk didn't say much. He didn't normally drink much, either, but that night he knocked back three glasses of wine, one after the other. Aunt Jackie kept massaging his shoulders. They had brought me a shadow puppet theatre from Turkey for my present that year. It could unfold and set up on a table, and it came with a set of shadow puppets—flat, jointed figures that could dance on the end of a stick, illuminated by a light held behind a cloth screen. Even though I felt too old for it, I put on a puppet show for the family, just to break the tension.

My parents and grandparents had played along, pretending to be entertained, but Berk, I could see through the cloth, wasn't even watching.

"Yeah, I bet he was depressed," said Sage. "Can you imagine going to school all those years and not being able to work in your field? That's why I want to take my time before I decide what to do about college."

Sage was giving me hope. Maybe my family drama would pass, or I could go somewhere someday and leave it behind. Life after high school? It was possible. Maybe.

"Just remember," Sage said, turning her empty glass round and round in her hands. "'The beckoning counts, and not the clicking latch behind you.'"

"Huh?"

"Freya Stark. I really have to loan you that book. Remind me tomorrow."

"Sure." Who *said* stuff like that? But Sage intrigued me. I suddenly wanted to read everything she had ever read, to know everything she knew, to see the world through her eyes. "I'm not the fastest reader," I confessed. "I don't know if I can finish before the cruise ends."

"No problem. Just return it to me in Istanbul."

"Istanbul?"

"Yeah. I have to go back to my host family, to pack up. I'll have a few days there. We can hang."

"Oh! Okay. Great." I hoped I didn't sound too eager.

Sage beamed. "It'll be fun! I'll take you to my favorite hammam—a Turkish bathhouse. There's one that I love by the Grand Bazaar. Oh, and we have to go to the Grand Bazaar. They have so many amazing shops there."

"Sounds good." I smiled, warmed more from her words than from the sips of raki that still burned in my veins. Sage was so different from anyone I'd hung with at my high school. Or anywhere. I mean, what kind of person went around spouting quotes from some dead British explorer lady no one had ever heard of, or geeked out over Ancient Lycians? She didn't seem to care how she dressed, or what people thought of her interests. She was just who she was.

Sage stood up, wobbling slightly. Then she slipped off her cover-up, revealing a black one-piece swimsuit.

"Wait. You're going in the water? In the dark?"

"Why not? It's the best time. It's gorgeous." She retrieved the ladder from its storage bin under the kitchen window. I watched, confused, as she hooked it to the side of the boat. Wasn't she going to invite me, after all we'd just talked about? After drinking together?

"Hey, wait up," I said, peering over the railing. The water was an inky indigo, not turquoise or teal like during the day. Where was she planning to go? Sage dropped into the sea with a small splash, and propelled herself away from the boat in a brisk crawlstroke.

I tore off my hoodie and sweats so I was just in my tank top and pajama shorts. I scrambled down the swim ladder, stifling a scream when I hit the cold slap of water.

I chased Sage, finally putting my face in the water and doing the crawlstroke, too. She was too good a swimmer, though. I realized she'd been holding back when we'd raced around the rocks earlier. Unleashed, with no rocks in her way, she was a torpedo. And now I saw where she was headed—the *Gulet Anilar,* which had moved sometime before dinner to the other side of an outcropping of rocks.

It was farther than I wanted to swim, so I started to turn back. Sage could handle herself.

But the alcohol might catch up to her when she was too far from either boat, or from shore. She could get a cramp. Or worse. Once, I'd drunk past my limits at a party and completely passed out, right on the edge of the swimming pool. The party host had called my mom. Mom's face had been the first thing I saw when I came to, and the first words I heard after "Are you okay?" were "Oh my God, you could have drowned!"

"Sage!" I called out, treading water. "Come back!"

She didn't hear me.

I couldn't leave her alone. Maybe she'd been drinking before I joined her—who knows how much she'd had. I plunged ahead, following her.

A few feet before the *Anilar,* gasping, I paused to tread water and get my bearings. A dim blue light shone from the hull of the boat, now just a few yards away. Everyone had gone to bed on that yacht too, except maybe one person. Light leaked out of a porthole.

I panicked. I couldn't see Sage. I was about to call out, when I heard voices. I swam to the back of the boat. Then I saw her, holding the anchor chain of the *Anilar* and eyeing the ladder a few feet away. What the hell? Was she actually going to go on board?

Rubbing the salt water out of my eyes, I lunged for the chain and held tight. "Sage!" I hissed. "What are you doing?"

She turned. "Oh! I didn't think you could swim this far."

"I was worried about you. Were you talking to someone just now?"

"The first mate. His name's Riza," she said. "I asked him to put out the ladder."

"But—but—how do you know him?" I felt a twinge of jealousy. I'd been trying to catch his eye all day, from afar, and had come to feel a weird sense of ownership toward him.

"I met him on the shore excursion this afternoon. He came down the Dalyan River with the boat's passengers, Ron and Judy Clarkson. They joined our tour of the ruins. Since we let them tag along, they said to come by anytime and say hi, and see the boat."

"It's kind of far to swim in the dark, don't you think?" I said. "And kind of late? Won't everyone be asleep?"

"I saw Riza on deck," she insisted. "And he saw me. He waved. I thought I'd get a closer look at him."

My face must have betrayed how I felt about being left

behind on her moonlight swim. She swam a few short strokes over to the anchor chain, grabbing on to a link near me. "Hey, I'm sorry. I would have invited you, but you said you had a toothache." Then she looked at me. Really looked. I saw her face register surprise. The slight upward lift of her eyebrows.

The moonlight. I was bathed in it. She was seeing my face, full on. I turned sideways, but knew with a sinking feeling that it was too late.

But before she could say anything, I heard a loud click above us, and looked up at the *Anilar*'s deck. At the unsmiling face of a man.

And a rifle pointing right at us.

9

Gun control was a big part of Dad's platform. I'd seen pictures of all the guns he wanted to ban. The semiautomatic rifle pointed at me now was one of them, ugly and huge.

The man with the rifle called out something over his shoulder, in what I assumed was Turkish. Then another man, similarly dressed in all black, appeared by his side, holding a pistol aimed at our heads. In his other hand, he held a flashlight, its beam searching the water until it came to rest on our faces. The light hurt to look at. I squinted and blinked, and tried to melt back into the shadows, but the light found me again.

My heart was pounding so hard. What if I hyperventilated, slipped underwater, and drowned? At least that sounded marginally better than being shot. I glanced at Sage. She too looked frozen with fear, hanging off the anchor chain.

The man with the rifle said something to us, in Turkish or English, or maybe some other language—I couldn't tell. Nothing made sense. Couldn't they see we were just two girls in the water? Who did they think we were?

And who were *they*? All day I'd seen only the hot first mate and the couple on the *Anilar,* and occasional glimpses of the captain and the cook. Did these thugs hide below deck all day? Or had they recently joined the cruise?

Worse—had they *hijacked* the boat?

Sage glanced back at our boat, as if gauging the distance. Then she took a deep breath and held up her free hand, as if in surrender, so I did the same.

"Don't shoot us!" she begged, a tremor in her voice. "Please. We're just swimming."

They didn't shoot, but they didn't lower their weapons, either. The guy with the flashlight and pistol shifted the beam so that it caught all of my face. Then they said something else to each other, harsh and guttural, that I couldn't understand.

Suddenly a light switched on in the boat's cabin. A string of tiny white lights hanging from an awning winked on. A woman wearing a filmy white bathrobe appeared on the deck. "What's going on?" she asked the two men in alarm.

"Oh, thank God. That's Judy Clarkson," Sage whispered to me while the man with the rifle talked to the woman in English. I could sense the relief in her voice. I felt the relief, too. If the woman knew who these guys were, this wasn't a hostage situation.

My relief quickly turned to annoyance. "She didn't happen to mention she had two armed thugs on their boat? I might have thought twice about swimming out here if I'd known."

"Actually, no, she didn't mention them. She said it was just the captain and the first mate on board. Oh, and the captain's wife, Elif, who cooks for everyone." Sage took another deep breath, as if about to go underwater, and shouted, "Judy! It's me! Sage Powell! From the *Gulet Yasemin!*"

"Sage?" Judy leaned over the railing. "My goodness! What are you doing out there?"

"Just out for a moonlight swim with my friend here."

Judy Clarkson turned to the two men. "Hey, those things really give me the willies. Do you mind putting them away?"

The men slowly lowered their weapons. But they did not lower their gaze. Their eyes seemed to pierce right through us.

"Come on up, girls," Judy called. "It's too dangerous to swim at night." I heard her voice tremble slightly with concern. "My apologies if our security staff frightened you. There's been some criminal activity in the area lately, and they're alert to every approach. We'll get you dried off and send you back to your boat in the tender."

"Oh, it's not so far. We can swim," said Sage. "We don't want to trouble you."

I stared at Sage in disbelief. "I want a ride back," I whispered. "It's dark."

"Are you kidding me? They almost shot us!" Sage protested. "You want to hop into a rowboat with a couple of trigger-happy thugs?"

"It's absolutely no trouble," Judy called down to us. "Really. I insist!" Then she turned toward the cabin: "Ron? Sweetie? There's two *kids* in the water!"

"Kids? Children?" said a male voice from the cabin.

"Teenagers. It's Sage, that girl we met on the ruins tour today. She's here with her friend!"

Her friend. I warmed. I had a friend. Hearing someone else say the words made it real.

"They've swum over from that other boat. You know, the *Yasemin*—the one that's been following us to the choice spots and hijacking our itinerary."

Wait. O*ur* boat was following *theirs*? I thought it was the other way around! But now it made sense. A private charter with wealthy passengers would gravitate toward the most secluded spots. Maybe Captain Mehmet was following the *Anilar* to give us some sense of exclusivity, as a way to compensate for the cancelled archaeological lecture. And there were a couple of other small boats not too far off, whose captains probably had the same idea to follow the private charter.

Judy beckoned to us again. "Girls, come on up. We have cookies, and hot tea."

"Come on," I urged Sage, in a low voice. "You wanted to see the boat, didn't you? Isn't that why you swam here? Plus, cookies." My own *mom* didn't call me in for cookies and tea.

Sage looked doubtful. But when I jerked my head toward the *Anilar*, she pushed off the anchor chain and crawlstroked to the boat's swim ladder. I followed.

We hauled ourselves up the swim ladder. The two men grabbed us roughly by the arms and pulled us onto the deck. Now, in the light, I could get a better look at them. I did a mental "You Are Here" journal entry. Both men wore black caps with some kind of white logo on the front. They also had on black windbreaker-type jackets, with the same indistinct logo, and black pants. I could also make out collared shirts and ties beneath the black jackets.

Up close, the guy with the semiautomatic rifle was really tall. He had an unusually long nose, a goatee, and a mop of dark, shaggy hair. He looked like he could be an indie rock star, with a guitar slung around his neck instead of a lethal weapon. He could even be handsome, or the kind of guy who wrote poetry in the back of class in high school—if his eyes didn't glitter in that unsettling way, and if the right side of his lip didn't curl up in a sneer.

The guy with the flashlight and pistol was shorter and stockier. He had close-cut hair and dark facial stubble, and a shapeless nose that made me think of a potato. With his broad shoulders and pissed-off expression, he looked like he'd make a great bouncer at a nightclub.

Then two more men appeared, looking at us like we were a very strange catch of the day. One slipped his arm around Judy, so that had to be Ron Clarkson, her husband. The other was a gray-haired Turkish man, short and stocky, who wore a white polo shirt and khakis just like Captain Mehmet, so I figured he must be the *Anilar's* captain.

And that hot first mate—the inspiration for Sage's moonlight swim? After all we'd been through to get on this boat, he was nowhere to be seen.

Judy Clarkson handed us enormous, lavender-scented white towels, two each, which we gratefully accepted. "Oh, to be young and crazy again," she said with a kind, almost wistful smile. "A moonlight swim. What a riot!"

Something inside me melted. Mom wouldn't have reacted that way. She would have launched into a lecture.

"It's insanity to swim here at night," Judy added, almost cheerfully, "but it's something I would have done in my carefree youth." She winked at us and smiled, revealing a gap between her two front teeth. My dad always said that he liked people with gap-toothed smiles, that they had a good sense of humor.

"Me too," said Ron Clarkson. "Those were the days. When you felt indestructible."

Neither Judy nor Ron seemed that old, I thought, as I wrapped one of the plush towels around me. They were both somewhere in their fifties. Judy was naturally pretty, like some classy British movie star. Unlike Mom and her friends, she didn't seem to be fighting her age with expensive products and procedures. Her honey-colored hair, swept back in a low ponytail, was silver-frosted. The lines on her face weren't Botoxed out. Ron, too, looked tanned and weathered, like he spent lots of time on boats or outdoors, and his muscular arms and legs suggested an active lifestyle. They fussed over us like my own parents hadn't in a long time. I hadn't realized how much I missed that. Being looked after instead of yelled at.

We dried ourselves while the security guards watched, their guns lowered but still in plain sight. I peeked at their hat and jacket logos while I toweled off. I couldn't read the Turkish letters stitched beneath, or even make out the design—a tree? A lion? A hand with claws? Before I could wrap my mind around it, Judy and Ron were leading us to a cushioned seat at the stern.

The stern area was similar to the one on our yacht, only bigger, cleaner, and overstuffed. All the furnishings were immaculately white except for the cushions, which looked like rich red Oriental rugs or tapestries. I had thought the *Gulet Yasemin* was an elegant yacht, but now, in comparison to the *Anilar,* I saw how tired our boat was. The *Yasemin* needed fresh oil on the teak, and its bolsters and cushions were ripped and stained. Some things didn't work right, like the medicine cabinet door in our bathroom that constantly banged around, and the floorboards that squeaked, and the toilet that had overflowed twice. It was still a more luxurious boat than I'd ever been on, and a vacation vessel that many people could only dream of. But everything on the *Anilar* was pristine, plush, and perfect.

Finally the first mate emerged from the kitchen carrying a steaming samovar and a tray of tiny glass cups with no handles. Hot tea. Hot guy. My hand flew to the left side of my face, where I pretended to be fidgeting with a stray lock of hair. Judy introduced us. "This is Riza," she said. "The captain and the cook on this boat are his uncle and aunt. He's trying out the family business."

"Hello," he said with a broad smile. He was even more gorgeous up close and in person. Tall. Plump lips. Dimpled cheeks. He wore his clothes effortlessly, his shirt untucked, and one lock of his wild, dark hair fell forward and hung in his eyes as he poured the tea. He was straight out of a Turkish Tommy Hilfiger ad. He smelled of fresh apples.

And there I was with half a face. I kept my head out of the light, sitting at a slight angle across from the Clarksons and from Riza. Not that it mattered. He was looking at Sage, with the same sort of lost-puppy look I'd seen Orhan use on Mom.

"We met Sage at the ruins today, but I don't believe we got your name," said Judy, looking at me.

"Oh. Um. I'm Zan," I said, pulling the towel partly over my

head, like a hoodie. The Clarksons were Americans. My dad's campaign, and his scandal, had made national news. But if they knew who I was, they said nothing.

Judy sent Riza to the kitchen for some cookies. Their captain disappeared below deck, taking the security guys with him. As I turned my head to watch them go, my makeshift hoodie slipped, suddenly exposing my face full-on. The Clarksons looked at me. *Really* looked. I could feel their curiosity, their gaze burning through me, wondering what was up with my Phantom of the Opera face. Was I a burn victim? A cancer patient? Fortunately they said nothing as I quickly readjusted the towel.

"You girls are very lucky, you know," Ron said, still kind but more stern now, sounding a little bit like a dad. Like *my* dad, before he got all weird about the campaign and about Victoria, back when my transgressions were less frequent. "You could have been hurt. Cut up on the rocks. Or you could have stepped on a sea urchin."

"A sea urchin!" Sage exclaimed.

"Oh, yes," said Ron. "You should always wear swim shoes. Be very careful on the rocks."

"Not to mention, sometimes the captains pull up anchor in the middle of the night to beat the crowds to certain beaches," Judy added.

I looked to the left, to see if I could still make out the two masts of the *Gulet Yasemin* over the outcroppings of rocks. I wasn't so sure that I could. Suddenly I ached for my little berth and my porthole, and my cool white sheets, even Mom's snoring.

Mom. What would she do if she woke up and saw I was gone? She would seriously freak.

"Or we could have been *shot* by your security guys," Sage added sharply. "Or had heart attacks from being held at gunpoint." I was surprised by her surge of anger. The Clarksons had put me at ease with their warmth and friendliness, and I understood that rich people sometimes hired their own security. There were often security guards at my dad's events, too. Although, come to think of it, their guns were always holstered.

"We're really sorry about that," said Ron. "I agree, it was an excessive show of force. But Lazar and Vasil heard a noise near the boat, and the radar in their cabin had picked up movement. The way the light was falling, they couldn't see it was two girls in the water. They were just doing their jobs."

"It seems weird that people would need that level of protection out *here*," I said, gesturing at the quiet water around us.

"I know. You'd think we wouldn't need armed guards in the Turkish Riviera," Judy agreed. "It's a shame. But it's not just Turkey that's heating up. Increased crime against tourists—especially if you look like you have a little cash—why, it's *everywhere*. We had a terrible experience in Egypt last year, being robbed at the pyramids, at knifepoint. We love to travel, to all the corners of the world, but after that horror show in Egypt, Ron and I decided, we'll pay for peace of mind."

"That was ghastly," Ron agreed. "But let's not scare the girls, or wreck our honeymoon with a bad memory." He smiled. "We're from Carmel, California. Where are you girls from?"

"Oregon," Sage mumbled.

"Portland?" prompted Judy. "I love Portland. It's come a long way."

"No. Rosedale. It's a pretty small town. You've probably never heard of it."

"I have not. But I do find small towns charming."

"Are you studying abroad like Sage, Zan?" Ron asked me.

"N-n-no. I'm here vacationing with my family," I replied, squirming under his gaze.

Riza returned at that moment, sparing me from explaining details. He set down a plate of cookies, pastries, and baklava. As Riza smiled at us, my hand automatically rose to cover my left cheek. Not that it mattered. His eyes danced at both of us, but it was Sage he looked at.

"This baklava is great," I said, biting into a juicy piece. Phyllo and walnuts crunched in my mouth, and honey dribbled down my chin. "Did you get it from one of those guys who comes around selling it in a motorboat?"

"We did. Just this evening," said Judy. "Isn't it divine? Please, have more! Otherwise I'll end up eating all of it myself." She patted her slim waistline.

I was about to ask if they'd bought anything else from him, too, but Ron wanted to know where we'd been in Turkey so far. So Sage and I told him while we finished our tea and cookies.

I felt increasingly at ease around the Clarksons. Ron sat with his arm loosely draped around Judy's shoulder as she leaned into his broad chest. They seemed genuinely happy together. Even Sage seemed wistful, watching them, and I remembered what she'd said about how her parents had handled—or not handled—her brother's death. How it had sent them in different directions.

"Sage mentioned something on the ruins tour about how your aunt has a hotel in Istanbul? You're going to stay with her?" Ron asked.

I nodded, but said no more. I liked the Clarksons, but Mom had said not to talk about our itinerary to people I didn't know. "And where are you guys going next?" I asked, deflecting their questions with a question of my own. A classic Dad move; I'd watched him do it in debates.

"We're off to Istanbul, too, for a few days, then on to Cappadocia," said Ron.

"For a romantic hot-air-balloon ride." Judy squeezed Ron's hand. "They say it's a once-in-a-lifetime experience. Have you girls ever gone hot-air ballooning?"

"Nope," said Sage. "I don't really love heights. Plus it's way out of my budget."

"I haven't tried it either," I said. "But it sounds fun."

"Got to live while you can," Judy said. "If it's on your bucket list, find a way to do it."

"I've noticed bucket lists tend to be expensive," said Sage, wiping honey off her chin.

"You're young. You have time," Judy assured her. "For us, it's different. Ron used to be a venture capitalist. He hit it big and was able to retire early. I was a software developer for an educational company. I did okay. But I had a little nest egg, some family money. A trust."

"Then we hit fifty, and I got cancer—survived it, by the way—and we realized time is precious," Ron chimed in. "We got married and pooled our resources."

"We realized what we really wanted to do was travel the world together. Have adventures," said Judy, nestling into the crook of his arm with a contented smile. "And now, life is but a dream!"

"That's amazing," I said, surprised to catch a sour look on Sage's face. Was she jealous? Why shouldn't these people spend their money on exotic travel, instead of acquiring meaningless stuff, like most of the rich people my family knew? The Clarksons were wealthy, clearly, since they could afford a chartered yacht and their own security for the cruise. But they weren't superficial like some of the people who came to Dad's fund-raisers. In fact, their real wealth seemed to be their love for each other, and their genuine appreciation of life.

I wished my parents could be more like them.

"Now we own a small art gallery in Carmel and travel when we have time," Judy said.

"Travel is something we love to do, and the gallery feeds our souls when we come home," Ron finished.

A wheel slowly turned in my mind. What if I studied in another country? Maybe even next year? Then it wouldn't matter if I had no friends back home; I'd just leave them all far behind. And an ocean between me and Dad and Victoria sounded pretty good, too.

Sage had struck out on her own to make a new life for herself. The Clarksons, too, had decided to put their money into travel and adventure. Why couldn't I do the same?

Before we knew it, we'd finished our midnight snack. Ron was asking the captain to get the tender ready for our transport, and Judy was wrapping fresh, dry towels around our shoulders. "These will keep you warm all the way back to your boat," she said, giving me a pat on the shoulder. "You can just send them back in the tender."

She led us to the swim ladder. I'd hoped Riza would row us back, but when I peered over the railing, I saw it was one of the security guys waiting below in the tender. The one who'd held the pistol and the flashlight. Crap. I glanced at Sage, who also looked disappointed at the sight of the glowering, balding, mustachioed man.

"Vasil will take you over now," said Judy, cheerfully.

We said good-bye to the Clarksons and descended the swim ladder, Sage leading the way.

We got into the boat and Vasil jammed the oars into the oarlocks. He rowed jerkily toward the *Yasemin*. Every time he pulled the oars, my teeth clacked together.

"What's his deal?" I whispered to Sage.

"He's probably pissed that he has to chauffeur us home," she said. "I'm sure it's not in his job description." But she didn't sound too calm, either, and she kept her eyes on his back.

It took a few minutes to get to the *Yasemin,* and I marveled at how far we had swum, when Vasil let us off at our boat. Sage and I wasted no time climbing up the swim ladder. It was good to be back on firm ground, even if that ground was a bobbing boat.

Vasil said something in Turkish. He seemed to be talking more to Sage than to me, though, since he was looking at her.

Whatever he said sounded kind of harsh. I was getting used to the sound of the language, hearing Selim and Captain Mehmet speak on our boat, but when they spoke, the Turkish sounded like gentle waves. This guy spoke a riptide.

Sage said something back that sounded brief and curt. When she turned from the railing, her face was clouded over. She stomped off to the opposite side of the boat.

"What was that all about?" I asked as Vasil rowed off, his oars slapping the water.

"He expected a tip."

"Okay," I said. "So why not tip him?" My parents always tipped generously when we went on vacations. Mom had been tipping since we got off the plane in Bodrum. "I know you said you were at the end of your cash, but I could get some from my mom's bag . . ."

"I didn't like his tone," she interrupted. "That's it. Okay? It's just not a big deal."

"Okay, okay."

Sage glared after Vasil, now a faint outline rowing away in the moonlight. I had to agree, it's not like the guy had been stellar on his customer service, ferrying us back to the boat only to demand a handout. I didn't like his tone either.

We went to retrieve our glasses and the bottle of raki, only to find someone had already done it for us. Mom? Oh, no. I pictured her confronting me with the evidence, just like she did when she figured out friends and I had been siphoning stuff in the liquor cabinet, or that I'd snuck off to a party and had a few beers, or that I'd lifted some makeup from our local CVS. The look on her face was always the same. Crushed. And it would happen all over again here, when she discovered I'd screwed up yet again. *Drinking and then swimming in the dark, Zan? Two bad decisions. Didn't you stop to consider the consequences of your actions?*

But nobody came out to yell at us as we went down to our

cabins. I slipped back into my cool white sheets while Mom snored on, oblivious. And that's when I started to shake. I'd been held at gunpoint. I'd been rowed back to our boat by a guy with a gun. I knew these were just security guys doing their jobs. Still, I felt like I'd dodged a bullet that hadn't even been fired.

10

The next morning, by the time I'd put on my makeup and sunscreen and dragged myself upstairs, Orhan was already clearing the dishes. The Geezers were propped up at their various stations. Nils and Ingrid were bird-watching. The British ladies were playing bridge. And the Lobsters were bickering. The only people still at the table were Mom and Aunt Jackie, paging through their books. I didn't see Sage anywhere. She was probably still asleep.

My head throbbed, almost as if I had drunk the "lion's milk" after all. I sank into a chair beside Aunt Jackie and rubbed my eyes.

Aunt Jackie smiled. "Hey there, Sleeping Beauty," she said. "Jet lag must be getting to you. They say the second day's worse."

Orhan brought me a plate of food. He also poured me a cup of coffee rather than the apple tea that was usually served at breakfast. I took the tiny metal cup gratefully in two hands, since there were no handles. Then I took a sip—and choked. It tasted like a cup of hot, thick dirt. I could see sediment floating around.

"Turkish coffee," Orhan reminded me with a smile. "We

usually have tea with breakfast in Turkey, but I know Americans often prefer something stronger. Especially after a late night." He gave me a long, knowing look.

So *Orhan* must have put away the raki and the glasses last night, knowing what Sage and I had been up to. But he didn't say any more about it. I gulped down the coffee and ventured a grateful smile at him.

"So what's the plan today?" I asked Mom between bites of breakfast.

"Cliff tombs," she replied, as the sleepy motor on the boat grumbled and sputtered to life. "Selim said we're heading to Fethiye now."

The boat began to move. I grabbed for my cup of caffeinated mud just as it slid away from me.

The Lobsters stood up from their sunny cushions and scuttled under the awning to join us at the shaded table. "Finally," said Maeve, wiping sweat off her brow with an embroidered handkerchief. "Blimey, it's really heating up early this morning. And I'm ready to see some more ruins. This spot was a little too secluded for my taste."

"Secluded is entirely fine by me," said Milton. "This is the first place we've gone in Turkey where no one's been trying to sell us jewelry or carpets. Honestly, you can't go anywhere without someone telling you they've got a brother or a cousin in the bloody carpet business. It does my head in."

"I don't mind it, really," Maeve said. "There are lots and lots of beautiful things to buy here. Is it so awful that they advertise them? I mean, everyone's got to make a living."

I thought of Baklava Guy and his tray of gold trinkets. Maybe he was just some guy trying to make a living, too, overcharging tourists—many of them probably drunk—on the water where his prices weren't regulated and his transactions went unrecorded. I wondered where he came from and where he had gone, and if we'd see other Baklava Guys at our next port of call.

As we pulled out of our sheltered inlet and away from the rugged coastline, I scanned for the *Gulet Anilar*. I didn't see the masts around the bend, just the two smaller boats that had been in the cove when we pulled up yesterday.

"Where's the *Anilar*?" I asked, standing up to look around.

"It's weird to look out and not see it, isn't it?" said Fiona.

"Oh, those Clarksons think they're too good for us," growled Milton. "We're always mucking up their views, I'm sure."

I thought of the Clarksons with their arms around each other and their adoring gazes, and wondered if Milton was right. Ron and Judy were traveling in their own happy bubble, with their own private staff, and they were probably sick of people from our boat swimming up to their yacht and disturbing their floating love nest. I really couldn't blame them.

As the captain steered us toward a new cove, the passengers—except for Sage—all gathered under the awning, seeking shelter from the sun, comparing notes on what was now, finally, coming into view. The Lycian cliff tombs.

My breath caught in my throat. There were way more of them than we'd seen in Dalyan. And I *totally* wanted to climb those cliffs. Of course, I had no gear. Or training on a real wall. Still, I'd never felt so drawn to rock.

"Look at that. They're like elaborate houses for the dead," said Nils, training his binoculars on the cliffs. "Carved doors and pitched roofs. Doric columns. Lintels. Extraordinary!" He passed the binoculars so everyone could have a look.

"Some of them look almost cozy, don't they," remarked Ingrid.

I took my turn with the binoculars, marveling at the honeycombs of doors and windows carved right into the cliffside. Some had little roofs; others had pillars and elaborate moldings. And yet they looked eerily unoccupied. I wouldn't have called them cozy at all. This was a housing project for ghosts.

"You'd think Selim or Mehmet or even Orhan could tell us a thing or two about the tombs," grumbled Milton. "Seeing how much money we're paying for this little jaunt. Believe you me, that's what I'll be telling Mr. Tabak when we see him in Fethiye, if he doesn't grant us that partial reimbursement."

"Oh, hush, Milton," snapped Maeve. "Quit complaining, will you?" She cast a worried glance at Aunt Jackie. "You'll hurt Jackie's feelings."

"I will not quit complaining," he huffed. "I am a consumer. The price of this cruise was dear. I don't appreciate being strung along with false promises."

"I have a guidebook, you will all be happy to know," said Nils, holding up a Norwegian travel guide. "It says a little bit about Lycian architecture. I will read aloud, in translation of course, if everyone is interested. Yes?"

Without waiting for a response, he launched into a lecture, translating in halting English. "The tombs were built around the fourth century BC. The house styles of the crypts were modeled after the wood houses the Lycians lived in, complete with windows and doors. The tomb chambers are empty, having been looted long ago, but they are accessible for viewing for those who have strong legs and care to take the hike."

"So dead people got the best real estate, with the best views," remarked Fiona.

Aunt Jackie was holding the golden urn with the rose petals very close to her chest, clutching each of the seahorse handles.

Mom moved her chair closer to Aunt Jackie.

"Was it right around here, then? Where Berk proposed to you?" Mom asked her quietly while Nils read on architectural details of the cliff tombs.

Aunt Jackie nodded, her eyes glistening.

"Are you ready to do the scattering ceremony?" Mom said gently. "We could find some privacy on the other end of the boat, now, just the three of us."

Aunt Jackie shook her head and looked up at the cliff tombs. The brown cliff façades glowed orange as the sun beat down upon them. "There," she said, pointing at a tomb on the top of the honeycomb. "That was where he proposed, actually."

Mom stared at her. "Not out on the water?"

"No. We hiked up there together, and he popped the question."

"Wait. Uncle Berk proposed to you at a *tomb*?" I asked. It was such an eerie premonition of how short-lived their marriage would be—just ten years—and how tragically he would die, falling off a cliff himself, though in a different part of the country.

"That's a unique place to propose," said Sage, who had quietly come up behind us.

I turned and she smiled at me over her cup of Turkish coffee.

"It was actually very romantic," said Aunt Jackie, a faraway look in her eyes. "There's a narrow trail way up there. Worth the hike. The view is spectacular."

I shielded my eyes from the sun and tried to make out the top tomb. It was pretty high up, almost a sheer rock face. The rock face interested me way more than the trail. There's almost always more than one route up a wall. I imagined which route I might take up that cliff if I had some gear, a rope, and a partner to belay me. I'd taken a lead climbing workshop last winter break at Burlington Boulders. I'd loved the feeling of not being anchored on top, plotting my line, and pulling myself up, bit by bit.

"Hey, would you like to invite Sage to hike up with us for the scattering ceremony?" Mom asked when Sage went to the kitchen to get a plate of food from Orhan.

"It might be good for her," said Aunt Jackie. "She seems so lonely."

Sage came back out, balancing two plates loaded with fresh fruit, yogurt, boiled eggs, and bread. "Any plans for today?" she asked.

I suddenly felt embarrassed. Maybe the family scattering ceremony was a little too weird. Aunt Jackie would be all emotional. Mom would be controlling. They might argue. And then they were going to fling dead flower petals over a cliff and pretend it was my uncle. The more I thought about it, the weirder it sounded. But Sage was looking at me questioningly. "My mom and aunt are going to do that memorial service thingy today. So, um, you probably don't, but if you wanted to hike up there with us, and hear a bunch of stuff about someone you've never met, you're welcome to join us."

"That sounds cool," she said. "I was actually going to hike up there anyway and check it out. I'd love the company."

"You *want* to come?"

"Of course. I'm honored."

"Great!" I grinned. Amazingly, nothing about my family so far seemed to weird out Sage.

While Sage sat at the table to eat, I ducked into the kitchen, hoping to catch Orhan. I wanted to thank him for putting away the raki and the glasses last night, and to make sure he wouldn't tell my mom.

Orhan was putting food in the refrigerator. He smiled when he saw me. "Oh, Zan! Hello! Can I help you?"

"Uh, I just wanted to say thanks," I said. "For the coffee, and for breakfast." I tried to remember what Orhan had taught me. "Tea sugar and a dream?"

His eyebrows relaxed a little. "Your Turkish is improving! And you are welcome."

I glanced at the bottle of *Yeni Raki*. He followed my gaze.

"You are welcome to anything in our kitchen," he said. *"Güle güle kullan*—that means, 'use it with joy.'"

"Thanks. And thanks for not telling my mom, too," I added. "She doesn't like me drinking. But you know what? I didn't even like that stuff anyway." I made a face at the memory of the bitter, burning taste.

Orhan chuckled. "Your secret is safe," he said. "And I can see you are not going to drink anymore." Then his expression became serious. "But I must ask you not to swim at night. It is not safe."

"We won't do it again," I promised. "And thank you for not

telling my mom about that, either." I smiled, my most winning, camera-ready smile. The smile that sometimes got me off the hook with salesclerks who suspected me when I slipped the occasional item from the makeup counter at Nordstrom into my tote bag.

It didn't work on Orhan. He remained dead serious. "I hope not. We are responsible for safety of our passengers. We need to know where they are at all times."

"I understand. I'm so sorry. We won't leave the boat at night again."

"Good. I am relieved," said Orhan. He held out a bowl of apricots. "Here. You hike today, yes? You should take these for extra energy."

"Thanks." I took four and put them in my cargo pants pockets. I turned to go, then realized Orhan might know the answer to something that had been on my mind ever since Mom and I had driven from Bodrum. And of all the crew on the boat, his English was the best. Maybe he could explain something that the Clarksons had alluded to last night. "So . . . are there police in this area right now because of the museum and mosque robberies?"

Orhan hesitated, then nodded. "Yes. Smugglers may be using porous borders to transfer stolen goods to their markets."

I frowned. The Lycian Tours representative, Erdem Tabak, had said that the police presence at the docks was a basic safety precaution. Clearly that was not the case. The problem was wider than the port of Marmaris, and connected to an ongoing series of crimes.

As if realizing his error in admitting the truth, Orhan looked down. "But you are perfectly safe on this boat," he quickly added.

"How exactly are we safe?" I spluttered. "If someone hijacks this boat, are you going to beat them over the head with a frying pan or something?"

Orhan stared at me.

"I mean, we don't have armed security guards on our boat like they do on the *Anilar*," I added.

Orhan raised his thick eyebrows. "They have guards on the *Anilar*?"

"Yes. Two. I actually had the pleasure of seeing their guns when Sage and I swam up to the boat last night. So I'd like to know how big a threat this is. Are we seriously in danger out on the water?"

Orhan met my eyes again, and this time he talked to me like a person—like an adult, even—instead of trying to sugar-coat his words.

"All right," he said, leaning heavily against the kitchen countertop. "This is what I know. The police are searching all coastal villages, trying to stop a smuggling network. Interpol is offering a large *ödül*—what is the word in English? Reward, yes. They offer reward for information leading to capture and arrest of leaders in this network. They are working with local police and private security firms. They ask the Turkish people to be alert to any suspicious people or activities in this area."

"That's good, right?" I said. "I mean, if everyone's on the alert, there's a better chance of catching the smugglers."

"In theory, yes. But it can also make people have bigger reactions to things."

I nodded, holding his gaze. "Thanks," I said. "I just wanted to know what was really going on." As I turned and left the kitchen, I thought of Lazar and Vasil on the boat last night, greeting Sage and me at gunpoint. That had been quite a welcome for two teen girls paddling around in the water. At least now I understood it better. They weren't just protecting the Clarksons; they were hunting for smugglers. They had probably meant to scare us and wouldn't have actually fired. Anyone connected to the criminal ring would be worth more alive than dead. But one of my dad's big issues was how ordinary citizens didn't need guns to protect them from perceived threats like home invasions, that the risks of owning a gun far outweighed the benefits. Much as I hated to give my dad any credit these days, his statistics haunted me now. I shivered. The idea that bounty hunters with itchy trigger fingers could be out here on the water creeped me out way more than the idea of thieves on the loose. I was up for another nighttime adventure with Sage, but maybe we'd have to stick to stargazing. I did not want to become a statistic myself.

11

Sage and I stood on the narrow ledge at the portico of a cliff tomb, looking out at the sparkling water of the bay. The tomb offered shade from the searing sun: a cool and dark room, beckoning to me. But it also seemed, well, tomblike in there, so we lingered in the doorway, between two crumbling and moss-covered columns carved into the rock face. I marveled at the warren of cliff tombs surrounding us, at how the morning sun transformed them into gold.

I shifted my gaze to the path we'd just hiked up. The narrow, winding trail of two hundred precarious stone steps had turned steep fast. Mom and Aunt Jackie were only about three-quarters of the way up, pulling themselves upward by grabbing onto bushes and tree branches that jutted out of the hillside here and there. A few switchback turns behind them were Nils and Ingrid, then halfway up the hill chugged Milton and Maeve. Still near the bottom were two gray-haired specks, Alice and Fiona.

They'd all wanted to come along when they heard why we were hiking to one of the highest cliff tombs. We'd thought it was because the tour representative hadn't appeared at the dock to meet us as scheduled. But it had turned out to be for a different reason, a nicer one. "We'd like to pay our respects," Nils explained on behalf of all the Geezers. "Even though we never had the pleasure of meeting Berk Yilmaz, we were very much looking forward to his lecture, and we feel so sorry for your loss."

"Think they'll all make it up here?" I asked Sage now, after I'd caught my breath.

"Not all. My money's on the Norwegians," said Sage. "And maybe Milton. Have you seen him swim? He may look like an old dude, but he's fitter than you think. Maeve worries about him, so she'll probably push herself." Keeping one hand firmly on the rock at all times, Sage shifted her body so that she was pressed flat against the side of the tomb entrance. I followed her wide-eyed gaze. There was less than a foot of stone ledge separating us from a fall down the cliff face of the mountain. This didn't bother me at all, but Sage looked almost green.

"Are you okay?" I asked.

"I hate heights," she finally admitted.

"Want to go back down?"

"No. I can handle it. It's good to face your fears. Right?"

"Yeah. Of course." I leaned against the cliff wall, more casually than Sage, and took one of Orhan's apricots from my pocket. I offered it to her, but she shook her head. I bit into it and sweet, delicious juice exploded over my tongue. I'd never tasted such good fruit.

"Besides, it's nice to be included in something like this," she added, with a wistful expression on her face. "My family never did anything special after my brother died. His body got cremated, but there were no services, nothing. They gave all his stuff to Goodwill one day. They locked up the empty room. And then both my parents sort of shut down, too. I feel like the house, and their lives, have been empty ever since."

"Sage, that's so sad."

She shrugged. "I guess that's why I bought them all those nice gifts yesterday."

I thought of the souvenirs she'd bought from Baklava Guy— the figurines, the earrings.

"But none of that stuff could replace your brother," I pointed out.

"I know. I guess I just want to bring my parents a piece of this magical country, and tell them about all the adventures I've had. I want them to see how fully I'm living my life. It's like I'm living for two people now. Me and my brother. I feel like I have this responsibility to live for him, too, and experience as much as I can, because he can't. Or maybe I just want one day where things are like they used to be, when we used to be a family."

I nodded. "I get it."

Sage sighed. "Anyway. I love what your aunt is doing, going to a place where she and your uncle felt most alive, and remembering her husband. It's a beautiful thing."

"Yeah, I guess it is." But I wasn't thinking about the ceremony. I thought about everything Sage had just revealed. She and I looked so different, but we both had sad family histories. I, too, longed for even one day where things could be the way they were back when things were good. Like when we'd sail *The Whisper* around Hingham harbor. Maybe it was all a façade, moments staged for family photo albums, but it had been real to me at the time: Mom with her legs stretched out, reading a book with a smile on her face; Dad at the helm grinning into the wind; me in between them, happy. Just the three of us, before the voting public and the media broke in and exposed our private lives, before Dad made all his stupid decisions that took him farther and farther away from us.

I drank in the air now, feeling clear-headed for the first time in a while. I hadn't realized how much I missed the way my family used to be. Or how much I missed being up high, where my brain seemed to work better. I ached for the climbing wall at the gym, where I felt in control. There, all you had to do was follow the colored plastic holds. There, the route was clear.

But an indoor slab didn't have anything like this view. I gazed out at it now while I polished off Orhan's apricots. The water gleamed a deep turquoise. The occasional speedboat raked a colorful parasail across the blue sky. And directly below us, the tiled roofs of downtown Fethiye tumbled down the hill and spilled out toward the beach and the harbor.

"Hey, just think," said Sage, following my gaze. "If you blocked out the buildings, this was the exact same view that ancient Lycians would have seen when they came up here to bury their dead."

"Minus the police boats," I added. "What's going on down there?" I took Nils's binoculars out of my backpack; he'd loaned them to us at the bottom. ("You kids are sure to beat all of us," he'd said. "Have a look for us when you get up top and make sure none of us have collapsed and died.") I trained the lenses on three blue-and-white speedboats that were zipping through the bay, gashing the water with their white wakes. They weren't towing parasailers; I recognized the police boats from the Marmaris docks. They were on a mission. They slowed at the small marina, where they cruised from one end of the dock to the other. I also saw a larger white boat with a diagonal orange stripe on the side. I focused the binocs and zoomed in: *Sahil Güvenlik,* it read on the side in thick black letters, and beneath it, in English: *Coast Guard.*

I ducked behind one of the Doric columns, melting into its shadow and hoping no binoculars from those boats were trained on us. Then I tried to brush off the guilty feeling once and for all. I hadn't done anything wrong. They weren't looking for me.

"Can I see?" asked Sage. I passed her the binoculars.

While she focused the binoculars on the boats, I told her what Orhan had explained about the trafficking operations the police wanted to shut down, and the reward money being offered. "I bet this is all about the smugglers," I said. "Look at them, swarming to the harbor. Like sharks drawn to the smell of blood."

"Could be," Sage said. She chewed her lip. "Or it could be something else."

"Like what?"

"Well, things are tense in Turkey lately for other reasons, too. Refugees are pouring in because of the situation in Syria. And there've been some protests against the government." Sage handed the binoculars back to me. "They're probably always looking for someone or something. This is a complicated country. But . . ."

I caught the look on her face: she looked as if she might cry. "What's wrong?"

"Oh." She turned so I couldn't see the look on her face, and cleared her throat. "I just suddenly got this stab of sadness. I know that must sound stupid . . ."

"No, it doesn't. I get that sometimes, too," I admitted.

She slid down to a squatting position against the cliff wall, then sat cross-legged on the ledge. I came out from behind the column and sat beside her, hanging my legs over the ledge.

"I'm going to miss Turkey so much," she said in a small voice, drawing swirly lines in the dust with her finger. "Even if it's unsettled right now, I've always felt at peace here. Like I was meant to live here all along, like I was born in the wrong place."

"Why don't you just stay, then? You could go to college here. Or work."

"It's not that easy. Visas and stuff. Money. God, money's a huge pain in the ass."

Again I thought of the stack of cash she'd handed over to Baklava Guy, and the fact that her parents had bankrolled her Blue Voyage.

As if she'd read my mind, she continued. "Yeah, my parents gave me what they could for this study year, and this farewell cruise, but now I'm being cut off. They want me home. You know how I mentioned my mom's been in and out of the hospital?"

I nodded.

"It's sort of a big deal. I have to go and be there for her."

"Wow. That's scary. What's wrong with her?"

"It's a heart thing." She cleared her throat. "Hey, speaking of heart things, did I tell you the story about the sultan's heart?"

I shook my head. There was that emotional whiplash again. A deeply personal confession by Sage followed by some breezy anecdote. Now you see her, now you don't. It was as if she sought safety in facts and stories. It was frustrating, but I understood it. Emotional conversations that went on too long could feel as if you were standing in too-bright sun: they'd leave you overexposed. So instead of pushing her, like my shrink had pushed me, I just did what Aunt Jackie would do and let her talk about whatever she wanted, trusting she'd say more when she was ready. "No. Tell me about the sultan's heart," I said finally.

"One of my international school teachers told us this story. There was this sultan in Ottoman Turkey. Suleiman the Magnificent. He was in Hungary with his troops, taking over a castle. A day before their victory, he died in his tent. Natural causes. He was old. But his death was kept a secret so the soldiers wouldn't lose morale. And his internal organs were removed to help preserve the body."

"Ew."

"I know, right? But they were at war. And they couldn't bury the body there. So, after the victory, his body was taken home to Constantinople. Which is now Istanbul. And his heart, they say, was left behind, in Hungarian soil." She paused dramatically, then smiled. "He fell in love. Not with a person, but with a place. He wanted his heart buried there. And researchers are looking for it to this day, or at least for the box that contained it. I guess the heart would be dust by now. Isn't that kind of beautiful? The whole leaving-your-heart-behind thing, in a country where you're not from."

"It is." I smiled.

"Turkey's way better than where I'm from." Then she added, almost fiercely, "I'd bury *my* heart here."

"What's wrong with where you're from?"

She picked up a small stone and hurled it over the cliff. We couldn't see or hear it fall. "It's just a small town, everything all fake old-time America." She sneered. "You know the type, I'm sure. All sandwich 'shoppes' and soda fountains, and civic parades for every possible occasion, and rallying around the local sports teams. And people are so narrow-minded there. They think they live in this perfect place, but it's a bubble. It's not real. They have no idea there's this whole world out there, and other people to learn about. But here?" She made a grand gesture. "It's a grand bazaar of *life*. Everything's on display, everything's waiting to be discovered. I've done Hawthorne to death. There's nothing there for me now."

Hawthorne? I could have sworn she told the Clarksons she was from Rosedale, or Roslindale, or something like that. But before I could ask her, I got distracted by my stinging eyes. Sweat was dripping off my forehead. It was getting really hot. I wiped my face, carefully, with my shirt sleeve, and then felt Sage's eyes on me.

"So is it vitiligo?" she asked gently.

I froze. I wasn't used to hearing that word aloud, except by my dermatologist and my therapist. Not even Mom and Dad said it aloud. Saying it made it too real, even for them.

"Vitiligo?" she repeated. "Is that why you wear all the makeup?"

"Um. Yeah."

"I knew someone in high school who had it," she said. "She was black, so it showed up more. I know sun was an issue for her, too. She used to cover it up, the white patches, but then she stopped."

"Why?" I asked in amazement.

"She said she got tired of covering up. It was a lot of work."

I thought about that. Covering up *was* exhausting some-times. And I suddenly wanted to reveal a little more of myself to Sage. Like about how hard it was to have vitiligo and wear certain kinds of clothes.

But at that moment, Mom and Aunt Jackie showed up, pant-ing and sweaty. Mom's pristine white capris and pale blue tank top were dirt-streaked, as was her face where she'd wiped off sweat. Aunt Jackie looked paler than ever.

Sage and I stood up.

"So gorgeous!" Mom exclaimed, taking in the view and extending her arms. "Can we go inside?" She ducked her head in the doorway.

"Sure. Berk and I did." Aunt Jackie leaned against the entrance. She mopped sweat off her forehead with her sleeve. She didn't look very good.

Nils and Ingrid showed up a couple of minutes later, col-lapsing their titanium walking sticks. They, too, marveled at the view.

"Why'd the Lycians have so much space in their tombs?" I asked, as we all filed inside to look around the closet-sized room. Shafts of light streamed in from the two windows. "This is way bigger than a coffin. Did they have more than one per-son buried here?"

"Nope. Just one," said Sage. "We studied these in school. These cliff tombs belonged to high-ranking people. They were rich enough to have nice houses and for their families to put their bodies here. All their valuables and gifts would have come with them."

I pictured Victoria Windham as an ancient Lycian in here, surrounded by her art objects, her weird cat and greyhounds whining outside. I imagined pushing a stone door shut. It made me kind of happy. Sometimes I wasn't sure who I was madder at: Dad or her. Both of them were cheaters and liars. Maybe they deserved each other.

"Those valuables are long gone, though," Sage added. "Even though some of the families put warning signs on their loved ones' tombs, or threatened eternal curses if any items were removed, looters ignored them."

"So where is everything now?" Ingrid asked.

"Museums, mostly, my teacher said," said Sage. "A lot of things went to American and European museums. Some are with private collectors. Some stuff's just lost to history."

"So disrespectful," said Mom. "Nothing should have left the tombs, or the country."

I knew Sage was talking about long-ago looters, but I thought of the local museum robberies, and the coast guard and police boats out in the harbor. Reward money for information leading to the criminals' arrest. I felt a quick prickle of fear. Could these old empty tombs be used as hideouts for thieves?

"Ow." Aunt Jackie suddenly doubled over in pain.

"Jackie? You okay?" Mom asked, frowning.

"Just a cramp. It'll pass," said Aunt Jackie. A moment later, she straightened up and took a long sip from her bottle of water. I guessed she still hadn't told Mom her news. I understood she was superstitious after having lost babies before, but how long could she keep it to herself? I was dying to shout out the news from the clifftop!

Milton and Maeve arrived next. Maeve was beet red, and wheezing. Milton was breathing better, but a bee had stung his nose, and it was swelling.

"Hey, you both made it!" said Aunt Jackie, grinning. "Good for you!"

"Not too bad a hike," huffed Milton. "For me anyway, since I swim all the time. Doctor says I'm more like sixty than seventy. But poor Maeve here's spent. Doesn't really have a hiking physique, does she."

Maeve, still panting, turned slowly and gave him a steely look.

"Oh, now, Milton, that's not nice," said Aunt Jackie, reaching over to pat Maeve's arm. "Maeve did great."

"Thank you," Maeve said. "Bit of a pull, that last part, but we're here." Her eyes traveled to the urn in Aunt Jackie's hands. "My, what an extraordinary vessel. Is it . . . oh, my." Her eyes grew wide and her pink lipsticked mouth formed a perfect O shape. "Is Berk in there?" she whispered.

"No," said Aunt Jackie. "There are no ashes inside. Just rose petals. See?" She removed the acorn-shaped lid and showed her.

Maeve leaned in for a closer look. "The seahorse handles are so unusual. Quite lovely. Solid gold, is it?"

"Gold plated," said Aunt Jackie, handing the urn to Maeve.

Maeve took it near the carved-out window to view the seahorse handles better in the light. "It must be quite old."

Aunt Jackie shook her head. "Just a replica. It's supposed to look like something from the famous Karun Treasure stash."

"Karun Treasure? What's that?" Maeve asked, handing back the urn. Milton, Nils, Ingrid, and Sage all leaned forward to listen with interest as Aunt Jackie began to explain.

"One of Turkey's most famous collections of artifacts," said Aunt Jackie. "Three hundred and sixty-three objects that were looted from the ancient tomb of a princess, back in the 1960s. Jewelry, pottery, things like that. They were sold to middlemen who then sold them to buyers at the Metropolitan Museum of Art. A Turkish journalist found them there, and after a legal battle, they were repatriated to this country in 1993."

I wondered about the princess who'd been buried with all that loot. For some reason I pictured her as a young dead princess. Even someone like Sage. Maybe the Sultan's heart story had stuck in my head and I was mixing the two things up.

"My husband used to do a lecture about the Karun Treasure," Aunt Jackie went on. "He collected replica artifacts like this one and used them for his lectures about the common motifs and styles. I found this replica in his office with all his lecture notes on the winged seahorse motif. The curious thing about it is that it's a replica of an urn that no one has actually seen."

"What do you mean?" asked Ingrid. "How can that be?"

"Many scholars believe the Karun Treasure is not just limited to the three hundred and sixty-three items that were illegally purchased and stored at the Met all those years," said Aunt Jackie. "Other items from the same tombs have surfaced in other countries since then. And the urn that looks like the one I am holding is rumored to be the most valuable missing item from the Karun Treasure. It has actually been spotted in different parts of the world. There are oral accounts from international art dealers who claim to have been approached to buy it—though no one would touch it without a clear history for it. Still, artists have sketched and circulated images of the urn based on these accounts. That's what this replica was modeled after." Aunt Jackie sighed. "Berk liked to tell this story in his lectures. But the real urn has never surfaced long enough to be handed over to the authorities. And Berk lost some credibility with his colleagues at the museum over this, unfortunately."

"How come?" I asked.

"Some experts don't believe the accounts of the missing Karun Treasure urn, and they liken it to Sasquatch sightings and things of that nature. It's almost a mythical being. A fantasy. Despite the eyewitness accounts by the dealers who are certain they saw it."

"I have read an article about this Karun Treasure," said Nils, nodding excitedly. "I understand that it is cursed."

I'd been touching one of the seahorse handles while Aunt Jackie was talking, admiring the details of the scales on the seahorses' tails, but at the word "cursed" I snatched my hand away. Then I remembered it was just a replica and so there was no way it could be cursed.

"Oh, no. That's just a myth. Like the cursed King Tut treasure," said Ingrid.

"No, many people do believe the treasure is cursed," Aunt Jackie corrected. "Everyone associated with the original Karun Treasure, from the original looters and tomb raiders to the middlemen who sold it off to the people who purchased items? They all suffered some kind of misfortune or died early. They say anyone who was ever involved in that looting, or who has possessed the treasure items for any length of time, had an unhappy life or very bad luck. Some people think the curse has been lifted since the Karun Treasure items returned to Turkey. But those who believe in the missing urn speculate the curse won't be lifted until the *entire* Karun Treasure is reunited—not just the three hundred and sixty-three items recovered from the Met but any other pieces of it that may still be at large."

"I see you *do* know a thing or two about archaeology," said Milton, almost accusingly. "Now I'm getting my money's worth!"

Aunt Jackie shook her head. "Honestly, that's the extent of it. It's all Greek to me. I just know about the Karun Treasure because it was Berk's most popular lecture topic."

Milton took a bandana from his pocket and mopped his brow. "Just don't get my Maeve started on tchotchkes," he warned. "She's quite the collector. Hits all the antique shops and rummage sales within a ten-kilometer radius of our home. She'll talk your ear off about them."

"Oh, Milton." Maeve gave him a withering look. "This urn is an objet d'art, not a tchotchke."

I backed away from the Lobsters as they continued to bicker. My stomach churned a little, as it sometimes did when my parents fought.

Mom looked uncomfortable, too, as if she was thinking the same thing. She changed the subject in her chirpy voice. "Where are Fiona and Alice?" she asked. "I worry about Alice with that cane."

"Fiona shouted up to go on without them," said Milton. "I don't reckon they'll make it all the way up."

"Maybe we should get started, then," Ingrid suggested.

"Okay. Let's go back out on the ledge, shall we? Back in the light?" said Mom. "It's a little gloomy in here, and this is supposed to be a celebration of Berk's life."

We all gathered on the ledge again. Sage went straight for a column and held on tight.

Aunt Jackie looked at all of us, then down at the urn in her hands. "Thank you all for being here. I just wanted to say a few words about my beloved—" Her voice broke.

The Geezers exchanged worried looks.

"There, there," Maeve said. "It's all right."

My nose twitched and my eyes watered. I almost felt as if I might cry, and I hadn't even known my uncle that well. But it pained me to see Aunt Jackie in pain. Her face made the whole thing so real.

"Shall I take over?" Mom whispered. "Get things started until you're ready?" Mom was using her event-planning voice, all business, but she rubbed Aunt Jackie's back.

Aunt Jackie blew her nose and nodded.

Mom stepped in front of the group. "Dearly beloved," she began. "We are gathered here today at this sacred site to remember Berk Yilmaz. Husband to my sister, Jacqueline Stern Yilmaz. Uncle to my daughter, Alexandra Glazer." Then Mom looked up to the sky. "We ask you to give us your blessing in this moment, and to look after the soul of Berk, who departed this earth too soon." She raised her arms in an expansive gesture, then teetered a little and looked down. She lowered her arms fast. "Holy crap. We are really high up, aren't we."

Aunt Jackie stepped forward. "Thanks, Kitsie. I'm okay. I'll take it from here." She stroked the lid of the urn. "I loved you so," she said at last, as if Uncle Berk were standing right there with us. "Your intelligence. Your sense of diplomacy. Your quiet reserve. Your sense of fun and mischief—that side of you that you seldom showed other people." Then she muttered, "And at the same time, I'm so furious."

"Jackie!" Mom whispered, stepping forward.

"It's all right," murmured Ingrid, holding Mom back. "Sometimes that's what people feel after they've lost a loved one. You should let her have her say." She nodded respectfully at Aunt Jackie. "Go on. Say what you need to say."

Aunt Jackie took a deep breath, then continued speaking, almost inaudibly, to the urn. "I'm not furious at you. I'm angry at whoever did this to you. I know you would never do something as unsafe as go hiking alone where you were. And that's why if I ever find any clue about who did this to you, I will make certain that justice is served."

"Oh, my," Maeve whispered to Milton. "Was there some kind of mishap?"

Mom smiled that tight smile of hers and put her arm around Aunt Jackie. "There are some complicated emotions," she said. "A few unknowns."

"Yeah, like who *pushed* him off a cliff," snapped Aunt Jackie. "For the hundred or so lira he might have had in his wallet at the time."

Mom whispered a few more things to Aunt Jackie, probably trying to do what she called "disaster control" like when something went wrong at a party or event.

Aunt Jackie nodded, cleared her throat, and continued in a louder voice. "Berk, I know your goal was to always provide for our family. So whatever choices you made on your last day on this earth, I forgive you. I miss you. And I promise I will raise our child to the best of my ability, and she will know our family and our country here, and she will know, above all, that her father, Berk Yilmaz, was a good man."

I caught her eye and gave her a thumbs-up. I'd heard so many speeches in my life, my dad's and those of lots of important people, but none had ever moved me like Aunt Jackie's simple words about her husband.

Aunt Jackie smiled back at me. Then she lifted the lid of the urn, removed the certificate inside, and shook the rose petals out. The dried, withered bits—ten-year-old petals—were immediately carried off by the breeze.

We all watched in stunned silence as Aunt Jackie calmly put the certificate back inside the urn and replaced the lid.

"There," she said, turning away from the ledge, toward the tomb. "It's done."

"Hold on a second," Mom said. "Did you say 'child'?"

12

The Geezers burst into applause and cheers, and Sage and I exchanged a knowing look.

Mom's hands flew to her mouth. "You're pregnant?"

Aunt Jackie grinned. She looked the happiest I'd seen her since we arrived in Turkey.

"But you—you said you couldn't!" Mom spluttered.

"Miracle of science. Took us four rounds of IVF and made us near broke in the process. But we did it. We actually did it." She wiped away a tear.

"Oh, Jackie!" Mom threw her arms around her sister. "I'm so happy for you! And I'm going to be an aunt! How far along are you?"

"Twelve weeks. I'm officially through the first trimester."

I went to give her a hug, pretending as if I was hearing the news for the first time.

"Hey, thanks for not spilling the beans," she whispered with a wink.

"Anytime." I grinned. Now it felt real. I was getting a cousin! Our family was growing. Maybe this would usher in a new era. And Aunt Jackie surely deserved some happiness after all she'd been through.

"A toast!" proposed Nils. "I've got a bottle of wine in my backpack." He pulled it out triumphantly. "Ingrid and I were going to have it on a picnic, but we'll share. And apple juice, of course, for the mother-to-be. Oh, but I see I've forgotten the corkscrew."

"I have one." Sage pulled a Swiss army knife out of her pocket.

While the Geezers and Sage gathered around Nils and the wine, Mom said quietly to Aunt Jackie, "Did Berk know? You know, before . . . ?"

Aunt Jackie nodded. "It's one more reason I'm sure he got mugged and led to his death on that trip. Knowing what we went through to conceive a child, he wouldn't have gone on a hike to such a remote place alone. No way would he take that kind of chance."

A vein in Mom's forehead pulsed. I could tell it was taking all her effort not to jump down Aunt Jackie's throat about the murder theory. "Well," said Mom, in a measured tone, "now I'm extra glad we're going to be in Istanbul for five weeks, to help you. You know, we don't really need to do any sightseeing there."

I looked at her. "We don't?"

"We're all about you now," said Mom to Aunt Jackie. "Helping you with the hotel is our number one priority."

Sage handed Aunt Jackie a bottle of apple juice. "Congratulations," she said shyly, looking at her with admiration. "I'm really happy for you."

Aunt Jackie beamed as she thanked everyone. But Mom watched her with a concerned expression. As soon as everyone finished their drinks, she steered Aunt Jackie toward the path as if she were suddenly breakable. "Now let's get you out of this heat," she said.

"Take this," Ingrid said, handing Aunt Jackie a walking stick. "You might notice your balance is off now that you're pregnant. I remember feeling that way with my first."

"I feel fine," Aunt Jackie protested. "Well, mostly. All the books I'm reading talk about this surge of energy you're supposed to get in the second trimester. I'm looking forward to that."

"I just want you on safer ground," Mom insisted, frowning. "What if you fell? Here. Take my arm."

"And let me carry that for you," said Sage, taking the now-empty golden urn.

"Thank you," said Aunt Jackie with a grateful smile at Sage.

Sage hesitated a moment, cradling the urn in her arms almost as if it were a newborn child. She looked from the urn to Aunt Jackie with an expression full of emotion that I couldn't read. I wondered if she was thinking about her brother and her own fragmented family.

Then, in the next moment, her expression was cheerful again. Sage's moods were like the birds Nils and Ingrid were always looking for: a flash of bright feathers, a rustle of movement. Before you could fully register what you'd glimpsed, it was gone.

Single file except for Mom and Aunt Jackie, we all headed down the narrow dirt path that led back to the stone staircase.

This time Sage and I trailed behind everyone else. Sage walked in front of me, slowly, holding the urn in both hands as if it were a precious artifact instead of a teaching tool.

"You'll have to rescue me in Istanbul next week," I said. "I want to help my aunt, of course, but I can't be stuck in a hotel all the time."

"Of course! Which hotel?"

"Hotel Mavi Konak. It's in Old Istanbul."

"Ah. The Blue House. I can remember that name."

"It's not really blue." I'd seen a postcard once; the hotel was a cream-colored building. "She has business cards with her. You should take one. Hey. Speaking of business." I smiled as an idea hit me. "My aunt might need an au pair, so she can keep working after the baby comes. What if you came back to Turkey and worked for her?"

Sage paused mid-step. She turned and looked at me, eyebrows raised. "Wow. You think? That's genius! Maybe I could ask her."

"I don't know if she could pay very much, though."

"Even room and board would be great."

"Yeah, maybe you could find some kind of work on the side. That paid money. Like translation. Or teaching English," I offered.

"Right. Right." Sage turned around again and walked faster now, as if fueled by the thought. "I think you're on to something, Zan. I'm getting all kinds of ideas."

"You could work at the hotel at night," I suggested. "Or you could give local tours to guests, since you know so much about Turkish history."

"Yes! Perfect! That'd be—"

Suddenly she tripped on a crumbling stone step. She pitched forward and fell off the steps to the narrow border of ground on the right side of them. She skidded for a few feet, her hands scrabbling at the ground in an attempt to stop the downward slide. The urn flew out of her hands and sailed over the cliffside, where it tumbled over and over, glinting gold in the sunlight, toward an outcropping of rock, and out of my sight.

13

I rushed to help Sage up. "Are you okay?" I asked. Breathless and unable to speak, she only nodded. Her hands were skinned, bleeding a little, but she seemed more startled than injured.

"Oh my God. Where's the urn?" she gasped, looking all around her.

"It fell over the cliffside."

We both ran a few feet back, to the place where she'd tripped, and peered over the edge of the cliff. It was a sheer drop, broken up only by a triangle-shaped precipice covered with brambly bushes. Beneath that precipice was another nearly sheer drop of cliff wall, then a pile of jagged boulders. Beyond that was the sea.

I felt sick and dizzy all at once. Partly because the urn was gone, and partly because I couldn't help thinking of Uncle Berk falling to his death. For the first time, I really thought about it: what it must have felt like for him to lose his footing, whether or not he had been pushed. The terror of sliding and not knowing when or if you would stop.

The terror of stopping.

The silence, after.

Mom and Aunt Jackie backtracked up the hill and joined us.

That's when Sage started to shake. Her eyes glistened as she explained what had happened. "I'm so, so sorry!" she finished.

"It's okay. It was an accident," said Aunt Jackie, reaching out and rubbing Sage's arm. "It could have been so much worse. You could have gone over the edge of the cliff. I don't understand why they can't put a railing up along this staircase."

"But I wasn't paying attention. I shouldn't have been carrying something so important." Sage wiped away tears, leaving a streak of dirt across her face. "I'm going to go look for it. Right now." She took a step off the stairs. A small avalanche of pebbles skittered down.

"No, don't," I said, pulling her back from the edge.

"Zan's right. It's too dangerous," said Aunt Jackie. "Maybe it made it all the way to the bottom of this part of the hillside. We can look around there, near the trailhead."

"Do you think it's intact?" Mom asked doubtfully.

"It's gold-plated, not solid gold," Aunt Jackie reminded us. "It won't get too dented. There's a chance the handles could break off. But *we're* breakable, all of us, so let's not take any unnecessary risks. We'll stick to the path for now."

We descended the rest of the stone staircase. The hill became a little less steep, and at a bench beneath the shade of a tree, just off the path, we caught up with Fiona and Alice, who were taking a water break.

Sage rushed up to them. "I tripped and dropped an urn that Jackie used for the ceremony," she said. "It fell over the edge of the cliff way up there near the tombs, and fell in this direction, I think. Did you see it?"

"No, my dear," said Alice. "I'm afraid my eyesight isn't what it used to be."

"I did see something," said Fiona. "Thought it might have been a bird swooping down at first, a hawk or something, but it was shiny. Maybe it was the urn." She pointed to the triangle-shaped outcropping of rock jutting out of the middle of the hillside, the outcropping I'd noticed from higher up on the path. "It might have ended up there. That was the direction. But the sun was in my eyes. I'm not sure if it landed there or if it glanced off and went further down the cliff or in another direction altogether. Or even into the sea."

Nils and Ingrid joined us, too, and then Milton and Maeve. Each of them said they'd seen a shiny object in flight. "I saw it go that way," said Nils, pointing to the left of the base of the outcropping.

"I'm pretty sure it went that way," Ingrid insisted, pointing to the right.

"A shame about that urn," Milton said, turning to Aunt Jackie. "I'm sorry for you, dearie."

"At least it wasn't too valuable," said Ingrid.

"Look. The whole ceremony was supposed to be about letting go. So I guess that's what I've done. Let go." Aunt Jackie laughed wryly. Then she gazed up at the cliffside again, with a hopeful expression, as if the urn might suddenly materialize.

"How can you say it wasn't too valuable? It had *sentimental* value," Maeve chided Ingrid. "It was a connection to Jackie's late husband. We must search for it. *Immediately.* Before the heat does us all in." She mopped her glistening face with a handkerchief.

"My Maeve doesn't let things go without a fuss," Milton muttered to Nils. "You ought to see the state of our house. Had to travel halfway around the world to get away from the clutter."

I glared at him. He didn't need to put Maeve down like that. Besides, it was a good idea. "There are a lot of us," I said. "We can cover more ground if we split up and look."

"Exactly," said Maeve. "Divide and conquer!"

"I suppose we could," said Aunt Jackie. "It's not quite so steep here. Better to look up at the cliffside than to try to creep down it from the top. We could split up and walk in different directions and scan the cliffsides. It might have gotten caught in a bush or stopped by a rock. If you see anything shiny, sing out."

"What is this *we*?" Mom asked. "You're not going hiking around off the trail in this heat. You stay here in the shade. We've got this."

Nils brandished his walking stick. "Ingrid and I will hike over to the left of that precipice, in case it went over."

"If you're all going left, Milton and I will look around the right side of the hill, at the base of the precipice," said Maeve.

"I'll look by the trailhead," Fiona volunteered.

"I'll join you," said Mom, walking over to the Lobsters. "Girls, you come, too."

"Zan and I can check out the front part of the precipice, where it sticks out," said Sage, pointing. "Doesn't it look like the front of a boat?"

Mom shook her head. "It looks too hard to get there. You have to climb over all those boulders at the base of it, and there's all those scratchy-looking bushes."

I rolled my eyes. "Mom. It's like bouldering. I can go over those no problem."

"And who knows, it might even have landed in those bushes," Sage added.

Mom sighed. "All right. But be careful, girls. Give a shout if you find anything. We'll just be on the other side of the precipice."

We all set off toward it together, leaving Aunt Jackie and Alice on the shady bench. Then we split up and walked in our different directions. Sage and I made our way up the steepest part of the hill, grasping the prickly bushes to help pull ourselves up, and then we scrambled over the boulders. I kept my eyes on the ground, hoping to see a glint of gold peeking between the rocks. But I didn't.

The boulders stopped about halfway up the precipice, leaving us at the base of a nearly vertical rock wall that rose about twenty feet straight up.

"I feel like the urn is up there," Sage said, her eyes shining with excitement. "I can see, behind the steps where I tripped, because there's that twisty tree growing out of a tomb. Looks like there's some bushes up on top of this ledge. It could have landed in one."

"Then we have to get up there."

"But how? If we go back to the steps where I tripped and follow how it fell, we could slip and slide all the way down this hill. It's way too dangerous."

"You're right, we can't get to the ledge from above. But I can go up from here." I tried to read the wall as if I were at the gym. Of course, at Burlington Boulders, everything was controlled: walls were sculpted by engineers; holds were manufactured from plastic, strategically attached, and routes set for a specific level of difficulty. The wall in front of me offered no such guidance or assurance. But there were some rock features jutting out here and there. I'd gotten to the advanced levels on top-rope climbs. I'd done climbs where holds were spaced far apart, or not directly on top of one another. Could this bouldering problem be so different? I put my foot up and reached out with one hand, when suddenly it hit me: This was *totally* different. With a wall height of twenty feet or so, this would be less like bouldering and more like free soloing. I'd be climbing twenty feet up with no safety rope, and a hard landing on jagged boulders if I fell.

"Zan, it's not worth it," said Sage. "If you fall, you could end up getting hurt. Or worse!"

"If it doesn't feel safe, I'll retreat," I promised. I shook out my hands and tied my hair back in a ponytail with an elastic band from my wrist. I fought back a wave of nervous energy and tried to steady my thoughts. I knew I had good instincts; my climbing instructors had told me as much. I took risks, but not needless ones. And I had a good sense of my body and what it could do. Climbing walls was kind of like working puzzles, which I used to love as a kid. It was just a series of problems to solve. Also, I'd watched videos of some famous climbers online. The one thing that always struck me was the look of calm confidence on their faces. If I could just avoid feeling fear, I would be okay.

I reached up for my first hold. I put my right foot on an outcropping, wishing I had my rock shoes instead of sandals. The flexible rubber soles weren't so bad—I could feel the rock through them—but I could tell my toes were going to get really scraped up. I reached for another hold, with my left hand. *Push up, pull up. Push up, pull up.* I could hear my climbing instructors' words in my head as I ascended, coaching me along, helping me spot the best holds. I made sure not to rely too much on my fingers, using my core strength instead.

This was real climbing! Just me and the rock. I had to listen only to myself, my inner voice, and trust my feet.

A soft breeze caressed my skin. Hope filled me. Aunt Jackie's urn could be up on that precipice. I might save the day! That would feel so much better than wrecking the day and disappointing people. I couldn't wait to see the looks on Mom's and Aunt Jackie's faces when I presented them with the found urn.

"Oh my God, Zan! You're amazing!" I heard Sage call. Her voice sounded far away, but it energized me. Feeling her eyes on me and enlivened by her admiration, I put more power into my limbs and sped up.

Push up, pull up. Now I was four feet . . . no, three feet . . . from reaching the top. Where I faced an interesting problem: how to haul myself up over the lip of the outcropping of rock. A gnarly tree root protruded from the sheer rock face a few feet away. If I leaned diagonally to the left, I could probably almost grab it. Yes! Now if I just reached a little farther, swung out my leg, and—

"Zan!" A shriek startled me. My left hand lost its hold. Stone that turned out not to be stone but a clod of dirt crumbled beneath my hand. Panting hard, throat dry, I scrabbled for a fresh handhold just as my left foot slipped.

"Sage? What happened? Did you see something?" I called down.

The shriek came again. And it wasn't Sage—it was Mom. Gripping a secure rock edge, I looked down and saw her scrambling over the boulders at the base of the cliff wall, toward Sage. She'd left Milton and Maeve. "Alexandra Glazer! What the *hell* do you think you're doing! Get down from there!" she shouted.

"I'm fine, Mom!" I called down. "I know what I'm doing!" What a nightmare. In front of Sage, Mom was acting like I was a misbehaving toddler.

"What? No! Absolutely no! This is a terrible decision! You will come down right this moment! Nothing is worth this kind of risk! Do you hear me? Zan!"

"Hey, you'd better come on down, Zan," called Sage. "Your mom is freaking out."

The fire I'd felt in my belly a moment ago, that pure energy, turned to black dust. I scaled back down the wall, feeling for the holds that had taken me up.

"I was so close," I grumbled after I jumped the last three feet to the ground. "If the urn got caught in those bushes up there, we'll never know it now."

Mom glared at me. "Back to the boat. Now."

"But oh my God, that was awesome, watching you climb," Sage whispered, out of Mom's earshot as Mom stomped back toward the path. "Where'd you learn to do that?"

I told her about Burlington Boulders as we descended the hill toward the harbor. It felt good to have done something that made Sage take notice of me. But I walked with empty hands and a heavy heart. I hadn't saved the day at all. I hadn't found the urn.

We gathered at the boat again, sweaty, exhausted, and empty-handed. Mom gave me an earful about my unsafe climb. Milton and Maeve said they'd seen no sign of the urn, and were giving up before they got heatstroke. Nils and Ingrid had no luck combing the rocky hillside either, nor did Fiona at the trailhead.

We all agreed the urn had most likely fallen into the ocean and already been swept out to sea. Aunt Jackie said everyone should just stop thinking about it. Still, I gazed up at the precipice with longing, hoping to glimpse the urn and prove I'd been on the right track. And yearning to be climbing again.

◇◇◇◇◇

The Lycian Tours representative showed up soon after with news that seemed to cheer everyone up: the company would award them partial reimbursements for the guest speaker who had never appeared. Feeling celebratory, everyone went into Fethiye to use the restaurant vouchers. Sage came to eat with Mom, Aunt Jackie, and me. "The boat is getting just a little too close," Mom confessed as we waved good-bye to the others and headed off for a café on the edge of the town. "Lovely people, but I think we could all use a little breathing room after this morning."

When we all met up again back on the boat, Orhan told us that the afternoon excursion was ready for us: a guided tour of some nearby archaeological ruins.

Mom signed us up for the excursion. Inspired, others on the boat signed up, too. "Safety in numbers, eh?" muttered Milton. "You figure they can't rip us all off at once, or drag us all to a carpet shop, right?" He inspected some long scratches that ran up and down his hairy arms.

Orhan immediately retrieved a first aid kit from under a bench and found some cream for Milton.

"We noticed the police and the coast guard are out and about," said Maeve, helping Milton slather on the cream. "They're all over this town."

"Yeah, Zan and I saw police, too, from the top of the cliff this morning," Sage said.

"We returned to the boat after lunch before you did, and there were three police officers here, along with a coast guard official. It was quite exciting," Alice chimed in. "Orhan says they're looking at passenger manifests and passport copies, just like they were in Marmaris. They haven't caught those smugglers, evidently."

We all looked at Orhan to elaborate.

"No specific threat," Orhan said carefully. "This is general security precautions."

I narrowed my eyes at him. I wanted to call his bluff, to ask what was really going on. How dare he tell me the truth this morning and then lie to all of us now? But I stopped myself. It suddenly hit me that this was his job. His income depended on people feeling safe on his boat. Maybe he'd tell me the real story later, as he had in the kitchen that morning.

"All the villages and towns along the coast must cooperate in this effort," Orhan continued, his face carefully neutral. "But please, ladies and gentlemen, do not let this affect the pleasure of your Blue Voyage! Your local guide, contracted by Lycian Tours, awaits you. You will then travel by *dolmuş*—by bus—to the ruins. It will be quite a nice adventure!"

Aunt Jackie said she would pass on the excursion, explaining that she wanted to rest.

To my surprise, Sage didn't want to go either. "I actually have a paper to write," she said when I gave her an incredulous look.

"A paper? It's July!"

"I know. But I have one assignment I didn't finish because I got sick last month and missed some school. I promised the teacher I'd hand it in next week before I fly home."

I gestured toward the turquoise water, the beach, the sun. "How can you write a paper under these completely brutal conditions? Do you even have a laptop with you?"

"I'll write it by hand. The teachers don't mind that. And then if I finish, I want to stop at a little market in town and see if I can find an urn to replace your aunt's. But have fun. You'll love the ruins."

Creeping around ancient ruins in the hot afternoon sun with Mom and the Geezers? I'd much rather hang on the boat with Sage and read while she worked on her paper. Or hang out with Orhan in the kitchen and see if he had more information about what was really going on with the search effort.

But Mom wouldn't let me back out of the excursion. "No way," she said when I tried. "I know the moment I leave, you'll be back trying to climb that cliff again."

"But—"

"I'm sorry, Zan. But like I said, if you want my trust back, you're really going to have to earn it. And I think today we took a giant step backward in that department."

Mom said all this in front of Sage, and I wanted to die. I boarded the tender with Mom and the Geezers and sat grumpily in the back. As we motored toward shore, I looked back at the *Gulet Yasemin,* and saw Sage unclipping two of her shirts from the clothesline near the prow, the breeze tossing her wild curls around and making her white sundress flutter. If a djinn came out of a lamp and let me have a wish, maybe I wouldn't wish for the urn back. I'd wish to be nineteen, and free, like Sage.

14

Somehow I survived the tour of the ruins. A *dolmuş*—a cross between a van and a mini bus—took us there from the dock at Fethiye. The village was searingly hot, no shade anywhere, and the remains looked like earthquake rubble. I tried to pay attention to our tour guide, but he talked so fast, condensing three centuries' worth of history into thirty minutes.

I looked longingly at a salamander scaling the wall of some former temple, wishing I could follow it on a climb.

On the way back from the ruins, the *dolmuş* driver routed us by a carpet shop at the edge of the town, where we had to spend an hour listening to the history of Turkish carpet-making and looking at carpet samples. The fibers swimming in the air made my eyes itch. These were no magical flying carpets, either. They were heavy, dusty, linty, and old, and the vendors kept dragging them out and throwing them down at our feet, piling them up one after another, until the air became so thick and close, I felt like I was being buried alive.

My gaze drifted out the window, to a caramel-colored building across the quiet street. RUŞEN KOÇAK MUSEUM OF ARCHAEOLOGY AND ETHNOGRAPHY announced the sign on the iron gate.

I nudged Mom. "Let's go over there," I whispered. Even though the name of the museum didn't exactly seem riveting, it had to be better than being imprisoned in a carpet shop. "Maybe there's a gift store. We could get Aunt Jackie some kind of replacement urn. I mean, it wouldn't be the same, but at least she wouldn't be going home empty-handed." I liked Sage's idea of finding some kind of replacement urn to give Aunt Jackie, even if there was no chance of getting anything that looked like the replica. I was feeling worse and worse about the fact that something dear to her had been lost. I'd played a role in that. After all, I'd gotten Sage distracted, firing off all those job ideas at her. If I'd just kept quiet, she could have kept her focus on the path, and held the urn safely in her hands as she had been, all the way down.

"That's a lovely idea. Let's go," said Mom. "I have a plan." She walked over to the *dolmuş* driver, who was standing by the door, the tour guide from the ruins having left us long ago. I followed her. "Excuse me," she said to him softly. "My daughter and I are just going to run over to that museum for a quick look. What time should we be back here? We don't want to miss the *dolmuş* back to the boat."

"Sorry, but this museum, it is closed," said the driver. "They have had a crime."

"Crime?" I asked. I peered out the window, and sure enough, three police cars were parked outside, a little bit down from the gate. By now I'd seen so many police officers, police cars, and police boats, in just a couple of days, that I was actually starting to get used to it.

"Were they hit by the robbers, too?" Mom asked. "Robbers," she repeated when the driver looked blank. "Stolen objects? Over there?"

"Yes, yes!" He nodded. "So, no reason to go. Is closed. But hear about traditional and historical rugs! You will not find weaving like this in all of Turkey."

One of the carpet sellers brought out a tray with tiny glass cups of tea, which smelled just like the apple tea the Clarksons had served Sage and me on their boat. Reluctantly, we all took the offered glasses. I wanted to ask the driver more about the robbery, but his English was limited. Mom asked one of the carpet sellers about it and got a little further.

"It was, how do you say, the basement?" said the salesman. "No damage or forced entry. But a large storage facility had some art objects. Some were stolen from there. It is very typical."

The tea burned my lips. "Typical? Why?" I asked.

"Small museums, they can easily be robbed. Most do not have alarm systems."

"I can't believe that," said Mom.

"It is true. And robbers know they do not have enough space to display all their items, so many things of great value can be found in a storage facility. But tell me, do you prefer hand-knotted or flat-woven carpet?" He held up two samples.

"No carpets," Mom said, her face tight. "We are not buying a carpet on this trip."

"But everyone needs a carpet for a floor."

"We don't have a floor."

I could tell Mom was starting to lose it. We were all losing it a little. I'd never seen such pushy salespeople. They didn't let anyone leave until Alice and Fiona finally broke down and bought a large *kilim* rug just to get us all out of there.

We returned, exhausted, to the boat, where we all helped the British ladies heft their awkward, unwanted, rolled-up rug up from the tender and into the boat. Then we pushed and dragged it, like a body, down to their cabin. "Bloody carpet sellers," Milton grumbled once we'd finally gotten the thing in their room. He gave it a spiteful kick. "They think every tourist is made of money. I tell you, if I bought a carpet or a knickknack from every man who offered me one here, I'd be broke in a day."

"Oh, I quite liked the carpets," said Maeve, licking her lips. "Wouldn't mind having one at home."

"Yes, but that would require actually having a clear floor

on which to display it," Milton said with a scowl. He swatted at the lint drifting in the air, and sneezed. Alice and Fiona looked miserably at their carpet roll, which now took up most of their cabin.

◇◇◇◇◇

After showering and changing for dinner, Mom and I went back up on deck to find that almost everyone else was seated already for our last dinner together. We took our seats, too, with apologies for being late. Mostly I apologized—I was always running late, because it took so long to put on my makeup. I wondered why I still felt a need to slather it on. Sage had already seen my real skin and not minded it. Others on the boat probably had some clue that I had a skin problem. Still, I applied my makeup with care.

As the sun sank lower over the water, floodlights turned on in Fethiye, gently illuminating the Lycian tombs. My breath caught in my throat. The beauty of it overwhelmed me. For a moment I almost let myself forget that the urn could still be up there somewhere, and that by morning we would be sailing away and leaving it behind.

Orhan, beaming, brought out steaming plates of meze— appetizers—and platters of rice and vegetables and freshly cooked fish. He served Mom first. "My specialty," he said as he bent near her ear. "I made this dinner with you in mind."

Mom blushed and choked out, "Oh! Well. Thanks. Um. Tea sugar and a dream."

The Geezer ladies giggled.

My cheeks warmed. Mom almost seemed as if she were flirting with Orhan! Then I realized that maybe that wasn't such a bad thing. Orhan could be a great distraction, and she'd finally take her eyes off me. I'd be free to hang with Sage, and maybe have another adventure tonight.

Where *was* Sage, anyway? I hadn't seen her emerge from the cabins yet, and her place at the table was still empty.

"Hey, where's Sage?" I asked.

"Sage had to leave," said Orhan, filling Mom's wineglass.

"Leave? What do you mean?" I asked.

Everyone stopped eating and looked at Orhan.

"She had a family emergency to attend to," he explained. "She asked me to say good-bye to you all for her, and to thank you for the pleasant company on the Blue Voyage."

Gasps rose up from all around the table.

"What kind of emergency?" I asked. "Did she say anything else?"

"I am afraid I do not know many details," said Orhan. "It was very soon after you went to your shore excursion, she packed and left," he went on. "She received an urgent email from someone at home. She had to get to the Dalaman airport right away and take an international flight on standby."

"Oh, no," said Aunt Jackie. "I wonder if it's something to do with her mother. She mentioned that her mother was in the hospital. I wish I'd had a chance to say good-bye. I'm so sorry I missed her."

Alice made a clucking sound. "Poor dear," she said.

I felt numb. Sage was gone! And while I felt bad that her mom must have taken a turn for the worse, part of me felt resentful. She'd spent time with all of us, gone to our ceremony, joined us for lunch . . . couldn't she have hung on another two hours and at least said good-bye?

Dinner conversations resumed around us. I tried to choke down my food, but nothing tasted right. Then I felt worse for having such selfish thoughts. Sage's mom was probably in some kind of medical crisis. She'd had to cut short a pricey cruise and go back to Oregon without even stopping in Istanbul to say good-bye to her host family.

Still, I felt like I'd started reading an interesting book that I'd never get a chance to finish.

I felt a little ripped off.

◇◇◇◇◇

After dinner, the adults hung out and sampled raki—except for Aunt Jackie, who stuck with tea. Bored with Nils and Ingrid's bird checklist, Milton and Maeve's quiet squabbling, and Alice and Fiona's tales of illnesses and bathrooms they'd experienced in their annual travels together, I went downstairs to my room.

The beckoning counts, and not the clicking latch behind you.

I thought of that Freya Stark quote as I flopped onto my berth. What the hell did that mean, anyway? It sounded like one of those journal prompts that my English teacher would write on the board and cheerfully command us to "expound upon, at length." I wondered what Sage's essay was about, and felt sad that I'd never know.

Or maybe I would. I felt something poking me and sat up and moved the pillow. Beneath it was a book, *The Lycian Shore: A Turkish Odyssey* by Freya Stark.

A name was written inside the front cover: *Amy Miller,* printed in neat, rounded letters. So the book had belonged to someone else first. A friend had probably passed it on to her, or she'd bought it used.

And the book was no loaner from Sage. It was a parting gift. I had no way to return it.

I felt something twist in my gut, or maybe up closer to my heart. I wasn't just sad that I'd lost someone close to my age to hang out with. Sage was unlike anyone I'd ever met. She challenged me, made me feel as if I might not have to hide my skin—or myself—all the time. She'd glimpsed the real me. Maybe it was crazy to miss someone I'd known for less than two days, but I did. And I'd had people vanish on me before; I should be used to it by now. But instead it felt worse every time.

I opened the book and started reading. At least I could maybe get to know Sage through these pages, by understanding why she was so into this Freya Stark person.

"Chapter One: The Voyage of *Elfin*." *Elfin* was the name of the yacht Freya Stark had traveled on with a team of explorers. Despite the intriguing chapter title, the book was hard to get into. It was more like a journey of the mind. Freya talked about reading the ancient Greeks and the adventures of Alexander the Great and how she decided to trace one of his conquering routes from the fourth century BC. I flipped ahead, skimming chapters. Greeks, Troy, Romans, the heroic age, Cnidus, bleah. I knew it was all important history, but it made a dull buzz settle over my brain. If I were writing a travel memoir, I'd focus on what I was seeing in the moment: useful stuff like where people could grab a bite to eat. Or I'd tell little stories, like Sage did, to bring the people in history to life.

The more I tried to read, the less I understood why Sage was such a fanatic about the book. My hope of finding her inside its pages was fading fast. The only thing the book revealed about her was how little we actually had in common.

◇◇◇◇◇

The next morning, we said good-bye to everyone at the dock, shaking hands with the crew and hugging all the Geezers in turn. Orhan held Mom's hand a little longer than necessary, I noticed, and then he slipped her a piece of paper with his phone number on it. Mom turned bright red and actually giggled. I rolled my eyes.

The Geezers chattered excitedly and shared their travel plans. It turned out that they were all following the same itinerary, arranged by Lycian Tours. They'd take a tour bus for three hours to Ephesus. They'd enjoy a guided tour from a university lecturer. Erdem Tabak showed up at the dock to make sure the bus transfer went smoothly. He assured everyone that this lecturer had been triple-confirmed and was eagerly awaiting them in Ephesus. They would spend one night on the Aegean coast, then fly to Istanbul for several more days of guided tours.

Aunt Jackie, looking slightly more energized, passed around business cards and brochures like a seasoned businessperson, telling everyone she was sorry we couldn't continue on the rest of the tour, but to look her up in Istanbul when they got there.

Our good-byes behind us, Mom, Aunt Jackie, and I made our way on foot to a travel agency. The commotion of Marmaris hit me like a slap of cold water after spending three days on a quiet boat. Aunt Jackie acted as if the streets weren't crowded, striding purposefully, her eyes straight ahead. I tried to follow her lead. When a man thrust a plastic bag of socks at me, demanding money, I lifted my chin and walked on by, looking right through him.

The plan, Mom explained as we walked, was to change our airplane tickets and catch an earlier flight to Istanbul. We didn't want to sightsee in Marmaris now that we knew Aunt Jackie was pregnant; Mom was concerned about the cramps she'd been having.

Aunt Jackie and Mom walked a bit ahead of me, talking about pregnancy stuff. The whole time we walked, I couldn't shake the feeling that we were being followed. Yet when I turned to look at the teeming crowds behind us, I didn't see anything suspicious.

We were waiting to cross a busy street when I felt something pull at my backpack. I whirled around and saw two men, one of them holding the string on the outer pocket of my pack to prevent me from taking another step.

I'd seen them before—it was Lazar and Vasil, the security dudes from the Clarksons' boat. Vasil, the stocky guy who reminded me of a bouncer, was the one holding on to my bag.

Lazar, the one with the goatee who reminded me of a rock star, glared at me down his long nose.

Mom and Aunt Jackie didn't seem to realize I was lagging behind. Like a scene straight out of a nightmare, I watched as they kept on walking and talking, oblivious, until they were out of my sight. I opened my mouth to call out to them, but Vasil yanked hard on my backpack straps, reeling me in closer. I was too startled to scream.

I looked around. "Where are the Clarksons?" I demanded. "Because I'm pretty sure grabbing people in the street isn't part of your job description."

"Clarksons not here," grunted Vasil. "Job over. They flew to Istanbul on early flight." Then he clapped both hands on my shoulders and shoved me roughly into an alley a few feet away.

My heart pounded. I'd seen enough movies to know good things *never* happened in alleys.

"Your friend Sage," said Lazar, while Vasil, behind me, continued to clamp down on my shoulders, as if trying to push me into the earth. "She is where?"

Lazar had a slight British accent, mixed with something else.

"Answer me!" he demanded, as Vasil shook me a little.

"I—I don't know," I stammered. "She went home. To the States. Family emergency."

"No. This I cannot believe," Lazar said, scowling. "She left you contact information. Yes?"

"She didn't," I insisted. "We were all on a tour. When we came back she'd just . . . left."

Lazar and Vasil spoke quietly to each other in Turkish.

Should I scream? I knew they were armed. Then I remembered that Orhan had said people wanted to find any lead on the smuggling ring, so they could collect the reward money offered by Interpol. My theory that these guards were also bounty hunters seemed even more likely now. What if they'd seen Sage buying stuff from the Baklava Guy and thought he—or Sage—was up to something? From twenty yards away, they could have easily observed that transaction, especially if they had binoculars. They might have seen enough to get suspicious, and not know that everything she'd bought was a trinket, gifts for her family. If they wanted her as a lead for reward money, maybe they saw me as a means to an end. They weren't going to shoot me.

I hoped.

Lazar's glinting eyes were on me again. "Before she left, did she give you something?" he demanded.

He couldn't be interested in the Freya Stark book, could he? He had to have seen the transaction with the figurines and that's what he wanted to know about . . . right? I shook my head. "She just bought some souvenirs," I said. "Cheap stuff."

Lazar and Vasil exchanged a look. Lazar translated for Vasil.

"If you're looking to catch thieves and smugglers, you might go check out the Ruşen Koçak Museum in Fethiye, across from the carpet shop," I said, trying to sound helpful. "I heard it got robbed yesterday. Maybe someone there has information."

They stared at me. Vasil did not loosen his grip on my pack.

"You are saying your friend went to this museum?" Lazar demanded.

A mistranslation of my English suddenly seemed like a great place to hide. I nodded.

He muttered something to Vasil.

Vasil shoved me out of the alley.

I stumbled, then ran to catch up with Mom and Aunt Jackie, not once looking back.

15

The Dalaman airport was even more crowded and crazy than the Marmaris docks. It was teeming with all types of people, tourists from all over the world, it seemed—the air was thick with a mix of languages. Inside, the place was boiling hot—no air-conditioning—and so crowded you could hardly find a clear path.

On top of everything, I was having some kind of delayed freak-out from my encounter with Lazar and Vasil. My hands wouldn't stop shaking. I gripped my backpack straps hard, half expecting someone to try to pull it off of me again.

What kind of security guards acted like that, grabbing innocent people in the street? Yes, at our first meeting Lazar and Vasil had thought I was up to no good, swimming up to a boat containing rich passengers, at midnight. But it sounded as if they weren't even working for the Clarksons anymore. Now that the cruise was over and the Clarksons were headed to Istanbul, they were free to be bounty hunters. Still, I was a teenager. Where did they get off scaring young, foreign travelers like that? I wished I could get in touch with Ron and Judy and tell them their security guards had accosted me in the street.

Accosted me. Because that's what happened. Wasn't that a crime? I had to tell Mom. But when? Aunt Jackie was having cramps, and she was in and out of the bathroom every few minutes. Telling her and Mom that two scary dudes had pulled me into an alley didn't seem like the best way to make her feel relaxed—and then I'd have to explain how I knew Lazar and Vasil, and tell them about my midnight swim with Sage. Besides, I reasoned, I hadn't been hurt. I was just scared. And those guys weren't after *me;* they were after Sage. Unfairly, I thought, because no way would she be involved in a smuggling ring. She was American! An exchange student!

I was suddenly so glad to be leaving the Turkish coast. The thought of never seeing Lazar and Vasil again made me feel deeply relieved.

After checking in for our flight, Mom, Aunt Jackie, and I got in the seemingly endless security line with our carry-on bags. We shuffled along like prisoners.

My backpack hung like a dead weight off my shoulders; the heat made it feel as if it weighed a ton. My hair clung to my face, and all my clothes stuck to me. I felt disgusting.

We finally reached the conveyor belt for the carry-on screening. I tossed my backpack onto it, relieved at having the pressure lifted off my shoulders.

I passed through the metal detector fast. I just wanted to get away from the crowd and on to our gate, where there might be some actual air to breathe. Especially for Aunt Jackie's sake. Her skin glistened with sweat.

Mom and Aunt Jackie gathered their bags at the end of the X-ray machine, and put their sandals back on. I put my shoes on, too, but my bag wasn't with theirs.

The conveyor belt had stopped. A red light was flashing.

At one of the X-ray machine monitors, a discussion was going on, in Turkish. The guy working it called someone over, then someone else, until there were four security officials gathered around the screen, looking and pointing at the monitor.

One of them held up the bag in question. "Whose is this?" he called out to the thronging passengers.

I hesitated, then raised my hand. It was my bag, though it suddenly looked strange and unfamiliar to me, hanging from this guy's hand.

"I must to open," he said.

I nodded. What else could I do?

"Oh, no," said Mom. "Do you think it's your sunscreens, Zan? You're supposed to put those in a clear plastic bag."

"I *did*." My face burned. Why did this situation have to be somehow my fault?

But the screener, who had taken my backpack over to a metal table, wasn't interested in my sunscreen. He flung the plastic bag of bottles aside without even looking at them. He had snapped on latex gloves and was rummaging through my bag now, unloading it item by item. Out came my wallet, my emergency tampons—how embarrassing!—and packets of tissues and hand wipes. A light sweater to wear on the plane. The Lonely Planet guide.

And then, from deep inside the pack, in the hidden interior pocket, he removed a black cloth bag with a drawstring. It was about the size of a book, only it was bulky and misshapen, not flat.

"What is that?" Mom asked.

"I don't know!"

"What do you mean you don't know?"

"I mean, I don't know! I don't know what that is!" This was getting scary. I did not own a black cloth bag with a drawstring.

The security official opened the bag. Onto the metal table, he poured out the contents, which made a loud clattering sound. Four shiny golden figurines.

Two security guards appeared at my side in an instant. "We have some questions for you, miss," one of them said, taking me by the arm. "We need you to come with us."

The whole room seemed to be spinning. "But those aren't

mine!" I protested. "I don't even know how that stuff got in my backpack! Please, let go of me!"

"We need you to come with us," the security officer repeated, more firmly.

"You can't just take her away!" my mom cried, jogging after us as they started walking and pulling me along. "Get your hands off her! That's my daughter. She's sixteen!"

"You must come too, madam," said one of the officers.

"Excuse me, there must be some mistake, some huge mix-up somewhere," said Aunt Jackie. She switched to Turkish, and I could tell from her gestures and tone of voice that she was explaining that I was her niece, that we'd just returned from a Blue Voyage, that I was just a kid. As she did, my thoughts pulsed. *Sage. Sage. Sage.* She must have slipped the figurines in my pack when she came to my room to leave me the book yesterday!

The guy holding my arm just shook his head when my aunt was done talking. "This is a very serious matter. Those figurines most likely are antiquities. They are forbidden to transport within or outside of Turkey." He looked at me with disgust, a look I remembered all too well from run-ins with security guards at various stores.

Only this time, I wasn't guilty.

"I'm innocent," I protested. "I can explain. My friend must have put them in there."

My friend. Some friend.

"I am sure it is a very interesting story," said the security official, "but you must explain it to the police."

16

The guards confiscated our carry-on bags, then marched us down a series of cinderblock corridors until we came to a small windowless room. This room was worse, way worse, than any holding area I'd been in at drugstores or in malls. The walls were painted a sickly green. The air was soupy, stirred by an oscillating fan whose metal blades were coated in dust. When the guards left, the door latch clicked loudly. Except for our luxurious furnishings—a metal table and some folding chairs—this room seriously felt like jail. I paced the steps to measure it: eight by ten feet. Slightly larger than my cell in juvie would have been. The size of our Pottery Barn living room rug back home. A rug I suddenly desperately wanted to see again in my lifetime.

"I want a lawyer," said Mom, talking loudly toward the closed door. "Or to talk to someone at the consulate." She banged on the metal door with her fist. "Hey! Somebody, help us! We are US citizens!"

"It doesn't quite work like that here, Kitsie," said Aunt Jackie, slumping in a chair. "They do have the right to question us at the airport if we have something suspicious."

Mom sank into the chair next to her. "I just hope we'll be released in time for our flight."

"I'm sure this is a bizarre misunderstanding," said Aunt Jackie. "Of course Zan wouldn't have knowingly carried real artifacts."

"Or *any* artifacts!" I said. "I didn't know they were in my bag! They belong to Sage!"

Aunt Jackie nodded. "I understand. And I'll call my attorney in Istanbul if things start looking bad."

"How?" Mom demanded. "They took away our phones! Our only link to outside civilization! They've cut us off!"

Welcome to my world, I refrained from saying out loud.

"We'll get to make a call," Aunt Jackie reassured her. "They'll have to give us a phone."

"By the way . . . what would be 'bad'?" I asked Aunt Jackie in a small voice. "I mean, bad enough to call your lawyer about?"

"Well, a conviction of antiquities smuggling can mean years in prison. And months in detention just waiting for a hearing," she said, a grim expression on her face.

Prison! Oh. My. God. Maybe Lazar and Vasil were really on to something, looking for Sage. Maybe *Sage* was one of the people the police had been looking for, too, on the boats. She could be someone working with a smuggling ring, and maybe Baklava Guy was, too! They'd sure talked a long time. They *had* to have been up to something that afternoon. Why else would Sage have sent me out of sight with a pastry delivery to the back of the boat, only to buy those earrings and figurines the moment my back was turned?

More strange facts began to add up. She'd boarded our boat very late on day one of the cruise, just before we left the dock—and only *after* the police and coast guard officials had finished with their dock inspections. Could that have been a strategic move? And could she have left the cruise early, making up a fake excuse, because the heat was on in Fethiye, too?

After a loud rap at the door, two police officers entered. They drew up chairs and faced us across the table, then introduced themselves as Inspector Kemal Turan and Sergeant Emre Aksu. I tried to convince myself that these were the good guys. Inspector Kemal looked like a history teacher or something, with graying hair and wire-rimmed glasses. One of his hands had a slight tremor. Sergeant Emre had tufts of gray hair growing in his ears and nostrils, and furry, caterpillar eyebrows. He also had a terrible cold; he sniffed constantly and dabbed his red, watery nose with a tissue. I reminded myself these guys were human, and their job was to get information. That's all. And this time I had nothing to hide. This wasn't the Athleta incident, Part Two.

Inspector Kemal set the four gold figurines down on the table, one by one, lining them up like chess pieces, his broad shoulders angling toward us. Then he sat back in his chair and looked at me, as if waiting for me to make a move—as if we were playing a game. I could hardly breathe. Finally he lowered his wire-rimmed glasses and asked me, in a stern voice, to tell him everything I knew.

As clearly and simply as I could, fighting to keep my voice steady, I told him about how Baklava Guy had sold Sage the figurines and a pair of gold and turquoise earrings on the boat. I explained how she must have put them into my backpack when we were on the ruins tour without her. Then I mentioned the security guys from the Clarksons' boat, and how they'd grabbed me in Marmaris and demanded to know where Sage had gone.

Mom let out a horrified little cry. "Those men laid hands on you? Pulled you into an *alley*? Oh, Zan. How could that have happened and you didn't even tell us?"

"Because—because—" I faltered. Now I was entangled in lies. Again. If I'd told Mom the guards had grabbed me, I would have had to explain how the guards knew who I was in the first place, and then I'd have had to explain about the nighttime swim to the *Anilar*, which would be more ammunition for Mom not trusting me.

"I didn't tell you because you were focused on getting us to the airport so fast," I finally managed to say. "And I didn't know about the figurines, okay? I had no idea they were in my bag."

"Why would they be so interested in Sage?" asked Aunt Jackie.

"Reward money?" I guessed. "Maybe they thought she knew something, or someone."

"What reward money?" Mom asked.

I told her what Orhan had said, about the reward being offered for anyone who could provide information about smugglers.

"It is true some security officers have become bounty hunters, American-style, since Interpol offered this reward," said Sergeant Emre. He sneezed loudly, mopped his nose with his crumpled tissue, and turned to me. "Perhaps they had good reason to suspect this girl was involved. Approximately how far was the *Anilar* from the *Yasemin* when you saw this strange transaction take place between Sage and the boy on the boat?"

"Maybe twenty yards? Twenty-five?" I guessed.

"That'd be about eighteen meters," said Aunt Jackie.

"This is not reliable data," Inspector Kemal said to Sergeant Emre.

"It is, I'm sure," said Aunt Jackie with a steely gaze. "My niece is a rock climber. She gauges distances all the time on the climbing wall. If she says it's between twenty and twenty-five yards, then that's what it was. With binoculars, those guards might have seen what Sage was buying, or seen enough to arouse their suspicions."

"I can see how they'd be eager for any lead that would get them closer to the reward," Mom added. "But here's what I don't get. Let's say Sage bought some spurious items from someone or was helping to transport them to a buyer. She must have known putting them in your pack carried a risk of getting you caught. And why would she want to take that risk? Or get you in trouble?"

"And why not put the items in your suitcase, which would have been less likely to trigger alarms at the security screening?" Aunt Jackie wondered aloud.

"I bet she put them in my backpack because my suitcase was locked," I said. "Mom told me to lock my suitcase all the time." I sighed. This was either Sage's sick idea of a parting gift, or she was setting me up to get caught. But why?

"Then I think it was a spontaneous and desperate decision on her part," said Aunt Jackie. "She knew the police were boarding boats and checking passenger manifests. She needed to offload the goods."

That theory made sense to me. I felt panicky around police all the time, and I hadn't done anything wrong here. And I knew how being skittish about police could lead to bad decisions. Like getting in a car with a drunk driver to get away from a party that police had broken up. Like ditching a bag of stolen clothes in a Dumpster because I'd sighted a police officer on patrol and felt sure he was looking for me.

"Yeah, I think you're right," I said. "Sage had already told me the figurines weren't worth anything. I can see how I'd be the perfect carrier, since I had no clue about them. I'd be acting normal and I wouldn't attract suspicion, right? And then she might try to get them from me in Istanbul later, since we had plans to meet up. Maybe she thought I could get them through security, with them hidden in my backpack."

"But her mother's sick," said Mom. "You wouldn't have met up in Istanbul."

The inspector and the sergeant had been watching the three of us try to sort out what had happened, turning their heads to watch each of us speak as if we were a spectator sport, but now Inspector Kemal cleared his throat and interjected. "Of course, it is entirely possible her mother is *not* sick."

Aunt Jackie nodded. "Maybe the sick mother was her excuse

for a hasty departure. And if that were a lie, she could find her way back to Istanbul at some point to try to get the figurines back from Zan."

A wave of nausea came over me. My God. *Everything* Sage had told me might have been a lie! Here I was again, burned by someone I'd let myself trust.

"So what about the baklava vendor? Why would someone sell valuable artifacts to a random American girl on a boat?" Mom asked the police.

"Smugglers and black market vendors work in many forms," replied Inspector Kemal. "The trade in illicit antiquities operates at many levels. Some vendors will sell less valuable black market goods at marked-down prices, from looters, because making some money is better than making no money at all."

"Well, if these figurines came from the kid with the baklava, we're off the hook, right?" Mom said. "And if there's anything suspicious about these figurines, it's that boy in the boat you should be after, not us."

I shot a grateful look at Mom. *Finally* she'd said something in my defense.

"We will certainly be looking for him," said Inspector Kemal. "Perhaps he had some distinctive identifying characteristics? Or his boat?" He turned to a fresh page in his notepad.

I mentioned the blue tarp I'd seen in the back, and he made a note of it.

"And now we've told you all we know, so you should let us leave," Aunt Jackie concluded. "Back to Istanbul. Our flight leaves in fifteen minutes. We might just make it."

"I'm afraid it is not so simple," said Inspector Kemal, his eyebrows knitting together. "Your descriptions and accounts are quite useful for us. But this remains a serious matter for your niece. Turkey has very strict laws about the purchase *and* transport of antiquities, which include any artifacts made before the year 1923. You did not purchase these figures, you say. But you are *transporting* them. This also can be a crime."

"What!" Mom exclaimed.

"You can only buy certain artifacts from authorized deal-ers who have a certificate from a museum for every item they sell," said Sergeant Emre, blowing his nose loudly. "You may not purchase or transport any antiquity or any questionable item in Turkey without a proper certificate. Even if you think you have only an inexpensive replica, you still need a certifi-cate to prove that it is not authentic."

"Jackie, did you know this?" Mom asked quietly, leaning in toward my aunt.

"I did," Aunt Jackie whispered. "It's why I carried a certifi-cate for the replica of that seahorse urn."

Mom looked at the inspector again. "And where does one obtain such a certificate?"

"If the vendor does not provide it at the time of purchase, then you need to consult a museum," said the sergeant.

"Okay, so we don't have a certificate for a gift we received. We weren't aware of the law, and we weren't even aware that we had received this . . . this *gift*. All right. So we'll pay the fine. We have a flight to Istanbul, and we need to be on it." Mom reached into her bag for her wallet. "How much is it? I have cash. I can get more."

"Ah," said Inspector Kemal. His mouth twitched. "I am sorry. You see, the items must be authenticated either as arti-facts *or* as replicas before I can let you go."

Mom slowly looked up from her purse.

"If they are determined to be fakes, you will receive a cer-tificate, and we will release you," he went on. "If they are authenticated, you will face charges. Five to ten years in prison."

"Five to ten years!" Mom exploded.

"You could expect at least one month incarcerated, pending a hearing."

Aunt Jackie looked sick again. She hugged herself and rocked back and forth in her chair. "I know all about this," she said in a grim tone. "My husband—my late husband—used to do this type of work. Listen, if you could show me a list of authenticators you work with locally, I can probably tell you if he knew any of them around here."

"I'm sure that won't be necessary," Inspector Kemal said smoothly. "We have our preferred contacts, thank you."

The walls seemed to move in on me. "Wait a second," I said to the police. "I had *no idea* these things were in my pack. Are you saying that if they turn out to be real antiquities, I'm still considered guilty for transporting them and I could be in jail?"

Inspector Kemal nodded. "This is how the law works," he said briskly, sliding each of the gold figurines into plastic bags. "Meanwhile, while we await the appraisal, I must detain the three of you here."

Mom, Aunt Jackie, and I exchanged alarmed looks.

"In the best of circumstances, I can arrange for a museum employee to come today," the inspector continued. "We have a detention facility at the Dalaman Police Station, where you can be relocated. They can accommodate overnight stays. Or longer."

"Wait a minute," said Aunt Jackie, her voice loud but trembling. "I'm a resident of this country. A business owner. And I'm pregnant." She switched to Turkish, speaking in a cool, even tone. Mom and I stared at her in awe. *Go, Aunt Jackie!* I thought. My next thought chased that away: *Prison. Holy crap.*

I felt like I'd lost my footing on a climbing wall.

I guess Aunt Jackie had failed to convince them. "I'm sorry," the inspector said curtly, as he and the sergeant stood up.

She stood up, too, so fast her chair fell. "I demand to call my counselor in Istanbul."

"Certainly. You may place a call." The inspector motioned to Sergeant Emre, who left the room and returned a moment later with a cordless phone receiver.

Aunt Jackie looked in her wallet, found a business card, and dialed a number. "No answer," she said, her face falling. "My lawyer's not in." She left a voice mail message, in Turkish, and hung up with a defeated look on her face.

"Call Berk's brother or sister," Mom suggested.

Aunt Jackie bit her lip. "I—I can't," she faltered.

"Jackie, they're still your family, even if Berk's gone," said Mom. "They should help."

Aunt Jackie shook her head. "We don't really get along. Right now." She paused. "Actually? They don't know I left the hotel. I can't tell them that."

I felt for her, remembering how badly she wanted the hotel to succeed, and how Serhan and Ayla were sniffing around it lately, looking for any excuse to sell.

Abruptly, Inspector Kemal and Sergeant Emre stood up. "I cannot sit here all day with you," said the inspector. "We must contact our museum consultants now." He picked up the cordless phone and the figurines, and he and Sergeant Emre turned and left the room.

Mom turned to me. "Zan," she said in a shaky voice, "are you sure, absolutely sure, that Sage bought the figurines from the baklava vendor, and that she put them into your bag?"

I stared at her. "What are you getting at?"

"Is there any chance you might have taken them from Sage's room—even to look at—and that you might have, well . . ."

"I didn't steal them, if that's what you're getting at. God, Mom! Why do you keep treating me like I'm the only criminal in the family?"

Mom folded her arms across her chest. "What did you just say?"

"Think back. The Athleta incident. What were you and Dad busy doing when I was there? You were holding a press conference, deceiving the good people of Massachusetts. *Lying.* About working on the marriage and the family. But I knew you weren't really going to. Dad was already packing his bags." I was shaking now. I'd never voiced these words; the thoughts had only been in the background of my mind. But now they surged forward like a strong tide.

Aunt Jackie came up behind me and put an arm around me.

Emboldened, I continued. "I couldn't stand there in front of TV cameras, wearing that ridiculous outfit and a hairstyle that wasn't mine, and pretend everything was going to be fine. So I swiped a couple of outfits that day. I admitted it. I said I was sorry. But Dad had an affair. And then you and Dad both lied to *the public,* saying we were all working on fixing our family. Just to win support for his campaign! So don't act like I'm the only bad guy in town. Just don't."

My mom's face twisted up. "Zan. A *lot* was at stake with that press conference. Not just for your dad, but for our whole family. I was trying to protect you, too."

"Protect me? Ha."

"Look, I know you're still processing all this stuff. It's hard. And we need to talk it through. But at the moment we have more pressing concerns."

"Well, I didn't take anything. I'm as surprised as you are to see those figurines in my bag."

"Of course Zan didn't steal the figurines, Kitsie," Aunt Jackie scolded. "Now can we all calm down a little, please, and just think this through?"

"Yes, let's just think this through," I said, shifting closer to Aunt Jackie.

"I'm losing my mind," Mom said, sinking into a chair. "They say interrogation rooms can do that to you. Make you crazy."

"Let's not catastrophize. We've only been in here for thirty minutes," said Aunt Jackie.

"But you heard the guy. We could be here much longer," Mom said. "And no offense? You look terrible. I'm really worried about you."

"I'm a little worried, too," Aunt Jackie confessed, as she and

I sat back down at the table. "In the restroom, I noticed I was bleeding a little. It's not just cramps now."

"What? Jackie! You need a doctor! And it's way too warm in here for you." Mom got up and repositioned the useless fan so that it stirred up the air around Aunt Jackie.

"I know. But we can't get out until the museum expert comes," said Aunt Jackie.

"And they're probably going to get authenticated as *real* antiquities," I added.

We all stared at each other glumly. We knew what would happen then. Prison. One month minimum just to wait for a hearing. Five to ten years if convicted.

Nobody wanted to say it out loud.

Two hours passed. Our flight to Istanbul left without us. Once, someone came in to bring us water, but otherwise we were left alone, with no updates, and no chance to make any more calls.

I studied my reflection in the chrome edge of the chair. I could see some white splotches emerging on my left cheek, and I reached for my backpack to grab for my cover-up on instinct, before remembering it had all been confiscated. Then I realized I didn't care so much about the cover-up, or even what I looked like right now.

Aunt Jackie sat as close to the fan as possible and closed her eyes.

"This is a nightmare," Mom said. "If you lose your baby, I'm holding the Turkish police responsible. The airport, too. And that baklava seller, while I'm at it."

Lose the baby! I hadn't seriously thought of that happening. But my aunt had miscarried before. Several times. It was a real possibility. My hands curled into fists. The baby was the one bright thing that had kept Aunt Jackie going through this dark time. If she lost her baby because she couldn't get medical attention in time, that would be *Sage's* fault, too.

Aunt Jackie moaned softly and leaned forward in her chair.

My heart thudded. "Should we call Dad?" I ventured. He'd be pissed, hearing I'd been caught with something stolen again. But I was truly innocent this time. All of us were. "Maybe he knows someone at the embassy," I added hopefully. Suddenly I remembered how he'd once saved a friend of mine from drowning in our swimming pool. We were kids, and my vitiligo wasn't so bad then, so I used to swim like a fish. My friend, who couldn't swim, had slipped and fallen into the pool. My dad had dived in after her, fully clothed, and saved her. I felt so proud to have a dad who could save people.

Mom massaged her temples. "I cannot call your father."

Aunt Jackie couldn't call her in-laws, and Mom couldn't call Dad—so much for pulling together as a family. "Oh, I get it. You just don't want him to know this trip was a bust."

"That is not true, Zan. This situation is way out of his jurisdiction. And if he does make calls, and the media hears about it, we'll be in the spotlight again. There's got to be some other solution."

I thought a moment about what Mom and I had just argued about. Maybe there was another way to look at the whole lying thing. As long as the people in my family were all masters of deceit, maybe we could swing that talent in our favor. "I have an idea. It's right up your alley, Mom. We'll stage an event. A *medical* event."

Mom and Aunt Jackie exchanged a look.

I explained my plan.

"It might work," said Aunt Jackie. "I'm up for trying, anyway."

"And there's a foundation of truth underneath it," Mom admitted. "You aren't well. We're just going to amplify your condition."

Minutes later, Aunt Jackie was stretched out on the floor, her head resting on a pillow made of jackets. We put water on her face to make her look even sweatier than she was. Mom moved a lamp slightly to cast dark shadows on Aunt Jackie's face. Then I pounded on the door and yelled for help. When Inspector Kemal came in to check on us, we explained that Aunt Jackie was ill. She *was* ill, but the lighting tricks and some acting skills on Aunt Jackie's part made her situation look more dire than it really was.

"She could lose the baby. We need help," Mom insisted when the inspector came in, wringing her hands like someone in an old-fashioned movie. "Please, let us go to a hospital."

The inspector took a long look at Aunt Jackie, who moaned convincingly.

"If she miscarries here, and that makes the news, it might not look too good," Mom added softly, lowering her eyes. "For Turkish tourism. You know? I have connections to the US government," she added. "My husband is attorney general of Massachusetts."

I stared at her. So she'd played the husband card after all. It was weird to hear her say "my husband" after everything that had happened. But technically he *was* still attorney general, and technically they were still married. She had every right to say that. And for a moment, it sounded nice to hear. I imagined my dad leaping for the phone, taking that call.

Inspector Kemal pressed his lips together while he thought. "All right," he said at last. "I will call her an ambulance to the local hospital. You two will stay here."

Oh, no. The possibility that we could be separated hadn't even entered my mind!

"I'm taking care of her," Mom insisted, holding Aunt Jackie's hand. "I'm her only family here right now. She's a widow. We can't be separated. And my daughter has to come, too. She's only sixteen." Mom put an arm around each of us, signaling that we were a family unit. I leaned in close to her for added effect. It would have made for a great family portrait.

Now Inspector Kemal looked exasperated. "That is out of the

question," he said curtly. Then he turned on his heel and left the room.

We waited, huddled together, whispering about what might happen.

"I'm not going without you," Aunt Jackie insisted, squeezing both our hands.

"Go," Mom told her. "You need medical attention. We'll be fine. We'll get through this." She looked doubtful, though.

"Just don't let them transfer you to another facility," said Aunt Jackie. "You don't want to end up in the police station, that's for sure. Then you're there with *everyone*." She shuddered. "And once you're in, it's hard to get out. It's best if you stay at the airport. And I'll keep trying my lawyer from the hospital."

"Okay," Mom whispered. She looked really scared, like the younger sister instead of the older. And Aunt Jackie looked terrible; I couldn't tell anymore how much she was faking versus how much was real. She looked worse than ever, as if she were truly uncomfortable.

The two of them hugged. Then Aunt Jackie embraced me, and stroked my hair. "Take care of your mom, Zan," she said.

"Hey. Don't act like we won't see you again," Mom said. "We will. Right? This will all get sorted out. I bet this happens to tourists all the time."

The door banged open. Inspector Kemal entered, flanked by two paramedics, one pushing a wheelchair. They loaded Aunt Jackie into it. She blew us a kiss and gave us a worried glance behind her as they wheeled her out of the room.

Inspector Kemal turned to us. "Now we will go," he said.

"Go? Go where?" Mom asked, wide-eyed.

"My boss, Inspector Lale Demir, would like to speak with you personally. She is head of Istanbul's department for investigating ancient stolen artifacts."

"So we're going to Istanbul?" I asked.

"Oh, no." He shook his head. "Inspector Lale is in town for

business. But she is busy at the local station, so I will take you there. Dalaman Police Station."

Mom and I exchanged an anguished look. Aunt Jackie had said not to leave the airport!

"Now," he insisted, holding the door open and ushering us out with his steely gaze.

17

The police station was an imposing white building encircled by a giant iron fence. Mom and I followed Inspector Kemal inside. We weren't handcuffed; it crossed my mind that we could bolt. But they had our passports. And if I'd learned anything from all my encounters with store security guards, it was that it was best to cooperate with the law and not dig yourself into a deeper hole.

We were put in a small, windowless holding room similar in size and furnishings to the one at the airport—better, in some ways, as it was clean and stark white. And it had air-conditioning. But it was like being stuck in a freezer. An hour passed, then another, and Mom and I found ourselves doing jumping jacks and jogging in place to stay warm.

"With my sister in the hospital, we're hardly a flight risk," Mom grumbled.

My stomach rumbled. It was close to dinnertime. "I'm starving," I said.

"Me too," said Mom. "I had snacks in my bag, but that's been taken. They're probably authenticating my munchies, too." She sighed. "You know, I kind of hate to admit it, but I'm missing

Orhan's cooking. Oh my God. That eggplant dish."

"I know. I'd give anything for some of that pita bread, too."

We reminisced about Orhan's meals, even the fish served with their heads and eyes intact.

"Mom," I said, when we'd run out of imagined foods, "what if we don't get out?"

"We'll get out," she said firmly. "We'll get the embassy involved if we have to. There are international lawyers. There is help. And there's always the media to help put the pressure on them to let us go. I could contact someone at the *New York Times*."

The media. Great. More exposure. Just what our family needed.

"And Aunt Jackie?" I asked. "Do you think she'll be okay?"

"I feel good that we got her to a hospital," said Mom. "And I don't think they'll bring her to prison. After all, the figurines weren't in her bag."

She didn't say the rest of her sentence, but I knew we were both thinking it: the figurines were in *my* bag. Even Mom would probably be let go. This potential prison sentence was mine alone.

Our door latch clicked, the handle turned, and Inspector Kemal strode into the room. "This is a most unusual circumstance," he said, spreading documents, a stamp, and an inkpad on the small metal table. "But Inspector Lale has authorized your temporary release."

I clapped my hands together and smiled at Mom.

"*Temporary* release? What does that mean?" asked Mom. "Were the artifacts fakes?"

Inspector Kemal stamped a few pages and scrawled his signature on others. "The artifacts have not been authenticated yet. The appraiser will not be available until tomorrow morning. Nor will Inspector Lale, for that matter. She is detained in another town, by an urgent matter. But she will see you two back here, promptly at nine in the morning." *Scrawl, stamp.*

Stamp, scrawl. "Sign here, please," he said, passing us a page and indicating blank lines to sign on. "Since your daughter is under eighteen, you must sign, too."

"What exactly are we signing?" Mom asked, reluctantly taking the pen he offered. "This is all in Turkish. I have a policy of not signing documents I can't read."

"You are agreeing to a travel restriction," he said. "Quite simply, you must not leave Dalaman. You may visit your sister in hospital. But you must report back to this station by nine tomorrow morning. Any violation of these terms will result in your arrest."

"If it's so simple, why is it a five-page document? I need a translator." She hesitated a moment longer, her pen hovering over the paper. "I'm not going be forced to sign some confession," she grumbled. Then she printed at the bottom of the document:

> *I was not given an English translation. I am signing and agreeing only to a temporary release from detention as explained to me by Inspector Kemal Turan.*

She wrote all the terms he'd stated, and only then did she sign on the line. I had to admit that was smart thinking on her part. I would have just signed.

"I have to confess, your dad told Aunt Jackie to do that when she first moved to Turkey," Mom explained to me after Inspector Kemal had left with the papers. "Your grandparents had seen this awful movie, *Midnight Express,* and they were convinced she was going to end up in a Turkish prison somehow. Your dad said that at least writing an explanation like this would buy you time in a court of law. They would have to look into it."

I wondered how Grandma and Grandpa would feel if they

knew how close Mom and I were to a Turkish prison now. But the next thing we knew, we had our bags again, our passports back, and we were walking out of the Dalaman Police Station. Free—for now.

◇◇◇◇◇

We went out to the street, stumbling down the steps in our haste to get out of there. We took deep breaths and relaxed into the warmth of the balmy early evening air.

"Thank God for that Inspector Lale," said Mom. "Hey, did you catch that she's a woman?"

I nodded. That was unusual here. I'd only seen two police-women, back in Marmaris.

"She must have had a heart, seeing we were detained females, and foreigners," Mom said.

Honestly, I was scared to meet with this Inspector Lale the next morning. And the release was only temporary. But for now, I'd be grateful, and drink in every moment of freedom. I focused on the feeling of my feet on the ground. The sound of a bird twittering in a nearby palm tree. The *put-put-put* of a moped passing by. The scent of diesel fumes from a bus. I did *not* want to be locked up in prison, or even in another holding room again.

"I really want to get to the hospital," said Mom, sticking her hand out as if we were in New York City. Three taxis instantly careened toward the curb, pulled up, and began arguing over who would take us.

"They're hailing us, not the other way around," I said.

"Oh, God," groaned Mom. "Why does it all have to be so complicated?"

Footsteps coming down the steps of the police station behind us made me spin around to see who was approaching. "Mom!" I whispered. "Look who's coming!"

Mom turned. "It's Orhan!"

"Kitsie? Zan?" Orhan broke into a wide grin and jogged over to us. "*Merhaba!* Hello!"

"Uh—hi! How, um, odd to see you here."

"Odd?" His brow furrowed. "In what way? Why odd?"

"I mean, it's nice to see you here. But unexpected. Were you brought into the station for questioning?" Mom guessed.

He nodded. "The police wished to speak with anyone who was on board the *Gulet Yasemin*. The other passengers have already left for Ephesus, and the boat has sailed again on a new Blue Voyage. But I came ashore for my exam. And they found me."

"I'm sorry," Mom said. "You probably know, then. Some figurines were discovered in my daughter's bag—figurines that she didn't put there. But she acquired them on the boat. We had to give your name as a potential witness."

"It is not a problem. I am happy to help and to share information. But I am concerned you are now involved in this. What exactly has happened?"

We quickly filled him in on the basics. "But I have to get to the hospital to find my sister," Mom finished. "If these gentlemen would just let us into a taxi."

Orhan said something to the drivers in Turkish.

"Oh, good," Mom said to me. "He'll sort it out."

All three drivers got into their cars and drove off.

Mom stared at Orhan.

"Come with me," he said. "I will drive you personally."

"Really? Wow. Thank you," said Mom, as we followed Orhan toward the visitor parking lot. "I'm sure this was not in your plans for this evening."

"It is my great pleasure to help," said Orhan. "I am happy that I live nearby!"

We came to Orhan's car, a white Ford Focus. He opened the front and back passenger doors for us with a grand gesture. I slid into the backseat and Mom got into the front.

The car reeked of some kind of intense cologne, but it was

spotless. A blue evil-eye amulet, suspended from a chain, swung from the rearview mirror. I watched the setting sun glance off it and hoped we were right to trust Orhan. So much for Mom's warning about not telling strange men our itinerary. But at this point, who else could we trust?

He sighed deeply. "I feel terrible that the three of you had to experience such a thing in my country," he said, though he only looked at Mom.

"It's not your fault," Mom said. "Airport security was just doing their job. I get that."

"But it is embarrassing to me. This is not how Turkey should treat tourists who come here to spend their hard-earned money. They should have taken the figurines and let you go. There was no need to treat you so rudely, or to detain you." He paused and shook his head. "We should not assume people are criminals."

I looked at him in the rearview mirror and something inside me melted. He couldn't know what those words meant to me. And maybe I had to think about those words before I blamed Sage for everything. I had complicated reasons for snooping and stealing stuff. And Mom and I had just staged an amped-up medical crisis to help Aunt Jackie and her baby. Maybe Sage had her own complicated reasons for doing the things she did, too. Maybe she'd do anything to help *her* mom, if her mom were seriously sick.

"Here we are," said Orhan, pulling up to a hospital. "Shall I go in with you?"

"We'll be fine," Mom said, opening her door. "Thank you so much."

"But . . . where will you stay tonight?"

"We'll find someplace," she said. "Don't worry about us. Good luck with your exam!" She gave a cheery wave as we got out of his car.

"Tea sugar and a dream," I added, following Mom.

The receptionist spoke enough English to understand

Mom's request to see Aunt Jackie. But Mom didn't seem to comprehend the receptionist at first.

"Visiting hours over," said the receptionist, making an X with her arms. "Tomorrow morning, yes, you come."

"But I have to see her now," Mom insisted. "It's urgent."

"I have doctor's note here. She is keeping for observation over one night," said the unsympathetic receptionist, clicking around on her computer.

"But is she okay?" Mom asked.

"Did she lose the baby?" I wanted to know, gripping the edge of the counter.

"I have only this note," said the receptionist. "I will try to translate. *Stable condition. No fetal distress. Keeping for observation.* Tomorrow, tomorrow. Now you must go."

"Stable condition, at least," said Mom as we went back outside. "But then why does she have to be kept overnight? That's what I'd like to know. I feel like what started as a medical drama on our part suddenly got too real."

"I really wish we could see her. Even sleeping, just to be sure she's fine," I said.

"I know." Mom sighed. "But I'm not busting in there and risking getting in trouble. We'll have to take their word for it, even if it is a translation. And we'd better get busy finding a hotel. I was counting on using Aunt Jackie's phone, though, since mine's completely useless here."

A horn honked. Farther down the curb was the white Ford Focus. Orhan rolled down his window and waved us over.

Mom's eyes practically bugged out of her head. "What? He stayed?" she exclaimed.

"Let's go," I said, hefting my backpack.

"I could not leave you here," Orhan explained when we got back into the car. "I worried you would have difficulty finding a hotel. I made a few calls for you, but all hotels are booked. High season. This is a problem. There is one Hotel Antalya near here, but not a nice place for ladies."

"We're not too particular," said Mom. "We'll go there."

"No." He shook his head. "There have been crimes in that area. I think you do not need more encounters with police, yes? Please, I insist. Come to my home. I will make you as comfortable as I can. You may have the entire upstairs."

Mom looked agonized. It was a tempting offer, but scary. How much could we trust him?

"My mother will be happy to have guests," he added, as if guessing our concern.

"Oh!" Mom looked relieved. "You live with your mother?"

"My mother lives with *me*," he said, straightening his shoulders.

Mom nodded. "All right, then. Thank you. We'll stay with you. That's very kind of you."

I'd rather have stayed in a hotel myself, but now I realized we were lucky to get this bonus time with Orhan. He'd spent some time on the boat with Sage, when were away seeing the ruins. Maybe he'd noticed something about her that would shed light on what she had done.

"So did you notice anything weird about Sage when she was on the boat?" I asked Orhan as he pulled back out onto the main road. "Any suspicious behavior?"

"I cannot say that I did," he said. "Except for her fast departure."

"What about the baklava seller? Do you know where he went after he came to our boat?"

Orhan smiled at me through the rearview mirror. He had a nice smile, I had to admit. Kind eyes. "You are more thorough an interrogator than the police," he teased.

"Sorry. I'm just curious."

He laughed. "Not a problem. Yes, I did see the same vendor who came to our boat. He also went to the *Anilar* after, and then to two other yachts in the cove," he said. "He did not remain at their boats long. I did not think much of it. These types of vendors are quite common along the coast. But this vendor was different in one way. He had a pile of, how do you say, *tarpau-lins,* I think?"

I nodded.

"Yes. Tarpaulins. This looked a little not so typical to me, so I mentioned it to the police."

"Oh, dear," said Mom. "The tarps were probably covering up all his stolen or black market artifacts. I hope that couple on the *Anilar* didn't get tempted to buy some. On the shore excursion to the ruins, they mentioned they had a little art gallery."

"Then I hope the police find them, and warn them," I said, remembering that detail, too. "If they bought something from him, they could get detained at the airport just like we did!" I shivered. Here were the Clarksons cashing out their retirement, living like free spirits, embracing life after their cancer scare. They didn't deserve to end up in a Turkish prison either. And they might not be so lucky to have this Inspector Lale let them go.

Orhan shook his head. "I do not think they bought objects," he said. "I was fishing, and I saw the vendor. He held up the tray to the two passengers. The couple. They bought pastries and ate them. But then, maybe he wanted to sell only pastry to them, and to get away quickly, because the *Anilar*'s first mate was standing nearby at the time. With a gun."

"A gun!" Mom exclaimed.

"You mean one of the guards on that boat, right?" I said.

"No, it was the first mate," Orhan said. "He was cleaning a gun. Sometimes the first mate acts as a guard on a boat. Especially these days when people have concerns about crime."

I frowned, thoroughly confused now. Why would Riza need to act as a guard if the Clarksons had hired Lazar and Vasil to do the job?

I wanted to ask Orhan, but then he pulled into a gravel driveway of a three-level house that clung to a bluff near the water. Just below was a narrow, rocky beach, where families with small children were gathering up towels and toys, fishermen were hauling in their nets, and the smell of fried food filled the air.

The house wasn't grand, it wasn't a mansion, and it looked a little run-down. But it also seemed cheerful and inviting.

"Oh, it's gorgeous," said Mom, gazing up at the decks, the potted roses, the twisting bougainvillea. "What a location."

"Wait, please." Orhan got out of the car, ran around to the passenger side, and opened both Mom's door and mine. "Welcome to my home! For now, please, consider it your home as well."

Orhan's mother was a woman in her sixties named Beyza. She wore a pretty green-and-black hijab, or head scarf, concealing all her hair, and simple but elegant clothes: a blue button-down shirt and neatly pressed black trousers. She had a dark mole on her cheek, and a twinkle in her eye. And she was kind to us. I hadn't felt so welcomed somewhere since the Clarksons made me feel at home on the *Anilar*. Just like Ron and Judy didn't treat Sage and me like the trespassers that we were, Beyza didn't seem to view us as criminal suspects out on furlough. And she really did make us feel as if we were home.

She showed us to our guest room—a sewing room with a pull-out sofa. It was a humble space, but comfortable and clean, and cozy with thick rugs and piles of pillows on the floor. Bright tapestries hung from the walls. After hours spent in interrogation rooms, I was so grateful to be in a real house.

After we'd washed up—I'd applied a fresh coat of foundation on my face from the emergency tube I had in my backpack—Beyza insisted we relax in the yard while she and Orhan cooked dinner. Relaxing seemed impossible while we still knew no details about Aunt Jackie's condition. But we stretched out on lounge chairs and played with four friendly cats, trying to distract ourselves.

Later, out on the patio, with a view of the sea, Orhan and his mother served up our dinner. Orhan handed each of us a small ceramic pot and instructed us to hold it with the top facing away from us. Then he pulled out a large knife and broke the end off each pot. Stew oozed out, glistening, onto our plates. It tasted even better than it looked. Orhan and Beyza beamed as we exclaimed how delicious it was.

Beyza spoke no English, but Orhan translated for her when she expressed curiosity about our conversation. Mostly, though, Orhan and Mom chatted together. They seemed to have a lot to say to each other, suddenly, about where they'd gone to school and how they'd grown up. I wanted to crawl under the table. It was one thing to be friendly with someone who was going out of his way to help us. But it was quite another to be flirting so openly. Which is what it appeared they were doing, even more blatantly than on the boat.

Every time I stole a glance at Mom, I seemed to recognize her less. Gone was the tensely smiling, über-chipper woman who had stood by Dad's side in her Talbots outfits. Mom looked . . . relaxed. She laughed openly, deeply, at Orhan's jokes, and told a few of her own. She even sat differently, seeming to take up more space, one arm draped around the empty chair to her right.

Beyza brought out a tray with rice pudding and tea. Conversation turned to our Blue Voyage and what we'd enjoyed about it: the cliff tombs and the rock tombs. The warm water. The ruins. And of course, Orhan's cooking. But as the moon rose up in the sky, and a chill mixed with the evening air, we were reminded of what was in store for us tomorrow.

Orhan explained the whole situation to Beyza, who nodded, murmuring under her breath, a grave expression on her face. Often that grave expression was directed toward me.

"Mother asks if you know the names of the guards who bothered you," Orhan said to me.

"Lazar and Vasil," I said.

Mom frowned. "How do you know that?" she asked. "Did they introduce themselves before they pulled you into the alley? Or after?"

I froze. I knew their names because the Clarksons had introduced them to me. "Um. Sage mentioned them," I said at last. "She'd swum out to their boat before."

Beyza frowned and said something to Orhan, who nodded.

"My mother says these are Bulgarian names, not Turkish. She is correct."

Mom scratched her head. "Why does that matter? It's a private security company, not the national police. Can't their employees be from anywhere?"

"Of course," said Orhan. "Bulgaria is our neighbor, and there are many Bulgarians in Turkey. They work in all industries, but many are in the security business. Like this Lazar and Vasil. And what I will tell you next, you must consider carefully. I myself have many Bulgarian friends. I do not wish you to think Bulgarians, or Bulgarian Turks, are bad people. They are not. But the Bulgarian mafia also has operations in Turkey. And the mafia is often involved in international smuggling operations. Sometimes they use security firms as their cover. Are you following me?"

Mom dropped her fork onto the table.

I stared at Orhan, my mind racing, trying to connect that idea to what had happened back at the Marmaris docks. Could Lazar and Vasil actually be *mafia* types who were involved in smuggling? Not bounty hunters at all, but the criminals whom bounty hunters, Turkish police, and Interpol were all looking for? Maybe hiding in plain sight, disguised as security guards, was the perfect cover. People like the Clarksons trusted them with their belongings, and their lives. There was a national call to get private security firms involved in anti-smuggling efforts. Lazar and Vasil were working on a boat and hanging out at a dock, places where stolen goods could be spirited out of the country. And they wore uniforms—which from a distance looked legitimate, especially to someone like me who'd grown up trusting people in uniform. But they had that unclear logo and no company name.

They also had weapons, which they had been just a little too eager to brandish.

A chill ran through me. I remembered Vasil dropping Sage and me off at our boat, how he'd refused to leave right away. How he'd said something to Sage, which she seemed to understand, and which she'd reacted so strongly to. What if Vasil had demanded something from her, something she didn't agree with?

What if Sage was working in a smuggling network with not just Baklava Guy but Lazar and Vasil, too?

18

The next morning, Beyza served us an early breakfast, and Orhan took us to the hospital.

Aunt Jackie was sitting up in bed, the color restored to her cheeks. "The baby is fine. I'm fine," she said, after Mom and I rushed up to hug her. "I just heard the heartbeat."

"Do you want to listen?" asked the doctor, smiling. She put a little wand over Aunt Jackie's stomach and turned a knob on the monitor beside the bed. Weird whooshing sounds, underwater sounds, crackled from the speakers. Then I made out the sound of tiny galloping hoofbeats. The baby's heart!

Mom wiped away a tear. "Thank God. So what's with the cramping and spotting? And why did they have to keep you overnight?"

"Just to be sure, given my history of miscarriages," said Aunt Jackie. "They gave me a progesterone boost. And they think I may have a low placenta. I'm supposed to take it easy for a bit. Not walk too much. But where were you two? I called the airport and they said you were moved to the police station. Then I called there and heard you were released, but they wouldn't tell me anything else!"

Mom and I quickly brought her up to date.

Aunt Jackie's smile faded when she heard where we'd stayed. "You stayed at *Orhan's*?"

"Yes." Mom lifted her chin. "Why do you have that look on your face?"

"You do want to be a bit careful, Kitsie. Much as I hate to buy into stereotypes, there is a thing here in Turkey with younger men preying on older foreign women. For their money."

"Older!" Mom's eyes flashed. "I'm not *that* much older."

"I didn't mean it like that."

"Besides, didn't you say not all Turkish men fit the stereotype? Orhan's a nice guy, Jackie. He's helped us a lot. His mother was at the house, for God's sake. And he's waiting for us now, outside in the car."

"Now?" Aunt Jackie looked surprised.

"We're due back at the police station in a half hour to find out about the artifacts," Mom said. "Are you free to leave?"

Aunt Jackie looked at the doctor, who nodded. "You may go," she said. "Just be careful not to overexert, avoid heat and stress, and please check in with your physician in Istanbul when you return. I will have the nurse bring your release papers."

"Great. I'll just change out of this stunning hospital gown and we'll be on our way." The doctor left and Aunt Jackie eased herself to a sitting position and swung her legs over the side of the bed. "I sure hope Inspector Kemal has good news for us. I'm guessing he does, since he let you go before the appraisal."

"Oh, he didn't let us go," Mom said. "It was his superior, someone named Inspector Lale Demir. We'll be meeting with her this morning."

"Inspector who?" Aunt Jackie almost fell off the bed.

"Inspector Lale Demir. If I heard correctly. I might be mispronouncing the name."

Aunt Jackie sucked in her breath. She grabbed for her clothes on a nearby chair.

"What's wrong?" Mom asked.

"Just a crazy thought that I might know this person. We'll find out when we get there."

⟨⟩⟨⟩⟨⟩⟨⟩

Mom, Aunt Jackie, and I waited in the holding room at the Dalaman Police Station. I stared at the evil-eye bracelet on my wrist, twisting it around and around so that the little glass eyes that made up the band seemed to roll and wink at me.

Beyza had given bracelets to Mom and me at breakfast that morning.

"This is a *nazar boncuğu*, or evil-eye amulet," Orhan had translated for us.

I'd immediately handed mine back. "Thanks, but I think I'm done with presents," I said. "They seem to get me in trouble."

"These are not valuable," Orhan insisted. "They are sold all over the country, in every gift shop. The amulets are supposed to protect you from the evil eye."

Mom had nodded, sliding her bracelet on. "He's right. Aunt Jackie has lots of these of her own. They're supposed to protect you from misfortune that results from envious people looking at you."

Envious? I didn't know who could possibly want to walk in any of our shoes, especially mine. Still, I'd had enough misfortune lately. So I'd slid my bracelet on, too, and secured the clasp firmly.

Inspector Kemal entered the room, and the door banging behind him startled me. He took a seat across from us at a desk, slapped down a file folder, and looked at us. "I have the authenticator's report. The four gold figurines are replicas," he announced. "Gold-painted lead. Skillfully made imitations. The gold paint contains some real gold, and the lead gives them their weight, so they are designed to fool the uninformed tourist and make them believe they are getting an item of great value for relatively little money."

Mom let out a long breath.

"Thank God," said Aunt Jackie. She closed her eyes for a moment, as if actually praying.

I looked down at my hands and realized they were trembling.

The inspector looked as though he couldn't quite believe it himself—and as if maybe he were just a little disappointed that three American tourists weren't headed for lockdown. "Inspector Lale will be in momentarily. She will give you the figurines and the certificate proving they are fakes, and you must keep it with you at all times, traveling within Turkey or leaving the country. Otherwise you will have this problem all over again. And you. Young lady." He turned to me. "I would advise you not to accept gifts from people you do not know well."

"I never accepted those gifts in the first place!" I burst out.

Mom jabbed me with her elbow.

"I mean, I won't. I never will. Thank you."

"And be careful in your interactions with police and security guards," he added with a stern look. "With a history like yours, people may suspect your motives."

"What history?" Mom demanded. "What motives? What are you talking about?"

"We are aware of your daughter's involvement with looting."

"Shoplifting," Aunt Jackie corrected. "Not looting. That's entirely different."

"Forgive me. I do not understand all the English idioms. There is a video that comes up on a search in your name . . ."

Oh my God. That damned video. So even Turkish officials could dig up the dirt on me! Was it a blight on my record forever, one that would grow instead of diminish, like the blotches on my skin? Would I always be trying to cover up the Athleta incident, too? I hated hearing him hurl that word: *looting!* I was getting lumped in with people like those tomb robbers in Fethiye, or the looters who'd stolen the Karun Treasure from the grave of the princess. I wasn't that kind of person. Was I?

Inspector Kemal stood up. "Inspector Lale will now speak with you." He exited the room, leaving us to sit in stunned silence.

The door opened again moments later, and a woman strode in. It took me a moment to realize this must be Inspector Lale Demir. She didn't look like a police officer, with her long layers of wavy dark hair, tumbling loose around her shoulders. Instead of a uniform, she wore a cream-colored pantsuit and pumps and was carrying a stylish leather satchel. She looked to be in her late thirties, and her makeup was impeccable—it seemed to have been applied less to enhance her beauty (she was obviously beautiful) and more as an attempt to soften her sharp features: high, angular cheekbones, a strong chin, and a cool, almost unblinking gaze.

Aunt Jackie stood up fast. "Oh my goodness! Lale? It *is* you! I thought I recognized your name!" She approached the woman as if she might hug her, but then stopped short as if she'd hit an invisible barrier.

The woman held out her hand, and Aunt Jackie shook it, confused.

"It's Inspector Lale now," the woman said brusquely.

"You're with the police?"

"I've been working in the anti-smuggling unit in Istanbul for the past three years."

"Oh. I see." Aunt Jackie drew back. "Well. That sounds . . . like an exciting career move for you," she finished softly. "Quite a change."

"Not really." Inspector Lale tossed her glossy hair over one shoulder and pulled back a chair at the table. "With all the museum budget cuts in this country, my PhD in archaeology wasn't opening any more doors there. And once the government purged the police departments of corrupt staff members, a whole lot of new positions in law enforcement opened up. When I saw they needed an expert to head the department of stolen artifacts, I jumped at the chance."

"Ah." Aunt Jackie stared at her a moment longer, then seemed to remember we were there, too. "Um. Well. This is my sister, Kitsie. My niece, Alexandra. She goes by Zan. I guess you know all our names already, though."

We all shook hands with Inspector Lale, who then took a seat opposite us at the table where Inspector Kemal had sat minutes before. I couldn't stop staring at her. She struck me as the kind of person who would have a corner office in a New York City high-rise. She seemed to control everything in the room, even the way the air flowed around us, just with her strong presence. Inspector Kemal had filled that chair up more than Inspector Lale did, but she radiated power.

"Thank you for releasing us yesterday," Mom gushed. "Jackie was not well. And we are completely innocent. As you can see, since the artifacts are fakes. What a huge relief!"

Inspector Lale nodded, rifling through her satchel and avoiding eye contact with us. "I'm glad I could help you. I would do anything for Berk Yilmaz. He was a wonderful mentor to me when we worked together at the Archaeological Museum in Istanbul years ago."

"Berk always spoke highly of you, too," said Aunt Jackie, who also seemed unable to tear her eyes away from the inspector. "Though I think he hadn't seen you recently?"

Inspector Lale's all-business mask shifted, just a little, as she shook her head. A small, sad smile leaked through. "I was so sorry to hear of his death. I wished I could have attended the funeral. I always had the highest respect for him. So when I saw your names on the report about suspected smuggling activity, I wanted to help you if I could. But I also needed to talk with you in person." She took some documents out of her satchel and handed them to Aunt Jackie. "First, these are your release papers. Second, I have the certificate from the authenticator." She patted her satchel. "But I need to retain it, as well as the figurines."

"Why?" I asked. "They're authentic fakes. And Inspector

Kemal said we needed to have the certificate if we're traveling around with replicas."

"Oh, no. *Please* keep them," Mom said to Inspector Lale. "Those things have caused us enough trouble. I don't want to travel around with them even with a certificate."

"The figurines need to remain in custody for now," said Inspector Lale. "They're evidence from a suspicious trans- action that is under investigation. They could be useful for prosecuting individuals within the smuggling ring we are after." She hesitated, as if about to say something else. Then she scribbled something down on a notepad and shook hands with Aunt Jackie, brusquely, and then with Mom and me. "Good to see you, Jackie. Nice to meet you, Kitsie and Zan. Safe trav- els." She picked up her satchel, pivoted on one heel, and strode out of the room, her hair bouncing on her shoulders. The door clicked closed.

"Are we free to go, then?" Mom asked.

"Look," said Aunt Jackie, holding up a piece of paper. It was the note Inspector Lale had scrawled. She'd slipped it to Aunt Jackie during their handshake! Mom and I stood beside her to read the tiny handwriting:

> *Meet me at Café Antalia around the corner in ten minutes. I need to talk to you.*

◇◇◇◇◇

"The statues are actually solid gold artifacts from the sixth century BC," said Inspector Lale, in a low voice. We had found her at the tiny café a few minutes after leaving the station and joined her at a corner table. "I could not say this in the office, since I am never sure who may be listening."

"Where were they stolen from?" I asked, while Aunt Jackie and Mom exchanged an anguished look.

"There was a security breach at the Ruşen Koçak Museum in

Fethiye the other day," Inspector Lale explained, "and these figurines were among some of the items reported missing from the storage facility."

I remembered that museum. I'd seen it from the carpet shop. I'd also misdirected Lazar and Vasil there, making them think Sage might have had something to do with that break-in. I hoped I hadn't made some colossal screw-up.

"The museum owners will be happy to see these again, once they are no longer needed as evidence," Inspector Lale went on. "I'll return these to the museum, hopefully soon."

"Hang on," said Aunt Jackie. "Someone signed a document saying they were replicas."

"Yes, I arranged for that," Inspector Lale said. "I have my own contacts here."

"You did this for us?" Mom shook her head in disbelief. "Had someone write a fake document? Put your reputation on the line?"

Inspector Lale nodded. "I believe your story, and I don't want to see a young girl in jail." She looked pointedly at me. "But I'm also in charge of this investigation and can override the local precincts. Who, quite frankly, are bungling everything."

"What are they doing wrong?" I asked. "We've been seeing police everywhere."

She smirked. "Acting like cops in some American movie! Roadblocks. Highly visible displays of power. It all only serves to drive the smugglers deeper underground and to scatter their own resources. And it makes museums, especially small ones, even more vulnerable to theft. This is what I came here to tell the police precincts, and I've been working around the clock to convince them to change their tactics. The smugglers are almost playing with police here. It's like a game to them."

"How are these museums more vulnerable to theft?" Mom asked. "I would think the strong show of force would help."

"Publicizing the thefts shows everyone which museums have stockpiles and storerooms, which ones can easily be robbed," the inspector replied. "The looters, the middlemen, everyone on the chain, they get more inside information when the events make the news. They get smarter at evading security systems. If there's a robbery reported in Göcek, smugglers go to Muşla, or to Fethiye, or to some other town. There are mosques and small museums everywhere, all with stashes of artifacts and art. Then even more smuggling gangs spring up, almost overnight. And all the while, as more police and coast guard boats patrol, and more security guards get hired, the tourists get frightened and avoid coming. The country loses money. It's a vicious cycle. But I wish to get to the heart of the organization. The masterminds. The people behind the largest, most powerful smuggling network that is leaking Turkey's treasures and stashes of Islamic art across its borders."

"Okay, I follow," said Aunt Jackie. "But Inspector Kemal doesn't know you're retaining the figurines?"

"No. My team in Istanbul has a special storage facility for these items. I'll keep them there. I trust and respect Inspector Kemal, but I don't trust all the police. We're having a problem with confiscated artifacts and other evidence being stolen from police stations, or sold off by corrupt officers who are willing to do business with smugglers."

Aunt Jackie pressed her lips together, not taking her eyes off Inspector Lale. "So you did us a favor, releasing us. But we're doing you a favor, too, in a way, by letting you quietly take these things back. Is that right?"

"Yes. I hope so," said Inspector Lale. "You see, in return, I need to know everything about what happened, and especially about Sage Powell." She turned her eyes to me. "Everything," she repeated.

I told her all the facts Sage had told me about herself. I told her about the brother who had OD'ed, the mother who had a heart problem, even about the paper she owed her teacher. For some reason, I was way more nervous now than I'd been around Inspector Kemal or Sergeant Emre. I felt like I should trust Inspector Lale, since she had worked with Uncle Berk and we owed her our freedom. But I couldn't read her face. And I could feel Mom's eyes boring into me. I got to the part about Lazar and Vasil accosting me in Marmaris, at the docks, but I stopped short of confessing that I'd previously met them, and been at the other end of their guns, on the midnight swim with Sage. Mom would definitely freak out if she knew that, and if she knew that I hadn't told that to the other police yesterday.

"Thank you," Inspector Lale said when I was done talking. "This is all extremely useful to know. Is that everything, then?" She continued to look at me, drumming her polished nails on the table.

"Yes," I said. "Everything." I swallowed hard. I averted my gaze while she continued to stare, and I picked at a hangnail on my own hand. Did she suspect I was holding back on one piece of information that might be useful?

"So what do you think Sage did?" Mom asked her, breaking the awkward silence that hung in the air.

"The question is not so much what she did as *who she is*," said Inspector Lale. "Or who she isn't."

"What do you mean?" I asked.

"There is no record of a Sage Powell having entered this country with a US passport. Or any passport," said Inspector Lale. "There is, apparently, no Sage Powell at all. We have been researching this since you gave us Sage's name yesterday."

"Wait. What? I don't get it," I said.

"I hope you're not suggesting my daughter invented her as a way to clear her own name," Mom said, crossing her arms in front of her chest. "We all met the girl. She exists."

"Then the name is false," said Inspector Lale. "The closest match we found is an Amy Miller, whose face came up in a photo recognition scan. We compared it to a security camera photo we have of Sage at the dock in Marmaris."

Inspector Lale took out a new paper from her satchel: a photocopy of a passport.

We all leaned forward to look. The girl in the picture was definitely Sage, or the person I'd met as Sage. Birthplace: *Hawthorne, Oregon.* She'd told the Clarksons that she was from Rosedale. Another lie.

I looked at the name on the passport copy again. *Amy Miller.* "I know that name!" I exclaimed.

"You do?" Inspector Lale looked at me intently.

"I forgot to mention one thing. Sage gave me a book before she left. A book by a writer named Freya Stark. This name, Amy Miller, was written inside the cover. I just thought it was a used book." I stared at that name on the passport copy now. Her real name seemed more like an alias than her alias did. Too ordinary a name for a complicated person. In my mind, she was still Sage.

"Amy Miller was an exchange student at the Istanbul International School earlier this year, taking some classes there, which she paid full tuition to enroll in," Inspector Lale went on, putting the photocopy back in her satchel. "But she dropped out of the program in January."

Dropped out! So the late paper was another deception. Facts soured into lies and swirled in my head. Sage had mentioned she'd been sick and missed some school, but that wasn't the same thing as dropping out. The story of her teacher who was obsessed with the Lycians—was that a lie, too? And why had she changed her name?

Disbelief gave way to anger. Sage—Amy—had *lied* to me and to my family about so many things. Here we'd been trying so hard to avoid hustlers, ever since we got to Turkey, but I'd been cruising with the biggest con artist of all, right on our own boat.

"Amy's extended student visa has become invalid," Inspector Lale went on. "Which means she has overstayed her ninety-day tourist visa. Passport control will be very interested in her when and if she decides to leave the country."

I ran through the facts in my mind. Fethiye had been

crawling with police and coast guard officials. Orhan had said they'd been boarding some of the boats, looking at passenger lists. If she'd gotten on the boat with a fake document, or if the crew had let her slide in, she could have been in serious trouble for that alone. And if she had something else to cover up—like criminal activity with a smuggling network—she'd be in even more hot water.

"She already left the country," Mom insisted.

"Or did she?" said Aunt Jackie, looking questioningly at Inspector Lale.

Inspector Lale shook her head. "Likely not. Passport control would have caught the alert on her. They should have given her a large fine for overstaying and for not reporting her change of circumstances to the Istanbul police. So either a lenient customs officer dozed on the job, or, more likely, Amy Miller is still here in the country, maybe lying low until all this blows over."

"So you want to haul her in about the overstayed visa?" guessed Aunt Jackie.

"Among other things, yes." Inspector Lale snapped her satchel closed. "She allegedly bought figurines of uncertain origin, with no paperwork, and then gave them to you, secretively, before disappearing. That is certainly enough grounds for me to desire a conversation with her. Besides, smugglers rarely work alone. She may be a low-ranking person in a network, but she may also know people higher up. I believe she could tell us a great deal."

"What about the security guards that grabbed me in Marmaris?" I asked. "They wanted to find her, too. Do you think they could be involved in some way?"

"They could be bounty hunters looking for smugglers," she said. "Or they could be smugglers themselves, posing as security guards. I am having my colleagues look into both possibilities. It is very helpful to us that you had at least their first names."

"If you trust first names," I grumbled, still pissed about the whole Sage/Amy alias thing.

I sank into my chair, deep in thought. If Lazar and Vasil, or whoever they really were, turned out to be smugglers, too, then Sage could have been running from them, not just from the law. She might have done something to go against them and needed to get away. Fast.

But if she'd been working with them, why would she be on *our* boat, and not on the *Anilar* with her coworkers? Or—I shuddered—was that really why the *Anilar* was near us so often? Did Lazar and Vasil have some kind of say in its itinerary? Did they need to keep Sage in their sight while she went around the coast buying stolen loot from baklava vendors?

I didn't know how to draw the line between circumstances and events and form a constellation that made sense.

"If she bought these figurines for someone else, then why would she put them in *my* bag?" I asked. "It's not like I'd know who to deliver them to. I feel like she *wanted* me to get caught with these."

"I have a theory," said Inspector Lale, leaning forward. "Let's suppose she thought the police were coming too close. She needed to unload some illegally purchased objects in a hurry. Smugglers are known for separating their caches, so that if they are caught, at least a portion remains, which someone else can be directed to retrieve. So she might expect you to have made it through security somehow—maybe assuming your aunt, as an archaeologist's widow, would be able to vouch for them and for you in some way if you ran into any trouble. Perhaps she is expecting you will return the figurines to her. You did say she planned to meet up with you again in Istanbul?"

I nodded. Inspector Lale had the exact same theory I did. Sage had seemed excited about meeting up with me in Istanbul; I'd assumed she was looking forward to showing me around and having fun. But she was probably planning her escape even then, and wanted to get her stuff back. So she set me up as an unwitting smuggler.

"Did she give you any contact information? An email address? A phone number?" Inspector Lale asked.

"None," I said. "I just know her host family was in Istanbul."

"I'll pursue that angle," she said. Then she slid her business card across the table to me. "I believe it is possible that Amy Miller will show up in Istanbul, attempt to contact you, and try to retrieve the figurines. After all, the two of you connected, you became friends, in a short space of time. And she knows the name of your aunt's hotel. I need you to get in touch with me the moment you hear from her. I can be reached by mobile phone. I will return to Istanbul in three days, and I would appreciate any information you can give me. Especially if you happen to recall anything else she may have told you," she added, giving me a meaningful look.

My neck itched. I nodded and put the card in my backpack.

Inspector Lale walked us back to the police station. After instructing us not to reveal our conversation to anyone, she went back inside the station and left us in the taxi queue.

A horn beeped. It was Orhan. He'd been patiently waiting for us.

He rolled down his window and grinned. "May I give you ladies a lift to the airport?"

Mom shot Aunt Jackie a look, but my aunt wasn't about to protest. We got in the car and slammed the doors behind us.

"Floor it," Mom said, her face grim.

Orhan looked down at the floor and then at Mom, confused.

"I mean, please drive quickly," she said. "I don't ever want to see this police station again."

While she and Aunt Jackie talked to Orhan, giving him only the most basic facts about our meeting with Inspector Kemal and Inspector Lale, I stared out the window, hatching my plan.

I was tired of following other people's itineraries. I wouldn't wait around for Sage to find me. I wasn't sure how I'd do it yet, but I'd find her on my own. Or at least find out about her by following some of her tracks in Istanbul. Who was she, anyway? And why had I been duped and dropped by a friend once again? Did it say something about her—or about *me*?

Part of me hoped she had a good motive behind her decisions. Like maybe she wanted to sell stuff with a smuggling ring to get money to help her sick mother in Oregon. After all, I had done some dumb things, too, broken laws, and I wasn't a horrible person.

Then a new thought seized me. What if *I* gave Interpol a big lead? I wasn't sure how much the reward was, but I bet it would go a long way in helping Aunt Jackie.

And if Sage didn't have a good answer to explain why she'd put figurines in my bag? Well, then, I wouldn't hesitate to turn her in and claim that reward money myself.

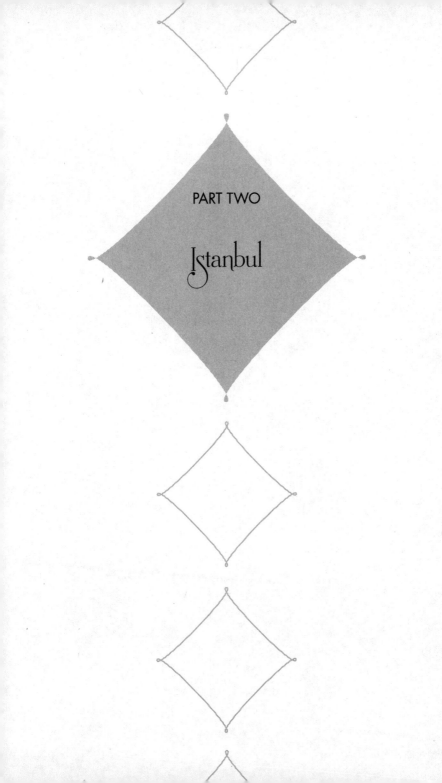

PART TWO

Istanbul

19

The taxi screeched to a stop and Mom, Aunt Jackie, and I got out. While the driver took our bags out of the trunk, I gazed around the cobblestoned street lined with crumbling buildings and mazes of alleyways, a mix of shops and homes. The air was thick with fumes from scooters that raced past us, cigar smoke, and *döner*, lamb, turning in a rotisserie nearby. Through the window of a café, I saw men smoking hookahs like the caterpillar used in *Alice in Wonderland*. I felt a little like Alice myself in that moment, as if I'd fallen down a rabbit hole. I'd never been in a place like this: the Sultanahmet district, otherwise known as the Old City. The heart of Istanbul.

Mom paid the driver, and I thought of something Sage had told me at the cliff tombs: that Turkey itself was a grand bazaar. Now I could see what she meant. All of life was on display—and most of it was for sale. Children strolled by selling candy and postcards. At the end of the street I saw an arched yellow sign that read ARASTA BAZAAR, the gateway to a local market, and brick walls lined with rugs hung on display.

Istanbul was sprawling, and even this cozy neighborhood was a labyrinth. Was I really going to be able to find Sage in this city? I looked up, wondering what I could climb, a tower or someplace I might go to clear my head and think. Then I turned and saw an enormous mosque not too far away. Seagulls swooped around the domes and minarets. My breath caught in my throat. The Blue Mosque. I remembered the image on the cover of Lonely Planet. It was even more dazzling in person. I hoped we'd get a chance to go in. I started to point it out to Mom, but she seemed fixated on getting inside the hotel and down to the business of helping Aunt Jackie.

"I still can't believe we got our bags so easily at the airport," said Mom, snatching Aunt Jackie's bag when she reached for it. Our suitcases had traveled to Istanbul without us while we were detained in Dalaman, and they'd been held at the airport overnight.

"Our evil-eye bracelets must be working," I said, following Mom and Aunt Jackie across the street.

I noticed some of the women wore black veils covering everything but their eyes. Others were dressed in colorful hijabs and long tan- or cream-colored trench coats. Some wore plain white or black scarves with long-sleeved T-shirts and jeans. Even those without scarves or veils were more modestly dressed than most girls and women I'd seen at the Marmaris docks. This was not the same Turkey where I'd just spent the past four days.

I had to smile, though, thinking of all those times my ex-friends had tried to get me to wear short skirts and tank tops, not understanding why I always covered so much skin. Here, strangely, I wasn't so out of place at all.

Suddenly the air crackled, stopping us in our tracks. A flock of pigeons shot into the sky with a *whoosh*. It took me a few moments to realize I was hearing music—someone was singing through a loudspeaker, or a bullhorn. The music sounded both piercing and muffled. Then I caught echoes of the song— no, many different songs—in the distance. A call and response. It was like nothing I'd ever heard, and strangely beautiful.

"It's the call to prayer," Aunt Jackie explained to Mom and me. "You're hearing the muezzin from mosques all over the city. The loudest is from the Blue Mosque over there."

I'd learned in Hebrew school that a muezzin is a Muslim who calls out the hour of daily prayers. We all stood still, staring at the Blue Mosque, listening to the muezzin. A few passersby stopped and turned toward the mosque, but most people hurried on, talking into their cell phones or hailing taxis.

"This is how I first fell in love with Turkey," said Aunt Jackie. "When I heard the call to prayers, something stirred in my soul. I loved the idea that five times a day you would hear this music, a reminder to hit the pause button on your life, even if you don't worship at a mosque. Berk laughed when I told him this. He said that after a while I wouldn't even notice the calls anymore. And you know what? He was right. I didn't."

"Uncle Berk didn't go to the mosque?" I asked.

"No," said Aunt Jackie. "He was very secular. Not all Turkish people are practicing Muslims."

"And this call to prayer, it happens *five* times a day?" I couldn't believe it.

"Yes," she confirmed. "You'll hear it next around dinner. Shall we go in?" Aunt Jackie led us across the street and stopped in front of a four-story cream-colored building with white trim. Some windows protruded, like square bay windows, but they were covered in wooden lattice. Flowers spilled out of pots by the heavy wooden front door, and a flowering vine crept up the side of the corner building. Looking up, I saw that both the hotel and the building next door had rooftop gardens. I made a mental note to check out the hotel's garden as soon as I could.

"*Hoş geldiniz!* Welcome! This is the Hotel Mavi Konak," said Aunt Jackie. She smiled, but her face tightened as she stood by the door.

"Oh, Jackie, it's so sweet!" exclaimed Mom. "Perfectly charming!"

Aunt Jackie frowned. "When people say *charming,* they usually mean *run-down.* That's what Mom and Dad said when I sent them pictures."

"But that's not at all what I meant." Mom looked hurt.

"Well, it's small even for a boutique hotel. It's just fifteen rooms. But Berk and I had all kinds of ideas for renovating and modernizing the place after his parents left it to us, and . . ." Aunt Jackie's voice quavered. "I just wish we'd finished it. Together."

"Is there much work left to do?" Mom asked. "The outside looks pretty spruced up."

"Outside is fine. But it's a bit tired inside," Aunt Jackie admitted. "It's an old Ottoman-era mansion, and it's got its quirks. There's always more to do. Constant updates. Maintenance and plumbing issues. No wonder we're getting all these bad online reviews lately."

Aunt Jackie led us inside and gave us a tour. There was a small lobby, a breakfast area with ten square tables, and a kitchen, which was closed and dark. Behind the front desk, made of gleaming dark wood, was a wall of wooden pigeonhole cubbies, each with an old-fashioned key hanging from a hook. The only modern touch was the computer on the front counter.

Mom exclaimed over the marble floor, the low divans encircling the room, the tapestries smothering the walls, and all the ornate Turkish rugs. I liked the little garden and patio outside, which were surrounded by crumbling, ancient-looking walls. Aunt Jackie said they were actually Byzantine ruins.

We were outside admiring a wall and the little stone fountain attached to it when a middle-aged man with wispy gray hair and a bristly gray mustache hurried up to us. He reminded me of a praying mantis, with his hooded eyes and the way he rubbed his hands together as if agitated, or cold—I couldn't tell which. He wore crisp black trousers and a maroon jacket with gold braiding and a double row of gold buttons. "I see you are admiring our ancient wall," he said, grinning, displaying tobacco-stained teeth. "Enjoy and appreciate. Our history appears on your bill!"

I couldn't tell if he was joking.

"No bill for these two," said Aunt Jackie. "They're family. This is my sister, Kitsie, and my niece, Zan." To us, she said, "This is Mustafa Polat, our guest relations manager."

Mustafa greeted us more warmly. *"Merhaba! Hoş geldiniz."*

"Merhaba," I said back. *"Teşekkür ederim."* He smiled, just as Orhan had when I first said thank you in his language. It was getting easier for me—and kind of fun—to say things like "hello" and "thank you" in Turkish.

"We are happy to have you here," said Mustafa. "You must be very tired from your journey. I hope Turkish Airlines will reimburse you for all of your delays and inconveniences."

Aunt Jackie shifted uncomfortably and looked down. I guessed she hadn't told Mustafa any details—or even the truth—about what we'd been through in the last twenty-four hours. Maybe she didn't want to freak out her staff.

"I'm happy to be here. Looking forward to a good night's sleep," Mom said.

"Ah, a good night's sleep! Yes! We charge double for that!" Mustafa said with a wink.

Mom gave him a tight smile.

Mustafa turned to Aunt Jackie. "Jackie Hanim. May I speak with you privately?" he said in a low voice.

"Of course." The two of them went back inside the lobby to talk.

"That's strange. Why did he use a different last name for her?" Mom asked.

"He didn't," I said, remembering some of what I'd read in Lonely Planet. "'Hanim' means 'Mrs.' in Turkish, and they use it after the first name. 'Bey' means 'Mr.'" I crept forward toward an open window leading to the lobby.

"Hey, don't you go snooping. This is none of our business," Mom whispered. But she followed me anyway, and we lingered by the window, pretending to admire some flowers.

"Pinar Hanim has quit today," Mustafa was saying in a low voice. "She and her daughter both."

"What? Did they at least give two weeks' notice?"

"No. They completed their workday and then left. I gave them what cash I could for the week's wages, but we will need to mail them their final check."

"This is a nightmare," said Aunt Jackie, running her hands through her hair until it stood almost straight up, like an alarmed cat's fur. "We have no more housekeeping staff! And we have that German tour group checking in tomorrow. They're a small group, but so *particular*." She sighed. "Can we advertise the positions first thing tomorrow morning?"

"Certainly. I have already written the advertisement. But there is more." Mustafa hesitated, then frowned. "Ayla Hanim and Serhan Bey came by this morning, at the very moment our Dutch guests in Room Nine were complaining about the toilet situation. They said they were eager to meet your family from Boston, but they also asked if the financial documents were ready for their review."

Ayla and Serhan—Uncle Berk's sister and brother. Mom and I exchanged a worried look.

"You didn't tell them I was on a cruise, did you?" asked Aunt Jackie.

Mustafa winced. "Not in so many words. But you know I do not like to be dishonest."

"That's okay." Aunt Jackie sighed. "I'll figure out some way to explain to them. Maybe they'll take it as a sign the hotel is in the black again, if I had enough money for a cruise." She didn't sound very convincing. And I knew those spreadsheets she'd pored over on the boat would tell a different story.

"Poor Jackie," murmured Mom. "This is way too much stress for her to come back to. Zan, we're going to ramp up our efforts. Full-time. I know it's not a glamorous job, but starting now, we're on duty. We're not sightseeing or anything until we get this place into shape."

I stared at her, suddenly comprehending. I was going to have even less freedom than I'd had on the Blue Voyage. How was I going to track down Sage and get the answers I needed? "We're going to work *all* the time?" I asked Mom.

She raised an eyebrow. "Would it really kill you to scrub a toilet for once in your life?"

"No! I totally want to help her. But—"

"Good. Just think of the great college application essay you'll get out of it. Here's a title for you: 'The Summer I Spent in the Tourism Industry in Istanbul.' Or how about this one? 'What Manual Labor Has Taught Me About the Value of Honest Work.' You haven't forgotten your dad's little life lesson in the garage, have you?"

I remembered it well. When I was in middle school and refused to do math, he once had me sweep out the entire garage. "Don't like this work?" he'd said when I'd complained. "Then study hard. Get a job so you won't have to do it. There are no free rides in life, kiddo."

What I couldn't explain to Mom was that I had urgent business: finding Sage and getting her side of the story, so I could at least understand why I'd fallen for her lies and been set up. Then, if she couldn't convince me there was some excellent reason behind it, I'd turn her in to Inspector Lale. If Sage turned out to be a good lead, some of that reward money might come my way, and I could help Aunt Jackie.

But in order to set all this in motion, I needed spare time. Just a little.

Mom hugged Aunt Jackie when she returned to the patio garden. "We couldn't help overhearing," she said. "So. Meet your new full-time housekeeping and hospitality staff." Mom slung her arm around my shoulders and beamed. "What do you think?"

I squirmed. Mom elbowed me.

"Oh, no. It's too much work," Aunt Jackie protested. "We'll find someone soon."

"We can handle it. No job too big. Right, Zan?" Mom gave me an encouraging shake on the shoulder. "Besides, you need to get to your doctor first thing tomorrow. And you need to deal with your contractors and maintenance crew. So there's no debate. Just give us a list, and we'll roll up our sleeves and tackle it."

"I really appreciate it," said Aunt Jackie, her eyes moist. "You guys are lifesavers."

Then I noticed someone else was in the lobby. At the base of a stairway, a guy in a white shirt was polishing a banister with a white towel. He looked up and caught my eye, then looked down, as if embarrassed, and started polishing faster, his hair hanging over his eyes.

Mustafa ushered him outside to the patio, and I saw he was actually around my own age.

"Allow me to introduce my son. This is Nazif," said Mustafa. He poked at Nazif's back to prompt him to stand up straighter. "He started working here with me two months ago, part-time, after school and on weekends. Now he is working full-time for his summer job. I am training him to be a bellboy, and introducing him to other exciting work in hotel management."

Nazif looked as if someone had given him a bellboy costume for a part in a play. He wore a crisp white short-sleeved shirt with gold epaulets. But the shirt was untucked over his black trousers, and his black shoes were scuffed, unlike his father's gleaming ones. As soon as Mustafa took his hand off his son's back, Nazif immediately slouched again. He didn't exactly project excitement about his dazzling career in the hospitality business.

I stole another glance at Nazif while Mom talked to him about his job. I noted his thick brown hair, messily parted to one side. He had a rounded chin and full lips, which worked into a slow, shy smile when Mom said it was nice to meet him. Above his lips was the faintest trace of a mustache. He wasn't model-hot, or stylish like Riza of the *Gulet Anilar*. Riza—I wondered who he was serving apple tea to now on that boat. But Nazif was cute, in a rumpled way.

"Nazif will take your bags and show you up to your rooms," said Aunt Jackie. "I've put you in the Harem Suite. I hope you'll be comfortable there. You can get freshened up and relax before dinner while I go over some business."

"You should be resting," Mom countered. "Put your feet up. That's an order."

Aunt Jackie smiled. "Okay, doc. I'll take my phone to my couch and work from there."

Nazif loaded our bags onto a gold luggage cart and brought us to an ancient-looking elevator with a sliding metal gate. "You are on floor four," he mumbled, his eyes downcast as he held open the elevator door and began to walk away.

"There's plenty of space," Mom said, backing against the wall. "Zan, squeeze next to me so Nazif can come in."

"There is not room for all of us and the luggage," he said, still avoiding eye contact. "Please, you two go first, and I will go after. I will meet you on floor four with your bags."

"Not the friendliest bellboy, is he?" Mom whispered as Nazif slammed the rickety elevator gate shut and sent us on our uncertain journey up to floor four. The elevator shuddered and moaned as we ascended. "And Mustafa's polite enough, but his jokes about overcharging tourists are way out of line." She shook her head in disbelief. "Grumpy and Son. It's no wonder this place is getting low marks for hospitality."

"Maybe we should take over their jobs, too," I said. "Seeing as we're taking over the entire hotel. I'm sure you have lots of ideas about how everything could be better."

"Oh, things definitely *could* be better," said Mom, kicking the shabby rug on the elevator floor. "This hotel has its charms. It could be amazing. But it's in dire need of updates. The staff is in chaos. And it's got terrible public relations problems."

"PR problems? Fits right in with our family."

Mom glared at me. "It's not funny. Your aunt's going to be a single mother. She needs this hotel to work. Otherwise she'll have to go back to teaching English, where she barely made enough money to get by. Or we'll have to twist her arm and get her to come back home with us. Which would thrill your grandparents, but I don't really see her doing it, do you?"

Alarms went off in my head. What if Mom decided not just to visit Aunt Jackie more often here but to *move* here? Could that happen? Maybe finishing my last two years of high school here would be okay, maybe an adventure, even—but what if I didn't see Dad anymore? Much as I didn't feel like seeing him now, the thought of being across an ocean indefinitely made me feel strange and kind of sad.

"This isn't your idea of what to do with the rest of your life, is it?" I asked, thinking of her self-help book. "We wouldn't, like, move here and help out permanently, would we?"

"How do you manage to go to these places in your mind?" Mom sighed. "Look. There's not much left of our family right now. Aside from your grandparents, Aunt Jackie, and this new cousin you'll have soon. So I am asking you to rise to the occasion."

Maybe she had a point. But I noticed she didn't answer my question.

The glint in her eye was still there when we stepped out of the elevator and she surveyed the peeling wallpaper. "What I could do here with a halfway decent decorating budget," she muttered under her breath.

Nazif came up the elevator with the luggage cart a minute later. He brushed past us and pushed the cart down to the end of the thickly carpeted hallway. Then he unlocked the door to our suite with one of those big, ornate keys I'd seen hanging behind the front desk. The door opened with a lot of clatter, squeaking loudly. He gestured for us to enter, then pushed the cart in after us.

"Oh, it's exquisite!" said Mom, clasping her hands together.

"A palace!" I exclaimed, looking around the living room at the plush furniture.

Nazif seemed surprised, and finally looked right at Mom and me. "It is not really so big," he said. "There is one bigger, down the hall. The Sultan's Suite."

"Should we move there?" Mom asked.

"No. That is used mostly by businesspeople. Sometimes it is rented for use during the day, for meetings or business functions."

As he talked, my view of our suite changed. He was right; it wasn't so big. Two strategically placed, ornately framed mirrors gave the illusion of extra space, and the divans and chairs were actually pretty faded and threadbare. The small living room separated two miniature bedrooms. Off Mom's room was a tiny bathroom with marble floors, which was mostly occupied by a white claw-foot bathtub. But compared to the boat and the two interrogation rooms we'd been in, the suite was spacious, even luxurious. The walls gleamed white, and all the furniture looked antique. And best of all? I'd have *my own room*.

Nazif showed Mom to her bedroom, then brought my bags to my room. The room had barely enough space for an old-looking wooden armoire, a narrow nightstand with an old-fashioned rotary-dial phone on top, and a twin bed with an elaborately carved headboard and footboard. But the place was cozy and inviting. The bed was draped with a lush bedspread embroidered with colorful tulips, peacock feathers, and twisting vines. It looked like the perfect bed to dive into and pull the covers up over my head—which I would totally do, if I didn't have a new job as a maid and a side job as a sleuth trying to find a missing person.

My room also had a built-in window seat next to a small bay window. The window was covered with those wooden lattices I'd seen from the street outside. But to my surprise, when I sat down on the cushioned seat amid the embroidered throw pillows, I was able to see outside between the densely slatted diamond shapes.

Nazif lingered at the door, leaning against the doorframe. When I looked at him, he turned abruptly, as if embarrassed to have been caught there.

"Hey, can you tell me why the windows are like this? Can they be opened?" I asked.

He turned back around. "The latticework is from the Ottoman era," he said. "This part of the house was originally the harem, the women's quarters. The women could see out of these shutters without being seen from the street. The windows cannot be opened. But you can always go up on the roof."

No curious stares. No blazing sunlight. Sounded good to me, after all I'd been through lately! Then I squinted through the lattice again. And gasped.

"What is it?" asked Nazif.

I was so stunned I couldn't answer. There were two men across the street, standing in front of a shop that advertised painted tiles and plates. One guy had a thick mustache. The other was bald. They wore street clothes, not uniforms: polo shirts and jeans. But I'd know those faces anywhere.

Lazar and Vasil.

Holy crap. Crap, crap, crap, crap. I shrank back from the window, though I knew they couldn't see me through the heavy latticework. Why here? Why now? They really must be smugglers. They must be looking for me, sure I was their ticket to Sage, who either knew something or had something they wanted . . . or they knew Sage had given me the figurines and now they were here to get them.

They were arguing about something. Vasil kept his arms folded while Lazar spoke with angry gestures. Sage must have seriously pissed off these guys if they were going to such lengths to find her. Maybe she'd reneged on a business deal.

I felt fresh waves of anger toward her, mixed with an undertow of confusion. I couldn't get the thought out of my head:

Maybe she had some good reason. I picked up the rotary-dial phone on the nightstand to call Inspector Lale. I rummaged in my backpack pockets, looking for her business card.

Just as I found the card, I realized there was no dial tone on the phone.

Nazif stepped forward and picked up the curly cord from the back of the phone, which went nowhere, and which ended in a tangle of exposed wires. "The phone is for display only," he apologized. "Decoration."

"Display only? Are you kidding me? Didn't my aunt pay her phone bill?" I meant it as a joke, even though nothing was funny right now, but Nazif just stared, and I knew it was true.

"The line to the main desk works. Not the individual room lines, currently," he said. "Will that be all your questions?" he asked hopefully, backing away.

"I guess that's all."

Nazif hurried away before I could tip him. Which was good because I didn't have cash anyway, and it seemed weird to tip someone my own age.

I replaced the receiver, and the useless phone jingled a little, hinting at a ring. Just as well. When I looked outside again, a crowd of gypsies was passing by, pushing wooden carts heaped with bags toward the Arasta Bazaar. Lazar and Vasil were gone.

I needed to move, to do something physical, or I was going to explode. As I started unpacking my backpack, my mind spun with options. Inspector Lale wasn't due back in Istanbul for another couple of days. I could have Nazif or Mustafa call her from the front desk. But then they would know we had a problem, and what if any guests in the lobby happened to overhear? Aunt Jackie clearly didn't want to reveal what we'd just gone through in Dalaman. Lazar and Vasil would be long gone by the time the police got here, and I didn't want the hotel to attract attention as a place where criminals lurked.

Anyway, they hadn't done anything except stand out in the

street, in a public place. They looked threatening, but they hadn't actually threatened me. Hopefully they wouldn't enter the hotel lobby. I just wanted to get to that working front desk phone and let Inspector Lale know I'd seen the two "guards" from the *Anilar*. She'd know what to do with that information, and I would have done the right thing by tipping her off.

I reached into my backpack one last time for my tube of concealer, thinking I'd freshen up fast before heading down to the lobby. My hand hit the Freya Stark book that Sage had given me. I held it, frowning at the cover with its photo of the cliff tombs. I didn't want the book anymore, just as I didn't want the gold figurines. Everything from Sage seemed tainted. I riffled through the pages. There was nothing in this book I wanted to read.

Then a little piece of paper fluttered out from near the back of the book. I picked it up off the floor.

It was a store receipt, torn at the top. On the back was a handwritten address: *25 Istiklal Caddesi, Beyoğlu, Istanbul.*

My heart began to beat fast. Maybe this was Sage's host family's address. Or a school address, or maybe a friend's. I clutched the creased and worn receipt, feeling its connection to her.

"Excuse me."

I looked up and saw Nazif in the doorway again.

"Oh. You're back?"

"I have shown your mother how to operate the shower. The hot and cold are reversed, installed incorrectly. It is important you use cold for hot and hot for cold. Do you want me to show you also?"

"Hot for cold, cold for hot. I think I got it."

"Good. I must go back downstairs now."

"Just one thing," I said, standing up. I showed him the address on the receipt. "Do you know where this is? Is it near here?"

He studied the address. "Istiklal Caddesi? This is the main

street in the neighborhood called Beyoğlu," he said. He handed the scrap of paper back to me, took a phone out of his pocket and typed something, while I shook my head in disbelief. Clearly I'd wanted to make a call a moment ago; why hadn't he offered his phone?

Then Nazif showed me a map on the screen. "This. It is a mostly touristic place. People like to climb the Galata Tower and visit Taksim Square. Some famous churches and monasteries are also there."

"Can you search for the exact address for me?"

He ran a Google search, but nothing came up. A little circle spun endlessly on the screen.

"We have weak Wi-Fi signal here in this part of the building," he explained. "Maybe you will have better luck in the lobby."

"Okay. Can I use your phone down there?" I asked, reaching for it. My hand accidentally brushed his. It felt incredibly soft.

He practically recoiled from me, stumbling backward. "My father needs me downstairs right away," he mumbled. "We have these Dutch guests who are having a difficulty, and—"

"Fine. Never mind." I didn't know why Nazif was allergic to me, but I didn't have time to figure it out now or even to be annoyed by it.

I needed more details about that address, and fast.

20

While Nazif went downstairs in the rickety elevator, I sped four floors down the carpeted stairs to the lobby. Mustafa was there, trying to pacify three Dutch travelers who were upset about a leaky pipe in their room. One of the guests was on the public computer, threatening to find another hotel if the problem did not get resolved immediately. I hung back near the kitchen, pretending to be fascinated by some old musical instruments on the walls. I became an expert on the design of the Turkish oud, memorizing its strings and contours.

The moment Mustafa went with the guests to inspect the pipe, I hurried over to the area with the low couch and the computer. There were two narrow windows on either side of the front door, covered by heavy wood blinds. Most of the light in the lobby came from the windows overlooking the back patio and garden. I peered out between the wooden slats and could see the plate and tile shop across the street. Lazar and Vasil weren't there, but that didn't make me breathe easier. They'd identified my aunt's hotel as the place where I was staying, which meant they could come back anytime. Before I looked up that address from Sage's note again, I *had* to tell Inspector Lale these creeps were in town.

I reached over the front desk and picked up the phone. But I hesitated as my hand hovered over the keypad. I thought about all the times I'd hidden from the police at malls. I'd dived into bushes, escaping the cops who busted up my friends' parties. I remembered dreading the sound of a phone ringing at home, wondering if it was someone calling my parents to haul me into the station. And now I was actually reaching out to the police, in a foreign country. I was reporting information, yes, but I was also inviting questioning.

Still, I had to let someone official know that these two thugs were outside my aunt's hotel.

I took a deep breath and called the mobile phone number on Inspector Lale's card.

"Alo," said a woman's voice.

"H-h-hello?" I stammered. "Is this Inspector Lale?"

"Yes," she said. "Is this Zan?" she added, almost eagerly, it seemed.

"Yes! How did you know?"

"The caller ID says Mavi Konak Hotel."

"Oh."

"So. Did you think of anything else you want to tell me? Or do you have any news?"

"Not about Sage," I said. "But I saw someone. Two people. Outside the hotel." I took a deep breath, and quickly told her about seeing Lazar and Vasil.

"I'm not surprised to hear they're in Istanbul," she said. "We ran a check on the *Anilar* to try to get information about them. Unfortunately, the *Anilar* is not properly registered, which means that American couple, the Clarksons, fell for some kind of scam."

My heart thudded. The *Anilar* was also a lie!

"There are unfortunately some yachts in the harbor offering unlicensed cruises for under-the-table cash," Inspector Lale went on. "So because the *Anilar* is not officially registered, we haven't been able to reach the captain or any other crew. The coast guard is looking for the boat now. It seems to have gone off the radar."

"Oh my God. Did you find Ron and Judy Clarkson?" I asked.

"We did. They're safe, staying at a hotel in Istanbul," she said. "I intend to meet with them in a couple of days when I get back to town."

I breathed a long sigh of relief.

"They told me the first mate on their cruise hired the security for them," Inspector Lale continued, "but they were not sure of the name of the firm. They were horrified when we told them the firm could be a scam, since the cruise itself was not a legal charter."

"So Lazar and Vasil are definitely not security guards," I concluded.

"Oh, no. They *could* be," she corrected. "It will just take us some time to be sure. The number of private security guards in Turkey outnumbers armies in some countries. We have more than two hundred thousand guards who have gone through some kind of training. And well over one thousand security firms. We are contacting all of them, but as you can imagine, this will take some time."

"So what should I do about these guys?" I asked, a note of fear creeping into my voice. "Whether or not they're really security guards, do you think they're looking for Sage at our hotel, and maybe the figurines, too? Will they come back?"

"It sounds to me like they're casing the place, waiting to see who comes out," she said. "Since they haven't gone inside. But it's worth paying attention to."

"Did you manage to contact her host family?" I said.

"No. The school said she lived on campus in a dormitory, not with a host family."

Great. One more lie.

"Listen, Zan, I'm detained here on the coast for two more days," she went on, suddenly sounding rushed. "But I'll send some of my team in Istanbul to inspect your area right away, undercover, and to keep a close eye on your hotel."

"Thank you." I was so glad I'd pushed past my fear of the police and called her. I was about to tell her about the address I'd found in the Freya Stark book, but she continued talking.

"In the meantime, please don't go out alone," she urged. "Stay away from those men if you see them. And call me at this number again—*not* the Istanbul police—if they reappear. This is *very important*."

"Is it because of what you said this morning? That some police are corrupt?"

"Partly that, yes. I don't want you taking any chances. But also because not everyone in the force takes me seriously. There aren't many women in my position within the national police—or any police department here. I can't take the chance that information might fall into the wrong hands and be used to take me down. Do you understand what I'm saying?"

"Got it. I'll call you," I promised.

"Thank you, Zan. You've been a big help. Every bit of information brings me closer to shutting down this smuggling ring, and if these men are involved, believe me, I will get to them."

Finally, I had done something right. But I still had Sage to find. I folded up the receipt with the address and put it in my pocket. If there was any chance I could get in touch with her first, on my own, I had to try. And if this address wasn't for a host family, what was it for?

After I hung up the phone, I faced the computer terminal . . . and froze. Everything on the screen was in Turkish. I finally managed to bring up a search engine in English. I typed the address I'd found on Sage's makeshift bookmark and it brought up a picture of a gray stone building sandwiched between two more modern ones. I enlarged the image and saw bars over the windows. Wrought-iron gates with elaborate scrolling covered the set of double wooden doors. On the wall to the right of the doors was a plaque, which I could just make out:

THE LYCIAN SOCIETY

I felt gut-kicked by disappointment. This wasn't Sage's host family's house, or a friend's house. It was the company that had arranged the Blue Voyage cruise. *Of course* she had this address written down. She was on the Blue Voyage herself, and would have set up the tour through them, too, even if she were working with smugglers. You had to book through the tour company in order to get on that boat. I felt like such an idiot, to think the address would magically lead me to some-one who would know exactly where to find her. It was a good thing I hadn't said anything about it to Inspector Lale—I would have felt silly.

But since I was already there, I clicked on the link to the Lycian Society website, wondering if they'd have a picture up of Uncle Berk, or some notice about his death. They didn't. It was just a simple, one-page website with information in Turkish, English, German, and Italian. I went to the English home page and read:

> We are an international organization of scholars,
> historians, independent researchers, and antiquity
> enthusiasts with interest in Turkey and Greece.
> We are devoted to the scholarship and interest of
> ancient civilization throughout Anatolia. We offer
> memberships at various levels. We also operate
> Lycian Tours, putting together educational package
> tours of archaeological interest along the ancient
> Lycian Way.

Sensing someone's eyes on me, I turned and noticed Nazif was back in the lobby. The moment I looked at him, he started watering a potted plant. Maybe he was nosy, or didn't trust me. But I didn't have time to think about Nazif. I finally had access to information. Ignoring him, I next Googled *Amy Miller, Hawthorne, Oregon.*

There were about twelve Amy Millers in Hawthorne. After I weeded out the obvious—the real estate agent, the librarian, the wedding planner—the only information for an Amy Miller close to my age was a list of swimming statistics from a few recent years. Turns out she'd competed for the Hawthorne High swim team. They'd made regionals, and she'd placed first on her team. I remembered how Sage had swum so strongly on the Blue Voyage, beating me in every race around the rock tombs, and fearlessly striking out for the *Anilar* at night—even after a couple of drinks. This must be the same person, and I'd been right to guess she was a champion swimmer.

Then my eye caught an obituary that dated back seven years.

> **Eric Miller** of Hawthorne, Oregon, left this world unexpectedly on May 25. Beloved son to Robert and Sheila Miller, brother to Amy Miller. Private memorial service. In lieu of flowers, donations can be made to the Rehabilitation and Substance Abuse Clinic in Portland, Oregon.

I stared at the page, and at the picture of the guy in a baseball uniform, holding a bat. This had to be Sage's brother. He had a mop of curly red hair the exact same shade as hers, and similar features. So Sage *had* actually told me the truth about her brother dying—and about how he'd died. And although it was an awful thing to read and to think about, it brought me some comfort to think that at least one part of Sage Powell/ Amy Miller had been authentic after all.

I dove down ten pages into the Google results, but got nothing else on Sage's previous identity. Her media footprint was strangely lacking. So next I searched her parents' names. Now that I had their names, phone directory entries, employers, or email addresses should follow.

I found two Sheila Millers in Hawthorne. One was a twenty-two-year-old college student. The other was a pediatric nurse at Hawthorne Hospital. Maybe that's what Sage had meant when she said her mother was "in and out of the hospital." Not sick. Working!

I found Sheila's photo in the staff directory, and immediately I knew she was Sage's mom. The same mane of curly red hair, the same cat-green eyes. Only she didn't have Sage's fullness and vibrancy. She didn't look directly at the camera but instead slightly off to one side. I recognized a similar quality in Aunt Jackie's smile. The look of grief.

I found an email address for the pediatric unit and immediately wrote to the head of the department:

> Greetings. My name is Alexandra, and I am trying to contact Sheila Miller, RN. I'm a friend of her daughter's here in Turkey, and I need to reach Amy Miller. I'm hoping that Sheila has some forwarding information for her. Please have Sheila contact me as soon as possible.

IT IS AN URGENT MATTER, I typed in all caps as an afterthought. That should get someone's attention. Only after I hit Send did it occur to me that maybe my note would freak her out. She'd already lost one child; she might think the worst.

But it was too late. I'd just have to wait for her response and hope I'd get some way to contact Sage, or some clue about where she might have gone.

Finally, I checked my email. There weren't many new messages, which was normal these days, since I had no friends anymore. There was an ad from Burlington Boulders about an outdoor teen rock-climbing trip I'd love to have been on, and a note from Dad, with the subject line: "Checking in with my world traveler!" I swallowed hard. It was surreal, seeing his name here, in another country, as if my two worlds were colliding. I didn't feel like reading his note, so I moved to delete it. But I ended up clicking Open by mistake, and I couldn't help myself.

> Hi Zanny! Are you and your mother at the hotel in Istanbul yet?? I've called there twice and nobody answered. Email me as soon as you get this. I want to know how you are, hear all about your exotic travels. Are you using the journal? Also would like to discuss the Victoria situation with you.

A flame of anger flared up inside me. I banged out a response.

> Yeah, we arrived. We're fine. But you want to talk to me about your mistress? Thanks but no thanks! I really have no desire to hear all the sordid details. Call your shrink.

I hit Enter so hard, the whole table shook.

I sensed, rather than saw, Nazif's curious stare as I stalked past him on my way back to the elevator. I punched the elevator button, and suddenly he materialized behind me.

I whirled around. "What is it?" I demanded. "Why are you following me?"

"Sorry. The address you showed me. I do know of this place. It is the Lycian Society headquarters."

"I know. I looked it up myself."

"I'm sorry. I did not make this connection until I saw what you were looking at. I must tell you, it is not a safe place."

"What? That's crazy!" I couldn't help laughing. "It's a

historical society. What are they going to do, bore me to death?"

He didn't laugh. "I am serious. There are some bad people there."

I didn't know whether to laugh or cry. There was no way a dusty historical society and an archaeological tour operator could be dangerous. And that tour representative, Erdem Tabak, had been perfectly friendly, bending over backward to make up for the missing guest speaker and following through on his promises. Nazif was just trying to play with my head. Or he was trying to be funny and failing. But I was still mad about my dad's note, and I was so discouraged that my one link to Sage had led to a dead end. So no witty retorts came to mind.

Then the elevator arrived, and someone in the lobby rang a bell for Nazif. To my relief, he hurried away. I had enough of a mystery on my hands right now. I didn't need to be analyzing and obsessing over this guy's every word.

21

I woke up with a start, to the haunting call from the Blue Mosque muezzin. I rolled over and read the clock on the night-stand: 10:42 p.m. I moaned and squished the pillow over my head.

Still, the chanting stirred me. In the darkness, I pulled on my hoodie and sweatpants and left the Harem Suite. I quietly pushed open the door to the stairwell and tiptoed up the wind-ing wooden steps, all the way to the rooftop garden.

The muezzin sounded so much louder outside. I walked through the trellis draped with grapevines, past a cluster of tables and chairs, and over to a white-cushioned sofa set off by large pots of geraniums. I sank into it and tucked my feet up under me.

Beauty was like this physical presence surrounding me. It changed the very air. One side of the roof offered a sweep-ing view of the Sea of Marmara, glistening in the moonlight, ringed by the lights of Istanbul that glowed like yellow gold. Was Sage out there somewhere? Was one of those gold lights hers? Was she hiding on the coast? Or was she somewhere in between?

I shifted positions. The other side offered a clear view of the Blue Mosque. The sky was still dark, but the six minarets were all lit up. A crescent moon hung low, clinging to the edge of night.

The building right next to the hotel also had a rooftop garden. There I saw the silhouettes of a family of three. They were sitting around a table, talking quietly, until the call to prayer ended. Then they turned their attention to the table, laughing and talking, pointing at things. I heard the roll of dice. They were playing a board game by candlelight.

I smiled to myself, watching them, and took a few deep breaths. I smelled food, cooking meat, coming from somewhere, and tasted the nip of sea salt in the air. Now I understood what Aunt Jackie had meant by using the call to prayer to hit the pause button on your life. I felt alive, my senses as finely tuned as the strings of a Turkish oud.

I usually only felt this way when I was climbing a rock wall and approaching the end of a route. I'd look down, and everyone below me appeared so small and far away. My worries would fall away, too. High on the wall, life became pared down and simple. Chalk on my hands. The click of carabineers snapping into place. The whizz of the rope through my fingers, leaving the slightest burn. The satisfaction of reaching a goal. Everything felt manageable and under my control. I made my own decisions, and was in charge of my own results.

A few minutes later, the family on the rooftop next door cheered and applauded. They stood up and began to put their game away.

The dad silhouette put his arm around the son silhouette. The mom silhouette, a willowy woman wearing a shawl with lots of fringe, laughed uproariously at something the dad silhouette said. Even after the three of them disappeared through a door and went back into their apartment, the rich notes of the mom's laugh hung in the air like thick perfume.

I swallowed hard, suddenly aching for my parents. For the family I once thought I had.

◇◇◇◇◇

Too soon, I was woken up again as Mom banged on my door. "Rise and shine! Kitchen patrol!"

Groggily, I sat up. "What?" The clock on the nightstand read 6:00 a.m.

"We're fixing a buffet breakfast for the guests. Apparently the staff who just quit were also the morning cooks. Chop chop! Up and at 'em! Let's go, let's go!"

Could she *be* more annoying? "*Unghh.* Okay. Let me just take a shower."

"No time. Shower later. We are needed *immediately.*"

I sat up and peered out through the diamonds in the window lattice. The world was already coming to life, with shopkeepers tossing buckets of water on the cobblestones outside their shops, as Selim used to do on the teak wood deck before we ate every meal. Suddenly I missed that routine. The Arasta Bazaar at the end of the street was awakening, too, with vendors arriving to work.

There was no sign of Lazar or Vasil. But what was to stop them from returning and simply walking in? If they needed to talk with me, they'd find a way—it was only a matter of time. I could only hope Inspector Lale had gotten some of her trusted colleagues on their trail.

I threw on some clothes—long pants and long sleeves, no surprise—and took a couple of extra minutes to slather on concealer.

When I got downstairs to the kitchen, Mom and Aunt Jackie were waiting for me. Mom was taking bins of food out of the fridge. Aunt Jackie was perched on a stool in front of a cutting board with onions, but she was massaging her lower back instead of chopping them. She looked pained and exhausted, as if she hadn't slept so well either.

Mom shot me a disapproving look. "You're late. Get cracking." She gestured with her chin to a bowl and the stove. "And by that I mean *not* cracking. I need you to hard-boil two dozen eggs. Guests will be coming down soon. We've got eight rooms occupied right now. Some Italians, some Swedes, and some Canadian guests. Early risers and big eaters, Mustafa said."

Yawning, I somehow got the eggs going in four separate pots of bubbling water. Then Aunt Jackie switched me to feta cheese duty, crumbling it into a bowl. After that, I put olives in bowls and sliced up halvah, which was thicker and softer than the kind we got at home, like a mocha-colored brick of sugar. It all looked amazing. Aunt Jackie picked up her knife and finally started chopping the onions. Working by her side, in silence, felt peaceful. It was satisfying to see the plates stack up with food and know that everything I did was helping her in some way.

"Do you always start work this early?" I asked.

"Only when the cook has quit." Aunt Jackie laughed. "We do run early around here in the summers, though, because guests usually like to start their sightseeing early. Mustafa and Nazif will get in close to eight," said Aunt Jackie. "And the cleaning staff soon after. That is, they would be arriving soon after, if they hadn't quit," she added, remembering yesterday's news.

Eight. That didn't leave me much time. Between Nazif's watchfulness and Mom's work schedule for me—which she'd written out and posted on my bedroom door—it was going to be a huge challenge to work on finding Sage. First, I needed to get to the computer to see if Sheila Miller had responded to my email. If she hadn't, I needed a new plan.

"Can I ask you something?" I said to Aunt Jackie, as soon as my mom went down to the laundry room to get some fresh towels.

"Anytime, Zan. What's on your mind?"

"Nazif said something weird to me yesterday." The Lycian Society remark was on my mind again.

She smiled. "Nazif's a good kid. He's an introvert and can be a little awkward with the guests, though, so I'm not too surprised. What'd he say?"

"He mentioned the Lycian Society had some bad people in it. Why would he say something like that, do you think?"

"Bad people?" Aunt Jackie thought a moment. "I don't know about *bad* people—maybe he's trying to translate from Turkish. Maybe he meant *dishonest.*"

"But it wasn't the tour packager's fault that neither of their guest speakers could make the cruise." I frowned. "And Erdem Tabak was really nice about getting the company to make up for it."

"That's the tour packager. That's a different part of it," said Aunt Jackie. "The society itself, the group of scholars and enthusiasts, must be what Nazif was referring to. I personally do find them dishonest. I never liked the way they treated Berk." Aunt Jackie sighed and set down her knife for a moment. She massaged her belly, wincing slightly, and then continued. "They paid their consultants and lecturers decently, so Berk did some work for them now and then. And he gave a guest lecture at their annual conference in April. That got him invited to talk on the cruise. But they always kept him at arm's length, and they rejected his membership application."

"I thought anyone could pay to join. That's what the website says, anyway."

"That depends. There are different levels of membership for difference price points and commitment levels," said Aunt Jackie. "The organization is financed mostly by donations and membership dues, and now these educational tours, which they started offering last year. But there's an elite level, called Onyx, which costs an arm and a leg to join and requires an application."

Onyx level. I knew onyx was like obsidian, a pitch-black gemstone. I thought of some of Mom's rich clients, and Dad's campaign donors, and the black credit cards they used—black was code for "loaded," Mom had told me once. Those were the people she went after most aggressively for donations.

"The Lycian Society is a complex organization," Aunt Jackie

continued. "And the Onyx level is a bit mysterious, kind of like the Masons. The members have codes of honor, and pass-words, and other ways for members to identify one another. Honestly? I think it's a little bit silly. Most members at the elite level are rich intellectual dilettante types who probably just toss the name around to impress their friends. But there are some serious scholars, collectors, and museum personnel in that group as well, and *that's* who Berk was really trying to con-nect with."

"Why?"

"For business-networking opportunities. He thought it might lead to a more permanent and stable job somewhere."

I frowned. "Yeah, but . . . why wouldn't they take him? I mean, he had a PhD. He wrote articles. I bet he could have run their whole organization!" I was surprised at how loyal I was starting to feel toward Uncle Berk, whom I'd hardly known when he was alive. Now that he was dead, I was getting to know him better, and I could see what he meant to Aunt Jackie and how much they'd loved each other.

"I suspect he wasn't independently wealthy enough," she said. "And he wasn't affiliated with any institution. It's a vicious cycle. He needed the society for networking opportunities, but he wasn't plugged into a network enough to be accepted."

"That's totally unfair."

"It was unfair," Aunt Jackie agreed. "And so yes, I do think some people in the Lycian Society are 'bad.' They're snobs. I'm glad I'm done with them. It's the only silver lining in this whole miserable business of Berk dying." She scooped all the chopped onions into a bowl in one swift motion. "Hey," she added, glancing toward the door, "do you mind giving me Lale—I mean, *Inspector* Lale's—business card? I want to give her a call."

"Sure. Why?"

She glanced at the door again. "Okay. I hate to ask you to keep another secret from your mom. But just between you and me? I want to get in touch with her about Berk's death."

I froze. This decision seemed huge.

"I know she's in the anti-smuggling division, not homicide," Aunt Jackie went on, "but I figure she might have some pull, given her title. And I know she's got her hands full with the racket on the coast right now, but maybe she can help me to get the case reopened. I mean, she was a friend of Berk's, and she did say she'd do anything for him. It can't hurt to ask her."

"Yeah. That's a really good idea." As long as Inspector Lale didn't tell Aunt Jackie about my seeing Lazar and Vasil outside the hotel yesterday, I thought.

"What's a good idea?" Mom came back in with a stack of fresh towels.

"Nothing," Aunt Jackie and I said together. We exchanged a quick, knowing smile.

Mom raised an eyebrow. Then she noticed I was no longer chopping. "What are you doing, Zan? Let's go, let's go!" She clapped her hands. "Guests are waking up. Time's running out!"

◇◇◇◇◇

Around seven-thirty, guests began trickling down to the tables, just as Mom and I had finished setting up the buffet. We greeted them in the small dining area off the lobby. Mom dashed outside to the patio garden to pick flowers for bud vases we'd set on the tables. She was smiling and humming to herself; I hadn't seen her so happy in a long time. Mom liked to work, and I could see that this lifestyle agreed with her more than a leisurely cruise. She bossed me around, and I scurried to get place settings on all the tables, managing to drop a whole stack of them on the floor just as Mustafa and Nazif arrived.

I was sure I saw Nazif smirk as I surveyed the scattered cutlery. I gave him my best glare.

But then he surprised me, stooping to help pick up forks and knives. "Let me help you," he said.

"I got it," I snapped. I bent down, too, and added, as we both picked up knives, "You know what you said yesterday? About the Lycian Society?"

He nodded.

"When you said there were 'bad people' there, you meant they were, like, snobby, right?"

"No." He shook his head. "I meant exactly what I said. I do speak English, you know. My father made me take English classes starting when I was five. And I watch a lot of American TV shows."

Now I was really confused.

"I cannot speak of it again," he added, looking down. "I should never have said anything."

"But *why*? Why are they 'bad people'?"

Nazif looked around, chewing his lip.

"Come on," I said. "You can't just drop something like that and walk away. Just tell me why you think they're dangerous. Or," I added, with a meaningful glance toward Mustafa at the front desk, "I'll tell your dad you were being rude to me."

His eyes grew wide. "When? When was I rude?"

"Right now. I'm a guest who needs help, and you're not helping me. I know how important hospitality is to him. Plus you could have offered your phone right away yesterday, when you saw that I needed to make a call and the connection didn't work in my room."

His face clouded over. "I thought maybe you were different, but I was wrong. You are a typical American."

His words smacked me in the gut. "What does that mean?"

"You think the world revolves around you. You feel entitled to demand things. Like so many of the Americans we see in this hotel."

"You don't even know me!" I burst out. "How can you say I'm just like every other person from my country? I don't think you're just like every other person in *your* country. And I do *not* think the entire world revolves around me. Anyway, you're changing the subject. This is really important to me. They hired my uncle as a guest speaker. I want to understand who he was working with."

At the mention of my uncle, his face changed. His eyes met mine, unblinking. "All right. Because I cared about your uncle, and you say it is important for you to understand, I will tell you what I know of this group. But we must talk outside this hotel."

"Why? What's wrong with talking here?"

He looked around again. "Voices carry," he said, "and I do not want guests to have the feeling that bad things could happen here. The guests are here to relax, my father says. We have had some negative reviews online and we must be careful to stay positive."

"Okay, but my mom doesn't want me leaving the hotel," I said, thinking more about Lazar and Vasil than her. I didn't want to meet those guys face-to-face in the street again.

"Sorry," said Nazif. "But that is my condition."

I hesitated. If I had Nazif with me, and saw Lazar and Vasil, maybe they wouldn't approach me. "Okay," I said. "We'll talk outside. At lunch."

"Good," he said. "I'll meet you at the front desk." He stood up, handed me a handful of cutlery to put away, and hurried back to the lobby.

Replaying our strange conversation in my mind, I couldn't believe the words that had come out of my mouth. I had acted like a snotty politician's daughter who was used to getting her way.

But I needed to find out what Nazif knew. If there was something rotten about the Lycian Society, I had to know what it was.

22

All morning, Mom kept me in constant motion, which meant I couldn't get to the computer to check for Sheila Miller's response. After clearing and washing all the breakfast dishes, we pushed the housekeeping carts down the halls and tackled the guest rooms. I was grateful that only eight of the fifteen rooms were occupied, but there was still plenty to do.

I learned a bunch of stuff, all right, but nothing I'd put in a college essay. For example, I learned that people leave hair in the sink, don't flush the toilet, swipe toiletries, smoke in non-smoking rooms, and expect maid service to pick up their underwear. I learned that if you're pushing a supply cart down a hallway, you are invisible. Guests chatting about their sight-seeing plans on their way to the elevator don't get out of your way, or say hello. They pretend not to see you.

"This hotel is operating at a total loss," Mom complained, flicking a feather duster over a mantel. "I mean, it's high season. This place should be full. People should be banging down the door and paying big bucks for this level of charm in the heart of the Old City. I looked at your Lonely Planet guide last night. The Hippodrome. The cisterns. The Blue Mosque.

Hagia Sophia. All this history right in their backyard."

"I know. And speaking of walking distance"—I snapped on a fresh pair of latex gloves and grabbed the toilet brush—"I was thinking of stepping out during lunch. Maybe go see the Blue Mosque, or even that bazaar at the end of the street."

"No. We have a lot to do here. Your aunt cannot afford one more bad review."

"I know. I'll be fast. I just want to walk outside, up and down the street. Nazif said he'd show me around our block, just so I know where things are."

Mom thought a moment. "I guess that would be okay. But no going over to his house. He seems like a nice boy, but you want to be careful not to step into a trap."

I stared at her. "Why would I go into his house?"

"Because he just lives next door and he might feel inclined to, you know, seize the day."

"Mom!"

"Pretty foreign girl? Empty house? It's an opportunity, and boys are boys, the same all over the world. So I'd feel more comfortable if—"

"Wait. He lives *next door*?" This revelation was so huge it blotted out, for a moment, the fact that Mom still didn't trust me enough to let me out of her sight for five minutes.

"Yes. I was talking to Mustafa earlier," she said. "The Polat family are the hotel's next-door neighbors. They have that gorgeous rooftop garden to our left."

I stared at her.

"In fact, that's how Mustafa originally got his concierge job," Mom went on. "He got laid off from another hotel and had trouble getting work at the same level. He said he was really happy to get this position, and to go home for all his meals and see his family."

So it was *Nazif's* family I'd seen playing a board game last night. *Nazif's* family I'd envied. And I'd traveled halfway around the world to meet the boy next door.

Now I was curious about Nazif for an entirely new set of reasons.

◇◇◇◇◇

Aunt Jackie came back from her doctor appointment just as the muezzin was singing the midday call. Mom and I were sweating it out in the basement laundry room, folding stacks and stacks of towels. Aunt Jackie sank into a chair, breathing heavily. "Bad news," she said. "My doctor's putting me on bed rest."

"Oh, Jackie." A towel slid out of Mom's hand and she didn't bother to pick it up. "I'm so, so sorry to hear this. For how long? Did she say?"

"Could be a couple of weeks, could be longer. It's kind of a wait-and-see thing." She sighed. "There might be a problem with the placenta. I don't have to be flat-out in bed all the time, but no lifting, no stairs. They want me to exert myself as little as possible and avoid stress."

Looking at my aunt and the dark shadows that ringed her eyes, I wanted to cry. What if she had to stop working for the remainder of her pregnancy?

I untied my apron. "Can I take my lunch break now?" I asked.

Mom nodded, pressing some Turkish lira into my hand. "Go ahead. I'll get Aunt Jackie settled in her room. If you could bring me back something small to eat, I'd appreciate it."

I ran up to the lobby, but I couldn't find Nazif. Or Mustafa. And one of the Swiss guests was on the public computer terminal, so I still couldn't check my email. I peered outside, looking in front of the plate and tile store. No Lazar or Vasil. That was good. But where was Nazif?

I stepped outside and looked up and down the street, in case he'd stepped away from the building. Suddenly the smell of fresh bread hit me. This was a welcome scent after a morning spent inhaling cleaning product fumes. So even though Inspector Lale had warned me not to leave the hotel alone, I decided to find that bread and get lunch for my mom and Aunt Jackie while I waited for Nazif.

I didn't have to look far. The bread was coming right toward me. A man was strolling my way, carrying a wooden tray on his head. Piled high on the tray were round brown things that looked deliciously like bagels. I had no idea how they stayed balanced up there, or how he walked with such grace under a board stacked high with bread. The man stopped in front of me, smiled, and pointed to the bread. "You would like?" he asked as he neared me.

"Yes. Three, please," I said. Turkey was amazing. All I had to do was *think* of food and here was somebody bringing it right up to me.

The vendor reached up and took down three breads from his platter, handed them to me, and accepted my cash. The bread looked like a pretzel-bagel hybrid, dotted with sesame seeds. *"Simit,"* he said in a friendly way.

"Zan. Nice to meet you."

"No." He laughed and pointed to the bagel things. *"Simit.* You like?"

I took a bite and gave him a thumbs-up sign.

"One more thing," said the *simit* vendor, lowering his voice.

"I'm good. Three is all I need," I said through a mouthful of bread. I started backing away. Great, I thought. He was just another pushy vendor after all.

"No. One more thing," he insisted. "I was sent to find you at this hotel. This is for you." He reached up to the platter again, felt around, and pulled out a folded piece of paper, which he handed to me. Then a large tourist group came up to buy *simit,* crowding me out, and he turned his attention to them.

I unfolded the piece of paper. It was a handwritten note. I immediately knew who it was from.

> *Zan, I know you must be really confused. I'm sorry for leaving so abruptly. I hope someday I can explain everything. But right now I can't. And I urgently need that package I left with you. I can't come out of hiding at the moment, so go get the package immediately and give it to my friend who gave you this note. Please. My life depends on it.*

My hands were shaking so badly I almost couldn't read the last words. Sage was reaching out to me, just like Inspector Lale had predicted! But I didn't have the package of figurines to give her. And even if I did, no way would I hand them over without getting her side of the story.

I studied the handwriting. It was a jagged scrawl that didn't look at all like the one handwriting sample I had from Sage: the name "Amy Miller" written in careful, rounded letters inside her Freya Stark book.

Wait. Maybe this was a setup, a way for Lazar and Vasil to get their hands on the figurines. The English was perfect, but almost too perfect—more formal than Sage would be with me. If the note were really from Lazar and Vasil, they could have commissioned some fluent English speaker to write it for them. They knew I was staying at this hotel. They could have had the vendor come deliver this note.

I pushed through the crowd of tourists and waved the paper at the *simit* vendor. "Do you know the person who wrote this?" I demanded.

"My English, not so good," he said with an apologetic smile.

"Male or female?"

"So sorry. But I cannot understand." He shrugged, and his *simit* tray didn't even wobble.

"Does anyone here have a pen?" I asked the tourist group.

They were from some other country and didn't seem to speak English either, as confused murmurs spread through the small crowd. I pantomimed what I was asking for, and a businessman finally handed me a ballpoint.

I put the three *simit* pieces on my left arm, like bracelets, since my hand could fit through the middle. Now that I had both hands free, I ripped the paper in half, pocketing the note that had been written to me. On the blank half, I scrawled a note of my own, a note that would work for either Sage or Lazar and Vasil because it was the truth:

I don't have any package.

The more I thought about it, the more strongly I suspected Sage hadn't written the note. This had to be some kind of trap. And I wasn't falling for cons anymore. I folded the paper and handed it back to the *simit* vendor.

He looked confused.

"That's all I've got," I said. "And I'm quite sure you understand me perfectly. Tell whoever sent you that I don't have anything they want, and to stay away from my aunt's hotel."

Now I was late to meet Nazif. I jogged back to the hotel, pausing at a trash bin to shake the *simit* off my arm. Then I went to a kebab stand to get some lunch for my mom and Aunt Jackie. I didn't get any for myself. The encounter with the *simit* vendor—who was possibly one of Lazar's henchmen in disguise—had left a sour taste in my mouth, and I'd lost my appetite.

23

Nazif was pacing in front of the hotel. When he looked up and saw me, he seemed annoyed. "There you are," he said. "I was wondering where you went."

"Where were *you*?" I countered. "I couldn't find you in the lobby." If he'd just been where he said he'd be, on time, I might have avoided that whole encounter with the *simit*-vendor-slash-bearer-of-creepy-notes.

"A guest needed room service items delivered. We can walk," he said.

"Great. Let's go," I said, eager to get the story about the Lycian Society. I was also eager to call Inspector Lale and tell her what had just happened. But Nazif pointed at his watch and said we had less than thirty minutes to talk.

"Is there somewhere a little less crowded where we could talk without people staring at us?" I asked. "I feel like people are always trying to sell me stuff here."

He looked confused, but my eyes pleaded with him not to ask questions. "Yes," he said at last. "We can go to a historic place, not a marketplace. Follow me."

We walked rapidly for a couple of blocks, in awkward silence.

It felt strange to be outside with Nazif. He was in his bellboy uniform, but not in a bellboy role. He was just a guy my age, probably wondering why I was furiously biting my thumbnail and glancing nervously over my shoulder every few seconds to see if the *simit* vendor—or Lazar and Vasil—were following me.

He led me to Sultanahmet Square, where we came to a track flanked by two looming obelisks. One obelisk was smooth. The other was made of stones stacked together like Jenga blocks—as if you might pull out the wrong one and the whole tower could tumble down. A paved oval path encircled the two monuments. "This is the Hippodrome," Nazif explained. "Even though the building is long gone, it still has the name, and the track marks where Romans once raced chariots." He made a sweeping gesture, as if trying to paint a picture of long-ago athletic events. "But now all that is left are these ruins. Please. Sit." He motioned for me to sit down. "I think no one will try to sell you something here."

I sank gratefully onto a bench beneath some trees.

A man came up to us, lugging a big silver container on his back. He was dressed like the other food and drink vendors patrolling the Hippodrome, in a white shirt, gold-braided vest, and a red fez. "No, please, send him away," I whispered to Nazif as the man approached.

"I know you do not want to buy anything, but I will buy it," Nazif insisted. "You should try this drink. It is very traditional in Turkey. Also, it is hot outside, and you look thirsty." Nazif spoke briefly in Turkish with the vendor, who then leaned over and poured red liquid from the silver container on his back into a paper cup. Nazif gave him a few coins and handed me the drink. Only after the man disappeared and I was satisfied he wasn't some spy sent by Lazar did I drink down five huge gulps. Nazif had been right. It was hot. I was thirsty. The drink was really delicious.

"Fresh pomegranate juice," he said. "Do you like it?"

"Love it," I admitted. "Aren't you having some?"

"I am not thirsty."

I drank while he waited, feeling kind of ridiculous, and then I set the empty cup on the bench. "So. Tell me about the Lycian Society."

"I will tell you what I know," he said. He took a deep breath and continued. "In April, the Lycian Society had its international conference. Some of the after-hours meetings were held at the Mavi Konak. In the evenings, a group of people would come from the conference. They met your uncle Berk in the lobby, and he took them up to the Sultan's Suite."

I sat up straighter. This was weird. Aunt Jackie had said the society didn't accept Berk. But they still booked meeting rooms at his hotel?

"Who came to the meetings? What kind of people?" I asked.

"International people. Mostly European. Two Americans, I think."

"Do you remember anything else about them?"

"Maybe eight or so came at a time. Their badges had black ribbons."

Onyx was black. Maybe this was that snobby group of Onyx-level members Aunt Jackie had mentioned.

"Did my uncle stay for these meetings?" I asked.

"He did."

"And where was my aunt? Did she meet with them, too?"

"No. She was away that weekend of the conference. She has friends who run a cave hotel in Cappadocia. Your uncle encouraged her to visit and to get some ideas for improving their business." Nazif twisted his hands in his lap and looked down. "I brought food and tea upstairs at these three evening meetings, and took the dishes away after. Your uncle made it clear to me that they were not to be interrupted, that they would ring for me when I was needed. But on the third evening, after I delivered tea and desserts, I realized I had left my set of hotel keys in the Sultan's Suite. My father would be furious if he knew I had been so careless, so I went back to retrieve them. When I walked in, nobody seemed to take notice. Of course, I am used to this. Guests only see you when they want something."

I nodded. Now that I was a part-time maid, I understood.

"But this time, they did not see me because they were all very busy," Nazif went on. "They were in pairs and groups around the room, having serious discussions. A man was taking art objects out of a black suitcase. One person was counting money. Other people were looking at documents, or iPads, or books. Still others were studying art objects with special glasses, and taking notes. It was like the Sultan's Suite had transformed into a museum."

"Were these things very old? Like antiques or something?"

"Yes, very old. I saw jewelry, coins, broken pieces of what looked like temples and buildings. Some pottery. Even a marble bust. I began to feel as though I should not stay in the room. But I wanted to see what was going on. I had never seen such a business meeting as this in the Sultan's Suite. So I quietly took my keys from the table where I'd left them and exited the room. But I left the door open a crack. I am a little ashamed to admit this, but I watched and listened through the crack."

"I would have totally done that myself," I said. "What happened next?"

"There was one square case on the coffee table, covered in black velvet. A man removed the velvet. Inside the case was only a pot, but everyone seemed *very* excited about it."

If actual horse-drawn chariots had been racing around the Hippodrome track, my heart would have been galloping louder and faster right now. "A pot? Like a cooking pot?"

"No. I think not for cooking. It was too decorated. I think the English word is 'urn.'"

I let out a breath. "What happened next?"

"Once people stepped aside, I could see it was the most beautiful object in the room," Nazif went on. "Especially when a man removed the case and the urn was passed around."

"Who removed the case?"

"I did not catch his name," he said. "But he had a Bulgarian accent. There were two Bulgarians there, or they may have been Bulgarian Turks. I cannot be sure. For now, though, I will call him the Bulgarian, since I do not know his name."

I sucked in my breath sharply. "Go on."

"This man, he could speak Turkish and English and Italian, fluently, and a little bit of French. He answered many questions from the people in the room," Nazif explained. "Some questions he avoided, such as where the urn came from. He said that he could not expose his contacts. This seemed to annoy some people. When they asked questions about the materials used in the urn and dating techniques, the Bulgarian made your uncle answer. Some people demanded documents for the urn, and the Bulgarian said your uncle would provide them within two weeks along with the 'proper packaging.'"

"So you think my uncle was *working* for this guy?" I guessed. "As an art expert?"

"Yes, I believe so. After some time, when people had inspected the urn and made notes, the Bulgarian and your uncle spoke privately. They were near the door, so I could hear every word. Your uncle said he felt uncomfortable about documenting the urn. The Bulgarian insisted that it had to be done, and soon, because the clients were expecting it to be included in their final order. This order needed to be prepared for shipping. They argued quietly about this, back and forth. 'An exception must be made. This item is far too valuable,' your uncle said. 'You have the opportunity to do the right thing. Come forward.' The Bulgarian responded that until museums in Turkey were equipped to properly store and care for all artifacts, he was going to keep the urn."

"What did my uncle say to that?"

"He said he would only provide documentation if it were taken directly to the Uşak Archaeological Museum to join the rest of the cache. That made the Bulgarian really angry."

I swallowed hard. A new theory was starting to hatch in my

mind. A theory so sinister I was afraid to even voice it.

"That's when the Bulgarian opened up his jacket and showed your uncle a long knife."

My hands flew to my mouth.

"He said that your uncle was putting the organization at risk, and that he'd better change his mind. Otherwise . . ." Nazif made a cutting motion at his throat. "Then the other Bulgarian came to stand by his side. And he was carrying a pistol."

I asked Nazif to describe the two men. The details he remembered—a tall man with a long nose and goatee, and a shorter, stocky man who seemed eager to pull the trigger— sounded like Lazar and Vasil.

I shivered. "So I bet my uncle agreed to the Bulgarian's proposal, right? He agreed to write up papers for something stolen. So that some illegal buyer could take it out of the country disguised and 'authenticated' as something else." Or maybe even so innocent people could get out of jail. Now that I'd been helped by the power of a forgery, I could understand why people might take advantage of any insider they could.

Nazif nodded. "After that, the Bulgarians packed up the urn in the clear case. Then they put that box into a black suitcase with padding. They gave the suitcase to your uncle. The meeting ended soon after, and the Bulgarians stayed while everyone else left. Your uncle took the suitcase with the urn inside. And then finally, the Bulgarians left. Unfortunately, they left so quickly I did not have time to get out of the way or pretend to be busy. They accused me of spying."

"That's ridiculous," I said. "You were doing what anyone would have done in your position. Listening at the door because you were concerned."

"No, it is true, I *was* spying on the meeting," he said, "because we had extra guests in the hotel and we knew nothing about them. And because your aunt and uncle could not hire proper security, I was acting as security. It was not just curiosity. I *needed* to know what was going on at that meeting. When the man confronted me, I thought to myself, this is good, now I can ask this man to his face. But he turned the tables around. He demanded to know what *I'd* seen and heard and who *I* was reporting this to."

"Oh my God."

Nazif folded his arms and hugged himself, as if he were cold. "He came right up to me with that knife. He laid the blade against my throat. He said if I uttered one word about that meeting to anyone, especially to the police, my father and I would both lose our jobs. He would see to it that we would be accused of stealing and would never work in an Istanbul hotel again. My father was out of work for many months, before your aunt and uncle gave him this job. My mother works as a dental hygienist, but only part-time. I could not put my father's job at risk."

I nodded.

"So until you came here and began asking questions, I have kept this secret inside me since that night. Three months." He patted his chest. "It feels good to talk about it. Finally."

My mind churned over all this information. "So let me get this straight. It sounds like some of the Lycian Society Onyx members were buying illicit artifacts, and the hotel room was like a private showroom."

"Correct."

"My uncle Berk was asked to appraise an authentically ancient urn as a fake." I considered this for a moment. "But you know something, Nazif? I think he double-crossed that Bulgarian guy."

"Double-crossed?" Nazif frowned.

"Went against him. By not providing the documents. Or by not returning the urn. Or both."

He nodded quickly. "Yes, you could be right."

"And the Bulgarian guy who did most of the talking—I think I know him. I think his name's Lazar." Lazar, on the boat, seemed to be the more talkative guy of the two.

"Why do you say this?"

I couldn't answer.

"Please. I have told you what I know."

He was right. It was only fair to tell him at least a little about why I was intensely interested in all this. I took a deep breath and began. "Okay. So here's the deal," I said. "The Turkish police are interested in me because I got caught with some artifacts at the Dalaman Airport. They weren't mine," I quickly assured him when his eyes widened. "I was set up. But the person who put them in my bag—her name is Sage—she went missing. I'm trying to find her, or at least figure out why she planted arti- facts in my backpack. So this Bulgarian guy we met on our Blue Voyage, named Lazar, followed me in Marmaris. He's some kind of private security guard. He asked me if I know where Sage is. And then I saw him and his partner, Vasil, outside of my aunt's hotel. Yesterday."

Nazif whistled under his breath.

"They stood in front of a store, watching for a while, and then vanished," I went on. "And look what I got just before I met you. I bought some *simit* right outside the hotel, and the vendor gave this to me. He said he'd been sent to find me." I took the note from my pocket and showed him. "I don't believe that this note was actually written by Sage. I think it's from Lazar, try- ing to use me to get to Sage."

Nazif looked startled. "But . . . but this is horrible! None of this is your fault, and now these people are looking for you?"

"For *Sage,*" I corrected. "As are the police. Both Lazar and the police think she'll seek me out, to get the figurines back. If she does, I have two choices. Hand her over to Lazar, or turn her in to the police. Now, I can see why the police want to find Sage, but I don't know why Lazar is so upset over the figurines. I mean, they're valuable, Inspector Lale said. But if he's really in the artifacts smuggling business, you'd think he could let a few things slip." Thinking of things slipping reminded me of the urn slipping out of Sage's hands on the path. "Can you describe the urn for me? The urn that was at the meeting?" I asked.

"Yes. It had this shape and this size." Nazif picked up a twig and traced an outline of an urn in the dust below our bench. "The handles were made to look like seahorses. Winged seahorses. And the handle was very unusual. It was a golden acorn."

I felt like the entire square around us disappeared. "That sounds exactly like the urn my aunt Jackie brought on our cruise!" I exclaimed. "She said it was a replica of a Karun Treasure artifact that some people think got separated from the rest of the cache back when the tombs were looted. She found it in Uncle Berk's desk, with a certificate of . . . oh."

Nazif and I stared at each other, and I knew we were both thinking the same thought.

The urn Aunt Jackie had brought on the cruise *wasn't* a replica of a Karun Treasure artifact. It was the real deal. Aunt Jackie must have believed the fake certificate Uncle Berk had made for it and didn't think twice about traveling with it.

"Sage knew that urn was real," I guessed out loud.

Nazif nodded. "She could have been working for Lazar and Vasil. I am guessing they sent her on this cruise to steal the urn."

"Then they chose the wrong thief," I said. "The urn is gone. We took it up a cliff in Fethiye for a memorial ceremony. Sage tripped and dropped the urn, and it fell over a cliff. We looked for it everywhere."

"Gone? Do you really believe that?" Nazif asked softly.

"What are you getting at?"

"If Sage were working for Lazar and Vasil, she might have come to the memorial ceremony intending to steal it back. Maybe she made her fall look accidental, to avoid making herself a suspected thief."

Maybe Nazif was on to something. "You could be right. She could have marked where it went, and returned to the cliffside later to get it. Maybe she even saw it when we were all search-ing, and she just hid it somewhere, when no one was looking, and then went back for it later." I thought about how she'd come up with the idea of looking at the base of the precipice. "Maybe she even misdirected people away from where she saw it land."

Nazif frowned. "I can see this happening. But real Karun Treasure items would not be gold-plated," he said. "They would be solid gold. And a solid-gold urn could be damaged, falling from such a height, onto rocks."

"But it would still have some value, right?" I said. "Is a Karun Treasure object, even dented, worth taking that kind of risk for?"

"Possibly. Its value would decrease, but not disappear."

"I bet that's why Lazar and Vasil want to find Sage so badly," I said. "It's not just about the figurines that she'd probably failed to hand over to them."

Nazif gave me a long look, his dark brown eyes searching mine. "What if she was supposed to get them that urn? And what if your uncle was not the only one who double-crossed Lazar and Vasil? What if Sage double-crossed them, too, and took the urn for herself?"

I swallowed hard. If our theory was correct, then there was a chance Sage might actually have the seahorse urn. A missing piece of the priceless Karun Treasure.

24

Having talked too long at the Hippodrome, Nazif and I had to run all the way back to the hotel. We burst into the lobby, where the tour group of Germans was converging at the front desk. Mustafa said a few words to his son harshly, in Turkish, an obvious reprimand for running late. Nazif, shoulders hunched and head hanging low, began loading luggage onto carts and ferrying it to the guests' rooms, careful not to make eye contact with me. I felt Mustafa's disapproving stare and was left alone with my new, dark thoughts about Sage, Lazar, and the priceless urn.

This situation was way bigger than me. I had to let Inspector Lale know what was going on: that Sage could have a long-lost urn from the Karun Treasure. As soon as the front desk was quiet and Mustafa was out of the lobby, I snatched the phone and took her business card out of my pocket. I dialed, and got her voice mail. I was afraid to leave too detailed a message, not knowing if someone might intercept it. "It's Zan. Call me back at the Mavi Konak as soon as you get this message," I said. "I have an idea I have to tell you about." I'd barely had time to spit out that sentence when Mustafa came back into the lobby, and I hung up the phone fast.

Maddeningly, Mustafa settled down at his desk to work, which involved making phone call after phone call. I assumed they had call waiting, but would he interrupt a work call to take Inspector Lale's? I could only hope. I might as well use the time to collect my thoughts about everything I'd just learned from Nazif. I ran up to my room, unable to listen to Mustafa talking. I needed some footholds, some facts and observations that I could nail down. Were we crazy to think Sage was a hired thief? Did she have opportunity and motive?

My hand brushed against my dad's journal as I riffled through my suitcase, looking for paper. It felt heavy, the pages too smooth, too intimidating. So I took out my Lonely Planet guide instead and flipped to the Notes section in back, to jot down what I knew so far.

As soon as I flipped to the Notes section, I saw my doodles and scrawled notes from the Blue Voyage. It was weird to see my sketch of Riza on the *Anilar*. It seemed so long ago since we'd been on the boat. But weirder still was to read my "You Are Here" entry, where I'd written about the heat, about Mom being mad, and about following Sage's lead to cool off in the water.

My heart thudded. This entry was written right after Aunt Jackie had taken the urn from her tote bag and showed it to Mom and me. Could Sage have seen it from her deck chair? And then she dove into the water and swam toward the *Anilar*. What if she'd gone to tell Lazar and Vasil that we had the urn? And were her other swims to the *Anilar* also to deliver news or goods to these guys? Had she bought even more trinkets from Baklava Guy than the ones she'd shown me, objects she was ferrying back to her bosses?

I grabbed a pen and jotted down my thoughts on a blank Notes page before I lost them:

1. Sage was probably working for Lazar and Vasil. Maybe they hired her to get goods from looters or thieves, like

Baklava Guy. Maybe they'd even put her on our cruise to look for the urn or find out what we knew about it.

2. As soon as Sage saw what Aunt Jackie had brought, she swam to the <u>Anilar</u> to tell Lazar and Vasil.

3. Uncle Berk had been working for Lazar, authenticating real artifacts as fakes, including the Karun Treasure urn. But he didn't seem happy about it.

4. Lazar worked for Onyx-level members of the Lycian Society, members who were into buying illicit antiquities. Maybe he had a client among them who was ready to buy the urn once its "official papers" were in order and it could be disguised as a fake— "prepared for shipping," as Nazif heard someone say at the big hotel meeting.

5. Uncle Berk died just weeks before a Lycian Society cruise!!!

I hesitated, then dared myself to write the darkest thoughts that were pulsing in my brain:

6. Could Lazar have killed my uncle because he failed to deliver the urn?

7. Could Lazar be looking to kill Sage next because she failed to deliver the urn???

I gripped the pen. Aunt Jackie probably had the right idea, thinking my uncle's death was no accident. She was just looking at the wrong group of criminals.

Now I had a new, more urgent reason to find Sage. I needed to get my hands on that urn. If our theory was right and she actually had it, but then sold it out from under Lazar, it would sink back into the black market. The trail that might lead to my uncle's murderer could forever be obscured. I stared accusingly at the useless phone on my nightstand. I tried to send Inspector Lale a telepathic message to call me right away so I could tell her about my murder theory.

I'd have to call her again and explain how urgent my message was. I flung open the door to the Harem Suite, nearly hitting Mom in the face as she stood right outside the door, room key in hand. "There you are!" she exclaimed. "You took a luxuriously long lunch break."

"I'm sorry," I said.

"And your work is not done. I have that napkin-folding project, plus silver that needs polishing. You can do it on the rooftop if you like."

I swallowed hard. I had to take the risk of telling her what had happened. "Mom, I have to tell you that there might be something to Aunt Jackie's theory about Uncle Berk being murdered. I—"

"Oh, Zan. Not you, too." She sighed. "The conspiracy theories are driving me crazy. Do you know how hard I've been working to keep your aunt off the Internet? She's obsessed. I'd almost rather have her working on hotel business, because every time I tuck her into bed and turn my back, she's looking at crime logs and old newspapers again, or calling up hotel operators in Cappadocia to find out what they know. I really, really need you not to get sucked into this drama, Zan. I mean it." She turned on her heel and flounced out of the room.

I trudged up to the rooftop behind her and sat at a table under the trellis of grapevines. Now I was even farther away from the phone. I hoped Mustafa would know to find me up here if she called me back.

"So. I found these in a storage box in a closet," said Mom, taking tarnished things out of a box and setting them on the table: trays, samovars, teacups, knickknacks. "Jackie said they could be displayed in the lobby."

"Are they ancient?" I asked, poking at a pair of candlesticks with suspicion. "Are we going to get arrested for having these?"

"They're not that old. They were just family items from Berk's parents. Wedding gifts. But they'd sure be pretty, with some shine," she said. "The lobby looks so gloomy. There's nothing interesting to look at except for a couple of instruments. These will help bring out its charm." She handed me some rags and a bottle of silver polish and went back downstairs.

As I polished an old lamp, I wished a djinn would come out of it and grant me three wishes. Find Sage. Get her story so I could either help her or turn her in.

And my third wish? What would that be?

Inspector Lale calling me back.

I gazed at Nazif's rooftop. Could I get a fourth wish? Once again, I was filled with a powerful feeling of envy, like a noxious smoke inside me. Then I remembered that envy was what the *nazar boncuğu,* the evil-eye amulet, was supposed to protect against. Was I giving Nazif the evil eye by longing for the family life he had? I wasn't superstitious. I didn't believe in Ouija boards or tarot cards, or daily horoscopes, or anything like that. I wasn't even sure I bought the idea of the Karun Treasure curse. Still, I turned my evil eye away from his rooftop, toward the Sea of Marmara.

My mom came back up to the rooftop and handed me a phone. I jumped up, heart pounding. I would tell Inspector Lale all about my theory and she would know what to do.

"It's your dad."

I let out a long breath and sank back into my chair. I picked up a platter and polished it vigorously. "I'm busy. I'm working."

"Zan," she whispered, cupping the receiver with her hand. "He is still your father."

"All right. Fine. But only for a minute." I took the phone, realizing I could call Inspector Lale again once my dad and I were done talking. Satisfied, Mom retreated toward the staircase that led back downstairs. Then I saw her hesitate at the door and look back with a sad expression.

"Hello?" I sighed more than spoke.

"Zanny!" My dad's cheerful voice sounded weirdly close, as if he were in the same building. "How's Turkey? Are you seeing lots of ruins?"

"Yeah. There are ruins everywhere." *Like my entire life, thanks to you.* "Aunt Jackie even has a Byzantine wall in her patio."

"That's great. I hope you're writing down all your impressions in that book I gave you."

"Yep." I hesitated, mouth open, on the edge of saying more. For a moment, I wanted to pretend he wasn't a big part of the reason Mom and I were in Turkey. I wanted to tell him about the situation I was in, that scary guys were stalking me. Maybe he could help.

Or maybe he'd just be pissed, or disappointed, that I'd made bad decisions again and was now on the radar of the Turkish authorities.

"Zan. Honey." My dad took a deep breath. "Listen. I hate the way we parted before your trip. I'm just feeling sick about it. We haven't really had a chance to talk."

I said nothing, while my breath caught in my throat. It was almost an apology. Almost, but not quite. The words didn't bring me comfort.

"Zan? Are you there?"

"Yeah."

"Your mother and I will always love you. We're still a family. That is fundamental."

I gritted my teeth. More lies. In no way did we resemble a family.

"Sometimes families rearrange. They shift, or divide, or

come together," Dad continued. "Sometimes in unexpected ways. Sometimes with new people. Sometimes families have to open their hearts a little, to make room for changes. Do you follow?"

"No," I said. I picked at the hangnail on my thumb. It stung, but I ignored the pain.

"What I'm trying to say, Zanny, is that Victoria and I have decided not to let the media and public opinion control our hearts and actions. We will not be puppets. I mean, if the good people of Massachusetts can't handle a governor who has a life outside the office, then I don't need them. They've figured it out in France. Their leaders aren't put under a microscope. A marriage ending doesn't bring down the whole country."

I froze. "You're moving to *France*?" I squeaked.

"No! No. What I'm trying to say, if you'll just give me a moment, is that Victoria and I, well, we feel something genuine between us, and we'd like to explore it and see where it takes us. And if it costs me my campaign, then so be it. At the end of the day, I'd rather be true to my heart, and happy, than Governor of Massachusetts. And I'll be a better father."

I felt cold. I thought of the story Sage had told me at the cliff tombs, about how the sultan had gone all the way to Hungary to battle, then left his heart buried there. Victoria Windham was freaking Hungary. Why had my dad dragged us through his whole campaign, then the whole scandal, only to end up leaving his heart with her?

"You must have some complicated feelings around this. I can understand," he said.

"Did some shrink tell you to say that?" I was angry.

"I just think transparency is best. I'm tired of living with my life under wraps."

"Is that a Fresh City Wrap joke? If it is, it's not very funny."

"Zan," Dad said. "You're sixteen. I think you're old enough to understand a little more. Listen to me. Your mother and I tried to work things out. But we decided we're just different people than we used to be. We've grown apart. Sometimes that happens. Sometimes lives take different directions, and the person you thought you married is no longer there. Or the person you thought you were on a trip with isn't on the same trip at all. I'm sure she feels the same."

I glanced at the stairway door again and saw Mom standing with her back to me. She was leaning against the doorframe, her shoulders shuddering. I was pretty sure she was crying.

Dad was just assuming that Mom was cool with this change, simply because he said so. And I hated that. He'd given me a blank notebook to fill up with my words, but in reality, he was the one always writing our stories. Spinning our situation to suit his needs and make people think we were this perfect family, not a ruined one. Now he was writing a new story: *We're unconventional! We follow our hearts! We live for love! That's how we roll! It was an amicable split! We're all better off!*

Not me. I was writing myself out of this one.

"I'm looking forward to this new chapter in our lives," Dad continued. "I know there'll be some bumps along the way. It won't always be easy. But not all change is bad. Your mom and I will work out a visitation schedule and you can have some say in it. I'm going to take an apartment near Victoria's place, on Beacon Hill. A two-bedroom. One's for you. You can decorate your own room however you want to. Won't that be fun? And Victoria—she's really excited to get to know you better—she's an amazing decorator. She knows all these hip design shops downtown, and she can take you shopping. And after that we can have dinner, and—"

"Thanks," I said, in an acid-tinged voice. "But I already have a nice room, at home, that Mom and I decorated. Mom's a great decorator, too, you know. You used to say so yourself."

Silence. I knew I'd touched a nerve.

Feeling empowered, I went on. "I don't get it, Dad. You bailed on Mom and me, and now you want me to have dinner with *Victoria*? And pretend to be some newly formed, happy family?"

"Okay, not dinner. Appetizers. We can go slow."

"Oh my God, Dad! Forget it! I'm not playing along. And I actually have to go now, because I have a job here. A real job. I'm very, very busy."

"Zan, wait. Please don't—"

I hit the End button on the phone. Then I got up and walked over to my mom at the top of the stairwell. She averted her eyes as she took the phone from me.

"Oh, Zan," she whispered. "I'm so sorry. I didn't think he was going to tell you that today. This isn't the ending I'd hoped for." She sighed. "Maybe I was wrong to think we could avoid his whole mid-life crisis drama thousands of miles away. We're all still in crisis. But we're going to power through this, and we'll come out stronger on the other side." She smiled wryly, and reached out to hug me.

I flinched and shrunk away. "Don't," I said. "Just. Don't. Touch. Me."

She held up her hands in surrender. "Can we at least talk? You might feel better."

"Jesus, Mom! I don't want to talk! Why does everyone want to *talk* all the time? Can't we just have some quiet for once? And can't people just leave me alone?" I pushed past her, down the stairwell, and then ran past an astonished-looking Nazif, who was talking with a German family in the hall. I felt a flash of humiliation, feeling his eyes on me, but I couldn't stop. I stormed into the suite I shared with Mom and slammed the door behind me. Then I slammed the door to my bedroom harder.

Through the thin walls, I heard the Germans murmuring.

No doubt they were drafting their TripAdvisor reviews, which would only drag my aunt's hotel deeper into the mud. *Proprietor's niece has tantrums. Steer clear.*

I flung myself onto the bed and wrapped myself up in the covers.

25

I slept heavily that night and woke up, startled, to the call to prayer just before dawn.

I was tempted to go up on the roof again to try to glimpse the family next door, but now that I knew it was Nazif's family, I felt weird about that. Like a spy.

Instead, I went to my window and peered out through the lattice as the call to prayer ended. A few dark silhouettes made their way down the street in the predawn light. People going to prayer or to work, I guessed. I hoped, anyway. Were any of those shadowy figures Lazar and Vasil? I couldn't tell.

But Nazif's story about the Lycian Society meetings haunted me. I really had to find Sage. I had to know if she had the urn, or, if she didn't, where it had gone.

After breakfast, I hurried to clear away the dishes, then found Nazif at the front desk. "Any phone messages for me?"

"No," he said. "But a written message came through the mail slot on the door. Your name is on it." He handed me an envelope.

I studied it. My first name was handwritten in block letters. There was no stamp or postmark.

"They did not send it through the post," he explained. "Could this be from your friend?"

"It's probably another setup from Lazar," I said. Still, my hands shook as I tore open the envelope and took out a piece of lined notebook paper. It was a short, handwritten note, in rounded letters—not unlike the way "Amy Miller" was written in the book. My heart beat faster as I read:

> *Zan—I have to talk to you. But I can't come to your aunt's hotel. Some people are looking for me. Meet me at Café Mozaik today at noon. It is in the middle of the Grand Bazaar. I can explain everything. I don't want you to think I am a bad person. I think when I tell you my story, you'll understand. Please come.*
>
> *Your friend, Sage.*
>
> *P.S. Please bring the package with you. It's really, really important.*

"Well?" Nazif asked, drummimg his fingers on the countertop. "Is it from her?"

"I think it could be," I said slowly. "But this reads different from the first note, the one the *simit* vendor gave me." And she'd signed it "your friend." "How far away is the Grand Bazaar?" I asked Nazif.

"Ten, fifteen minutes by taxi," he said. "Will your mother let you go?"

"I don't know. If she won't, I'll have to find some way to get there." I was certainly an expert in the art of sneaking off. But Mom was watching me like a hawk, and if I got caught, I'd have zero chance of getting out of the hotel ever again.

Mom interrupted us just then, walking in with a huge cardboard box overflowing with brochures and flyers. "Project time!" she sang out. "I need a display table set up with tourist information in the lobby. Can you believe what a gold mine your aunt's been sitting on? These things come in the mail and they've just been piling up. They're not doing anyone any good out of sight. And she should totally be contracting with some of these tourist organizations, booking excursions for her guests and taking a cut. Once this is set up, Zan, you're going to help me make some calls."

Calls. I'd have phone access. I could try Inspector Lale again. Why wasn't she calling me back?

Mom set me up with a table and told me to weed out anything for events that had already passed, and to arrange all the other stuff neatly. I set out flyers and brochures for all the amazing things in Turkey that I was probably not going to get to do because we were now hotel workers. Historical tours. Bosphorus river cruises. Balloon excursions in Cappadocia. My hand paused on a brochure for a company called Voyager Balloons, and Judy Clarkson's words came back to me: *A once-in-a-lifetime experience.* She'd been so excited about the balloon tour she and Ron would take, and now I could see why. The colorful balloons hung over what looked like a landscape made of soft-serve ice cream.

I was nearly done when I found a stack of maps for the Grand Bazaar. I snatched one up. If I were going to meet Sage at the Grand Bazaar, this would be the perfect way to bring up the topic with Mom. I went to the kitchen, where she and Aunt Jackie were going over grocery lists, and showed her the map and brochure.

"Hey, Mom. Can I take a taxi to the Grand Bazaar?"

She glanced at the brochure and gave a short laugh. "Uh, no. Sorry."

"Why?"

"Well, the Grand Bazaar is basically a shopping mall. And you are so done with malls."

I stared at her. "Mom. You have to trust me. I'm not a klepto. And it isn't a mall."

"It's a historical site," said Aunt Jackie. "And you know, Kitsie, there's a fantastic spice market right there. I could have her pick up some paprika, which I'm all out of. You could go along with her. I'll be fine. I promise I'll be good and stay sitting down."

"No way," said Mom. "I know you're going to research those Cappadocia crimes the moment I leave, and I don't want you getting all worked up. Besides, Mustafa has three housekeeping candidates coming for interviews today. You should at least meet them."

"Maybe I can go with Nazif," I suggested. "Please?"

Mom shook her head. "You do need to see something historical. I know you shouldn't be so sequestered here. But you can't take Nazif away from his job. And I can't let you run off on your own in this city. Now please go take one brochure from each place and we'll get a database started of tour packagers to contract with."

God. Mom still didn't trust me. I stomped back to the brochure table and did as she asked. Nazif, sensing something was wrong, kept his distance. Fuming, I set out brochures for the Topkapi Palace, the Bosphorus river cruises, and the Galata Tower—all the amazing sights I probably would never get to see on this trip. I stared at one brochure about a whirling dervish performance. It showed men wearing white robes and tall white hats. These men were the whirling dervishes, I guessed. Their pictures were almost blurred, showing them spinning around, with their eyes closed and their arms held out wide, one palm turned upward and one turned down. I felt like a whirling dervish myself, spinning in circles, dizzy and lost. In two hours, Sage would be sitting at Café Mozaik in the Grand Bazaar, waiting for me. I had to find a way to get there.

Mom set me up with the database project on the front-desk computer, where I created a spreadsheet of tour operators we could contact about possible group rates for hotel guests. I had just typed in "Voyager Balloons" when the door opened. I jumped a little, half expecting Lazar and Vasil to burst in and half expecting Inspector Lale's forces.

But it wasn't either of them. It was the Lobsters.

Milton and Maeve walked in, looking slightly dazed and lugging enormous floral suitcases. I almost didn't recognize Milton without his Speedo. He was wearing a loose, tropical-print shirt, better suited for Hawaii, and khaki pants. Maeve wore a pale blue warm-up suit and a visor. She also had on a little more makeup than before, and her short, frosted blonde hair looked as if it'd been touched up in a salon.

"Well, well!" cried Milton. "It's Alexandra the Great! How are you?"

"Good," I said, coming out from behind the front desk to greet them. "How are you two?"

"Homeless," said Milton, making a face. "That's why we're here."

"What do you mean?"

"We're looking for a room," said Maeve. "Lycian Tours put us at the Swissotel, but we had to leave. Bedbugs." She shivered. "Mr. Tabak offered to transfer us anywhere we wanted. Your aunt's place sounded cozy, so we thought we'd give it a go."

My mom came in at that moment and greeted the Lobsters with hugs. "Milton! Maeve!" she exclaimed. "What a wonderful surprise! I can't wait to hear all about your tour of the Ephesus ruins. Nazif, can you check the reservations page on the computer and see if we have a room available?" She winked at him. Of course there were rooms available—the entire second floor and half of the third were available. But a full-seeming hotel was always more desirable.

Nazif went behind the front desk and began typing away on the computer, playing along with my mom's act and even scratching his head. "I might be able to move someone," he said doubtfully.

"Oh, we don't wish to be a bother," said Milton "We'll look elsewhere."

"But wait. Nazif, what about the Sultan's Suite?" Mom asked.

Nazif gave her a strange look. He didn't seem to be playing along anymore. "It's usually reserved for corporate groups. For business functions," he said.

"Well, we don't have a corporate group at the moment, do we? But we *do* have Milton and Maeve." Mom beamed at them and clasped her hands together. "Oh, you'll absolutely love the Sultan's Suite. It's huge and luxurious. You'll feel like royalty in there."

Nazif and I exchanged a look. The Sultan's Suite seemed almost haunted to me, now that I knew all about the secret Lycian Society meetings that had taken place there. It was where Lazar had threatened my uncle over the Karun Treasure urn.

"Are you sure?" Nazif said. "Maybe we should check with Mrs. Yilmaz first."

"Nazif," said my mom, through a clenched smile, "these are my friends. They need a room. The room is vacant. Please, let's just book the room for them."

"Hold on a second. I'm not paying the sultan's rate," said Milton, looking worried. "Exactly how much is this going to run me?"

"Milton's right," said Maeve. "It sounds lovely, but if that's all you've got, maybe we should look elsewhere. We've got some serious shopping to do today. At the Grand Bazaar. I promised all my children and grandchildren I'd bring home souvenirs, and I'm not going back to Sydney until I've seen the place."

The Grand Bazaar! I perked up and looked at Maeve intently. A plan began to form in my mind.

Milton uttered a little moan, and Mom offered him a chair. "Please charge them *regular* room rates," she instructed Nazif.

"But that's half the—"

"Don't worry," she said to him, just under her breath. "If we can show we've booked that suite, Berk's siblings will be impressed. Even at a reduced rate, it brings in a lot of money, and it will look like business travelers are attracted to this place. They don't have to know the occupants are actually retirees."

When I realized how badly Mom wanted Milton and Maeve to be happy, and to keep the hotel looking full to help out Aunt Jackie, that's when I saw my chance, my little bit of leverage. I turned to the Lobsters with my warmest hotel-hostess smile. "So you're going to the Grand Bazaar? I've been dying to go there."

"We are," said Maeve. "I'd love to get a young person's eye on things to help me pick out what I should bring home for my teenage granddaughters. You're just their size—you could try things on!"

"Wonderful idea!" said Milton. "What do you say? Care to join us?"

"I don't know. I have to ask," I said, looking slyly in Mom's direction.

"All right," Mom said. "As long as you all stay together. Sometimes Zan needs a watchful eye," she added quietly to Maeve.

Normally that comment would have pissed me off, but now I didn't care. I was trembling with excitement. I was going to the Grand Bazaar. Hopefully, I would meet with Sage and get some answers at last.

26

I shivered with excitement as the Lobsters and I walked beneath a large, ornately decorated stone archway: the main gate of the Grand Bazaar! According to my tourist map, it was a labyrinth of squares and corridors, roughly divided into zones—textiles, jewelry, ceramics, clothing, and more. In real life, the bazaar was overwhelming, stretching out in all directions and teeming with shoppers. The vaulted ceilings rose so high it hurt my neck to look up.

"Seems like anything you'd ever want to buy can be found in the Grand Bazaar," Maeve marveled. "My goodness. Where to start?"

"How about we don't start," said Milton. "Let's quit while we're ahead and not buy anything here."

"Oh, don't be such a yobbo, Milton," said Maeve. "You act like I've got no self-control, and that couldn't be farther from the truth."

"Oh, come on," groaned Milton. "I don't give a rat's arse about this stuff. You're bleeding me dry, Maeve, with all this bloody spending."

While they bickered, I studied my map carefully and found

Café Mozaik. It was a tiny box practically in the center of the Grand Bazaar.

"Milton," said Maeve. "Wake up. We're in *Turkey*. We live in *Australia*. I'm seventy-one years old, and I'm likely never coming back here, so I intend to enjoy myself. These are unique items. And what we don't have room for or what we can't give to the kids as gifts, I can sell online and get some money back."

"You always say that, Maeve, but it never happens! You're a right hoarder!"

I checked my watch. I was due to meet Sage in ten minutes. "Maybe you guys could start browsing, and I could pick up some coffees to go, for energy. And I'll come find you."

"Oh, no, dear. I'm afraid you might get lost," said Maeve. "Let's all stick together."

"Then let's start shopping at the heart of the bazaar and work our way outward," I suggested. That way I could pretend to get lost, and duck into the Café Mozaik to find Sage.

Milton sighed. "Fair enough. Lead the way. Let's get this over with."

We ventured a few yards down a corridor, and were instantly followed by men hawking their wares. It was like the Marmaris docks all over again.

"Hello! Bonjour! Excuse me! What language do you speak?"

"Can I offer you some tea?"

"Family! Nice family! Come and see our carpets, nice family!"

"I swear," said Milton, "if I have to see one more carpet in this country, I am going to go out of my bloody mind."

"Oh, stop. You'll do no such thing," scolded Maeve, who seemed to be perking up now that she was in shopping nirvana. "You'll buck up and see what there is to see."

"We're in the seventh circle of hell. Or square of hell, I should say," Milton muttered.

As we walked deeper into the bazaar, I realized that Aunt Jackie was right: this wasn't a regular mall. There were lots of Turkish crafts, including all types and sizes of *nazar boncuğus,* and textiles galore. Also, there were hustlers everywhere. Drink vendors with those giant cases on their backs, like the one who'd served me in Sultanhamet Square yesterday, pouring juice into cups. We passed stalls selling all kinds of spices, mounds of rich red, yellow, and bright green powders. Some spices were labeled "Aphrodisiacs" and "Turkish Viagra," which made Maeve blush and Milton chuckle. We also passed some strange things for sale: Jars of leeches. Live chickens and rabbits in cages. Sets of false teeth laid out on silver trays. One vendor shook a whole tray of glass eyeballs at me. I shuddered and hurried on.

But something about the bazaar felt familiar at the same time; not everything about it seemed sinister. There were plenty of regular people like you'd see in any shopping center. Mothers, some in head-to-toe black veils, pushing strollers and gazing at window displays. Little kids, racing around and pushing each other. Teenagers loaded with shopping bags, laughing, talking, and texting. I felt an aching sensation. It was like seeing my old life on display in some parallel universe.

Maeve paused at a pashmina stall to admire some cashmere wraps hanging on a rack.

My eye caught sight of a rack of scarves nearby, and with a start, I noticed that some of them were indigo with little white stars. Exactly like the scarf Sage had worn on the boat! Maybe she'd even bought it here, at this very stall.

Maeve selected five pashminas, and Milton tried to haggle with the vendors. He was fighting a losing battle, turning red now not from sunburn, but from a smoldering rage about being overcharged. I checked my watch again. Five minutes to noon. Realizing this transaction could take a while, I took the opportunity to slip away. The café wasn't so far.

I broke into a jog, then a run. Vendors called after me:

"Slow down, beautiful girl!"

"Stop, stop! Why in such a hurry, my friend?"

Then it dawned on me that maybe I looked as if I'd stolen

something. I could attract the wrong kind of attention if I kept running. I slowed down to a fast walk, my eyes fixed forward. One more corridor and I would be at the Café Mozaik, according to my map. And finally I would see Sage again.

Suddenly, I heard a hissing sound off to my right. Like a cat, or maybe a snake. I looked all around me, and the hissing continued. I saw a small, dim shop filled with elaborately decorated plates and tiles, and ornate hanging lanterns made out of glass. In the doorway was a rack full of blue *nazar boncuğu* amulets. There were tiny earrings, bracelets, and necklaces; amulets hanging from strings; and even glass eyes that were the size of dinner plates.

The hissing sound came again. And then, from behind a rack of dangling evil-eye amulets, another set of eyes emerged, blinking slowly at me.

Eyes that belonged to Lazar.

27

I stared back at him, paralyzed with terror.

"Come here," he said, looking down his nose at me and beckoning with one long finger. "I must talk to you."

He must have followed me here, and waited for an opportunity to corner me. I couldn't talk to him now, or I'd miss my chance to meet with Sage. I shook my head and backed away. My eyes darted around. Tourists were admiring wares, and vendors were tidying their stalls or chatting on cell phones. No one seemed to have any clue that I was in danger.

Lazar stepped out from behind the amulet rack. The glass evil eyes clinked, clattered, and danced. "This is my friend's store," he said, gesturing to the storefront behind him. "We can talk inside, in confidence. This is the easy way." He opened his leather jacket, and I glimpsed the hilt of a knife sticking out of an inside pocket.

I glanced longingly in the direction of the Café Mozaik, just three doors down. What if I just brought Lazar directly to Sage? Then I could wash my hands of this mess.

Catching my look, he laughed. "Your friend Sage, she is

not there. But the writer I hired did an excellent job with her English, yes?"

My face burned. I'd fallen for yet another con. "You wrote both those notes, didn't you," I whispered. He'd wanted me to come to a place where he could confront me, where my family wouldn't be in the way. Where everyone would be too busy to notice us talking, or where maybe nobody would care because strange business transactions happened all the time.

Lazar smiled, pointing at the backpack slung over my shoulder. "You have a package with you?"

I didn't answer. I felt numb. Sage was still missing. She hadn't tried to get in touch with me at all.

His smile fell. His eyes glittered. "You did not bring the package?"

I lifted my chin. Fine. Let him wonder about me and about the gold figurines.

"Come with me," he said in a low voice. "And do not run," he added sharply when I turned toward a shop that sold water pipes and tobacco, thinking I'd ask for help. "I have many friends here."

I swallowed hard and followed Lazar into the tiny store.

I looked in all directions, trying to scope out an escape route. For a place that sold crafts and souvenirs, the store was weirdly empty of people, unlike all the other shops and stalls I'd seen in the Grand Bazaar so far. This store was dimly lit, the air thick with a haze of pipe smoke. What the shop lacked in people it made up for in clutter and goods for sale. Shelves along the walls and in the middle of the store were bursting with glassware, ceramics, and painted plates that swirled with red tulips, blackberries, and vines. From the ceiling hung lanterns made of cut glass and iron, in all shapes and sizes and various colors, casting strange and colorful designs on the walls as the dim ceiling lights shone through them. It was like being inside some strange cave, a treasure trove hoarded by dragons.

As Lazar led me deeper into the narrow, hallway-like room, I spotted an old man smoking a pipe behind the counter. My other non-favorite person these days, Vasil, was sitting across from him, his bulky frame somehow balanced on a delicate stool. They were playing backgammon, and the dice clicked on the board as they rolled. Vasil gave me a long, dark look, so cold that it made me shiver. The old man just ignored me.

At the back of the store, Lazar cornered me, breathing heavily, staring at me with an expression I couldn't read. The only sound I heard was the roll of the backgammon dice, as if the roll were deciding my fate. I pressed myself against a shelf of pottery to put as much space between us as I could.

"If you have the package, give it to me, now," he said.

"I don't have it," I said, unzipping my backpack and showing him the contents.

"Then talk to me about your friend," Lazar said. "What do you know?"

"Sage and I weren't friends!" Now I knew for sure that the "Your friend" part of her forged signature in the note wasn't real; it had all been Lazar's doing. Friends didn't make up their names, their hometowns, their entire histories. Real friends didn't offload stolen goods on you and set you up to get interrogated by police at the airport.

Lazar took a step closer. "I ask you again. Where is she?"

"Look, I'm as confused as you are. All I heard was, she went back to the States."

"She did not," snapped Lazar. "My police contacts would have alerted me. She has not yet crossed a border."

Police contacts. I froze. Inspector Lale had mentioned there were some police who worked with smugglers. Inside jobs. Now Lazar was suggesting the same thing.

"So you came all the way to Istanbul to see if *I* could lead you to Sage," I guessed. "Because you think we're such good friends, right?"

"That is correct. She will return and look for you, because you have something she gave you. Temporarily."

"Why would she have given me those gold figurines if she wanted them back?"

"She thought you would be a better carrier for them. You were traveling with an antiquities expert's widow. The contents of that package could be easily explained at an airport."

"Not really, it turns out."

He made a dismissive gesture. "All right. Fine. These trinkets, I can let them go. But Sage I must find. And I have no doubt she will come to you to try to get them back."

I felt light-headed. It was clear to me now that Sage had gotten in over her head with Lazar. My anger toward her lessened as my anger toward Lazar grew. And I thought, suddenly, of how all my friends had bailed on me when I needed them most. Maybe we weren't real friends, after just two days, but even though I was disappointed that Sage hadn't reached out to me yet, I wasn't going to bail on her until I heard her side of the story. I'd have to keep trying to find her.

"I don't have the figurines. I don't know where Sage is. Are we done here?" I said.

"Not quite," he said, licking his lips. "I also came to give you a warning." Abstract shapes of light from one of the lanterns splayed an odd pattern across Lazar's angular face. He opened his leather jacket again and slowly drew the knife out of the interior pocket. It had an ornate handle, encrusted with colorful gemstones; it was almost beautiful. Except for the fact that it was a knife.

No. A *dagger*. I gasped as the crescent-shaped blade came fully out of its sheath.

"In case my English is not so clear. You will not communicate with police about this conversation," said Lazar. "And when Sage returns, you will bring her directly to this shop. My friend at the counter will alert me. I will come for her personally. Do you understand me?"

My throat was dry, my tongue as rough as sandpaper. "I—I understand," I managed to choke out.

"Good." He slid the dagger back into its sheath and inside his jacket pocket.

I pushed past him, knocking my wrist against a shelf in my haste to get away. My *nazar boncuğu* bracelet broke, scattering little blue eyes all over the floor as I ran out of the shop and back into the crowds of the Grand Bazaar.

It took me almost forty-five minutes to find Milton and Maeve. Still shaken, I took one wrong turn after another. I pushed past men who offered me leather jackets, purses, slippers, candy. Finally, almost in tears, I found the pashmina stall, where Milton and Maeve were talking to a police officer.

"Crap," I hissed, ducking behind a rack of shawls. I pressed myself into them, willing myself to be invisible. Then I worried the police officer or a shop owner would see me and think I was trying to steal something.

I stepped out from behind the rack, and Maeve's face relaxed the moment she saw me. "There she is!" she cried, pointing to me. "Oh, Zan, where were you? We've been so worried."

"Any problems, miss?" the policeman asked me.

Yes! I wanted to say. *There's a high-level antiquities smuggler lurking here in the middle of the bazaar, and he just flashed a dagger at me!*

But I remembered Lazar's warning, and Inspector Lale's words of caution about police who might be working with smugglers, and I shook my head. Inspector Lale was the only person I'd tell about my scary run-in with Lazar—and as soon as we got back to the hotel, I'd be placing another call to her. "Sorry," I said to Milton and Maeve. "I just wandered a few stores away to see something, but I took a wrong turn and got lost."

"Yes, this is very easy to do," said the police officer. "I am glad you are all right now." Satisfied that there wasn't a major issue to deal with, he gave us a sympathetic smile and a more detailed tourist map before walking away.

I let out a long breath. The officer hadn't detained me, or wanted to search my bag, or looked at me in any other way than as if I was some lost kid.

"Thank God you're back," Milton said. "Your mother would have had our hides. What do you say we get ourselves a treat? I saw an ice cream stand outside at the gate."

We hurried outside and found the stand. The ice cream vendor wielded an absurdly long scoop on a stick, dipped it into a bin of ice cream, and handed the cone with the scoop of ice cream on the stick. When I reached for it, the stick and cone flipped upside down. Strangely, the ice cream didn't drip or spill. He swooped his arm down, flipped it up, turned it, and offered it to me again. I reached for it, and it darted out of my grasp again. Up high, down low, too slow, just like that old grade-school game. And the ice cream never changed. A crowd of onlookers started to gather, laughing, and I felt as if they were laughing at me. My cheeks burned. Finally the guy took pity on me and let me have the cone from the scoop.

I didn't even feel like eating it anymore. Instead I wanted to cry. The ice cream game reminded me of my whole experience with Sage and the lost urn. You're close, you're far, you're hot, you're cold. It's real, it's fake.

I wished I knew where she was staying, or if she was even in Istanbul right now. Where did a girl with dwindling funds, an expired visa, an alias, a police warrant, and a gang of criminals breathing down her neck seek refuge?

And why hadn't she reached out to me yet, when that's what everyone seemed to think she was going to do?

28

The Lobsters went out to a restaurant that evening, and Mom and I had take-out dinner in Aunt Jackie's apartment, since she wasn't up to going out.

While we ate, we watched a Turkish version of *American Idol*. Or pretended to watch, as we each grappled with our private problems. Aunt Jackie looked a million miles away, massaging her belly, clearly consumed with her health and hotel worries. She'd had a financial check-in from Uncle Berk's siblings that afternoon, which sent her blood pressure soaring; she said they wanted to see real numbers in three days. And I'd seen the paper on the coffee table before Aunt Jackie stuck it between the couch cushions, out of Mom's sight. It was a map of Zelve National Park in Cappadocia, with trails she had highlighted and notes she had scrawled. I couldn't let her keep going down wrong roads and dead ends. I had to get to the bottom of this. And it looked like I might have to do so on my own. Mustafa said Inspector Lale had called the hotel while I was at the Grand Bazaar, but when I called her mobile number again all I got was voice mail. I'd left her a quick message about the new run-in with Lazar, though I didn't dare leave details about the urn or my Uncle Berk murder theory in case some corrupt person on the police force intercepted her phone.

Remembering Lazar's warning to me today, I suddenly sat up straighter. A new theory jolted me. What if there were no undercover cops watching out for me in my neighborhood, or protecting me from that encounter with Lazar, because *she'd never sent them*? Because she was working with Lazar, too?

The parts of this new theory clicked into place, making my breath come fast. Maybe that was why she'd told me to call only her, and not the main number at the Istanbul police station. Maybe *she* was the corrupt one, not others in her department. And maybe that's why she was in no particular hurry to call me back. She was helping to run this show!

I glanced at Mom, wishing I could tell her all this. But she looked miserable, probably still processing the conversations with Dad and me, which her self-help books had obviously failed to prepare her for.

I wasn't going to waste another thought on Dad or Victoria. I was done giving him the power to use me as a convenient prop in his life. I was here, in Turkey, with a stalker-slash-murderer on the loose in my neighborhood, a police inspector I suddenly didn't feel I could trust, and a missing person to find before she became the next victim.

The three of us blinked slowly in the hot-pink glow of the screen, watching some wildly attired Turkish band singing some kind of synth-pop song.

"This show is inspiring me. I'm getting a vision, you guys," said Mom.

"Oh, God," moaned Aunt Jackie. "A vision."

"A party!" Mom said, clapping her hands together. "We need to blow the dust off this place, and put you on the map of hot destinations. We'll have a party. On the rooftop, in the evening, with music and dancing under the stars."

Aunt Jackie blinked at Mom. "I'm on bed rest."

"You can recline on a divan. We'll dance around you!" Mom

was getting that glint in her eye. "I could hire a band. Caterers could serve all kinds of meze. We'll throw the doors open and people will come. They'll see that this isn't a crumbling, run-down place, but hip and romantic—"

Aunt Jackie looked horrified. "Don't," she begged. "Please. Just don't."

"Jackie. Hear me out. Mustafa told me you have no advertising budget, and your social media presence is dismal. You're at barely fifty-percent occupancy in high season. Your brother- and sister-in-law are ready to bring in the bulldozers. If you want to stay in business, and support your baby, people have to find out about the Mavi Konak! You have to stand out in some way from the other boutique hotels around here."

"But it doesn't work like that," Aunt Jackie protested. "You can't just wave a magic wand and have a party."

"Publicity is my profession. I know what I'm doing. There are international business councils I can contact. I can find people with deep pockets and get invitations out. Not to mention tourist bureaus. You want not just businesspeople but also travelers. You want them to go home and tell all their friends about this charming boutique hotel in the heart of Old Istanbul. I could get it organized and spread the word in two days flat. I'm that good, Jackie. Come on. Give me a shot."

"I don't know." Aunt Jackie looked skeptical.

"Neighbors and local shop owners can come, tour opera-tors can bring information. We'll even raffle off a couple of great prizes and solicit donations for hotel renovations. It'll be great!"

"Oh, Kitsie." Aunt Jackie rubbed her forehead. "You've just had a stressful phone call from Marcus. If you have something to prove, please don't choose my hotel as your platform."

"That's not what this is about! I'm not trying to prove any-thing. This is all about helping you!"

I shifted uncomfortably as the two of them argued. Party planning right now seemed so pointless. Sage and the urn were still out there somewhere. The urn could be linked to Lazar and to Uncle Berk's death. I couldn't get sucked into Mom and Aunt Jackie's drama.

Looking at a closed door down the short hallway, I realized I was sitting mere steps away from Uncle Berk's office. There was probably a computer in there. I could see if Sheila Miller had written back about Sage. But also, Uncle Berk had kept the urn in his office. And he'd been hired by Lazar to write up fake documents for it. Maybe I could find those documents, or even some kind of business agreement between the two of them. I wasn't yet sure whom I'd bring them to, now that Inspector Lale was on my list of suspicious characters, but I could worry about that later. Right now I just needed some proof that Lazar had hired my uncle to help with his smuggling operation.

"Hey, Aunt Jackie," I said, "I need to check my email."

"You can use Berk's office," she said. "That is, if you dare. The place is a disaster. It's just a converted closet, and it's heaped with relics of his old career. He never could get rid of anything."

She rose slowly to her feet, with a grunt.

"No, don't get up," I protested. "I can just go in." My heart pounded, but I tried to look calm. If Uncle Berk never got rid of anything, maybe the documents were still in there!

"I can walk a few yards. I'm not paralyzed," she said. "And I keep the office locked," she added, fumbling for a key chain in her pocket as she led me to his door. "I didn't want any of our cleaning staff to get in there, and Berk never did, either. It drove him crazy if people moved his papers around. Now, don't trip over anything," she advised me as she unlocked the door and switched on the light. She stared around the small, messy office and sighed heavily. "Someday I'm going to have to deal with all this stuff."

"So you never came in here to look for any clues that would maybe explain how he really died?" I asked her.

"I sifted through a few things. But it was too painful. And anyway, Berk and I didn't have secrets between us."

I studied her face carefully. She must not know about Lazar and Vasil at all, then, or my uncle's consulting gig with them. Nazif had said she was out of town, at her friends' hotel in Cappadocia, when the Lycian Society Onyx group held their secret meetings here. Had Berk not told her about those? Why would he conceal all that from his own wife?

Because the business he was in with Lazar and Vasil, on behalf of the Lycian Society clients, was illegal. Shady, and shadowy. No wonder he encouraged her to go out of town.

But Uncle Berk wasn't shady and shadowy himself. Was he so desperate for money that he would sell himself out like that? If he had done it for his wife, for his family, did that make it all somehow okay?

"Oh, I meant to tell you. I called Inspector Lale," Aunt Jackie added.

A chill ran through me. "Oh, no. I mean—you did?"

"I realized it was silly to keep bugging you for that business card, so I looked her up online," said Aunt Jackie. "I invited her to come over here and have a chat with me."

"Did you leave her a voice mail?"

"No, I got her on the phone."

I frowned. Why was Inspector Lale taking my aunt's call but not mine? That in itself seemed suspicious.

"So when's she coming over?" I fought to keep my voice steady.

"She said we'd set up a time as soon as she got back in town. She's still on the coast, where there was another robbery last night."

"Another one!"

"Yes. She's really got her hands full with the crime situation there. Another mosque and another small family museum were looted. She has to investigate their storage rooms and interrogate a local suspect they managed to take into custody.

Anyway, when she comes, I plan to hand over my whole file and explain my theory. Maybe you can keep your mother busy with party planning or something while I do that. You know how she tends to have big reactions."

"Uh. Um. Sure, I can do that," I said, mentally adding this information to my theory that Inspector Lale was working for the other side. True, I'd had trouble with the police in my past, so maybe it was in my nature not to completely trust them. But it now seemed entirely too convenient that Inspector Lale's work kept her on the coast, with all these robberies taking place there. Maybe on these storage room inspections and police station interrogations she was confiscating other artifacts for "evidence." And funneling the artifacts right back into the black market, or perhaps even to Lazar himself!

I was getting so worked up about this idea I didn't realize Aunt Jackie was already out of the office. "Hey, Zan," said Aunt Jackie, looking back in through the doorway. "Thanks."

"For what?"

"I know your dad had certain opinions about me, and probably your mother does, too," she said. "But I know I'm not crazy. I knew Berk so well, and I knew his habits, and it makes no sense to me the way his life ended. So thanks for believing me." She came back into the office and gave me a quick, warm hug. I hugged her back, tentative at first—afraid to squish the baby—then firmer. It felt good to hug someone, and be hugged back. Mine was not a hugging family. Maybe we were missing out on something.

If you only knew how much I believed you, I thought as Aunt Jackie went back to Mom and the TV show. And if only she knew how worried I was, especially now that I couldn't trust Inspector Lale.

When my aunt left, I sat down at the computer, which was on a desk heaped with papers and books. Talk about an antiquity. The computer had a huge monitor and a hard drive tower—it was probably fifteen years old, at least—and it took forever to boot up. When it finally did, I pulled up my email right away. Nothing from Sage's mom.

Then I looked around the office, wondering if any clues might offer themselves up to me. Something to do with the urn and the work Uncle Berk did for Lazar. Nothing was going to be obvious, that was for sure. The walls were lined with file cabinets and bookshelves, and the shelves were sagging with books. College textbooks and reference guides, in both English and Turkish. Guides to ancient civilizations and art, bristling with sticky notes. I turned and nearly tripped over a stack of cardboard file boxes. When I dislodged the lid on the top one, I saw that it was crammed with three-ring binders and spiral notebooks. I chose a notebook at random and paged through it. It was filled with Uncle Berk's small, cramped handwriting. It looked like lecture notes from his time in grad school at BU.

I sat in the middle of the floor for some time, hugging my knees, immobilized. What was wrong with me? I'd never had any trouble snooping before, or going through other people's stuff, whether it was in someone's house or in a store. My shrink had always tried to get me to understand why I might be doing it—a need for attention, a cry for help—but none of her theories had ever sunk in. It was like autopilot when I went through other people's things, like a part of my brain clicked off and left this buzzing sound in its place, and my body acted on its own. It was the opposite of the climbing wall, when I was in complete control, when I could command the tiniest of muscles in my fingers to keep me from falling. The worst of my falls, it seemed, had always happened on the ground, when I'd get caught for doing stupid things.

I felt awful lying to my aunt to get into Uncle Berk's office so I could go through his stuff. I had to remind myself that this time was different—wasn't it? I was a detective now, not a thief.

I pulled books and files off the shelves and flipped through them, scanning for any reference to the seahorse urn from the Karun Treasure. I opened desk drawers stuffed with tissue boxes and office supplies. I sifted through files on the desk, which held things like receipts for contractors at the hotel and copies of bills. Nothing jumped out that had any connection to the Lycian Society, the seahorse urn, the Karun Treasure, or Lazar.

I did, however, see invoices from an assisted reproduction clinic. Bills for thousands of dollars, all marked "paid." So there had been some money coming in, from somewhere.

I sat on my uncle's office chair and looked around in despair. It seemed as if he'd saved every scrap of intellectual work he'd ever produced or consumed. The office was a monument to my uncle's failed hopes and dreams—or a tomb for his intellectual life. It would take an entire archaeological team to get to the bottom of this. No wonder Aunt Jackie felt overwhelmed just walking through the door.

But I had to do something, chip away where I could. So next I scanned the jumble of icons on his cluttered computer desktop. Folders with labels in Turkish and English. Video game icons next to virus protection software next to several search engines. PowerPoint presentations. Resumes. I found a bunch of spreadsheets created in the past year that contained digital photos of antique objects, and notes on dimensions, all in Turkish. I couldn't read all the file headings, but each spreadsheet seemed to be a kind of database for an art and artifact collection. It looked like museum names on some files and mosque names on others. I figured it was all from the consulting work Aunt Jackie had mentioned—non-criminal work, I imagined.

Then it occurred to me that if he'd been writing fake appraisals or false histories for Lazar, he'd probably been smart enough not to do it on his home computer. Feeling increasingly guilty, yet unable to stop, I opened a few files to check out his most recent Word documents. I saw nothing about ancient artifacts or appraisals, just hotel information, spreadsheets and purchase orders for food and supplies, and employee records

An electronic copy of *Hotel Management for Dummies*. A document dated back in January listed four pages of repairs and improvements the hotel needed. The numbers in the outgoing expense column were way higher than those in the incoming column.

Clearly, despite having some guests, the hotel was struggling. *They'd* been struggling, too, with the fertility treatment bills. Yet Uncle Berk had somehow raised enough money for four rounds of IVF and managed to keep the hotel sputtering along. Lazar must have come along with an offer—or offers—that my uncle couldn't refuse. So maybe Uncle Berk and Sage had something in common: a desperate need for money to make their problems disappear and their dreams come true. And when Lazar produced an artifact that needed to have a story behind it—a fictional one to cover up its true origins from looters and sketchy dealers, and to distance himself from it as well—maybe my uncle realized he was in deeper than he wanted to be. It was one thing to authenticate "trinkets" as replicas, but it was a whole other level of crime to be passing off a lost part of the Karun Treasure as a fake in order to sell and transport it illegally. Maybe that's why he'd been holding on to both the urn and the fake certificate he'd created for it. He couldn't let Lazar get away with this one.

Working faster, I sifted through more files and papers. Near the top of a stack was a copy of a British archaeology magazine, with a sticky note. I opened it and found an article called "Rich as Croesus" about the Karun Treasure—written by my uncle!

I snatched it up with both hands and read it fast. It described the origins of the looted treasure, and explained that "Karun" was the Arabic version of "Croesus," after King Croesus, the legendarily wealthy king of Lydia. It then went on to tell how the Karun Treasure hoard had passed through a series of middlemen and eventually made its way to deep storage at the Met in New York. When some of the objects were finally displayed, they were labeled as "East Greek artifacts." A

Turkish journalist got suspicious and investigated. Eventually the objects were all shipped back to the Uşak Archaeological Museum, a small museum in a village near Ankara.

One of the key pieces of the collection, a gold seahorse brooch—"The Hippocampus Brooch"—was later discovered to have been replaced by a fake. The director of the Uşak museum, who had helped to bring back the treasure to Turkey in the first place, was found to be responsible for selling the one-of-a-kind item right out from under the museum and arranging to have it swapped for a fake. He was now in jail. The original brooch had been tracked down in Germany, but it had yet to be returned.

Uncle Berk went on to explain how the scandal angered a lot of archaeologists and museum curators. Some thought Turkey had blown it—their treasures had been returned from the Met, but they didn't look after them properly, so they didn't deserve to keep them. A lot of people thought the artifacts didn't belong to Turkey at all, since they were created by civilizations that had lived on the land long before the Turks got there. These objects belong to the world, some art collectors argued, and should be cared for in countries with the resources to display and secure them properly. Still others felt that anything found on Turkey's land must belong to Turkey, and stay in its place of origin no matter what, even if it meant not as many people got to see it.

I studied a picture of the original golden brooch that went along with the article, and could hardly breathe. The brooch reminded me so much of the urn! The smiling, winged seahorses on the urn looked the same. The brooch had tiny acorns dangling from gold chains, and the acorns looked exactly like the lid of the urn. The brooch was beautiful; I could see why someone would want to own it. But stealing it from a museum and replacing it with a specially made fake? That was so wrong. It meant that all the people who'd come to the museum to see the treasure were robbed, too. Seeing the fake was not the same as seeing the real thing. If I went all the way to France to see the *Mona Lisa,* only to find out later that what I'd actually seen was a forgery, I'd definitely feel ripped off.

Uncle Berk's last paragraph hinted that there might be even more lost Karun Treasure items out there, in museum storage in other countries, or in the homes of private collectors who didn't know what they'd acquired. He encouraged any museums or collectors who found artifacts in their storerooms matching materials or motifs from the cache to come forward. He felt as if the treasure should be reunited, in Turkey, once and for all.

"Any single item of the Karun Treasure is priceless," Uncle Berk concluded. "But until all its items are recovered, authenticated, and brought into the light of day for everyone to know about, no museum or private owner will be rich as Croesus. The real curse of the Karun Treasure—indeed, the tragedy—is that tomb raiders and their accomplices have stolen history. And in doing so, they have robbed *all* of us."

I stared at the page, letting those final words burn into my eyes. I pictured the urn sailing over the cliffside, and the look on Aunt Jackie's face when she realized another connection to her husband had been lost. That had been really sad. But it was even sadder now that I realized the urn's value wasn't just sentimental, and the urn didn't belong just to her. It meant a lot to Turkey, and to the world. A piece of history could be completely wiped out because some people wanted to own stolen artifacts and other people wanted to profit from that.

And then I thought of how this article fit perfectly with what Nazif had seen and overheard at the Lycian Society meeting. My uncle hadn't felt comfortable working to get this lost item out of the country, when it could have been reunited with its companion pieces instead. By aiding the robbers, he was becoming one, too. And maybe his only reason to help Lazar and his group had been to get enough money for all those fertility treatments. Or to save the failing hotel.

But he hadn't followed through on the last job. He had been hiding the urn in his desk—a supposedly *cursed* urn—with the fake certificate of "inauthenticity," for weeks. How long would he have kept it there? Was he planning to hand it over to museum officials eventually, or to the police? What was the reason for the delay? And if Uncle Berk were around right now, what would he want me to do?

I sighed and put the magazine back on the stack of papers where I'd found it, and that's when I noticed what was beneath it. It was a large envelope addressed to Inspector Lale Demir, at the Istanbul Police Station. I snatched it up. Maybe he meant to mail her a copy of the article—they were, after all, old friends and colleagues, and maybe he trusted her. I picked up the envelope and noticed it wasn't empty. Inside it were hard copies of those database spreadsheets I'd seen on his computer, with the photos and dimensions and notes—all in Turkish.

I chewed my lip. I wanted to believe through all of this that Uncle Berk was a good man, doing the wrong thing for noble reasons. But I was afraid there was more to his story. Why had he been sending this information about museum and mosque collections to Inspector Lale? Was it to help her trace stolen goods? Or to help her and a bunch of thieves *acquire* them? How deeply was Uncle Berk involved in this smuggling ring anyway?

29

Later that night, the muezzin woke me from my fitful sleep.

"*Allahu Akbar . . . Allahu Akbar . . .*"

I put on my hoodie and sweats and made my way to the roof, where I faced the minarets.

"*Ash hadu al laa llaaaha illal laah . . .*"

As the voice took twists and turns, I found myself wishing I had someone or something to pray to. But I'd never been very religious. Mom had grown up Christian but secular, and didn't spend much time learning about Jewish traditions with us. Dad was raised Jewish, and he talked a good game about faith and God, but remained carefully neutral, to get votes. I'd gone through the basics of Hebrew school and survived my bat mitzvah, but never felt a personal connection to the Torah text I'd learned to read. And after three sessions of temple youth group in ninth grade, I dropped out, preferring to sleep in or see school friends on Sundays.

I didn't know who or what I could count on anymore. Not God. Not my family. Not my friends. It was as if I was up on the top rope, looking down, and nobody was there holding the end.

When the call to prayer ended, I turned to go, taking one

last look at the Blue Mosque. It was a cloudy night, the moon obscured. The blue lights beneath the minarets gave off an unearthly glow. Then a movement on Nazif's roof caught my eye. Was Nazif's family out there again? Maybe that's why I'd come up to the roof. Not for the call to prayer, but for a glimpse of a happy family.

But it wasn't the family I saw.

A white cloth had been strung up on the trellis where Nazif's family grew grapes. A light shone from behind it. Suddenly two black figures appeared on the makeshift screen. Shadow puppets, flat and hinged, controlled from behind by a stick. They were just like the puppets my uncle had given me a few years ago for Christmas, in a kit that now lay somewhere under a bunch of outgrown toys and board games in our basement back home.

I walked to the edge of the roof, drawn to the two puppets as they danced jerkily. They seemed to fight, then come together and embrace; then dance, then fight, then flip and tumble. It was almost like watching a cartoon; the characters were in constant motion. Until one of the puppet's legs broke off and the show stopped. The broken puppet limped offstage and the other one chased after it. The screen went blank. I waited, holding my breath.

The next puppets that emerged were different. One was wraith-like and reminded me of a ghost, until I realized it was a bird. The other puppet was a boy. The boy shadow tried to catch the bird shadow, doing somersaults and handsprings and vaults while the bird darted just out of reach. It was a beautiful chase scene, and even in two-dimensional paper, the shadows managed to convey a sense of longing. Then the shadow bird flew away. The boy puppet sank to his knees, watching it go, slowly hanging his head and bringing his hands to his heart. Then he sank below the stage.

I clapped, softly.

The light winked off, and the puppeteer emerged from

behind the screen. He nearly dropped his armful of shadow puppets on sticks when he saw me.

I was startled, too. It was Nazif standing there.

He laughed—nervously, it seemed, as if he'd been caught doing something ridiculous or wrong. He ducked his head a little.

He slowly crossed over to the edge of his rooftop.

In the moonlight and out of uniform, he looked ordinary, like the guy next door. Wearing jeans and a T-shirt, he looked like anyone I might know at school. But he was also so different from anyone I might know at school. Back home, I didn't know bellboys or puppeteers. I didn't know guys who got up before dawn to eat and pray. We were now separated only by a five-foot gap between our buildings, yet we were worlds apart.

"So. You're a puppeteer?" I said. Then I winced. I could see he was embarrassed, as if I'd just said he played with dolls in his spare time.

"I know it must seem like a children's game," he said. "But actually, shadow puppetry is a serious tradition in Turkey. I practice up here sometimes, at night, alone." He stole a glance at me. "I don't usually have an audience. I did not know you were watching."

"I didn't mean to spy on you," I said. "I wasn't here long. I came up because I couldn't sleep. But it was really good. Like having a show put on just for me. And you know, as a typical American, the whole world does revolve around me, so . . ."

"I am sorry I said that the other day. I was a little bit wrong about you."

"You were?"

"You are so concerned with your aunt, and with finding out the truth about your uncle's death. You are also concerned about a friend you made after only two days on a boat, even though she did something bad that got you in trouble with the law. By the way, I found one of her former teachers."

"What?" I took a step forward, eager to hear every detail,

and then remembered there wasn't a full railing to catch me. Four stories below, a stray cat leaped off a garbage can.

"Careful," said Nazif. "Please don't fall. Your aunt is hoping to build a fence here. Until she does, guests are not technically allowed on this roof."

"I won't fall. But tell me about the teacher."

"Her name is Gamze Inan. She teaches history at the International School."

"I can't believe you looked up Sage's school!"

Nazif shrugged, though he seemed pleased by my reaction. "It was not a big problem for me. I had a little extra time this evening. First I found an Amy Miller of Oregon, USA, in the student directory. It said 'withdrawn' by her name. Then I looked at faculty to see which history teacher she might have had. This is how I found Gamze Inan. She teaches a class on Ancient Lycia. This topic interested your friend, right?"

"Definitely," I said. "Sage geeked out over Ancient Lycia."

"I sent this teacher an email asking if she knew where Amy Miller might be. Hopefully she will reply."

"Wow. You didn't have to do all that, you know."

"Your aunt and uncle were good to my family. So I want to help you. This problem, it seems too big for one person."

Suddenly it was as if neither of us knew where to look. I remembered that I was completely without my face makeup, uncovered and exposed. Probably the moonlight and my hoodie obscured the blotches on the left side of my face, but I couldn't be sure.

I pointed to the puppets in his arms, which looked like a pile of shadows. "My uncle Berk gave me a set of Turkish shadow puppets once, when they came to visit us. Thick paper on sticks, not as elaborate as yours."

Nazif looked pleased to hear this. "Really? Did you try using them?"

"Sure. I did one show for the family. I was behind the screen, so I never saw it from the other side. It's amazing how lifelike those puppets are when you see them from the audience. I'm sure I couldn't make mine do half the things yours did."

"Do you want to see them?"

"Sure!"

"Wait here. I will bring them and pass them over, if you— Oh! What are you doing?"

It was like something took over my body. I backed up a few steps, then ran forward and leaped onto Nazif's rooftop. I easily cleared the five-foot gap and landed on my hands and knees.

Nazif shook his head in disbelief. "Did you really do that? You are crazy!" He gave a rich laugh, tossing back his head. "Wow. That was like from a video game!"

"Yeah, I guess I did just do that." I stood up, brushing the dirt off my hands. I felt a slight twinge in my left knee, but otherwise I was fine. And Nazif was fine, too—fine to look at. I noticed the way his eyes danced in the moonlight, the languid way his body moved now that it was free from the binding structure of his bellboy uniform. I took a deep breath. I hadn't felt this alive, this awake, since the night of my midnight swim with Sage.

"So impressive! You are not afraid of heights?" said Nazif.

"No. I'm actually a rock climber, so I'm used to heights. Hey, can I see the puppets?"

"Of course." He took me over to the screen he'd rigged up. I could smell roses, sweet and strong, and I could just make out the outline of bunches of grapes hanging from vines threading through the trellis.

Nazif reached behind the screen and turned on the light.

I jumped back, hitting my head on part of the grape arbor in my haste to get away from the harsh light. "Are you all right?" Nazif asked, peering around the side of the screen.

"Yeah. It's just bright," I mumbled, covering the left side of my face. "Can you turn that down?"

But it was too late. He'd seen me. Full-on. I let my left hand slowly fall to my side.

"Well, do you want to see these puppets or not?" he finally asked.

I nodded.

"Then come. You have to see them in the light."

I came closer, dragging my feet. A far cry from the girl who'd just leaped between two buildings in a single bound.

Nazif held up the two puppets from the first show I'd seen, using a stick attached to the back of each one. Up close, in the light, they were surprisingly colorful. The puppets were of two men, both with beards. One beard was pointed, the other rounded. The puppets were seen in profile. They wore elaborate hats, ornately decorated knickers, and pointy shoes. The pointed-beard puppet was wearing only one shoe, as his leg had come off during the show. The puppets' joints had hinges, and when I reached out to touch them, I was surprised that they felt as if they were made of dyed leather. The hinges had an almost translucent look.

Nazif ducked behind the screen with them, making them grow to twice their size. "Meet Karagöz," he said, shaking the puppet with the rounded beard in a type of jig, "and Hacivat," he went on, making the one with the pointed beard appear to lurch drunkenly.

"Nice to meet you both," I said.

He came out from behind the screen and put the two puppets into my hands. When I looked at their faces, I recoiled in horror. I could swear they looked exactly like Lazar and Vasil. I shivered. It was weird how a pair of puppets sent my mind straight to the thought of Lazar and Vasil, reminding me they could pop up anytime.

"These are Karagöz shadow-theater puppets, traditional in Turkey," Nazif explained. "But maybe you know that already?"

"I didn't know what they were," I said. "Uncle Berk just handed me the package. He never explained it." There was a lot Uncle Berk had never explained, not even to his own wife. Aunt Jackie seemed clueless about Uncle Berk's side dealings with

Lazar and the Lycian Society, and what was probably the true source of funding for their expensive baby-making project.

"These two puppets are from maybe the 1940s," said Nazif. "They belonged to my grandfather. He was a shadow master, a highly respected puppeteer. He left them to me when he died, thinking I might become an apprentice to this art. But my father has other ideas. He believes that puppetry is a dying tradition, and there is no future, no money in it. He wants me to go into hospitality. He thinks tourism has a better future."

"But you'd rather be a puppeteer?" I guessed.

"An animator, actually. The puppetry interests me, too. I'd like to help keep this tradition alive. But I'd also like to make contemporary stories and media that people can relate to better." He set down the pair of Karagöz puppets and pulled out the boy and the bird. "These I made," he said, handing them to me.

"No way. You *made* these?" I turned the puppets around in my hands, marveling at the delicate cutting of heavy black paper, the perfect hinges and joints.

"Yes. I am still learning puppet-making techniques. Mostly from books and YouTube." He sighed and ran his hand through his hair, making it even messier.

I resisted a sudden impulse to reach out and smooth it back down.

"I wanted to attend a youth arts conference in the city of Bursa this summer," he went on. "I told my father I would work extra hours at the hotel and pay for it myself. But tonight, he told me no. He thinks it is a distraction and will only fill me with impossible ideas. He thinks it will not prepare me for a career in hospitality."

"Well, hospitality is a reliable business," I pointed out. "People always need a place to stay and food to eat when they travel."

"Yes, but this is not a business that holds any interest for me."

I nodded, smiling in sympathy. I handed back the puppets, then sat down opposite Nazif and leaned against a potted rosebush, hugging my knees to my chest. For some reason, I didn't care about my face now and the light exposing my white patches. Nazif seemed completely unbothered by it, too. I wondered what he'd think if he knew there were white patches on my arms and legs as well, if he knew I was practically disintegrating even as I sat there.

"I know how you feel," I said. "I didn't get my ideal summer, either."

He raised his eyebrows. "No? You did not want to come here, to Turkey?"

I shook my head. "I wanted to do an advanced teen climbing program this summer, and maybe teach little kids in a climbing camp."

"So why didn't you?"

"My mom thought we should come here and help my aunt."

"And your father?"

"He's, um, a little tied up."

"With work?" Nazif looked at me expectantly, as if waiting to hear my story. As if he had all the time in the world.

I took a deep breath and told him the short version of my dad's scandal, leaving out my whole shoplifting incident—I wasn't quite ready to show him all of myself. It was a big deal just to tell him who my family was, and what had happened, and why Mom and I had run so far away.

"Basically, my family thinks mostly about themselves," I concluded. "I guess we're a bunch of self-entitled Americans. To the extreme."

Now it was Nazif's turn to smile sympathetically. "Not you," he said. "I can see you are different." As he talked, he made the shadow bird come to life in his hands. It preened and fluttered its tail feathers. "At night, when my parents are asleep, I come out here sometimes," he said. "It is peaceful for me, maybe like your rock climbing."

I nodded. It was comforting to think he had conflicts with his parents, too.

We sat across from each other in contented silence for a while, and he continued to play with the puppet, making the bird's feathers flutter as if it were flying. Our feet seemed to gravitate toward each other's and suddenly his shoes touched my bare toes. He jerked his feet away.

"It's okay," I said, longing for them again.

"I should probably go," Nazif mumbled. He stood up and turned off the light behind the screen. Then he took down the screen and wrapped the puppets inside it. "It's getting late. And those German tourists, they are killing me. So many things wrong with their rooms, so many misunderstandings. Two of them are threatening to leave, and if they do, the others will follow. Your aunt will be out a lot of money if they go."

"Oh, no. Maybe she should take my mom up on her crazy idea after all."

He paused in his folding. "What is this crazy idea?"

I tried to draw out my words, to keep him on the roof with me. I didn't want the evening to end. "She wants to throw a big party, with a band and caterers and stuff. She says we could sell raffle tickets and encourage donations toward renovating this historic building."

"Can she really do all that?"

"Sure. She was an event planner in her past life. And she's good at it. I just don't think my aunt's too into the idea."

"No, it's good, this party," said Nazif. "The hotel is invisible here, on a mostly residential street. And if people can see what is good about the hotel, maybe they will be inspired to help pay to fix it. When will it be?"

"Two nights from now. Hey, you know what? You could have an audience for your show, if my Mom got a bunch of people up here."

"Oh, no." He waved away my comment.

"Why not? Your show was beautiful! A perfect blend of traditional Turkey and modern Turkey, just like this hotel could be. And the puppets are amazing—do you have more?"

"A few," he admitted. "Okay. In confidence?" He lowered his voice to a whisper. A whisper that made my skin tingle. "I have made close to twenty."

"See? You need to get your real work out there, Nazif. If you did a performance at a party, you could show your dad how good you are. I'll mention it to my mom. I have a feeling this party's going to happen whether my aunt wants it to or not." I realized I was babbling now, nervous at how close he was, but I couldn't stop talking. "When we left Aunt Jackie's apartment tonight, Mom mentioned inviting everyone who'd been on our Blue Voyage, since almost all of them are in Istanbul. Even if she can just get six people, believe me, she'll call it a party." I sighed as reality hit me. "I wish I were in more of a partying mood."

He nodded, somber. "Have you told anyone about Lazar?"

"Just you." And then I told him about my encounter with Lazar at the Grand Bazaar.

Nazif whistled under his breath. "Not good," he said. "He is following you."

"He's *trapping* me," I said. "He thinks I'm hiding something. And he's writing me fake notes from Sage to get me to talk. The one in the door wasn't really from her, but I fell for it."

He looked worried. "Have you called Inspector Lale to tell her all of this?"

"No," I said, a little too loudly. "I don't know if I can really trust her. And I'm thinking of going to the embassy, because someone there must know who to trust. My dad is in government back home, so I'm guessing people at the embassy will be more willing to help me. But I have to have something more specific for them to investigate. I can't just say that a creepy guy is stalking me when I have no evidence or witnesses, just these two notes. And I can't say Sage has the Karun Treasure urn because we don't even know for sure that she does. I mean, she *might*, but what if she doesn't?"

"Yes," he said, deep in thought. "You need to find something to link Lazar to the urn and to your uncle's death."

"Right."

"And Sage is that link."

"But what if she doesn't have the urn?"

"Still, she will know something, and she is useful to the authorities. But she may have connections who can help her cross a border. We must work faster to find her."

We. We were in this together. I felt a warm stirring inside me, almost like what I'd felt on the Blue Voyage when Sage wanted to be my friend. I'd trusted her, and I'd been burned. Was Nazif different?

My thoughts were interrupted as a yellow light flicked on from the door to the stairwell on Nazif's roof. I shrank back into the trellis, the vines concealing me from view.

Mustafa talked to his son in Turkish. He said something that seemed like he was still vaguely annoyed—like my own dad might—before he switched off the light and went back inside.

Nazif turned to me. "I must go," he whispered.

"Did he see me?" I said.

"No. I told him I came up here for the evening prayer and that I am going to bed soon." He chewed his lower lip. "How will you return to your room?"

"Same way I came." I flapped my arms. "Don't worry. I'll be fine. I'll see you tomorrow."

He grinned and tipped an imaginary hat.

Wow. He didn't care about my skin. Which meant that for the past fifteen minutes, I hadn't cared, either. As I took my running jump back to the Hotel Mavi Konak rooftop, I felt my heart soar a little bit, too.

30

The next morning, I flew through my breakfast prep tasks fast enough to earn a five-minute break. I swung by the front desk just as Nazif was arriving for work.

"Hey, did you hear from that history teacher?" I asked.

"Well, *merhaba* to you, too," he said, his dark eyes twinkling. "Don't Americans say hello?"

"Oh. Sorry. *Selam.*" I stared at him. Had I dreamed last night on the rooftops? I hadn't, because he suddenly gave me the biggest smile, and I couldn't help smiling back.

"Yes. She replied." He turned on the computer and brought up his email. "I will translate for you. Amy Miller was her student in the fall. She was a good student and eager to learn, and she was paying for the exchange program herself. But then something happened to her money. The teacher was not sure what happened, but Amy said she could not afford to continue the program. Ms. Inan offered to give her a spare room in her home, so that Amy could avoid paying fees for the dormitory, hoping that would help, but Amy declined the offer. The last she heard from her, Amy had taken a job with a tourism company that was hiring English speakers for video tours of Istanbul. She expected to earn enough money to pay for the course and come back in the spring, and she said she had friends she could live with."

I shook my head in disbelief. "I can't believe she would have earned enough making tourism videos to pay for all her living and school expenses." *Let alone a Blue Voyage cruise,* I thought. And what about that stack of cash she'd used to buy stuff from Baklava Guy? No, the job that paid for such things had to have come from Lazar. That money came from smuggling antiquities.

"So now what?" Nazif asked.

I shook my head. "I don't know, Nazif. I really don't know."

At that point, Mustafa came into the room and spoke to Nazif, somewhat harshly.

"I'm sorry. I cannot talk now," Nazif explained with apologetic eyes. "I talked to my father about doing a puppet show at the hotel party. He did not like this idea, or the fact that I am practicing late at night instead of resting up for work. We had an argument this morning."

"I totally get it," I said. "I have parents, too. But please don't give up on the puppet show idea. Your dad has to change his mind. People would love your work."

He shrugged. "Thank you. I will try."

While Nazif went back to work with his dad, I checked my email on the lobby computer, even though I expected Mom to come haul me back to work any moment as well. Two new messages popped up. One was from Dad, which I ignored; I was so not up for an emotional package bomb. But the other was from Sheila Miller. Sage's mom!

Hand trembling, I clicked to open the email.

Dear Alexandra,

I am sorry I cannot help you. I have no contact information for Amy at this time. Amy was declared an emancipated minor when she was seventeen. Her father is not in the picture. I have not been responsible for her, financially or otherwise, since her legal emancipation from us. I was aware that she had gone to Turkey to study last year, but we have not been in touch since. Is she in some kind of trouble? It would not shock me. Amy has an impulsive streak, which has sometimes gotten her into trouble. If you do find her, tell her I would not mind if she checked in. I would like to hear how she is doing.

Sincerely, Sheila Miller

I gazed at the screen, blinking back tears. I felt so bad for Sage. What a horrible email. I didn't know what would make Sage want to separate legally from her parents, but there must have been good reason; I knew from my dad that emancipation was a hard thing to get approved. (I knew because in the heat of an argument once, I'd threatened to do it myself.) A brother dead from a drug overdose, a dad who was AWOL, and a mother who didn't care that her daughter was wandering around Turkey by herself. Whatever I had going on in my family, it wasn't half as bad as Sage's situation. No wonder she'd said she couldn't go home.

Out of her enormous pack of lies, her sad family situation was actually authentic. My heart ached for her. Sheila Miller's daughter was way more lost than I was, having fallen a much farther distance. Even if I had to turn her in as a thief, I wanted to do something to help her, reach out a hand and try to pull her back up. I wanted to save her if I could.

The problem was, with Lazar breathing down my neck and no clear person to trust on the police force, I had to worry more about saving myself.

31

All morning, I was stuck working with Mom on the database project, surrounded by lists and brochures. Mom went through my spreadsheet and called every organization I'd entered to ask who might be willing to offer a raffle prize for our party or discount rates for hotel guests.

"This Voyager Balloon company in Cappadocia is the best," Mom said as she finished her one-billionth call. "They're going to offer a free balloon trip for the raffle. It's worth five hundred dollars!"

"Awesome," I said, glancing at the brochure for the whirling dervishes. Then the address of the dervish show caught my eye: Istiklal Caddesi, the main drag in the Beyoğlu neighborhood. I'd heard of that street before. A new plan for tracking down Sage came to mind. I couldn't wait to run it by Nazif.

A half hour later, I was pushing a cart with freshly laundered sheets down a hall on the second floor, and Nazif was pushing a cart with ladies' dry-cleaned dresses hanging from it. We almost collided.

Laughing, we maneuvered our carts around each other in

the narrow hallway, until we were finally standing side by side and mere inches apart.

Nazif's eyes were shining. "He said yes!"

My mind was on the Lycian Society and my new plan. "Sorry. What?"

"My father. He said I can do the puppet show at the party! I convinced him that it would be good for tourists to experience some Turkish culture they might not often see."

"Oh, Nazif! That's wonderful!"

"What about you? Anything new?" Nazif asked.

"The Lycian Society," I said. "I've decided I need to go there in person. Maybe I can find out something about Lazar and Vasil. Or the clients they buy artifacts for. If I can't get to Sage myself, maybe I can find something about the smugglers that I could give to authorities at the embassy. Maybe I can get a list of the Onyx-level members and find out who might have been dealing with him, or even who was buying the Karun Treasure urn!"

Nazif nodded excitedly. "And if you find anything that links the Onyx clients to Lazar, investigators could arrest him."

"Exactly. And then Sage might come out of hiding."

"This plan sounds good. Except how will you get the list of Onyx members?"

"I'll go into the office asking for tour information for our hotel," I explained. "I have the perfect excuse. I met a tour representative on the boat cruise. I'll go into the tour office asking for him. Mom's looking for raffle prize donations. I'll ask what they can offer us. And I'll tell them we'd like to offer a special package for Onyx-level members of the Lycian Society. I'll need their email addresses. Even though Mr. Tabak works on the tour business side, I bet he has some connection to a society staff member who could give him that information. He feels so bad about Uncle Berk dying and the guest speaker thing not working out on the cruise, he might be willing to bend a rule for us and get me a membership list."

"It could work," Nazif said slowly. "But will your mother let you go out again?"

I handed him the brochure I'd folded up and put in my pocket.

Nazif looked puzzled. "The *sema*? You wish to see the whirling dervishes? How are men spinning in white robes going to help you find Sage?"

"Stay with me, Nazif! The whirling dervishes do their performance in a hall that is *practically next door* to the Lycian Society."

"Ah!" He smiled, comprehending.

"I'm not going to stay there and watch it, but it will get me close to where I need to be. And as far as my mom's concerned, it's the perfect evening activity to do with my pretend grandparents, Milton and Maeve."

◇◇◇◇◇

The Lobsters loved my idea of seeing the whirling dervish ceremony that evening. So did the entire German tour group, who overheard us talking in the hall and decided to come along.

"The more, the merrier!" I said, beaming at them. Mom would have to let me go now! And it would be easier for me to slip away unnoticed from a larger group.

Mom did let me go. But then Aunt Jackie insisted that Mom go, too. "Mustafa, Nazif, and I can hold down the fort," she said. "Half the guests will be at the show anyway."

Mustafa nodded. "The *sema* is a beautiful religious ceremony, and the dervishes are an important part of Turkish culture," he said. "The Mevlevi Order is the oldest group. Zan should not miss this, and you should not either. We will take care of Jackie."

My heart sank a little, and I was sure a look of disappointment crossed Nazif's face, too. His dad wasn't going to let him come. And I had let myself imagine, for a moment, sitting beside Nazif—close to him—in a taxi, or at the performance hall, our hands touching, legs brushing against each other.

I shook off my fantasies. In the past, I had been a master at orchestrating romantic encounters with guys in the dark. A dimly lit corner at a party? The backseat of a friend's car? Shadows and darkness were my friends. So were guys who drank too much. If they kissed my makeup off, they weren't likely to notice. The problem was, none of those relationships, or whatever they were, lasted too long, because they couldn't survive in the light of day.

But I didn't have time to swoon over Nazif. I would barely be at the whirling dervish ceremony before I'd have to duck outside and begin my mission.

Up in our room, Mom had second thoughts about the plan as we got dressed for the evening. "Did you see that file Jackie was carrying?" she said. "My God. More of those articles about crimes in Cappadocia. Plus email printouts from correspondence with lawyers and local business owners out there. I don't know how she keeps unearthing all of this information."

My stomach twisted.

"You see what happens the moment I turn my back? She gets obsessed with her murder theory, and then she's agitated. It's not good for her health or the baby." Mom set down her purse. "I can't do it. I won't enjoy myself, worrying about her the whole time. You go on without me. I'd better stay here to distract her."

◇◇◇◇◇

Mustafa called four taxis to take the Germans, the Lobsters, and me to the performance. As I got into one of the cabs, Nazif ran up to the car and pressed a cell phone into my hand. "Here. It is mine," he whispered. "You can use the camera app. If you see anything important, take a picture. And please. Be careful."

"I will," I said. "And thanks," I added, touched by his concern for me.

He closed the taxi door, and I felt a tugging sensation inside me as I watched him go back inside the hotel. I wished he were coming with me. I was starting to get used to the idea that we were solving this mystery together. I felt like I was off to a climbing wall to use the auto belay, when it was always more fun to belay with a partner.

We arrived about fifteen minutes later at the Galata Mevlevi Lodge, a large performance hall where the dancers would do their *sema* ceremony. I set my plan into motion almost immediately, complaining of a stomachache. "Too much hummus," I apologized.

"Oh, honey." Maeve looked alarmed. "We should get you right back to the hotel."

"No, I'll be okay. But if I leave partway through, I'll just be in the restroom."

The hall was almost full now, with crowds seated in a circle, about five chairs deep, around the perimeter of the room. The lights dimmed, and a quintet of musicians appeared beneath the spotlight and began to play. I recognized the oud, and a hand drum, but I'd never seen what looked kind of like a flute or the other stringed instrument before. The music was strange to my ears and hard to follow, like a tangle of musical threads, winding and unwinding. Like the different paths to finding the seahorse urn. Lazar. Vasil. Sage. Uncle Berk. Maybe Riza, too, and the captain of the *Anilar*. All of them connected to the urn. An urn I was sure my uncle had died for.

The five dancers—the Mevlevi dervishes—walked slowly toward the center of the floor, arms crossed in front of them. They were dressed in long black robes and wore tall brown hats on their heads; it almost looked like a funeral procession. "They're supposed to be from the grave," whispered Maeve, her eyes wide. "The hats represent tombstones."

"Guess this is someone's idea of fun," Milton muttered grimly. "But not mine."

Maeve shot him a look. "This is a spiritual ceremony, not a Broadway show. It's a meditation. They go into a trance and purify their souls."

The dancers walked in tighter circles, stopping every few steps to bow deeply. Then they removed their robes, revealing white jackets and long white skirts. Slowly they stepped into the circle again, crossed their arms in front of their chests, closed their eyes, tipped their heads to one side, and began to pivot.

I knew it was time to feign illness and get to the Lycian Society building while it was still open. But I was transfixed by the dervishes. Their arms unfolded and extended, until each man had one hand raised, palm up, and the other extended to the side, palm down. Their faces were serene, emotionless, even as the music sped up and their whirling intensified. They seemed to carve the air with the scoops of their hands and the flare of their white skirts. Their heads were tilted, their eyes still closed, as if resting on a pillow.

I brushed aside a tear, the sudden appearance of which surprised me. This was no time for emotions to get in my way. And then, through the blur of the spinning white skirts, I glimpsed a familiar face across the room. Nazif! He had come after all!

He was standing by the back wall, not far from the main door, and clearly looking for me.

I clutched my stomach and stood up, muttering an apology to Milton and Maeve, who gave me a sympathetic look. I threaded my way through the audience, ignoring the annoyed stares, and ran out into the early evening light. A flock of pigeons scattered.

Nazif joined me a moment later on the steps of the Mevlevi Lodge.

"Wow. You actually came?" I said. "I mean, your dad let you go?"

"The hotel was quiet," he said. "I suggested I come help everyone get taxis and return safely to the hotel afterward. My father thought that was an excellent idea. What did you think of the *sema*?"

"I loved it," I said. "I have no idea how they do that without getting dizzy! And they look so peaceful. I can't believe they're going to keep that up for almost an hour! I wish I could stay and watch the whole thing."

"You still could," he said.

"No. You know I have to get this done. But if we solve this mystery? I'll come back here and see the whole thing."

"I'll take you," he said.

"Oh." I smiled. "Thanks."

"I thought of another plan," he went on. "We go in together. I am still in uniform. This will leave no room for doubt that we come from a hotel."

"Good plan," I said, giving him a thumbs-up. "Let's go."

Maybe I only imagined the electrical current between us. *Focus!*

As we sprinted down the steps and ran down the street, I felt a twinge deep inside me, like the taut string of an oud, reminding me that at this very moment, I was deceiving the Lobsters, whom I'd blatantly lied to in order to get away. And I'd lied to Mom, too, acting exactly like she thought I would act and giving her no reason to trust me.

But this situation was different. We'd come all this way to help Aunt Jackie, and that's exactly what I was doing.

32

Two blocks from the performance hall, Nazif and I stood before the Lycian Society headquarters, the narrow, gray stone building I'd seen on the computer screen. On the left side loomed a taller and more modern office building. On the right side there was a tiny, dark alley, and then another modern building with a restaurant on the ground floor and tables out on the sidewalk. A smiling host approached us with menus, but we shook our heads and waved him away.

"This is not the kind of restaurant I would take you to anyway," Nazif said. "It is touristy, this place. I would take you for a more traditional meal."

Was he asking me out? Would we go to a restaurant sometime, like a couple?

No swooning! "I think we're fine to go in," I said, stepping forward toward the front steps. "It's an office building. Nothing's going to happen to us here," I added when Nazif hesitated.

We went up the sagging stone steps and tried the door. It was locked. The wrought-iron gates barricading the heavy wooden doors were as impenetrable as a fortress, even though it was just after five o'clock. I took a deep breath and pressed the buzzer. I could hear it reverberating somewhere inside. I pressed it again, twice, but no one buzzed us in or came to the door.

"It's just after five," I said, checking my watch. "I guess they already closed for the day."

Nazif frowned. "In Turkey, most businesses are open until six or seven. This is strange. Maybe we must find a way to come tomorrow and try again, earlier."

"But we're here *now,*" I pointed out. "And I came up with this whole complicated way to get to this neighborhood tonight. I can't pull it off two days in a row." I surveyed the building. "There must be some way to get in."

Nazif looked alarmed. "But the building is closed."

"To some people, yes, you could say that." I recognized the feeling coming over me that I sometimes got when I shoplifted. It started with a buzz and a tingle, as if my nerves were waking up. It was like being in a gray space, somewhere between being seen and not seen, kind of like a ghost. And once I started, and the buzz got going, it was hard to stop.

I went back down the steps and walked to the narrow alley on the right-hand side of the building. Nazif shadowed me; I could hear the quietly reassuring *tick-tick-tick* of his shoes on the cobblestones. I gasped as a huge rat scuttled by, and quickened my steps. Looking up, I could see windows caked with grime going all the way up to the top. Near the back of the building, three stories up, were four windows covered in black paper. "Hey, look!" I said, pointing. "That one's open!" One of the blacked-out windows was cracked open. A rusting fire escape led to it. If I could jump high enough and crawl onto it, I might be able to get inside.

"I don't know about this," said Nazif, glancing back toward the street.

"I can do it," I insisted, jumping for the fire escape and missing. Repeatedly. Nazif tried, too, but he wasn't much taller than me.

Then I realized that the walls of the two buildings on either side of me were made of brick. Brick was basically a rock. When I thought about it, I wasn't in an alley, but in a canyon. I pushed my back against the wall of the neighboring building and put my feet on the façade of the Lycian Society, and began to inch my way up while Nazif watched in awe. I scraped my back on something but ignored the sting and pressed on.

When I got close to the edge of the fire escape, I leaped for it, just barely grabbing on to the iron railing. The whole structure creaked ominously. I held my breath, tested my weight, and then continued onward and upward, toward the open window. *Push up. Pull up. Trust your feet.*

"Zan! Are you all right?" Nazif called anxiously.

"I'm good!" I turned my attention to the window. The glass was covered with black paper, but where it was cracked open a few inches, I could see a metal window screen behind it. If I could raise the window higher, maybe I could see inside through the mesh screen. Grunting, I tried to pull it open some more, pushing up, in, out—and finally managed to move it up six inches. That was as far as it would raise, evidently hitting some kind of security lock from inside. But it was enough for me. I lowered my head to peer through the widened section of window screen that I'd exposed. And I nearly gagged.

It smelled *so bad,* like toxic paints and chemicals. Now I understood why the window was open: someone must have cracked it to try to let out some of the noxious fumes.

The room was dim, since most of the windows were covered with dark paper, but a couple had been left uncovered, and they let in just enough light for me to see inside. It appeared to be some sort of workshop or artist's studio. I could see wooden drying racks stacked with paper, almost like in the art room at my high school. There were a couple of drafting tables, cardboard boxes flattened and folded, and wooden storage crates. Floor-to-ceiling industrial shelves were filled with ceramic busts, mosaic tiles, pottery, rugs, and, just below the window a low shelf with what looked like loose manuscript pages covered with calligraphy and intricate, colorful illustrations. The shelves were almost like you'd see in a shop, though the contents were more of a jumble than an attractive display.

I blinked slowly, trying to understand what I was seeing. I noticed the window screen had a slight tear near the bottom. I poked it. It ripped a bit more. Then I took up a corner and yanked it, pulling it out of the frame on the bottom. Now the glass was cracked just high enough, and the window screen ripped almost long enough, so that I could just manage to squeeze inside. If I could just rip out a few more inches of screen from the bottom, I'd be in.

I started working at the screen again until the fire escape rattled behind me. It was Nazif. He'd managed to climb up the walls, and now was crawling across the iron grate platform to join me.

"There are rats in the alley," he said, making a face. "From the restaurant next door, probably."

"Ew. But hey. Look inside," I said, shifting so he could see under the torn part of the screen.

Nazif ducked his head and looked through the screen. He whistled under his breath.

I pointed to a small statue on a table. It was half dull gold and half bright gold, with a paintbrush sitting beside it. A smaller bust next to it looked to be made of some kind of oxidized metal—except for the neck, which appeared to be plaster. "That kind of reminds me of the figurines Sage put in my bag. Could all these things be replicas of ancient artifacts that someone is trying to make look real?"

"Or ancient artifacts being made to look fake?" Nazif countered. "You see those crates? And those black boxes and the plastic cases?" He pointed all these things out to me. "This is exactly the kind of packaging that Lazar brought to that meeting. The urn was in a clear box just like that one."

I stared at him. "Wait a second. Didn't you tell me the other day that Lazar's clients were going to use disguised packaging for anything they purchased?"

"Yes."

"So they could take stolen goods across borders more easily." My brain was practically humming now as I made the connections.

"Along with fake authentication papers certifying the real artifacts as replicas," said Nazif, his eyes shining.

"Right. Fake papers like the ones my uncle was commissioned to write. And I bet Lazar uses this workshop to prepare shipments for his Onyx-level clients." I stared intently through the window, trying to make sense of what was in the room. Toward the back, there were shelves filled to bursting with gold-colored animal figures, bowls, and some familiar-looking shapes. Small, human shapes. I couldn't hold myself back any longer.

"What are you doing?" cried Nazif, wide-eyed, as I started pulling at the broken window screen. "You should not be doing that!"

"I have to go in," I said, tugging the screen harder. "I have to see what's on that shelf over there." I worked at the frayed screen, pulling as hard as I could.

"What if an alarm goes off?" There was mounting panic in Nazif's usually calm and measured voice.

"Then we run for it," I said. I put my hoodie up over my head and pointed to Nazif's bellboy cap. "Pull your hat down lower over your face just in case there's a security camera somewhere."

His eyes widened, but when I gestured again for him to pull the brim lower, he did.

I finally managed to tear the screen enough so that I could push on it, slide beneath the cracked-open glass window, and get inside the room. But first I picked up a twig that had fallen from a tree and landed on the fire escape, and threw it in. "No motion detector," I said. "Are you coming?"

Nazif hesitated, then pushed at the screen. "I'm too big to slide under this without tearing it more," he said. "I will wait out here and keep watch. Do not turn on the lights."

"I won't," I promised. I held the screen aside and squeezed myself through the window, then ran to the shelf with the gold bowls and figurines. I picked up a bowl, then some of the golden animals. They weighed next to nothing. They were made of plaster. Fakes.

Then my breath caught in my throat. Near the back of the shelf were about twenty gold figurines. There was also a photo printout next to them, showing pictures of figurines from all different angles. "Look at these, Nazif!" I breathed, bringing two figurines to the window to show him. "They look exactly like the ones Sage bought on the cruise. But those were real, and these are obvious forgeries. Feel them. They're so lightweight."

Nazif touched one gingerly, then looked at his hand as if it had been burned.

I picked at the paint on one of the animals; it flecked off. "Gold-painted," I said. "At a glance they look real, though. I bet if someone had a box of these, and you mixed one or two real ones in—and you had papers certifying they were souvenirs—you could get past a security checkpoint."

Nazif nodded. "Carrying things out in the open might attract less attention," he said, looking nervously over his shoulder. "Do you think we can go now?"

"Just a sec. I want to take one to show someone at the embassy," I said, handing him a figurine. "Can you put it in your pocket?"

"What? No! We can't take this. It's stealing!"

"It's not stealing. It's collecting evidence."

"We're not professionals. It's illegal. And we are breaking the law just being here." Nazif's voice broke. "Use the camera instead to document anything you think is suspicious. And hurry."

"We're fine," I assured him. "No alarms went off. I'm sure

no one saw us come up here." I took out his cell phone, which was still in my pants pocket, and walked around the room, snapping pictures. Nazif watched me work, with an expression I couldn't read. When I'd photographed all I could and handed him back his phone, he took it wordlessly.

I felt exhilarated, filled with boundless energy, as I slipped out the window and we made our way down the fire escape.

But by the time we got back to the performance hall for the very end of the *sema,* I felt deflated. Nazif had said little on the way back. Maybe he'd seen a side of me that was even less attractive than my vitiligo: my talent for breaking the law.

He sat next to me in the taxi on the way back to the hotel, his knee touching mine. Or mine touching his—I wasn't sure how they'd come together. I wanted, with every fiber of my being, to lean against him, to rest my head on his shoulder. But he sat carefully, as if aware of every inch of his body and trying not to cross an invisible boundary. "Hey," he finally whispered while the Germans in the taxi talked.

"Yeah?" I whispered back. I wanted him to tell me I'd been brave to find Lazar's workshop and get those pictures. But his face was serious. "I am wondering if you are too quick not to trust Inspector Lale," he said. "When we get back to the hotel, maybe you should contact her again. Tell her what we found."

I pulled away from him and gave him a long look. "Are you serious? She said she'd get undercover police in our neighborhood, and she hasn't. I'm being stalked and harassed. Lazar was able to lure me to the Grand Bazaar without any interference. How has she helped me?"

"Maybe she has undercover police in the area and we just do not know," he said. "If you can trust her, and show her these pictures, she can take over the case right away. I think you are in too much danger to keep quiet any longer. What if there were hidden cameras in that workshop and Lazar finds out you were inside?"

My stomach lurched. He had a point. I'd thought my hoodie

would disguise me in case the staff at the Lycian Society reviewed the security tapes. But Lazar had probably figured out that I was a girl who wore hoodies a lot. And part of me agreed with Nazif that I should just trust Inspector Lale. But I'd been around too many liars in my life. Maybe that was why I assumed the worst about her.

No. I would stick to my plan. Once I had solid evidence on Lazar and his organization, I could go to the embassy with it and bypass her completely.

And if all my efforts to find Sage were unsuccessful, at least I would have found a way to nab Lazar without having to drag Sage into it, too.

33

The next morning, I woke up with a cold, hollow feeling. For a moment I thought I might be getting sick. But then I remembered the fire escape, and the secret workshop Nazif and I had discovered and broken into last night. And I remembered Nazif's face in the taxi, the way our conversation had dissolved into an awkward silence. The way he'd so quickly said good night and hurried home with his father. I buried my head under the pillow and groaned. Nazif hadn't looked at me with awe when I tore the window screen and went inside the building; he'd looked scared and uncomfortable. I'd dipped back into my old life—breaking and entering, ignoring the law—and even though it was for good reason, it didn't sit right with me anymore.

But the day wasn't going to magically disappear if I stayed in bed, and neither would my problems. I got up, showered, dressed, put on my makeup, and slunk downstairs, dreading the moment I'd run into Nazif. I vowed to push him out of my mind and focus only on getting to the next step of my plan: going to the American embassy to show someone the photo evidence I'd taken.

To my surprise, escaping the hotel wasn't so hard this time. Apparently I'd scored points with Mom by showing the Lobsters a good time the day before. As we prepared breakfast for the guests, she asked me to pick up some things for the party at the Arasta Bazaar. "Some nuts, fruit, Turkish delight, whatever you think sounds good to set out in the candy dishes," she said, handing me cash and a list. "And you can go alone," she added. "Since it's right down the street."

"Really?" I glowed a little. It felt good to be earning back her trust. Although I felt a twinge of guilt, too, knowing what I'd pulled off at the Lycian Society, all because of a lie. And now I was about to lie again. The moment I got outside, I was going to hail a cab and race to the embassy with Nazif's cell phone and the pictures I'd taken.

"Yes, really." Mom managed a small smile. "Though you should probably go before I change my mind. Oh. Here." She reached over to a table and handed me a stack of papers and some duct tape. "I distracted Jackie last night by making flyers for the party. Why don't you post a few of these along the way, and leave some at neighborhood shops."

I glanced at the flyers ("Open House at the Mavi! Appetizers! Music! Authentic Turkish Karagöz Puppet Show!"). I put them in my backpack along with the list and the money, grateful to have an errand that would take even more time and help explain what was going to be an unusually long absence.

Truthfully, I was scared to go outside alone and risk being accosted by Lazar or Vasil. But I was sure I couldn't get Nazif to go with me to the embassy. Even if his dad let him out, he probably didn't want to be around me anymore, now that he'd seen my true colors.

I finally had to confront him, though, because I needed to take his cell phone with me. That's where all the pictures were.

Nazif was at the front desk, sorting the mail. I could see his cell phone on the desk beside him. Part of me just wanted to snatch it and run off to avoid seeing the look on his face.

I approached slowly, not sure what to say. Act cheerful, as if nothing had happened? Or tell him what I was really thinking, which was this: the way Nazif had acted around me last night made me think I didn't want to break into anything, anywhere, ever again. Even if it were for good reason.

Hearing me, or sensing me, Nazif looked up. "You have a message," he said.

"*Merhaba* to you, too," I said, going for the cheerful approach. "I thought you liked to start with hello."

"Sorry. *Merhaba,*" he said. "A call was left for you, on voice mail."

I was so relieved that he wasn't ignoring me or treating me coldly that it took me a minute to process what he was saying.

"From whom?"

"A girl," he said.

"I bet it's another setup from Lazar. No way am I falling for it this time," I said.

"This seems different," said Nazif. "She really sounds like an American girl. You must come and listen."

I joined him behind the front desk. Nazif dialed into voice mail on the phone and handed me the receiver. For a moment, all I heard was Nazif's breathing, so close to me; I swore I could hear his heart beating. Or was it mine? It took all my powers of concentration to focus on the voice mail.

"Zan, it's me," said the voice.

I gripped the phone. It was unmistakably Sage's voice. Of course, she'd had my aunt's businesss card. Why had she waited so long to call me? Had she been too deeply in hiding to risk making that connection? If insider police like Inspector Lale were working for Lazar's side, they might have even wiretapped the phone. So if she was taking the chance to call me now, she must be really desperate.

"We have to talk. I'm at Cajagoogoo. Meet me there at two o'clock today. Bring the package. Come alone." Her voice sounded rushed, and scared. There was a weird echo in the background, and something that made me think of water spraying.

I replayed the message three more times.

"Is it Sage?" Nazif asked.

"It's definitely her voice," I said. "I have to meet her. Before I talk to anyone at the embassy about those pictures, I have to get her story and see if there's any chance she has the urn. Cajagoogoo. Where is that?"

Nazif frowned. "I do not know this place. It does not even sound Turkish." He Googled it on the computer and shook his head. "Nothing comes up."

"Um, by the way," I said, as he ran a new search. "Last night, when I broke into the workshop, I didn't want you to think that I—"

"You did what you had to do," said Nazif, not taking his eyes off the computer.

"But you think it was wrong."

"Honestly? I think you should have called Inspector Lale as soon as you saw what was inside the room. I think you should not have gone in. But." He shrugged. "It is done."

I looked down. "I want you to know something. I'm not really in the habit of doing stuff like that. Anymore. I mean—"

"Zan!" Mom strode into the lobby. "Why are you still hanging around here? We need those ingredients."

"While you are gone, I will keep researching this," Nazif whispered, still not looking at me.

"Thank you," I said. My face burned as I left the hotel. Nazif seemed to like me enough to help me solve my problem, but the spark I'd felt between us was gone. And that was my fault.

I quickly bought the food for Mom at the Arasta Bazaar, then considered going straight to the embassy. But I'd forgotten to take Nazif's phone; the voice mail from Sage had thrown off my plan. I could go to the embassy without the phone and just tell them what I'd seen. But I couldn't shake the feeling that I was being watched. So I hurried back to the hotel with bags full of figs and apricots and other ingredients, pausing every few feet to hastily tape a flyer to fences, poles, and building sides. I swear I didn't breathe until I was back in the hotel lobby.

When I got back, there were more eyes staring at me in the hotel lobby. But these at least were friendly and familiar. Nils and Ingrid, and Fiona and Alice!

They all hugged me and exclaimed over me, as if we were old friends—which I guess, in a weird way, we were. And even though only several days had passed since our cruise, so much had happened since then. The Turkish Riviera felt far, far away.

"What are you all doing here?" I asked, handing my mom the bags of food. "Are you staying at the Mavi Konak now?"

"Yes! Milton and Maeve raved about this place," said Fiona. "Said it was full of historic charm, good customer service . . . and a fun activities coordinator." She winked at me.

"And the Swissotel has bedbugs. Awful." Alice made a face. "They said the problem was contained, but it wasn't—it's in all the rooms. Thank goodness your aunt had enough space for us all and Lycian Tours could honor our transfer and refund the hotel rate difference."

"We hear there will be quite a party tomorrow night," added Nils.

I was dying to ask Nazif if he had figured out what or where Cajagoogoo was. But he was busy with the Geezers, and Mustafa was watching him closely.

Mustafa was a worse taskmaster than my mom. When he wasn't giving his son orders, he would brush lint off Nazif's shirt, or tell him to tuck in his shirttail, or fix his hair, or stand up straighter. Every critical comment from his dad just seemed to chip away at Nazif. By midday, he was slouching so much he was the shape of a question mark. It was strange to see all this, how different they were up close. From across the rooftop, I'd thought they were a totally together family. Now

I just wanted to give Nazif a huge hug. But he probably didn't want to be hugged by someone like me.

When Mustafa finally went out for a break, Nazif rushed over to me.

"Cağaloğlu," he said, showing me a piece of paper where he'd written out the word. "This is a neighborhood near the Grand Bazaar. I think it is where you will find your friend."

"I can't just wander around a whole neighborhood looking for her, can I?"

He turned the paper over and showed me a list of more names. "These are all businesses in the neighborhood that also use the name Cağaloğlu," he said. "Do any of these sound like a place where Sage would go?"

I studied the list of restaurants, clothing boutiques, jewelery stores, and cafés. Then, near the bottom, Cağaloğlu Hammam caught my eye.

"A hammam!" I exclaimed. "Now I remember she mentioned there was a hammam near the Grand Bazaar that she loved. And I thought I heard water on the voice mail message."

"I can understand why she would hide there," said Nazif. "The men's and women's quarters are separate. Lazar and Vasil cannot enter the women's side."

"But they could send a female to get her, couldn't they? I mean, if they can find someone to write a note that sounds like Sage, I'm sure they could find someone to go look for her in a bathhouse."

"Of course," said Nazif. "This is why you must go there as soon as possible."

"I will," I said. "Oh, and I'm going to do it without breaking and entering this time. I know how I can get in the front door this very afternoon."

Nazif smiled, the warmth returning to his face and filling me up as well.

I bounded up the stairs to the roof, where Mom was oiling furniture in preparation for tomorrow night's party. She had plenty of company. Fiona and Alice were pruning the roses and the geraniums. Ingrid was sweeping, and Maeve was polishing a samovar. Milton and Nils were setting up a makeshift wire fence around the perimeter of the roof, unrolling the wire and nailing it to stakes. And Aunt Jackie was sitting on a sofa, working on spreadsheets on her iPad.

"Oh my God, you guys," I said. "You do realize you're not on a boat anymore, don't you? The city awaits. Adventure beckons." I wished I could remember the Freya Stark quote about the clicking lock.

Everyone stared at me with blank expressions.

"I mean, should we all go somewhere? Do something?" I persisted.

"We have explored, sweetie. And I'm knackered," said Maeve. "All that shopping yesterday and the sightseeing this morning did me in. I need to recover."

"And we had quite a tour already today," said Ingrid. "Erdem Tabak took us personally around the best of Istanbul."

"Where'd you go?" Mom asked.

"We all met at the Galata Tower, then went on a Bosphorus cruise," Ingrid replied. "After that, Taksim Square. Oh, and we even saw the Lycian Society headquarters, which happened to be nearby."

I chilled at the mention of the Lycian Society. I now thought of the place as a crime scene—partly because of the workshop I'd seen there, partly because of my own actions last night.

New worries took root in my mind. What if someone had reported seeing two kids on the fire escape last night, maybe someone from the restaurant next door? What if I'd left behind my footprints in the gold dust, or my fingerprints on the windowsill? The police could be called. Legitimate police might investigate the break-in and find the workshop in the process— so that was good—but if any evidence got traced back to me,

I could get in serious trouble. I already had a rap sheet in Turkey. And if corrupt police answered a call about a suspected break-in? They would tip off Lazar and he'd be after me in a heartbeat. Either way, I was screwed.

I eyed Nazif's rooftop longingly. I wanted to break down that makeshift fence, leap to his roof, hide myself in his family's lush grape arbor and never come out again.

"Anyway, we got here, and we thought we'd help your mother," chirped Alice. "Kitsie has so much to do with this party, and your aunt was so generous booking us into these rooms at a discount. Helping out is the least we can do. Though I wish you'd let me help cook. I'm pretty handy in the kitchen."

Mom smiled mysteriously. "Oh, we're covered on the food," she said. "Jackie's going to make a special dish, and the rest we're having catered." She passed me a cardboard box. "Zan, will you please look through this party box of your aunt's and see if there are any decorations?"

I opened the box and started pulling out strands of little white lanterns, thinking frantically about how I had to get to that hammam to see Sage. I was so nervous imagining how the police or Lazar might come haul me out of here at any moment that I could hardly work my fingers. I tried to untangle a strand of lights and ended up only making it worse.

Mom sank into a chair. "My God. I don't know when I've felt so exhausted."

I spun around eagerly. Maybe a little too eagerly. "Yeah, you look tired," I agreed. "Really tired."

"In what way? Like, older?" She patted her face. "That's not good. The local press is coming to the party. We're going to be putting pictures up on the website, too."

"You just look like you could use a good night's sleep. Or a spa day."

"Oh, a spa day." She smiled wistfully. "Doesn't *that* sound nice."

"I know of a spa," I said carefully. "A Turkish hammam. It's near the Grand Bazaar. Just a short taxi ride away. We could *all* go. As a treat to your volunteers," I added, gesturing to the ladies.

Mom got that glint in her eyes. "Yes. We could. What a lovely idea. And we'd have just enough time to do it before my meeting with the caterer."

◇◇◇◇◇

It was raining when we got into the taxi, and pouring by the time we pulled up in front of the hammam. Water raced down the streets, beat down on us, and rushed into grates along the sidewalks. I followed Mom and the women from the Blue Voyage, who giggled and whispered as they filed into the stone stairwell.

All the women had come except for Aunt Jackie; her doctor had advised against steam baths. She didn't sound too upset about staying behind. I had a feeling she was going to pick up the phone and call Inspector Lale, and I couldn't afford an untimely visit from the police wrecking my plans. So I'd crept under the front desk and unplugged the land line, and then—feeling sick to my stomach about it—I'd taken Aunt Jackie's cell phone out of her purse, powered it down, and hid it in a potted plant. I just needed to buy myself some time, and it was the only way I could be sure I would get it.

In the taxi, I felt relieved to be zooming away from the hotel. Even though I'd taken nothing but pictures, I knew I'd committed a crime by entering the Lycian Society building after hours. I wanted to deal with embassy officials, not the police. But Lazar might come looking for me, if I'd been caught and identified on a hidden camera. The idea tied my stomach in knots. If Lazar suspected that I knew too much, he'd stop at nothing to silence me.

I hurried after the other women, down the narrow stairwell that led from the sidewalk entrance into the bowels of the Cağaloğlu Hammam. The place smelled like soap. Old photos lined the walls by the doorway, showing various Turkish celebrities smiling. I also saw a framed sign from an American publication declaring it "One of 1000 Places to Visit Before You Die."

To visit *before* you die? *How long* before? I suddenly pictured Lazar and Vasil ignoring the rules about the women-only entrance and showing up, brandishing daggers and guns.

I tried to concentrate on the fact that I was now mere steps away from Sage, and possibly the Karun Treasure urn. I was so close to getting all the answers I needed.

We came to a tiny foyer at the bottom of the stairs, where Mom slapped her credit card down on the check-in counter and paid for everyone. I watched the attendant at the front desk carefully as, between drags on a cigarette in a long holder, she gave us each a locker key, a towel, a washcloth, slippers, and a flimsy plaid wrap, which she explained was called a *peştemal*. The *peştemal* was to be used for covering ourselves as we walked from the changing rooms into the bathhouse. I looked at it doubtfully, knowing it would never cover all of my white spots. Even though Nazif had accepted my face the way it was, none of the hotel guests had seen me in my true skin.

Scared of what I was getting myself into, I started to tune out the attendant's instructions. I watched her speak, but I couldn't hear what she was saying. Her mane of dark hair was pulled back in a messy ponytail, and the black kohl ringing her eyes was running from all the moisture in the room. I checked my own face in a mirror on the wall, wondering how soon my makeup would melt. The foyer itself was so warm it felt kind of like a sauna.

"So this is a communal bath?" I asked when she was done talking. I'd been expecting private steam rooms. And if this place was so communal, where would I talk with Sage?

"Yes," she said, opening a door so we could see the women's spa. Steam escaped from the door as we all peered inside. It was a huge round room with a high, domed ceiling and small windows way up by the top of the dome. There was no actual bathtub, not even showers. The floors and walls were marbled, white streaked with black and gray, and faucets were spaced out every few feet all around the room. A huge stone slab in the shape of an octagon took up the center of the floor. On it, bath attendants were vigorously scrubbing down two women, who were lying on their stomachs, naked. I felt self-conscious, but I took a second glance at the bathers, and both women were plump, with black hair. Sage wasn't in the room.

"This ought to be an adventure," said Fiona, doubtfully.

I backed away. I was so not doing this. I would let everyone else go in, then I'd double back and ask the attendant if she knew where I could find Sage.

I hung back as the ladies disappeared into the changing rooms. Then it was just Mom and me standing there. "You don't want to do this," she guessed.

"Not really," I admitted. I had more pressing business. And I wasn't ready to expose my body to the world. Sure, Sage and Nazif had been cool with it. But showing my skin to all the hotel guests, to strangers, and being stared at . . . whispered about . . . discussed behind my back? No thanks.

"It might be fun," said Mom. "I'd hate to have you miss out on an awesome life experience. And all the ladies will wonder what happened to you."

I peered inside the spa again. The bath attendants were exfoliating the naked bathers. What if they rubbed all my skin off? What if I came out blotchier than ever, my countries and islands turning into vast continents and drifting all over my body? What if I came out bone white, without a trace of pigment? Dr. Shaw had assured me that pigment couldn't actually be rubbed off—the disorder didn't work that way—but I wasn't convinced.

"I'll say I got my period. They'll leave me alone. Really. I'm fine with skipping this."

My mom looked at me. Then she did a bizarre thing. She put both hands on my shoulders, and brought her face closer to mine. "It's okay," she said. "You don't have to go."

I smiled, relieved. "Really?"

"Really. I get it. This isn't your thing."

"Thank you. I'll just sit out in the foyer. I saw some magazines."

Mom disappeared into the steamy corridor, and I ran back out to find the attendant. She was perched on a stool, flipping through a tabloid, still smoking. "I'm looking for my friend Sage Powell," I said. "Is she staying here?"

The attendant looked up at me. "I have a question for you," she said, in a husky, thickly accented voice. Tendrils of smoke writhed around her. "Who is the passionate nomad?"

I thought a moment while I coughed. Sage was a passionate nomad. But if this was a security test to screen me, there had to be a better answer. "Freya Stark?"

The attendant closed the magazine and stood up. "Follow me."

34

I followed her back into the corridor, where we pushed through a thick wall of steam. We went past the bathhouse and all the way to the end, where the corridor forked. Veering left, we walked through an enclosed garden. We passed through another door, and another, then made our way down a steep staircase. I tried to remember where I was going so that I could find my way back; this place was even more confusing and labyrinthine than the Grand Bazaar.

Finally, the attendant opened a door to a small room that looked like an office, with a desk and a fan and a bookshelf. There were blankets on a couch in the corner. And lying on them, sleeping, was Sage.

The door clicked behind me. Sage and I were alone.

The room was moist, the walls beaded with dampness, and water dripped in the corner. I stared at her for a moment, unsure if I wanted to hug her or slap her. Here she was at last, the girl who'd nearly sent me to prison. Finally I just shook her leg gently. "Hey. Wake up."

She sat up with a jolt. "Zan! Oh my God. You have no idea how glad I am to see you. Do you have the package with you?"

I folded my arms in front of my chest. "As a matter of fact, no. Do you have the urn?"

"Wait. What? You don't have the gold figurines?"

"Kind of a long story," I said. "But I'm not going to tell you where those figurines ended up until you tell me about the urn."

She pressed her lips together. I took a step closer to her. "Here's the deal. My uncle might have lost his life over that urn. I know you know its true value. So tell me. Do you have it? Did you drop it on purpose and then go back for it on your own?"

A look of pain crossed her face. "I don't have the urn," she whispered.

I started pulling books off the bookshelf, yanking out desk drawers, looking under the makeshift bed.

"You have to believe me, Zan. Your aunt's urn isn't here."

"It's not my aunt's urn. It's Turkey's urn. It's part of the Karun Treasure." I slammed an empty desk drawer closed. "And I know all about your business. I've met your friend Lazar."

"Lazar! He came after you? Oh, God. That was my fear. That's why I stayed away from the hotel. Look, I'm broke. I need to sell those figurines. I know someone who will buy them. If you don't have them, where did they go?"

I gave her a long look. All this time I'd held on to the hope that Sage wasn't an evil person, but hearing that she wanted to sell the figurines, and that she'd used me to transport them, pissed me off— even if she *was* broke. Now was the moment of truth. "First, tell me about the urn," I said, my voice icy.

"Sit. Calm down." Sage sank back onto the couch, patting the seat next to her.

I sat down, gingerly, as far from her as I could.

"Okay. I did go back on my own to look for the urn after I dropped it," she admitted. "But not for the reasons you think. I was supposed to get it for Lazar, after confirming his suspicion that your aunt was taking it on the cruise your uncle was supposed to be on. For weeks Lazar had been sending maids and cooks into the Mavi Konak hotel to spy, and that's how he knew."

Maids and cooks as spies. No wonder there was high staff turnover at my aunt's hotel!

"He suspected it was an artifact your uncle had in his possession for a consulting job and had never returned to Lazar," she went on.

Nazif and I had been right that Sage was commissioned to retrieve the urn. "So when you tripped and fell, did you plan that?" I asked.

Sage nodded. "After I dropped the urn, I memorized where it landed. I knew it was at the base of that boat-shaped precipice. While you were climbing up that cliff wall, I picked it up and hid it in a crevice between some boulders on that big pile. I marked the boulders with my hair clip so I could find it later. When I went back, though, the urn was gone."

She looked down at her lap. "At first I just wanted to get out of that job with Lazar. I wanted the urn to literally disappear off the face of the earth. I was going to tell Lazar someone else dropped it and it vanished. I thought losing the urn this way was the perfect solution to my problem. But then I freaked out. I knew Lazar would kill me. That's why I went into hiding."

"Didn't it occur to you just to hand in the urn to the police and turn in Lazar right away?" I said. "There were tons of police officers crawling all over the coast. Any one of them would have been happy to take the urn off your hands. Or you could have just told us what was going on. I'm sure my aunt would have helped you to do the right thing."

"I thought of all that. Believe me. But I was too scared. Some police work as insiders, with Lazar's group. I wasn't sure who to trust. And I have an expired visa. I thought I'd be in all kinds of trouble."

"So you want out of the smuggling business, but you still want to sell those figurines?"

"It's going to be my last deal," she insisted. "Just enough to pay someone to help me get out of the country without passport control giving me hassle." She reached out and clutched my arm, a wild look in her eyes. "Where are they? If I can't sell them to my buyer in the Grand Bazaar, I can't get anywhere. I'm serious."

"I got detained at the Dalaman Airport when they were found in my bag," I said. "The police confiscated them and interrogated me and my family."

Her eyes filled with tears. "Confiscated! Interrogated! Crap."

"Did you honestly think I wouldn't get caught?"

"I did," she said. "I wrapped them well and put them way down in the bottom of your bag. And I figured you had your aunt with you, and having been married to an archaeologist, she'd know what to do or how to get you out of trouble fast if your bag was searched. I thought it wouldn't be a big deal."

"Well, it *was* a big deal," I said. "It was actually a huge pain to get out of there, and really stressful for my aunt—she ended up in the hospital. And I could have gone to prison."

"What?"

"I have a record of shoplifting. I am, actually, a suspicious person."

Sage stared at me, her mouth open.

"Hi, my name's Zan, and I'm a former shoplifter. Google me sometime. I went viral."

Sage shook her head. "I had no idea. But why does that matter here?"

"The police weren't going to let me off easy for having those artifacts on me. I think they questioned me harder and kept us longer because of my record back home."

"But you got out."

"I got *lucky.*" Suddenly I thought of Inspector Lale, and Nazif's suggestion that I might consider trusting her after all. Maybe he was right. I could still be back in that holding cell if it weren't for her.

"And you know what?" I went on. "I'm extra lucky because even without my criminal record back home, if those figurines had been authenticated as real—which they really are—then I would have gone to prison for sure. Did you even think of all that when you put them in my bag?"

Sage sighed and buried her face in her hands for a moment. Then she looked up with a pained expression. "Honestly, I had no idea you would have so much trouble. I bought the figurines with Lazar's money and was supposed to give them to him. I didn't expect him and his partner Vasil to show up on the *Anilar*. They weren't on the boat the whole time. I was supposed to deliver them to Riza, and he would give them to Lazar. It all got so complicated, so fast, especially when the urn came into the picture and Lazar asked me to get it."

"Riza? He's in on this?" So that's why that hot first mate had been interested in Sage and not me. He already knew her. But my flash of jealousy faded almost instantly. Who cared how hot the guy was? He was an antiquities smuggler, too.

Sage nodded. "He kind of got me into this mess in the first place."

"Okay. Go on. Lazar showed up on the Clarksons' boat?"

"Right. I don't know why. But I realized I wanted to get away from all of this. Seeing your family, and you—I just missed my normal life so much. And I felt like everything I was doing was wrong."

Something inside me softened, remembering how I felt around Nazif, how I felt this powerful urge to be normal and honest and good.

Sage twisted her hands in her lap. "So I thought I'd sell the figurines out from under Lazar and get out of the whole business after that. I swam to the *Anilar,* the night you came with me, to tell Riza I didn't have the figurines. But he'd seen me buy them, through his binoculars, and he told Lazar and Vasil. That asshole." She shuddered. "That's what Vasil was demanding when he dropped us off at the boat. Not a tip. The figurines, and then the urn."

I remembered how harsh Vasil had sounded that night, and how rattled Sage had seemed.

"I got scared," she said. "I knew I had to get out when the police started closing in. So I put the figurines in your bag, thinking I'd get them from you later, sell them, and buy my way out of the country, away from Lazar."

"You don't just have an expired visa," I pointed out. "You have a fake name. What's that about, anyway?"

"Like I said. It's complicated."

"I understand complications," I said. "Better than you think. And I might be able to help you find a way out of all this. But maybe you'd better start from the beginning."

35

We left the room to get away from its stagnant air, and Sage led me up to a tiny enclosed garden. It was about the size of my hotel room, with only a bench and some potted plants, and surrounded by stone walls. Like a prison yard, I couldn't help thinking. But at least we could see the sky, and an overhang from the roof provided shelter from the rain. We dragged the bench beneath it and Sage began to speak while the rain poured down in front of us.

She started at the beginning—the very beginning. In ancient history: Hawthorne, Oregon.

"So my dad drank. A lot," Sage said in a small voice. "He hit my brother and me. I got out of the house as much as I could as soon as I was old enough. Worked part-time. Saved all my money. I had an uncle who was a lawyer, and with his help I got emancipated at seventeen. I moved in with him and my aunt until graduation. I changed my name. Sage was my late grandmother's name. It means 'wise,' and she always said I was. Plus, I like it. I never felt like an Amy. It's an ordinary name, and I've never felt very ordinary."

"Where'd Powell come from?" I asked.

"Powell's Bookstore, in Portland. I liked to read and to hang out there. Anyway, after graduation last year, I just wanted to get as far away as I could. I applied for every scholarship I could find. But I didn't have a great GPA because of everything I was dealing with at home, and working. The only place I got a partial scholarship was the Istanbul International School. I still had to pay some money, but at least it seemed possible to go there. So I went for it, even though I didn't have all the money yet. I figured I'd just find some under-the-table work. And it started out great. I fell in love with Turkey right away. My town was so ugly. My family history was so ugly. But everywhere I looked around me in Istanbul, I saw beauty."

I nodded. I'd had glimpses of that beauty. On the rooftop at night, staring out at the view and listening to the call to prayer. Glimpsing the silver slice of the Bosphorus River and the mansions on either side of it. Breathing in the intoxicating mix of smells at the Grand Bazaar. Watching the whirling dervishes. Dining outside at Orhan's house on the coast. Turkey had a surplus of beauty.

"I ran low on money sooner than I'd expected," she went on. "Turkey is expensive. Then I got conned."

"How?"

"I went out with this guy, and he came up short for the bill. He asked if I could loan him money, and he made me go to an ATM with him. Then he pulled a gun on me and made me empty out my account. I had to hand over everything to him—not that it was a lot, but it was all I had—and he ran off. I reported him to the police, but the money was gone forever, and I didn't even know his real name. I couldn't afford the next quarter of school. So I dropped out and found a job with this tourism company that was looking for native English speakers for videos to use in a phone app game. They needed actresses. I'd acted in high school, and I thought it'd be fun. And it was, for a while."

"Is that where you met Riza?"

She nodded. "We hit it off right away, and started going out. He found me a group apartment with some of the other foreigners who worked for the tourism company. Then he said there was a way I could make more money. He said he did some contract work for this guy Lazar and his team, easy money, and I could do the same."

"Who else works with Lazar?" I demanded.

"Lots of people. But the main players are Vasil, his right-hand man, and some insiders in the police force who give him confiscated artifacts or look the other way, for a fee. And he has a whole team of artisans he works with to disguise real objects as fakes so they can be sent to his clients or moved around the country without attracting attention. Repackaging artifacts so they can be smuggled is an art in itself. He works with pros and pays them well to keep quiet about it. And if they don't keep quiet?" She swallowed hard. "Every once in a while, someone ends up dead. And that keeps everyone quiet."

"Except you," I said softly. "Why are you telling me all this? You know I could turn you in. I could even get reward money for it. Interpol is behind all the efforts to crack this case."

"I know." She sighed. "Assuming I can't leave the country now, since I'm broke, I figure either you'll turn me in, or Lazar will find me eventually, or the police will track me down. I'm in checkmate. But someone should know the truth. I want it to be you."

I thought of the workshop Nazif and I had broken into the night before. "Is Lazar's lab in the Lycian Society headquarters?"

"That's only one of them. He has a few others around the country. That way he can cater to clients in all different regions."

"And are his clients in the Lycian Society? These Onyx people?"

"Some of them, yes. Riza told me. I'm not supposed to know their names. Lazar kept us low-level smugglers away from the clients, to protect them. Riza only knew more because Lazar was grooming him for a better position in the network."

"Where is Lazar getting all these artifacts from?" I asked.

"Museum warehouses and storage rooms, mostly, with the help of local looters that he contracts. They also get confiscated items stored at police departments. Insiders there pass them back to Lazar."

Thunder rumbled overhead. "And do you know if an Inspector Lale Demir is one of these insiders?"

"I honestly don't know who the contacts are," Sage admitted. "Riza doesn't either."

"So why do the clients want these illegal things?"

"The Onyx members are a weird group," she said. "They actually don't consider these artifacts Turkish."

"But that's crazy. The artifacts come from here."

Sage shrugged. "Some people want to own a piece of history. But a lot of them truly believe that the artifacts belonged to past civilizations, before the Turks were even here, so they belong to the world."

I thought about Uncle Berk's article in the British archaeology magazine. "And I bet they believe Turkish museums aren't taking good enough care of these treasures, right?" I guessed.

"Exactly. So these collectors call it 'recovering,' not 'stealing.' Most of them think they're actually doing something noble, saving objects from neglect or invisibility. They're working with smugglers and looters and mafia types in Lazar's organization to get them and move them, and they're paying them big bucks for their help."

"And they're disguising the real artifacts as fakes?"

"Yes, or packaging them among fakes," said Sage. "Then, once the goods are out of the country, they end up in private collections or other storage facilities. The ones who see themselves as heroes probably take good care of them. They might restore them, or take special steps to preserve them, because they feel that's where Turkish museums fell short. Some of the members travel around the world to view each other's private collections. Eventually, they might get 'discovered,' like someone says, 'Wow, my grandfather had this rare sculpture in his attic! Turns out it's worth a lot!' And then it gets sold at auction or donated to a museum in their own country, and they get a little plaque with their name on it and some fame."

I gave her a long look. "Did you know all this when you started?"

"No," she insisted. "I just needed enough money to stay in Turkey and to finish my program. I thought I'd quit when I earned it. Then this cruise job came up, and Riza was going to go on that other boat, and I thought, great, paid vacation! But then I realized how wrong this business was, and all I could think about was getting out of it."

We sat in silence for a moment, listening to the rain, not looking at each other. The storm was intensifying, washing dirt into a grate in the center of the small patio garden.

"Where'd you go when you left the boat?" I asked next.

"I ran. I camped out by a small beach hotel down the coast. I went back to the cliff tombs to look for the urn. When I was absolutely sure it was gone, I came back to Istanbul to figure out what to do next, because I knew I could stay with my friend here at the hammam. I sold the earrings I bought from the baklava seller to a guy I know at a gold shop, but that gave me just enough money to buy food. The earrings weren't worth much." She sighed. "Also, I thought I'd be harder to find in a big city. Obviously I'm not. Lazar and Vasil are here. I was sure they'd stay on the coast longer."

"Not if they thought you might come here with the urn," I said. "They think I'm a magnet and that I'll draw you out. They're stalking me, watching for you, hoping you have the urn, too."

"Ugh. The urn." Sage picked up a pebble from the ground and hurled it at one of the stone walls. "I wish I'd never heard of that urn. It really is a cursed object. I should have just lied and told Riza it wasn't even on the boat! Then all of this could have been avoided."

"I hate the urn, too," I said. "If it weren't for that urn, my uncle would still be alive."

"I thought he died hiking."

"You don't really believe that, do you? Did you know he did a job for Lazar?" I told her what Nazif had told me.

Sage paled. "Oh my God, Zan," she said. "I'm sure Lazar has something to do with your uncle's death. It makes sense. Especially since Lazar's headquarters are in Cappadocia!"

"They are?" I jumped up from the bench. "Not at the Lycian Society?"

"He does some water transport on the coast, but it's easier to be inland and escape through less vigilant border controls over there. And a lot of the coastal smuggling is just smoke and mirrors, to distract the authorities and keep them busy while his real work goes inland. The seahorse urn is supposed to be in Cappadocia with the rest of a cache of artifacts. One of his top clients is expecting to pick it up there, just two days from now."

My head was spinning. *Cappadocia.* Had Uncle Berk traveled there to deliver the urn with the fake documents? Had he failed to do that, fought with Lazar, and lost his life? I could see how my uncle needed money, like Sage, and could have agreed to do a simple appraisal—but then the game had changed on him, and he found himself in over his head.

"If we could get the urn," I said, thinking out loud, "and give it back to Lazar—in front of an embassy official, and maybe some museum expert who can authenticate it on the spot—we could shut down his whole operation."

"Perfect," said Sage. "Except for one problem. I lost the urn. Remember?"

"Maybe not. Let's go back in time," I said. "Is there anyone else who could have gotten to it first? Or come back to look for it before you did?"

"There weren't any other tourists out that morning," she said. "It was so early in the day. Only the people from our boat were there. It would have to be one of them."

"Okay. What about Fiona and Alice?"

"Alice doesn't walk so well. And her eyesight's poor, she said. But Fiona walked around near the trailhead. The boulders where I hid the urn could have been seen from there. So I guess there's a chance she could have seen me getting the urn from the base of the precipice and hiding it. It's a possibility."

"Maybe," I agreed. It was hard to picture Fiona, this nice English lady, taking the urn and not immediately returning it to Aunt Jackie. It was harder still to picture her sneaking it past Alice when she went to take her mother back to the boat, but at this point we couldn't rule anyone out.

"What about the Lobsters?" Sage asked. "Milton seemed pretty sure-footed, for an old dude."

I remembered the scratches I'd seen on his arm, and how Selim had given him an antibiotic ointment. I hated thinking these stand-in grandparents might have found the urn and kept it quiet. "It's possible," I agreed, reminding Sage of the scratches. "They could have pushed through those bushes near the front part of the precipice, if they went back after lunch. So they're on the list. But what about Nils and Ingrid? They like finding stuff. They spent half their time hunting for rare birds."

"True. They also had binoculars and walking sticks," said Sage. "So, yeah. I guess that makes five people who could have the urn in their luggage, even as we speak!"

"But everyone likes my aunt. If they'd found the artifact, they would have given it to her."

"You don't know that," said Sage. "Sometimes people do bad things even if they start out with good intentions. And sometimes they do bad things for reasons that are just . . . complicated. It doesn't mean they're evil."

I understood all too well how someone who was basically

good could make a poor decision and get in too deep. I had done it. Sage and my uncle had done it. Even my dad had done it, I realized, although it pained me to think it. It was a stupid decision to have the affair. If he wanted to leave Mom, he should have done that first instead of cheating on her. But he hadn't set out to hurt anyone. It had just ended up that way.

"Fortunately," I said, "all the suspects are in one place now. The Hotel Mavi Konak."

Her eyes lit up. "They're all at your aunt's hotel? Why?"

"Bedbugs infested the Swissotel. My aunt had given them all her card, so they ended up with us."

"So you're thinking of, what, just asking them if anyone took it?"

"I doubt anyone would admit it," I said. "If they didn't take it, they'd be insulted I asked them. If they did take it, they'd probably lie and cover it up, because they'd be too embarrassed."

"Or because they'd want to keep it for themselves," Sage said. "So how are you going to find this thing?"

"I'm a part-time maid these days. I'll look through their stuff when I'm working."

"Great idea. And what do I do?"

"Lie low here. If I find the urn, I'll call the embassy right away. Then I'll set up a meeting with Lazar, like he asked me to do if I found you. Only it'll be like a sting operation. I'll get an embassy official and one of their police contacts to witness the handover of the urn. They'll have to arrest him on the spot. Then you can come out of hiding."

"And then what?"

"Then you can talk to the authorities, once someone at the embassy tells us who, and tell them everything you know about Lazar and his operation."

"Oh, God, no."

"I know it's scary to talk to people in uniform. Believe me. But if you're honest and helpful, I bet they'll let you off easier."

"I guess I can do that," said Sage, but she still looked worried.

"By the way, where's Riza now?" I asked. "Is he going to pop up somewhere and throw a wrench in our plan?"

"I don't know," she said. "Riza and I are done. That's the one thing I know for sure. I can't believe I let him persuade me to work for Lazar. I don't want to see him ever again."

"Good," I said. "Don't. You could definitely do better."

Birds were flying overhead. The rain had acted like one of those white noise machines outside my shrink's office, masking our conversation, but now that it was letting up, I worried we might be overheard. We went back to Sage's hideout office.

"I should go," I said. "Some of the Geezers are actually here, and so's my mom."

Sage smiled sadly. "How's your aunt doing?"

"Better. I'd tell her you said hi, but—"

"I'm in hiding," she finished. "I know."

"We'll get you out," I promised, trying to sound confident.

"Hey," she said, softly, as I turned to go. "Some of what I said on the cruise was true, you know. I'm not a total liar."

"I know." I smiled. "I'm not a total liar, either."

"Like, I really do love Freya Stark. Have you had a chance to read the book yet?"

"Um, no? I've been a little busy looking for you and for an ancient cursed artifact, and trying to save people's lives. I haven't quite gotten around to it."

"Right." She smiled wryly. "Got it. Well, anyway, thanks. And Zan?"

"Yes?"

"Be careful. There've been a couple other kids who got recruited by Lazar's organization, for their language and acting skills. There was this Russian girl, and a guy from Chile . . ." She trailed off and bit her lip.

"And?"

"They went to Cappadocia on a special assignment for him. And they never came back."

"He killed them?"

"Presumably, though the deaths looked accidental. Riza says Lazar is famous for never shooting at close range or getting his hands covered in blood. Their bodies were found in a car. A car that had gone over the edge of a cliff. These guys mean business, Zan. And they're masters at the art of the cover-up. You have no room for errors."

36

The spa party returned by taxi to the Mavi Konak. The ladies shared their stories, all except for me. I sat in the backseat, wedged between Maeve and Fiona. As they chattered away, I looked closely at each of their pink faces, glowing from their exfoliating scrubs, and wondered which of these women might have the urn in her room back at the hotel. I wished they'd been scrubbed one more layer down to reveal a guilty look. But their faces betrayed nothing, except for good spirits and health.

"So the woman tells me, 'We'll wash your hair just like your own mother used to, when you were a child,'" Maeve spluttered between laughs. "Then she proceeds to pour bucket after bucket of scalding hot water all over my head! I tell you, my mother never washed my hair like that. If she had, I'd have run away from home!"

"Me too!" Ingrid exclaimed. "Oh, it was horrible! I couldn't see! I couldn't breathe!"

"And what about that massage?" said Fiona. "Where you're lying on that slab, like a piece of meat being tenderized?"

"I think I went down six layers of skin," said Mom.

"Look at this," said Alice, displaying her chafed arms. "It's me at age twelve! I'm back!" She nudged me and winked. "You think we're a bunch of old coots, don't you, dear? But beneath all these wrinkles, we're still us."

"Yes, appearances can deceive," said Maeve, waggling a finger at me.

"Oh, youth is wasted on the young," sighed Alice when I didn't respond.

Everyone laughed. Mom looked especially happy. She seemed younger, healthier, more relaxed, as if the spa really had returned some past version of herself and she'd gone back to the serene and beautiful mom I used to like hanging out with. The mom who'd seemed happy with my dad, happy with her family around her, back in the days before Dad ran for office, before I got sticky fingers in stores and developed a taste for booze and parties. Back when life was easier for her, for all three of us.

Maybe the things Dad had done and the things I had done had changed Mom, too. I only noticed it now that she seemed to be changing back.

But my mirth evaporated and deep dread returned as we neared the hotel. I closed my eyes, not wanting to face what surely awaited me.

Opening my eyes when we pulled up to the curb, I immediately saw a familiar car parked in front of the hotel. A white Ford Focus.

And a familiar face. Orhan got out of the white car, smiling at my mom.

"Orhan!" Mom said, fluffing her damp hair and exiting the cab. The other women and I got out, too, all of us staring at the two of them. "You made it! How was the drive?"

"Long," he admitted. "But I am so eager for this wonderful opportunity! I will not let you down." He grinned wider at Mom, clearly admiring her hip-hugging capri pants and her loose blouse. Spotting me, he said cheerfully, "Hello, Zan! It is nice to see you!" Then he greeted the Geezer ladies, who looked dumbstruck at the sight of the chef from the Blue Voyage cruise.

"Opportunity?" asked Aunt Jackie, who had come to the front door to greet us.

Orhan gave a little bow. "Your catering service has arrived!"

We all looked at Mom. "Kitsie?" said Aunt Jackie. "What's going on? And by the way, has anyone seen my cell phone? I can't find it anywhere."

"Let's all go inside and get out of the traffic fumes, shall we?" said Mom.

In the lobby, while Mustafa got Orhan his room key, Mom and Aunt Jackie pulled off to the side of the room to talk. I followed at a short distance. They talked in near-whispers, but I hid behind a tall potted plant and managed to hear every word.

"*This* is the surprise caterer?" Aunt Jackie whispered. "You brought him all the way from the coast?" She glanced at his suitcase. "And he's staying here, too? For how long?"

"Please don't be mad, Jackie. I called at least ten caterers, and they were way out of our budget. Orhan's barely charging us anything, and you know he's an excellent cook. We're just paying for his ingredients, a free room for a couple of nights, and gas money for the drive."

"Really? That's it?"

"That's it. He's not after money. He wants job experience. And we owe him, don't we? He put up Zan and me when we were stranded in Marmaris. He's so excited to help us with this event, and he'll have a chance to interview for some high-end Istanbul restaurants while he's in town. It's a career move for him."

"That's true, he was good to you and Zan, to all of us," said Aunt Jackie. "But he's still a stranger in many ways. We know so little about him. Why is a man in his thirties, who isn't married and is living with his mother, just now finishing a school program? That's a bit unusual in Turkey. What's he been doing for the last ten or fifteen years?"

Mom frowned. "I don't know. I never thought of that."

"Well, I have. You're my sister, and I worry. Even if I am the younger, crazy one. I've dated guys on the rebound before, in my past, and I know that can blind you to certain things. Like people's motivations."

"This isn't what it's about." Mom looked hurt. "I mean, yes, okay, I wouldn't mind having a date for the party. But I brought him here to help *you*."

I'd heard enough. Maybe Mom deserved a couple of evenings of feeling like some guy was interested in her. I liked Orhan well enough. But it was too weird, having him here. And I wasn't ready for *both* of my parents to be dating other people.

"What's with her?" I heard one of the Blue Voyage ladies ask as I dashed up to my room.

"Teenager," said Maeve in an ominous voice, as if I had a disease.

As I fumbled with my room key, I heard footsteps behind me.

"Zan, wait," said Nazif, coming up behind me just as I pushed the door open. "Did you talk to Sage? Do you have the urn?"

I looked down the hall left and right. "Can we talk in my room?"

He hesitated. "My father is concerned we are spending so much time together."

"Are *you* concerned?"

"No. The opposite! But—"

"I won't keep you long. I just don't want to discuss this in the hall."

I held the door open for him, and he came inside. I shut the door behind us, all my senses alive as I realized we were alone together in a hotel room with my mom and all the adults downstairs.

But Mom could come up any minute, and with the clock ticking on finding the urn, the stage was hardly set for romance.

We stood on opposite sides of the couch, Nazif venturing into the room only a few steps.

I pulled myself together and told him, quickly, what Sage had told me about working for Lazar and how our theory about her had been right: she had tried to double-cross him, but then chickened out and had the urn stolen out from under her. "We're pretty sure the urn is right here in this hotel," I said.

His eyes widened. "How could that be?"

"All the passengers on our boat were in the area when it fell over the side of the hill, and we were all looking for it. Sage thinks someone found the boulders she'd hid it under and quietly took the urn."

"So you're going to interview all the guests?"

"No." I sat on the edge of the couch and played with the fringe on a pillow so I wouldn't have to meet his steady gaze. "I know that would be the most honest thing to do. But if someone's kept the urn this long, there has to be a reason. I can't expect them to tell the truth. I need to look in their rooms. In their luggage. Which, I know, is technically breaking and entering," I added quickly. "But I don't have strong enough evidence to get the police involved in a search. I don't see any other way."

"Of course," he said. "This is what you must do."

"Really?"

"Yes. I don't want to see you become Lazar's next victim because of this business. We know he had a hand in your uncle's death. If you have a chance of finding the urn, you should look. And I will help you." He took the ring of room keys off his belt and jangled it slowly.

"Right now?"

"No. The guests will soon be in their rooms," he said. "And not while you are working, either. It is too risky to search in three separate rooms when guests may be on the premises, coming and going at any time. You could be caught. And if you are, and if you do not find the urn, it will reflect badly on the hotel."

I nodded. I didn't want that to happen. I couldn't do that to Aunt Jackie.

"It is best if you search during the party tomorrow evening, when everyone will be out at the same time," he went on. "I will perform a twenty-minute puppet show. You can take my key ring then and search the three guest rooms."

"It's a plan." I smiled. Even though it meant delaying the search a little bit longer, and I was dying to ransack everyone's bags right away, we had to be careful. Like Sage said, I had no room for errors. "Thanks, Nazif. But if you don't feel comfortable with it, you can get off the train here, you know. I mean, this doesn't have to be your problem."

"But it *is* my problem," he insisted. "This smuggling situation, this is all of our problem here in my country. Lazar is stealing our history. And if we are very careful, and we get that urn, I believe we can stop him."

◇◇◇◇◇

Orhan cooked his signature eggplant dish for Mom, Aunt Jackie, and me that night. We brought dinner to the rooftop and feasted beneath the stars.

I looked up at the indigo sky and thought how lucky I was to be able to enjoy that view. I wasn't in hiding like Sage, or in a police station or jail. No one had shown up to question me about the Lycian Society break-in yet. I was sure that soon Lazar would be off the streets.

"I have news from the coast," said Orhan. "Remember the other yacht that was near us a lot on the cruise? The large one with the American couple on board?"

"Of course," I said.

"The *Gulet Anilar*," said Aunt Jackie.

"It was found off the coast of Bodrum. Abandoned," said Orhan, in a dramatic voice.

"Abandoned!" I cried, almost knocking over my water glass.

"Oh my God," said my mom.

"It was not a legally registered yacht," said Orhan. "It also had gone through several name changes and paint changes. Before it was the *Anilar,* it was called the *Altin.* And before that, it was something else," said Orhan. "The captain is missing now, as is the crew. The coast guard and police in Bodrum have taken the boat into custody for further inspection into its history, so the original owner can be traced."

"That boat must have been worth so much money!" Mom exclaimed. "Who would do such a thing? The captain?"

"He may have abandoned ship because he did not want to be arrested," said Orhan. "Same with the first mate and the cook. But the owner of the boat, not being registered, is unknown. The boat in fact may have been stolen from some other place, even another country. This is all over the news back in Dalaman."

My mind raced. Riza was gone, then. Probably deep in hiding like Sage. So who was in charge of the boat and its strange itinerary during our Blue Voyage? Had Lazar and Vasil boarded the boat to take command of it until Sage produced what they'd come for? And had they ordered it to be abandoned when they realized the police might be closing in?

Now I had an even stronger feeling that Inspector Lale could in fact be trusted. And should be trusted. After all, when we'd spoken on the phone before, she had told me she was looking into the *Anilar* and its crew. Maybe she'd come so close that they were all forced to sacrifice the boat. An insider wouldn't sabotage a smuggling ring that way. Whatever was happening on the coast right now was definitely upsetting Lazar's plans.

"Excuse me," I muttered, shoving my chair back from the table.

"Everything okay?" Mom asked.

"Stomach problem," I said, and I ran down to my room and got the business card out of my backpack. Then I ran down to the lobby. Mustafa was busy in the back office, talking to the new maids he'd just hired that day. I glanced at them through the office window as I passed by with the phone. They didn't look like spies at all, just two plain-looking older women. But I wasn't taking chances. I took the receiver to the outdoor garden where I could talk in private.

This time, Inspector Lale picked up on the second ring.

"It's Zan," I said. "Can we talk?"

◇◇◇◇◇

Later that evening, the other guests joined us on the rooftop for dessert and conversation. I didn't converse, though. I sat alone on an outdoor sofa in the corner, near Nazif's roof, trying to reassure myself that I'd done the right thing by inviting Inspector Lale to the party tomorrow night.

She'd apologized for not returning my calls quickly enough and for being hard to reach. "We've uncovered the connection to the *Anilar*," she said. "We are one step closer."

I wasn't ready to tell her about Sage yet, since I now felt protective of her again. But I did tell Inspector Lale about my uncle's possible connection to Lazar. My secret plan was to make sure Lazar was at the party by sending him an official invitation through that neighborhood *simit* vendor, whom I'd seen walking around the street off and on ever since he'd delivered that first forged note from Lazar.

"It'd be good if you could come and bring some backup," I said to Inspector Lale. "I can't say much right here in case anyone overhears me, but I think you should come to this party, just in case Lazar or any of his friends show up. We advertised all over the neighborhood, so I'm sure he knows about it. He might take an open house as an open invitation to look around the hotel for Sage, or the urn he thinks she might have."

"I will definitely be there," she assured me.

I finally felt some degree of relief. Part of me wanted Inspector Lale to interrogate all the cruise guests about the urn and go through their luggage. But without clear evidence that any of them had taken it, I knew she'd be powerless to search their belongings. And if she questioned a guest who was hiding the urn, that guest could get scared—and get rid of it. The risk was too great.

But with both Lazar and Inspector Lale at the party, all I had to do was get the urn from whichever boat guest had it and deliver it to him with Inspector Lale as a witness. Then he could be arrested on the spot. And if my theory about the urn proved incorrect and I couldn't find it in the guest rooms, I could at least tell Lazar I'd looked for it. That conversation alone, witnessed or recorded by Inspector Lale, would be enough to book him. Even though the urn would remain at large, we'd have a murderer off the streets. It seemed like a fail-proof plan.

Mom was waving me over to join her and the other guests under the little white lanterns we'd strung up for the party. "Don't sulk alone in the corner," she said. "We're party planning. It's happy stuff. Come and talk with us."

I reluctantly took a seat near the cruise guests.

"I hope one of us wins the raffle," Ingrid was saying. "Did you all hear about the prizes?"

"I want the balloon ride," said Fiona. "Wouldn't that be a dream!"

"Booby prize, if you ask me," said Milton. "You've got to buy your airfare out there. They don't give you anything for free in this country. Everything's got some hidden cost."

"What about you, Zan? What are you looking forward to about the party?" Aunt Jackie asked, trying to draw me out.

Oh, not much. A successful sting operation. Clarity. Justice. Little things like that.

"Orhan's cooking," I said carefully.

Everyone murmured their agreement, and Orhan beamed.

I listened to the rest of their conversation closely, hoping something would be revealed in their conversation after all the wine they were drinking, some clue about who had found the urn on the cliffside and kept it. But the darkness soon settled around us, cloaking the guests, and any secrets they might be keeping, in shadows.

37

All evening, and into the next morning, Mom kept me busy decorating, helping Orhan with food prep, and moving furniture. I managed to get out briefly to the Arasta Bazaar for an errand and found the *simit* vendor. I wordlessly handed him a note with Lazar's name written on it. The vendor nodded and slipped it into his pocket. "I bring this to him," he assured me.

As I worked, I thought about the plan, visualizing all the steps in my mind—getting the keys from Nazif, listening for the opening musical notes of the puppet show, then sprinting to the first guest room. It excited me to think this whole business might be resolved this very evening.

In the late afternoon, I hit a glitch in the plan, which turned out to be my party outfit. As in, I had none. Expecting to have zero fun on this trip, I hadn't packed any party clothes, or formal clothes, or even semiformal clothes. The closest thing I had to something fancy was my decidedly non-festive Laura Ingalls Wilder getup. Or my black beach cover-up, which looked exactly like a black beach cover-up.

Mom tossed clothes at me from her suitcase and made me

try them on. Everything looked awful. Too bright, too tailored, too preppy, too . . . Mom.

Then there was a knock at the door, and Aunt Jackie came in. She was wearing a chic black halter dress that showed off her growing baby bump. She looked a little healthier today, though she still had dark circles under her eyes. Her doctor had given her the go-ahead to attend the party, as long as she avoided dancing and excessive stair-climbing. At breakfast, she'd admitted it was nice to have something fun to look forward to, and she was pleasantly surprised by the donations that were already coming in for the hotel's renovation. I had to hand it to Mom; she really knew how to plan an event and get people buzzing about it. Even in a foreign country.

Aunt Jackie interrupted my thoughts, shaking a hanger with a long teal-colored gown at me. "I found this in my closet. I'm not squeezing into this thing anytime soon. Want to try it on?"

I took the dress into my room and put it on. It hung perfectly on my body, the hem of the gown just brushing the floor. And it completely covered my legs. The only problem was on top. I turned around in front of the full-length mirror on my door, frowning. It was a sleeveless dress with a low cowl-neck that exposed the blotches on my arms and a small patch on my chest. If I wore cover-up on my arms, the makeup would get all over the fabric. I'd have to wear it with a sweater, or go with bare arms.

I smirked at my reflection. I was about to pull off the most high-stakes snooping expedition of my life, and bring a police officer to confront a murderer . . . and I was concerned about my skin? Seriously?

I lifted my chin. In the light leaking through the lattice windows, my arms didn't look so bad. They actually looked kind of good. I felt like an ancient figurine, mottled and weathered in places, but still holding together.

"Well?" Aunt Jackie called through the door. "Let's see."

I stepped out into the living room. Aunt Jackie and Mom

both applauded. "You look gorgeous," said Aunt Jackie. "That dress was made for you. You wear it well."

"Stunning," Mom agreed. "Now let's see about that hair." She sat me down by a mirror and fussed with my hair, pulling it back into a neat bun at the nape of my neck and jabbing in pins. She combed my long bangs forward, but I stopped her. "Maybe to the side," I suggested.

She nodded, and brushed them over, exposing my forehead and the white patch there that I hadn't covered up yet. I smiled at myself. I felt brave. I was going to this party as no one but myself. Tonight I would face everyone with my actual face.

"You'll have to do my hair for me next," said Mom.

"You don't need to do anything to it," I said. "Seems like Orhan likes you just the way you are." I stole a glance at her in the mirror. "So is he going to be hanging around here the whole rest of our vacation?"

"Of course not. He's got things to do." She set down the brush. "Zan, this isn't anything serious. I just haven't had fun in a long time. Your dad and I were under so much strain, with his campaign and even before that. I've been thinking it's time for me to get a life. Your dad and I aren't going to get back together, sweetheart. We know that now. Adults make mistakes. Parents aren't perfect. I'm sorry you had to learn that lesson in such a hard way."

I looked down at my lap, fighting back tears. I didn't want to admit it, but I kind of got her point, about getting her own life and rebuilding. I'd been angry for so long, feeling as if my life had been stolen from me. Maybe I was ready to move on, too.

Mom went back to combing and pinning my hair, and we laughed over a story about her bad eighties prom hair. For a moment there, it almost felt like a party. Almost. Then I swallowed hard, remembering the huge climb still ahead of me.

◇◇◇◇◇

An hour before the party, I was dressed and in the patio garden picking flowers for vases, when I heard the front door to the hotel open slowly and close softly. I didn't hear Mustafa greet anyone—he might have been in the back office—and I knew Nazif had gone home early to get ready for his puppet show. Wondering if Lazar or anyone from his gang had arrived yet, I peered into the lobby through the window.

A girl stood there, looking around. She wore a long, chic tan trench coat and a long dark skirt. A navy blue head scarf was pulled low over her forehead, casting most of her face in shadow. But then I noticed one stray red curl escaping from the hijab.

I flung the flowers aside and ran inside. "Sage! I thought I told you to lay low until you heard from me! Why are you here?" My mind raced. If Sage was still here when Lazar or any of his cohorts showed up at the party, that could throw my whole plan. I did not want Lazar to find Sage. I wanted to leave her out of this business as much as I possibly could.

"I got discovered this afternoon," she said, her voice shaking. "I went to get a drink from the vending machine, and saw Lazar and Vasil coming down the stairs from the street. They were with a woman, someone they were probably sending in to look for me. I don't know how they figured out I was there, but they did. My friend gave me some clothes from the lost and found bin, and a hijab to hide my hair, and I escaped out the back. I'm sorry I came here. They're probably going to find me here, too, eventually. I feel like *I'm* a cursed object. But I didn't know where else I could go."

I didn't know what to do either. But I needed to get her out of the lobby. "Come up to my room," I said, leading her toward the stairs. "You can hide there. The windows will shield you from the street."

I brought her upstairs to my room. "Are you hungry?"

She nodded.

"I'll bring you some meze. We have tons of food for the

party. And Orhan's cooking." I lowered my voice as the sound of my mom's shower stopped. "Lock the door from the inside. I'll knock three times when I come back so you'll know it's me."

"Thank you." Sage sat on the bed and drew her knees up to her chin. "This might all be over by tonight, right? If one of the guests really has the urn?"

"I hope so. But I invited Lazar, through one of the street vendors. I wanted him to take the urn, with Inspector Lale as a witness. I don't want him taking *you*."

"You're right. I shouldn't be here. I'll go." She started to stand up.

I pushed her gently back down. "No. Stay. Now that you're here, you shouldn't go. It's too risky to just run out into the street again. I think you can hide here, but you cannot come out of this room, and I'm keeping the doors to the room and the suite locked. Understand?"

She nodded. "But I insist on helping you look for the urn. If everyone is at the puppet show on the rooftop, no one will see me, right?"

"All right," I said. "You can help. But don't even open this door. I'll come get you when the show starts and I have Nazif's keys."

She nodded. "I'm so sorry, Zan. I keep dumping all my problems on you."

"You're not dumping your problems on me," I said, thinking of something Nazif had said earlier. "What Lazar's doing with this smuggling operation is *all* of our problem. But I'm also going to have a real problem with my mom if I don't finish what she asked me to do for the party. Here." I handed her the Freya Stark book. "At least now you won't be bored. Try to relax, if that's even possible."

She took the book from me and smiled at it, as if it was a long-lost friend.

38

At sunset, after the call to prayer, the band arrived, and then the guests. As I slowly made my way down the stairs, trying not to trip in the long gown, I heard them streaming in. I paused on the landing to watch. Couples and small groups of people came through the front doors, where they were greeted warmly by Aunt Jackie, Mustafa, and Mom. Some were local business owners and salesclerks. There were also tourists, mostly Europeans, dressed in chic cocktail attire. I heard a mix of languages—Greek, Italian, French, German—and breathed a heady mix of perfumes.

Some people went to the patio garden for drinks and hors d'oeuvres and others, directed by Mom, headed up to the roof garden. Others lingered in the lobby to listen to Aunt Jackie talk about the planned renovations; Mom had made an information sheet for her to hand out to people. Most of the guests went directly upstairs to the rooftop, where music from the Turkish band could already be heard; it was some kind of fusion of jazz and Turkish folk music, and it was catchy. Mom had actually found a good band. I started to get a fluttery, panicky feeling inside, wondering if Lazar would dare to show up in person. Would he come alone or with Vasil? Would he have a whole gang of people to protect him?

I took a deep breath. I couldn't waste time imagining failure. I had to be confident. I came down the stairs a little farther, scanning the crowd of arriving guests, and then spotted the Geezers hanging out on the long, low couches in the lobby. The Blue Voyage guests, I corrected myself. Since the spa trip, I felt bad thinking of them as "geezers." Alice and Fiona were right—there was more to them than their old age and their appearance. Just like there was more to me than my appearance.

The Blue Voyage guests were dressed up fancier than I'd ever seen them on the boat, in suits and linen dresses. They were sipping wine and chatting. I watched them for a moment, suddenly feeling terrible about my plan to go through all their personal stuff. It almost felt like seeing family again, relatives gathered together at a holiday party or something. I wanted to imagine that these were my grandparents, my great-aunts and great-uncles. I had to remind myself that one of them might have the Karun Treasure urn in their luggage, that at least one of them might have deceived my aunt. But people were complicated. Watching the Blue Voyage guests now, I hoped that if one of them had taken the urn, it was for a very good reason.

Noticing me, Milton whistled. "Ah, there she is! Alexandra the Great!"

I turned and looked at the group. There was silence. I knew what they were thinking. What was wrong with my skin?

But I rode it out. I stood there smiling bravely, even though I didn't feel very brave.

Then Maeve, wearing a floral halter dress a few sizes too small, beamed at me and told me to come and join them, so I did. Nils and Ingrid complimented me on my dress, as did the British ladies, and then . . . the *Clarksons*?

Ron and Judy Clarkson were there, too! They perched on the end of a divan, just under the overhanging staircase, which was why I hadn't seen them at first. They were the best-dressed of the group. Judy wore a fuchsia-colored sheath dress. Her hair was slicked back in a sleek twist at the nape of her neck, not windblown like it had been on the boat. Ron wore a crisp dress shirt, blue tie, linen trousers, and buttery brown leather loafers with tassels—the expensive brand my dad always bought. They looked like real businesspeople, people with some serious money. And they smiled warmly at me, as if were still hanging out on the back of the Anilar.

Which none of the other cruise guests here knew I had done. My whole body tensed up.

"Ron and Judy, I don't believe you have had the pleasure of meeting Zan," said Nils. "Zan was our youngest blue cruiser. She's the daughter of this hotel owner, who was also on the cruise."

Judy beamed at me. "Oh, of course, we—"

I shot her and Ron a pleading look, channeling all my mental powers to beg them not to tell about the midnight swim with Sage.

Judy nodded. "Of course, we are delighted to meet you, Zan." She stood up and shook my hand, as did Ron. "We had the pleasure of meeting your mother on the Dalyan River shore excursion."

"So when are you two lovebirds off to Cappadocia?" Milton asked the Clarksons as they sat back down.

"We fly out tomorrow morning," Judy said. "And the day after?" She squeezed Ron's hand and smiled at him. "Our hot-air-balloon adventure."

Ron made a face showing mock terror. "I'm not wild about heights. Or about the prospect of a six a.m. balloon launch. Which means arriving at the launch site at five thirty."

"Oh, but honey, that's when the light is best." Judy patted his arm. "I spent months researching this. Voyager Balloons has the best views and the best photographic possibilities. Not to mention the highest safety standards."

"She's right," I said to Ron. "Voyager Balloons is one of our raffle prize donors." I gestured toward our raffle table and the sign I'd made myself.

"Don't get me wrong. I'll be a good sport about it when the time comes," said Ron. "Besides, how often will I go ballooning in Turkey? You only live once, right?"

"I'll toast to that," said Maeve, raising her wineglass and taking a sip.

"Every day's a gift," Nils murmured in agreement, lifting his glass as well, and the others followed suit. "We'd do well to remember that."

"Amen," said Alice, draining her glass. "And may the best man or woman win." She looked at the raffle table. "We've all entered, you know. That balloon-ride prize would be worth extending our stay for."

"Agreed! And good luck to all of us," said Nils, clinking glasses with the people sitting on either side of him. "Even if one of us doesn't win, we should all go together on a group rate. One last voyage together, up into the blue sky. What do you say?"

"Bloody expensive," grumbled Milton. "Now they're charging for the very air."

"Nonsense," scolded Maeve. "You're paying for experienced pilots, and spectacular views." She turned to the Clarksons. "Anyway, you two certainly deserve your lovely balloon ride considering the near miss you had on the *Anilar*. To think you were cruising around with criminals all that time!"

"We were just talking about the news before you got here, Zan," said Ingrid. "Have you heard? The Clarksons' yacht was found abandoned in Bodrum!"

"Crewed by criminals!" said Nils.

"What a waste of a grand vessel," said Milton. "They had a Jacuzzi on it, can you believe it? And a full bar. And flat-screen TVs in all the cabins."

"Yeah, Orhan told me it had been abandoned," I said. "Were you guys totally shocked?"

"Oh, we were out of our minds," said Judy. "We didn't suspect a thing. The whole operation seemed quite legitimate, and we had a lovely cruise. The captain was a fine navigator, always seeking out private coves for us and the best snorkeling waters. The cook served delicious meals. The first mate was awfully young, but competent. Shame he got arrested. He seemed to have so much promise."

"He was arrested?" I squeaked. Wait till Sage heard about this. I wondered if she'd be relieved, or freaked out, or even a little bit sad. After all, Riza had been her boyfriend, not just an accomplice to a smuggling ring, and things between them had probably been happy at one time.

"They found him trying to stow away on a ferryboat bound for Greece. He's wanted for antiquities smuggling," said Alice.

"And the guards?" I couldn't resist asking. "What happened to them?" I didn't want to let on what I knew yet, or what had happened to me since. I was curious what they had to say.

"Oh, those Bulgarian security guards we had?" said Ron. He made a twirling motion by his head. "Wackos. I was happy to cut them loose in Marmaris."

"Really? Why?" I asked.

"Where to start?" he groaned, and Judy gave a nod of commiseration. "Let's see. They arrived late, first off, and then they left the boat, going off in the tender a lot more than we would have liked, considering what we were paying them to, you know, *guard* us."

Fiona made a *tsk*ing sound. "Do you think they were in league together? The guards and the crew of your boat?"

"Who knows," said Judy. "I think I'm through with cruises for a while. I'm so ready to take to the skies. Do you mind if we change the subject? I'm a bit rattled by the whole boat situation."

"Of course," said Alice. "We're at a party. We should be festive."

"How'd you hear about our fund-raiser, anyway?" I asked the Clarksons.

"We saw a flyer when we were touring the neighborhood," said Judy.

"And we recognized your aunt's hotel name, since your mother had mentioned the place that day we all went to the Dalyan ruins. Thought we'd check it out," said Ron. "We're always on the lookout for charming boutique hotels and off-the-beaten-path experiences."

"Are you staying here, too?" I asked.

"No, we're perfectly happy where we're at. The Inter-Continental," said Judy. "It's like home away from home for us. We stay there every time we're in Turkey. But we'll certainly tell all our friends about this little hidden gem," she added warmly.

"Oh, I hadn't realized you were repeat travelers to this part of the world," said Alice.

"Occasionally. New to the coast and to Cappadocia. But we sure love Istanbul," said Ron. "Hey, it looks to be a fun party," he added, surveying the guests still streaming through the front door. No Lazar, no Inspector Lale. "We can't stay long, on account of our early departure tomorrow, but we'll be happy to make a donation to the cause."

"They're a bit skimpy on the wine, though." Judy set down her empty glass. "Is there a full bar?"

"It's just wine or beer," I said, remembering that Mom didn't want to cause offense by emphasizing alcohol too much; some Muslims, she said, didn't drink at all. "I can get you a refill, though." Again I scanned the growing crowd in the lobby. A new worry stabbed me. What if Lazar showed up but Inspector Lale didn't? I trusted the inspector with information now, but she had a pretty lousy record for returning phone calls in a timely manner. She got distracted a lot by crimes needing her attention. She seemed to have understood that I was serious about needing her to come to this party, but what if something pulled her away tonight, something beyond her control?

"Oh, no, you don't need to serve me," said Judy. "You need to be a hostess. Chat with your friends from the cruise, and I'll go help myself. Some wine for you, too?"

"My mom would kill me," I said. "I'm not allowed to drink."

"Your mom's a wise lady," said Judy. "And you've got plenty of time for all that."

As I watched her go to the drinks table, I remembered something I'd really liked about Judy on the cruise: how she didn't assume the worst about me. I glowed a little. And standing by the stairs near the Blue Voyage guests, I suddenly felt kind of grown-up. Kind of . . . elegant. If I didn't have a search to try to pull off, I might actually have some fun. This was a whole different kind of party from the usual fund-raisers Mom threw. This party felt so much warmer, and genuinely festive. It wasn't a bunch of people crammed into stiff clothes, drinking stiff drinks, trying to impress one another.

Even Aunt Jackie seemed to be enjoying herself as she chatted with guests about the renovations. "We'll bring the Mavi Konak back to the splendor of its Ottoman days," I heard her say to a smiling couple.

Judy came back with her refilled wineglass, and a large glass of pomegranate juice for me. "I hope you like it over ice," she said. "I always prefer it that way."

"Oh, thanks." I took it gratefully. The evening was warm and the air in the lobby close with the growing crowd of guests.

Then I remembered that I'd promised Sage I'd bring her some snacks and something to drink. So I excused myself from the cruise guests, grabbed a plate, piled it high with appetizers and my half-finished juice glass—and nearly bumped into a woman in a chic white sheath dress.

Inspector Lale! Her hair was pulled back in a slick French twist, and she wore long gold earrings and a ton of eye makeup. I hadn't recognized her at first.

"Zan!" she exclaimed. "There you are."

"I'm so glad you came," I gushed. I looked behind her and all around. "Are you alone?" I wanted her to be flanked by beefy, legitimate security guys—or real cops.

"I wouldn't have missed this. It sounded so important to you that I come. Can we talk somewhere more private? It's been hard to talk on the phone, hasn't it."

I nodded. I couldn't take her to my room because Sage was there, and I didn't want to turn in Sage until I was sure we could get Lazar taken into custody. Still holding the plate of meze and the juice, I led her to the garden. We found a quiet corner by the Byzantine wall, where the splash of a fountain would mask our hushed voices and a row of potted trees hid us from view.

"I've been worried about you," she said. "You called and left messages, but when I called back I didn't hear from you for a long time."

"I didn't know if I could trust you," I admitted. "I thought you might even be working with Lazar. You know, like from the inside. You told us back in Dalaman that his ring used some operatives inside the police force."

Inspector Lale looked astonished. Lines appeared in her forehead. "They do, but not me," she said. "I assure you, I'm working around the clock to apprehend Lazar and his team. All the crimes I was investigating on the coast were potentially related to their vast smuggling network. Which I am trying to bring down. I certainly do not work for them. Whatever made you think that?"

"I'm sorry," I added, suddenly embarrassed. "It's just, all these things happened to me—Lazar sent me two notes pretending to be Sage, and he followed me to the Grand Bazaar—and I never saw any sign of undercover police officers. Nobody ever came to ask me what happened, or to stop Lazar."

"Oh, Zan," she said, sadly. "I'm sorry. I can imagine you were really frightened. I can see why you stopped calling for a while. But you see, I *did* send police after you called me the first time."

"You—you did?"

"Yes. At least, I thought I did." Her face hardened. "No one came in to introduce themselves? Or to speak with you in my place?"

I shook my head.

She pursed her lips and let out a long breath. "I'm supposed to have a team of three men on the ground here. Three men—that's all my superiors would give me. But that should have been enough for basic surveillance. However, I just learned this evening that somebody didn't think it was all that important. I couldn't even get backup for this party. This is so typical." Her eyebrows knitted together. "I don't know what I have to do to earn the respect of my own department."

Now I felt ridiculous. Nazif had been right. I should have trusted her all this time, and if I'd just persisted in calling her a bit more, she might have learned earlier that she had no one on the ground here and come back to Istanbul sooner. I'd gotten myself in over my head with this situation, all because I couldn't trust people.

"So I get the feeling you've been holding back on the phone a bit," she said. "Tell me, what's been going on?"

I took a deep breath and told her about the secret workshop I'd seen on the third floor of the Lycian Society building, taking care to leave Nazif's name out of it. "I have pictures on the bellboy's phone, which I sort of borrowed for the expedition," I explained, unable to meet her stern gaze. "I know it was wrong to climb up there, and to go inside, but—"

She shook her head. "Wrong, maybe. Dangerous, definitely. But nobody has reported an incident, and I'm certainly not going to press any charges. I will be quite eager to see those photos. Does this bellboy know they are on his phone? And do you think they're still there?"

I nodded. "But he didn't have anything to do with it. Really."

She put up a hand. "He will not be in any trouble," she assured me. "You have my word. Listen, Zan. " Her face was a bit softer now, but still serious. "You've given me some extremely important information. I've suspected for some time that there's a workshop where these replicas and packing materials are being put together. I'm amazed, and grateful, that you found it. I'll look into this personally, right away."

"I'm glad you came to the party, too," I said. "My aunt really wants to talk to you. She has a theory about how Uncle Berk died." Even if Aunt Jackie had the wrong kind of evidence, she had the right idea, to think he'd been murdered. And if I let her plant that seed now in Inspector Lale's mind, she'd be ready to move fast on the evidence I'd be bringing to her soon enough.

"Yes, Jackie mentioned something about that," said Inspector Lale. "Can you find her for me?"

"Of course," I said, and we left the private corner of the garden and reentered the noisy lobby. I walked Inspector Lale over to where Aunt Jackie was sitting.

The inspector and Aunt Jackie went off to my aunt's apartment down the hall. Meanwhile, I carried the plate and the half-finished glass of juice up to my room, where a grateful Sage took them and dug in. "No Lazar yet," I said. "But Inspector Lale is here."

Sage choked on her appetizer. She looked really scared.

"It's okay. We want her here. Once we get the urn, I'll tell her I've found it, and then we'll look for Lazar."

"She brought backup, right?" asked Sage.

I shook my head. "She couldn't get anyone to join her. The men on the force don't all take her seriously, I guess. But she's official police, and all she has to do is see Lazar take or even ask about the urn, and she has enough to take him into custody."

When I rejoined the cruise guests downstairs, they were comparing notes about what to see and do in Cappadocia. That's when Nazif came through the front door.

He was carrying a large box. A thrill ran through me, knowing it contained his beautiful handmade shadow puppets and his screen, which he'd be setting up on our roof tonight. And as for Nazif—oh my God, he looked amazing. He wore a black suit for the occasion and looked somehow put-together and yet slightly, adorably rumpled: he'd missed a button on his white button-down shirt. But his hair was neatly combed back from his face, like an old-fashioned movie star's. And he turned his dazzling smile to me, like a spotlight, even though I didn't have a speck of makeup on and was standing by a lamp.

Then, in an instant, his smile faded. Instinctively, I put my hand to my face. My skin burned. He must have seen something he didn't like; it was written all over his face. It had been one thing to see my face exposed in the moonlight before, but now he could see my arms. The patches. The continental drift. This had been a stupid idea, thinking I could go around looking natural. I should have covered myself up after all.

"I have to do something upstairs," I mumbled, and I turned and ran up the stairs, tripping over the hem of my dress.

But Nazif followed me. "Wait, Zan!" he said.

I kept going. He kept following. We were in the stairwell now, approaching the roof. The voices and laughter trickled down to us, as did the sounds of the Turkish band.

Finally I stopped and whirled around. "You don't have to pretend anymore. It's okay. I'm a freak. Now you know. It's not just my face, it's my arms, too. And my legs. Eventually it might be all over my body. It's an autoimmune disorder, okay? I can't help it. Somehow I got a weird gene. Get over it."

"Zan, no! It's not that. How horrible. I don't think you are a freak. Not at all," he continued. "I think you are . . . the opposite of that. An un-freak."

We both laughed, a little nervously. Then he reached out and touched my face, softly. Then my arm. Then my other arm. "I do not like this word, 'freak.' I stopped and looked at you because you were . . . because . . ." He faltered. "Because your eyes were shining. And you looked so beautiful standing there."

I shivered, even though his touch was soft and warm. I felt that magnetic pull of attraction to him, the impulse to fold him into my arms and lean my head on his shoulder. Then I felt sweaty. I looked down at my arms and saw goose bumps, even though I felt overheated.

I had never fallen for any guy before, not like this. I shook my head, trying to stay focused. *No swooning!* I scolded myself.

I had to get that urn and take it to Inspector Lale, and get Sage out of hiding. Then I could be free to have feelings again.

I leaned against the wall. I didn't remember it being at a slight slant. Maybe it was from some earthquake damage in the past.

Nazif checked his watch. "I must begin my show in five minutes. That means it is time for you to look for the urn." He handed me a piece of paper listing all the cruise guests' room numbers, and his ring of keys.

"Good luck," I said. "I'm sorry I'm going to miss it. I hope your mom and dad love the show."

"Thank you. Good luck to you," he said. "I'm afraid you need it more." He reached out and stroked my face, the left side. He looked deeply into my eyes, and I looked back into his, unafraid. We stood there for a few moments like that. Then Nazif took a deep breath and let it out in one long, slow sigh. "I want to stay here and look at you all evening. And more."

I shivered. "Really?"

"Yes."

"You mean, you want to look at me more or . . . do more?"

He hesitated. "Both. Look more." He looked down. "And do more." He reached for my hands and held them for a moment, then squeezed them softly and released them. "But it is time for me to go. We have our plan."

"I know. The show must go on, right? So. Go." I gave him a small, playful push on the arm. "I'll be okay. You know I always land on my feet." I tried to smile, remembering my rooftop leaps and how he'd laughed in amazement.

"Yes," he said. "You do land on your feet." He held my gaze a moment longer. Then he turned and ran down the hall, disappearing into the stairwell. I stood pressed against the wall, listening to his footsteps spiraling upward and to the pounding of my own heart.

39

Sage and I peered down the hall both ways. I felt a dull throbbing in my head, but ignored it. This was no time for a headache. "All clear," I said. "Room 214 first. Nils and Ingrid." We went to the stairwell and ran down a flight, ignoring guests who brushed past us. Already I could hear the strains of the oud that signaled the start of Nazif's performance. He would be doing his show to the accompaniment of an oud player and a hand drummer from the band, he had said. When we stopped hearing the music, we would know that the twenty-minute show was over and that guests might be filtering back down the stairs.

We scurried down the second-floor hall, unlocked the door to room 214, and got busy. I was glad Sage had insisted on coming to help me. The Norwegians had a ton of luggage. We went through everything, every compartment. We opened armoire doors and closet doors. We found clothes and outdoor gear and basic souvenirs from tourist shops, including a whole bag of evil-eye amulets. Gifts, I guessed. I was tempted to take one, for any protection it might offer me—I never had replaced Orhan's. But I closed the bag and shut the suitcase. I was no longer a thief.

"Nothing," we agreed minutes later.

"Next room. The Brits," I said, locking the door behind me. "Room 215."

We went through all their things, too, even faster, but found no seahorse urn there, either.

"That leaves Milton and Maeve," I said. "Sultan's Suite. Top floor." We locked the door to 215 and dashed into the stairwell, where I nearly collided with Orhan, who was balancing a large tray of small glasses filled with tea.

"Wrong way!" he cried out, as the tray teetered.

"Sorry!" I said, reaching out to stop it from falling.

Meanwhile, Sage darted around the corner, out of sight.

Orhan smiled at me and wiped imaginary sweat off his brow. "Whew. A close call, yes? I need some more hands. And I do not trust that old elevator. Can you please take this up to the roof for me?" He handed me the tray before I could protest. "I have something in the oven. I am afraid it may burn." He dashed downstairs, back to the kitchen.

Sage crept back around the corner. We exchanged an anguished look.

"Put the tray down. You can deliver it later," Sage said. "We need every minute."

"I can't leave a tray of drinks on the floor. I don't want to make Orhan worried and looking for me. I have to go up near the roof garden anyway to get to the Sultan's Suite. I'll be fast." I didn't want to admit that also a part of me wanted to glimpse Nazif in his element, doing his show.

"Okay. But *hurry*."

The tray was awkward to carry with all those glasses, but I managed to carry it up to the roof and open the stairwell door. My legs felt heavy and my heart was pounding as I stepped outside. All the glasses on the tray wobbled and made soft clinking sounds.

Outside, except for the gentle plucking sound of the oud and the rhythmic thud of the drums, a hush had fallen over

the rooftop. A spell had been cast. Everyone's eyes were on
Nazif's show. He was using his handmade puppets. I recognized the bird; it was soaring against a backdrop of the Blue
Mosque. A sultan shadow puppet appeared, bowing before the
bird, and the bird bowed back. Everyone laughed with delight.
I saw Mustafa and Nazif's mother standing to the side, smiling
along with the audience. I didn't know if Nazif could see them
through the screen. I would have to tell him later that his parents had looked so proud.

I set the tray down on the food table. Much as I wanted to
see the show, I had more pressing business. I quickly turned
to go, then lost my balance a little and knocked over a vase of
flowers on a plant stand. Bending down to right the vase, I wobbled in the high-heeled sandals I'd borrowed from Aunt Jackie.
That's when my mom came striding over to me, a furious look
on her face.

"You've been drinking, haven't you," Mom whispered, glaring at me.

"What? God, Mom. No!" I whispered back.

"You're acting funny." She grabbed my arm, then sniffed
me. "I don't smell anything. But that doesn't mean you haven't
been at the wine."

"*Mom.* I've only had pomegranate juice tonight. I might
have eaten something funny. I just want to go lay down for
a few minutes and maybe it'll pass." I wrenched free of her
grasp. "Besides, I thought you'd decided to trust me." I winced
as I said these words, realizing I was still lying. I wasn't trust-
worthy. Sage was on the other side of that door, and my mom
had no idea what kind of scheme we were really up to.

She gave me a long look, then felt my forehead. "You do seem
clammy. Go lie down. I'll come check on you in a few minutes."
Her voice was softer, but she still didn't seem convinced.

I took my clammy, wobbly self into the stairwell and down
to the Sultan's Suite as fast as I could manage. Sage was there
already, leaning against the door and massaging her temples.

I fumbled with the ring of keys, dropping it twice on the rug.

"I think I might need to sit for a moment before we search the rooms," Sage whispered. "I'm not feeling too well. I've missed my workouts lately. I can't even make it up the stairs without getting winded. Ridiculous."

I held her steady by the arm and peered at her anxiously. Sage looked oddly pale. Sweat beaded her upper lip.

"We can't sit right now," I insisted. "There's no time to rest."

"Of course not. You're right," she murmured. Her eyes fluttered, as if she might fall asleep on the spot.

I got the lock to turn and pushed open the door to the Lobsters' room. "Let's go!"

Milton and Maeve were not the neatest people, that was clear. Clothes and Maeve's boundless shopping bags were strewn around the room. Sage seemed to rally a little. She pawed through Milton's suitcase while I ransacked Maeve's.

"Nothing in Milton's," said Sage. "Want me to help look through Maeve's?"

Together, we rummaged in her second suitcase, through plus-sized lingerie and nightgowns. Both of us kept dropping stuff. Then I felt my hands hit something different. It was a jogging-suit top, zipped up, with something heavy inside it.

"Unzip it," whispered Sage, her eyes shining.

I did, my hands trembling. Inside was a sweatshirt, balled up, the sleeves tied in a knot. I untied them and shook out the shirt, and into the suitcase slid the seahorse urn.

"Maeve!" I said, my jaw dropping. "*She* had it all along!"

Sage reached out and touched it. "She and Milton must have gone back to hunt for it, like we thought. I have to say, I didn't suspect her at all."

"Same here," I said. "She's so sweet and grandmotherly." I looked up. "But she's obsessed with shopping, and bric-a-brac, and anything collectible. See those bags from the Grand Bazaar? She bought all kinds of crap there."

Sage nodded excitedly. "And at the cliff tombs, she seemed

really interested in the urn, asking about the seahorse design."

"And Milton said she goes to rummage sales, and antique shops, anywhere. She's like a hoarder. I don't even think she had a clue this was the lost piece of the Karun Treasure. She just likes shiny things! I bet she and Milton did go back for it after our hike. She probably sent him crawling up the pile of boulders at the base of the precipice and rummaging in the bushes. I bet that's why his arms and legs were all scratched up after lunch!"

Sage nodded. "And he was always talking about being ripped off, and being owed something. Maybe this is the prize he thought he'd claim."

I held the urn up to the light. There were the smiling, winged seahorses, and the acorn lid, and the filigree. And a scratch I remembered seeing at the base. I lifted the lid and pulled out a piece of paper. It was the certificate, typed in both English and Turkish, saying the urn was a replica. A fake certificate for a real antiquity, I now knew. Beneath the paper were a few lingering rose petals from Uncle Berk's proposal, ones that hadn't fallen out during the scattering ceremony. I touched them softly, then replaced the paper and the lid.

"Zan, we really should go now," said Sage. Her voice sounded kind of slurry and far away, like an echo, as if we were still in the stairwell. "But we made such a mess."

"Leave it. And leave the door unlocked," I decided. "Let's let Milton and Maeve think they forgot to lock the door and some random party guest came in and stole the urn. They won't report it missing because they won't want to admit that they stole it first. Now let's get you back to my room, and I'll find Inspector Lale, and together we'll look for Lazar or for someone who can take us to him!"

We closed the door behind us, and hurried down the hall to the Harem Suite. *Stupid floors,* I thought. Why were they so uneven? It was like running on a freaking roller coaster. Or being on a boat all over again.

"Zan," said Sage, behind me. "I really feel weird. Are you sure there wasn't any booze in that pomegranate juice?"

I stopped in my tracks and leaned against the wall. Or what I thought was the wall. Now the wall looked like the Turkish floor runner. I gazed at the swirling patterns, the flowers and vines stretching and pulling and spinning around.

The urn rolled out of my hands. The lid fell off, and I dropped to the floor. I crawled forward, unable to stand, reaching out to grab it.

The pomegranate juice. Sage and I had each drank half of a tall glass of juice. Had Orhan spiked it first, in the kitchen? No. Orhan wouldn't do that. He was a good man. A helpful man. At least I thought he was. But could he have spiked our drinks? Wait, "spiked" wasn't the right word. *Laced.* Lacey. Lady. Lazy . . .

Urn. Get the urn. Seahorse smiling at me. My fingers closed around the base.

"Sage?" I called out.

A man's shoes appeared, a pair of tasseled loafers, the butter-brown leather gleaming. "I'll take that, if you don't mind," said the shoes.

Hands reached down and pried the urn from my fingers.

My head hit the floor. And then everything went black.

PART THREE

Cappadocia

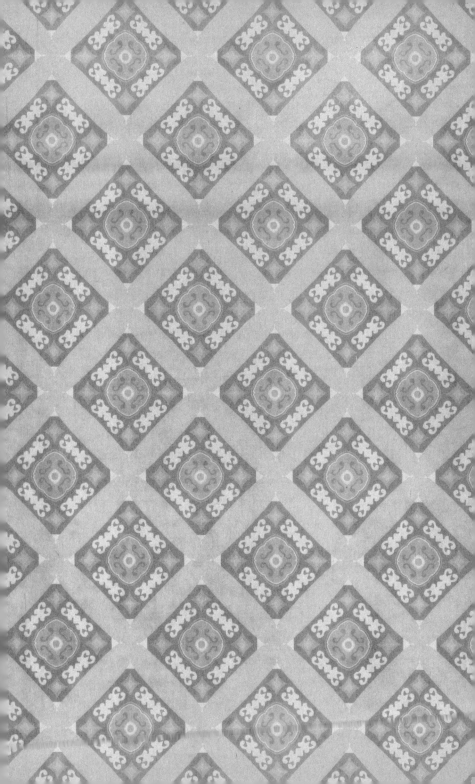

40

Dark. Dank.

These were the first words that came to my mind when my eyes finally fluttered open. I groped around, feeling for anything to orient me. Someone had replaced Aunt Jackie's hall runner with a dirt floor.

A dirt floor? I slowly sat up. The darkness was intense. Onyx black. No light at all.

"Zan?" someone whispered. A hand clutched my arm.

I screamed.

"Zan, it's me! Sage! Shhh! Calm down!"

I turned to the right and squinted into the darkness. My muscles ached. I felt like puking. My tongue was thick and papery, and there was a sour taste in my mouth. "Oh my God," I rasped. "Where the hell are we?"

"I think we might be in a cave."

"A cave! There are no caves in Istanbul." I'd read the whole Lonely Plant section about the city. There are cisterns under the street in Istanbul, but no dirt caves.

"But there are thousands of them in Cappadocia," said Sage.

"Cappadocia!" I spluttered. "But how could we have gotten

there from my aunt's hotel?" I'd had to get all the travel details for the balloon company raffle, so I knew Cappadocia was at least an eight-hour drive from Istanbul, and an hour away by plane. "Sage, we are so not in a cave." I stood up, and promptly whacked my head on the ceiling. "Oof. Ow."

"Feel around," Sage said. "The walls. They're crumbly. It's a cave all right."

I ran my fingers over the rough surface of the wall. It scraped my skin, like an exfoliating scrub at a hammam. Little bits of wall skittered between my fingers and fell to the ground.

"That's volcanic rock, called tuff," said Sage. "I've seen it before. I've been to caves in Cappadocia. With a light, though."

I walked in a circle, stooping, keeping my hand on the wall and taking mincing steps—I was still wearing Aunt Jackie's gown and her high-heeled sandals. I walked as far as I could until I tripped over Sage and sat down again. "Cave," I agreed. "Small. But *how*?"

"We were drugged, Zan. Poisoned," she said. "Laced drinks are a common scam in Turkey. In some of them, you can't smell or taste the drug in the drink at all. Someone must have given us enough Nembutal or something to knock us out for a few hours. Long enough to get us here."

Shards of the evening came back to me in a jumbled rush. The party. Nazif's hands holding mine. The shadow puppet show. Maeve's suitcase. The urn.

"We found the urn in Maeve's suitcase, didn't we?" I recalled. "We were taking it to my room. And then—then—Sage! Where's the urn?!" I groped around frantically, my fingers scrabbling at the dirt.

"Gone," said Sage. "You fell and dropped it in the hall, right before we got to your room. And that's the last I saw." She stifled a sob. "We came so close to shutting down Lazar. All we needed was to get the urn to Inspector Lale—and she was *in the building*! How could all this have happened with a police officer in the hotel?"

"She was talking to my aunt privately," I said. "About my uncle's murder. She wasn't exactly patrolling the hotel at the time we recovered the urn from Maeve's luggage."

"And who drugged us?" Sage asked in an ominous tone. "Or who drugged *you*?"

"What do you mean? We were both affected."

"Yeah, but you shared your drink with me while I was hiding out in your room. I mean, no one knew I was there. Somebody wanted to take you out. I was just a side effect."

My stomach seized as I thought through the suspects. "It couldn't have been Nazif," I said. "He's been on my side with this from the start. And not Orhan," I added. "Even though he was in charge of food and drinks, he's helped us so much. I don't know why he'd drug me."

"Who handed you the drink?" Sage asked.

"Judy Clarkson." Suddenly I sat up straighter. "Wait a second. She went to the drinks table for a refill and came back with juice for me. Oh my God. Unless it was one of Orhan's helpers in the kitchen, *Judy* could have laced it." Then I remembered the shoe with the tassel I'd seen just before I blacked out. "And I think Ron was right on our tail when we got the urn. I'm sure I saw his shoes, and I'm sure he's the one who took the urn!"

"The Clarksons," breathed Sage. "Oh my God. I never would have thought."

"You didn't ever suspect they knew anything?"

"No," Sage insisted. "Riza said they were using a boat that Lazar owned, or probably stole—he'd gotten it in Greece through some chain of connections he had—and he said the Clarksons were real paying passengers. Lazar told me never to speak of the urn or any of our business around them. He didn't want them to suspect a thing." She paused. "Now I see he didn't want *me* to suspect they all knew each other."

"They were lying, all of them," I said. "*Everyone* on that boat was involved in Lazar's smuggling ring. It all makes sense now. Nazif said there were two Americans at the Lycian Society meeting at my aunt's hotel, the meeting where Lazar first showed off the urn and gave it to my uncle to make up those papers. I bet those Americans were the Clarksons."

"Not only that," said Sage, "the Clarksons could be the ones who are buying the urn from Lazar once it's packaged and ready to go! He probably told me not to say anything about the urn around them because he didn't want them to know it had gone missing, that he'd screwed up the deal."

"Sage." I swallowed hard. "If the Clarksons somehow figured out the urn went missing, maybe they came to the hotel to look for it themselves. They could have drugged me to get me out of the way."

"Yeah, but how would they have any clue that the urn might be at the hotel?"

"I don't know. Maybe Lazar had a spy in the hotel who heard us talking about the plan."

"Nazif knew the plan," Sage said slowly.

I shook my head, and the earrings I was still wearing jangled loudly. "I can't believe he'd betray us. He's as scared of Lazar as we are. And he's been helping me so much." Nazif was the first person I completely trusted—I couldn't believe he would be a spy. "But anyway, it doesn't even matter how the Clarksons found out about the urn, because they have it now."

We fell silent for a moment, letting this horrible fact sink in. The urn was gone again. "Not only that," I continued, counting off new problems on my fingers, "Lazar's still on the loose, free to run his smuggling ring. The urn won't be reunited with the Karun Treasure. No one will be held accountable for my uncle's death. And, oh, yeah—we've been drugged, kidnapped, and left in a cave to die."

"Why would someone leave us here?" Sage moaned.

"Because they knew we were a security risk for this whole operation. This was a way to silence us. I just can't figure out how we got put somewhere so far away. I mean, if I couldn't get four small gold figurines through airport security, how did *they* get through with two passed-out foreign girls?"

"Lazar has access to a private plane," said Sage. "That's how I got to the coast for the Blue Voyage. His personal pilot took Riza and me. The pilot is involved in the smuggling ring, too. Transporting us wouldn't be so hard at all, as long as he could sneak us out of the hotel without attracting attention."

My head throbbed. "How long do you think we've been gone?" I wondered if Mom and Aunt Jackie were frantic by now, looking for us. I wondered what Nazif was doing and if he'd told anyone about the plan, since it had clearly gone awry.

"No idea," said Sage. "And who knows if it's day or night outside. If we did have Nembutal, that drug lasts several hours."

"Since when are you such a drug expert?"

"I had to learn about drugs as part of my student orientation at the international school. And you know, having a brother who OD'ed made me extra cautious about drugs. So I've done my research. I can tell you that some other drugs they could have used might last a little longer, or he could have slipped us a second dose and we were too out of it to know. But one thing's for sure. We have got to find a way out of here. We're going to need water soon. All these types of drugs they can mix with drinks to knock you out are really dehydrating." I felt her stand up beside me, and I heard her start feeling the walls with her hands.

"What are you doing?" I asked.

"Checking for exits. Ancient civilizations made entire underground cities in the volcanic rock. They'd retreat down here when intruders came. There are supposed to be about thirty-six of these underground cities in Cappadocia. But they all have interconnected rooms. That's what I'm looking for."

I stood up too, wobbling on my heels. "Damn shoes," I grumbled, kicking them off. "So if you find an exit, and we get out, then what?"

"Riza told me the headquarters of Lazar's smuggling ring is based in one of these underground cities," she said. "One that hasn't been fully excavated or opened to the public for tours. He told me they use caves and tunnels to store their loot. They take it to artisan workshops nearby to have the artifacts disguised as replicas, or to have them deceptively packaged. Then the goods come back to his headquarters, awaiting shipments or pickups."

"So you want to go spelunking in Lazar's underground cave city?"

"I'm just saying there has to be a way out," she said. "Whoever put us in here had to use an entrance, right? They didn't build the cave around us. And these cities were all warrens of rooms and tunnels. Sometimes long tunnels can even connect one settlement to another."

"You sound so sure. I thought you didn't trust Riza anymore."

"It's not just Riza," said Sage. "I once went to one of the cave cities that's open to the public, when I did some filming for that tourist video company. I had to do a whole narration about it. I know that some of the rooms have rocks that sealed the doors or windows. Others have small holes for entry or exit points, where families used to push big rocks to seal themselves off from intruders."

"So there has to be an exit here."

"Exactly. You check the floor, and I'll do the walls. See if you feel any cracks. If there's any movement, if anything gives just a little, push as hard as you can."

We searched in silence, feeling every inch of floor and wall. I stretched my arms and felt around on the ceiling, wincing as the crumbly rock and dust fell into my eyes. Then I pushed on the ceiling and felt it give way. Like a hidden ceiling panel. "Sage! I think I found it!" I cried out. "Help me push this thing. It's really heavy!"

Together we pushed with all our strength until the panel heaved up and off. A round slab of rock had been covering a hole. By feeling around, we could tell that the portal was as wide as our bodies. Just wide enough to drop two girls in, cover them up, and leave them for dead.

"They were trying to bury us alive!" I exclaimed in horror.

"I know," said Sage. "Still, they might come back to check on us, and make sure their attempt was successful. We can't waste time. Let's go."

41

Sage gave me a boost, and I pulled myself up through the hole. Then I reached down and pulled Sage up. We found ourselves in an identical prison. No light. Same dimensions. Also, apparently, sealed off. But now we knew the kind of blocked portal we were feeling for. After a few minutes of scrabbling around, we found another rock seal that gave way when we pushed, this time in the wall. We found ourselves in yet another cave, staring into more inky blackness straight ahead.

I went in a little farther.

"Come back," Sage called, her voice echoing off the walls.

"It's a tunnel," I said. "We'll have to crawl. I can't stand up all the way."

"Wait," she said. "It's completely dark. We can't just crawl off into darkness."

I came back. "You'd rather sit here? And see who pops by for a cozy chat?"

"No. I don't know. I just wish we had a flashlight or something. It's creepy."

"Of course it's creepy!" I said. "Evil people dropped us into a cave and left us to die! They weren't going to send us to

Disneyland. Anyway," I added, softening my tone, "the only way out is through. I didn't find another exit in this room, did you?"

"No," she admitted.

"Okay. So we're going to go through this tunnel. Let me just tie my dress somehow. It's dragging me down." I tied two knots in the skirt to hike it up a little and free up my legs.

"Good idea," said Sage, doing the same. "And I'm going to lose the trench coat. It's just getting in the way."

I heard only rustling sounds as we made our adjustments, and then Sage cried out.

"What? What?" I exclaimed. "Are you okay?!"

Click-click. Whoosh. Sage was bathed in the soft white glow of a cigarette lighter!

"Coat pocket," she said, smiling. "My friend at the hammam is a heavy smoker. These are her clothes. I suddenly realized she might have a lighter in her pocket!"

I'd never felt so grateful for someone being a smoker.

"There's not a lot of fluid left, but let's see how far we can get. And there's this." She passed me a stick of gum. "Dinner's on me. Thank me later."

I popped the gum in my mouth and nearly cried as my mouth watered in appreciation. Water. This gum might have to last me awhile. I remembered one of my climbing instructors telling me about a time he'd gone rock climbing and dropped his water bottle—he'd sucked on pebbles to stimulate his saliva glands. We could do that, but it would only bring temporary relief. Eventually, if we didn't get out from underground and get water, the dehydration would do us in.

We started crawling. Sage led the way this time. Progress was slow, as she held the lighter with one hand. Our shadows loomed and flickered alongside us, as if ghosts were following us. I knew I shouldn't feel afraid. I tried to imagine what kind of story Nazif would turn our shadows into, if he were to do a puppet show. I conjured the image of his beautiful bird puppet, leading me out of the cave. Maybe I was dehydrated, or the drug hadn't worn off completely yet, but at times I could have sworn I saw Nazif's shadow bird, flitting just ahead of us, around the corner, leading us back to safety.

The tunnel seemed endless. It took a few twists and turns, and went slightly uphill, which seemed encouraging, but then it dipped sharply and went downhill again.

"Fluid's getting really low," said Sage as the lighter flame sputtered. *Shick, shick, shick.* She flicked it a few times, and sparks flew out.

"Then I think we should save it for emergencies," I said.

"I would consider this to be an emergency," said Sage.

"Maybe not, right? Things could always be worse," I countered. "That's our family motto, anyway." *Mom's* motto, which I now wanted, more than anything, to believe . . . and to hear her say again. I'd been so annoyed when she used the phrase on our first day in Turkey, when we'd gotten lost driving. But now I understood why she said it. Her optimism was her way of keeping herself together—and maybe keeping our family together, too, in some way. Because if you didn't have hope, what was left? You would just crumble inside. You'd give up.

Sage flicked the lighter off and put it in her skirt pocket. We crawled through the darkness, moving a little faster now that Sage had use of both hands. "I love that your family has a motto," she said. "I wish my family had had one." She paused. "I wish I'd had your family."

I couldn't help laughing at that, even though there was nothing funny about our situation.

"I'm serious." Sage sounded hurt. "I saw you and your mom and your aunt on the boat, that first day, and I was just so jealous, I could barely stand to be around you guys at first."

"Jealous!"

"I probably gave *you* the evil eye. So now all this bad stuff happening to you is my fault." She thought a moment. "Actually, it *is* all my fault. I'm sorry. I destroyed your vacation."

"Apology accepted," I said. "But you have to understand, I never considered myself on vacation in the first place. And it's *not* all your fault. Remember, my uncle Berk was mixed up in all this. Maybe he's the one to blame. You see? My family's a complete mess. There's not much to be jealous of."

"Just because your uncle got entangled with a smuggling ring and might have gotten murdered doesn't mean your family is a complete mess."

"That's not even the half of it." I hesitated, then told her more. "My parents are splitting up. My dad's the Massachusetts attorney general. And he's running for governor. He had an affair with a campaign donor, and it went public."

"Oh my God," she said.

More words tumbled out. Unstoppable, like rocks rolling down a cliff. I told her the rest. About my friends dropping me. The Athleta incident. Everything. It felt good to talk about it out in the open at last—even though this cave wasn't exactly out in the open, it felt good to *talk*. Not to a shrink, but to someone my age. To a friend.

"That's really horrible," Sage said. "You've handled it so well, though."

"I have?"

"Yeah. And I'm still going to say it: I'd take your family over mine. Any day."

"Why?"

"You guys actually like each other," said Sage. "You want to be around each other. So you're not perfect—who is?—but you keep trying to connect with each other. I mean, you and your mom came all the way to Turkey to see your aunt! And then you dropped everything to help her! My family just gave up. And I gave up on them, too. You know the story I told you about the suitcase my parents gave me?"

"Yeah. How it encouraged you to be a world traveler?"

"Right. I told you they said 'Just go,' like 'Just go off and have adventures.' But that's not what they actually said. They said 'Go' as in 'Get out.' They said, 'If you don't like this house, you can go try to make it on your own.' So that's exactly what I did."

We crawled in silence after that, each of us lost in our own thoughts. Or maybe we were conserving our strength at that point. We'd been creeping for a long time now, and there was no end in sight. But at least we were in it together.

The tunnel ascended again. "Good sign," said Sage, her voice raspy. "Up leads to out."

"I like up, too," I said, thinking of my climbing walls. Would I ever see Burlington Boulders again? Or my mom? Even my dad would be a welcome sight right now. I'd have those stupid appetizers with him and Victoria if I could just get out of this endless maze.

Suddenly Sage stopped short, and I crashed into her.

"Oof. Why'd you stop?"

"Shhh. Hear that?"

I listened, and heard a scraping sound. "Rats," I guessed, shivering. "Or bats?" My skin crawled. Sage flicked on the lighter. No rats swarmed around us. No bats hung above. But the weak light showed that the corridor made a Y. One tunnel went left, the other right. We listened carefully. Murmuring. Tapping. Footsteps. Voices.

"I hear men talking," Sage whispered. "Off to the left, I think."

"Is it Lazar and Vasil?"

"I don't know. They work with a lot of people. But we don't want to end up in some office here. Let's go right. And we'd better stop talking." She shut off the lighter.

We resumed our crawling, in silence now, and went on as quietly as we could. Suddenly the tunnel widened and got taller, and we were able to stand up and walk, stooped over and pushing ourselves along off the walls. My hands stung, and I knew they were scraped and bloodied. But the wider tunnel made hope surge inside me. We had to make it out of here alive! I thought of all the things I still had to do. Like find a real boyfriend someday. Like be a counselor at a climbing camp for kids—I'd be really good at that. And I wanted to be an awesome older cousin to Aunt Jackie's baby. And travel more—maybe even with my mom again.

Suddenly we heard men's voices echoing down the hall. Behind us, and not far.

"Oh, no!" hissed Sage. "They're on to us!"

Then we heard feet pounding on earth, coming after us— or were they echoes of our own footsteps as we began to run, too? I couldn't be sure. I just bolted. The tunnel went up, and up, and up, slanting at a forty-five-degree angle. Was I imagining it, or was it just a little bit lighter now?. A man began shouting at us. We scrambled faster, forward, onward . . . turned a corner . . . and found ourselves staring at a narrow crack in the wall, where a bit of light leaked through. We flung ourselves against the wall, feeling around the crack for anything that might give way. The footsteps behind us grew louder.

"This part of the rock wedged in here is fake!" Sage cried, grabbing hold of a crudely cut rectangular wedge of stone that was about her height. She slammed her body against it, and more light leaked in around the edge. I joined her in slamming my body against it, too, and after three tries the slab door groaned open.

We ran outside. Into air. Sweet, fresh air! I drank it in great gulps.

"Don't stop!" cried Sage, and we ran on.

Pink sky. The sunrise hurt my eyes, but it felt good. I didn't care what it was doing to my skin. I stumbled, and gaped at the landscape. I'd seen pictures in Lonely Planet, but in person it was so much more intense.

I could hardly breathe. I motioned to Sage to stop, and I tried to catch my breath. Then I looked up and saw we were surrounded by tall mounds of pink and gray earth made of volcanic material. They were long and slender, paler and rounded at the top. "Holy crap," I said, managing a laugh between gasps. "It's a land of giant . . . male . . . um . . . phalluses?"

Sage coughed violently and spat some dust she'd inhaled. "They're called fairy chimneys, actually," she rasped, "sculpted by hundreds of years of wind and erosion. But this is no time for nature appreciation. We have to get out of here."

"So soon?" Lazar came running from behind a fairy chimney. Alone. "You ladies are quite the escape artists."

Rage boiled up inside me. "Is this the place you brought my uncle to?" I yelled. "Is this where he fell? After you *pushed* him?"

He regarded me coolly. "Your uncle was a liar. He was supposed to bring me that urn when I summoned him here. But he gave me an empty backpack, and for that he paid the ultimate price. I am a businessman. I do not play games."

"I don't play games, either," I said. "Like cave hide-and-seek. You had no right to lock us up in there."

"We know your client has the urn now," said Sage. "We know Ron Clarkson got it at the hotel before we passed out. So if he has the urn, and you got your money, you can just leave us alone!"

He took a step toward us, a vein twitching at his temple. "You have damaged my business!" he shouted. "My clients heard that silly Australian woman talking to her husband in Fethiye. They heard her mention a golden seahorse urn she found. This urn was found on a hillside. My clients got worried. I was forced to tell them they might leave Turkey without the urn. This was unacceptable to them. And to me. Now they worry about information leaks. They do not feel safe doing business with me anymore." He paced, his hands balling into fists. "I know you talked to police. Maybe to your father. Maybe to other people. I must know everyone you talked to." He stood directly in front of me, so close I could feel his breath hot on my face. "If you want to save yourself, you will come talk to me now. Back in my office." He gestured toward the narrow crevice that looked like a crack in a mesa wall, through which we had managed to exit his underground lair.

"Wait. How did the Clarksons know we were looking for the urn in the hotel?" I demanded. I didn't know where I was finding my courage, but as long as he didn't have a weapon in his hand, and Vasil wasn't with him, I wanted answers. Besides, the longer we stood outside in the open talking, the more hope

I had that someone might come by and save us—despite the completely desolate landscape stretching out in all directions.

"Zan, what are you doing? You don't have to ask him all this. Let's get out of here!" Sage hissed.

"We helped get the urn back, in a way," I said to her. "So I think he owes us an explanation." I folded my arms across my chest and glared at Lazar. At my uncle's killer. "So. Did you have spies following me around or something? Who told the Clarksons about the urn in the hotel?" *Please don't let it have been Nazif.*

"Smart girl," he said, narrowing his eyes at me. "Yes. Too bad I didn't get to you earlier. You're just the kind of young person I like to hire. You are correct. The new maids at the hotel worked for me."

I felt sick to my stomach. The harmless-looking old ladies I'd seen Mustafa talking to in his office the day before the party? Spies. I should have known. I should have found some reason for Mustafa not to hire them. Sage had said Lazar had used hotel staff spies before for information and for attempts to find the urn. Lazar seemed to have an endless supply of hired help to give him inside information. I could have prevented the Clarksons from coming to the party if I'd just remembered all that and spoken up. Once again, just like not telling anyone about my dad and Victoria, my sitting on information had caused an avalanche of bad results.

Lazar smirked. "You are wondering how they heard, yes?"

I nodded. They'd barely had time to start their jobs, they were such new hires.

"They heard you and the bellboy talking, through a heating vent in the wall. Never trust old houses. Once I had this information, I told the Clarksons that you planned to search for the urn in the guests' room during the party. They insisted on coming to the party to get the urn themselves. Then we discovered a new problem." He took his eyes off Sage and looked at me, and his gaze, so full of hatred and even disgust, seemed to pierce my soul. "I learned that you have a famous father. A politician. Yes?"

Mutely, I nodded, as he took a step toward me.

"Government connections. Maybe embassy connections. We knew you would talk, and maybe you had talked already. I gave Judy something to put in your drink. What a lot of extra work you made for us!"

"How did you get us out of the hotel?" Sage demanded. "That party was full of people."

Lazar laughed, though it came out more like a sharp bark. "The band that came to the party? They work for me as well. Some musicians took a break during the puppet show. They rolled you up in carpets. They took the carpets, with you in them, out the front door to make room for a dance floor. Nobody questioned this."

Wait. We'd been *rolled up in rugs*?

"Then, before anyone even knew you were missing, you were on your way to the airport and to my company's private plane," Lazar concluded.

"You're right, we did make a lot of work for you," I said. "Why not just take us out into the alley and slit our throats?"

"Too much risk. I needed to kill you because you know too much about my business. You could talk to officials. Okay, so I kill you in Istanbul. But then there are problems. Your father would use his political connections for a long investigation. I am an expert at avoiding such things. But the Clarksons, they were afraid. They said if I killed you, I must make it look accidental."

I glared at him. "We accidentally got sealed up in a cave city?"

"Yes." He looked at Sage. "Your friend Sage from the cruise contacted you, inviting you to Cappadocia to go rock climbing. You boarded a bus and went to meet her. You left a note for your family."

"Well, they'd never believe that. They know Sage doesn't like heights. She wouldn't go rock climbing." This was true. They'd seen her turn green, I was sure, at my uncle's cliff tomb ceremony in Fethiye. I felt a surge of hope and tried to signal that to Sage, who flashed me a stricken look. My family would find the fake note. They'd know something was wrong. They'd send help to Cappadocia. Maybe Inspector Lale herself.

But how soon?

Lazar looked back at me, his eyebrows knitting together. "I didn't intend for you to die in there immediately," he said. "You owe me something."

I held out my empty hands. "I have nothing."

"Information," he said. "I need to know everyone you girls talked to. I will give you this chance to come on your own, to my office in the cave city, with no force."

"No way," said Sage. "We're not going back in there with you. Or ever again."

Keep him talking. Buy more time. My family, or Nazif, will send a search party. How big is Cappadocia, anyway? I tried to steady my voice. "And the Clarksons? Where did they go?" I asked. Movement from behind a fairy chimney filled me with momentary hope, but then I saw it was only a bird. A large bird resembling a vulture, nothing that Nils or Ingrid would have wanted to find. It uttered an ugly squawk and flapped away.

"With us," Lazar said, frowning, clearly getting impatient with my twenty questions game. "They picked up their other parcels at my office and departed. But now I have told you enough. You owe *me* information. Your turn. Maybe you need some motivation." He reached into his back pocket. I gasped, and clutched Sage's arm, expecting to see the dagger with the jewel-encrusted hilt.

Instead it was a wire brush. He held it in one hand and tapped it in the other. Then he reached down to the ground and brushed away some of the footsteps he'd made in the dust. I watched in horror as I realized what he was doing, and how the signs of a scuffle at the top of a cliff could so easily be erased in the volcanic dust.

Lazar looked up at me and smiled. "You see? Erasing people is not so difficult," he said. "Cleaner. It is more my style, to create an accident. Fewer questions later. Come back to the cave and we talk, or we take you with force."

Vasil came running around a fairy chimney from the opposite direction.

"Oh, good, Vasil is here." Lazar smiled. "Vasil, it seems these girls do not want to visit with us. What should we do?"

Vasil reached into his pants pocket and took out a gun. "I went back for this. We need?" He cocked the gun and pointed it at us.

Sage stifled a scream. I sucked in my breath as we clung to each other, backed up against a tall boulder.

Lazar said something harsh to Vasil in Bulgarian or Turkish.

Sage slipped down to the ground. Was she fainting? I pulled her up, and realized she had something in her fist now. She'd picked up something from the ground.

Lazar and Vasil continued to argue, even though Vasil still had the gun trained on us. I imagined Lazar was warning him not to take our lives yet. He didn't have his precious information from us.

Nor was he going to get that information. Sage wound up her arm and threw the rock directly at Vasil's head. The baseball-sized rock with jagged edges struck him on the forehead, drawing blood.

"Run!" Sage shouted at me, grabbing my arm and pulling me sideways while he staggered backward, confused.

We ran and ducked behind another fairy chimney, bullets exploding behind us. My feet seemed to move on their own. Blood coursed through my veins. We ran to the next fairy chimney and the next, trying to confuse our pursuers by weaving a crazy pattern. Ducking behind the chimneys helped us avoid the gunfire that occasionally burst from Vasil's gun, followed by Lazar's shouts.

We came to a ledge with a slope leading about ten feet to the ground.

"What now?" Sage cried out.

"Slide!" I said.

We jumped and slid on our backs to the bottom.

Lazar and Vasil followed fast. But when I glanced back, I saw they both tripped getting up from the slide, which bought us a little more time. We ran on, through the forest of fairy chimneys.

They were larger now, some rising over a hundred feet high. My long dress came unhitched, and tore on bushes that we thrashed through. My bare feet stung. Still I ran faster, Sage by my side.

There was no sign of a road, or any human life-form. It was like we had landed on Mars. The landscape had changed slightly, too, the earth turning redder. The fairy chimneys widened into hills and mesas with fatter bases. Some of the hills had dark holes for windows. Unoccupied caves from a long-ago time, built into the rocks instead of underground. I felt like an ant surrounded by anthills. An ant that was going to get stomped on by giants.

"I really need air. And water," I said, stopping to lean on a fairy chimney.

"Me too," said Sage, doubled over. "I don't know how we pulled that off, but I think we lost them. I haven't heard gunshots or footsteps for a while."

"Where are we, by the way? What is this place?"

Sage shielded her eyes and scanned the area. "I'm guessing we're in Zelve. It's a national park. Zelve is famous for its fairy chimneys and its red dirt."

"And for crimes against hikers and tourists," I added grimly, thinking of the map Aunt Jackie had in her file, the highlighted routes twisting like veins. "This is where my uncle was. Should we shout for help?"

Sage made an expansive gesture. "Who would help us? Birds?"

She had a point. The landscape was totally desolate. Why on earth would Uncle Berk have chosen to hike in this creepy place all alone? He wouldn't have. Aunt Jackie was right. He was coerced into coming here.

"I don't want to shout," said Sage. "I'm sure Lazar and Vasil are still nearby and looking for us. We need to hide."

"What about there?" I pointed to a rounded entrance to what looked like a tall, narrow anthill.

"That's a cave," said Sage. "But look at the sign."

Right by the entrance was a Ministry of Tourism sign with words written in English, Turkish, French, and German. In English, it read: DANGER. DO NOT ENTER. THIS CAVE CLOSED TO THE PUBLIC DUE TO EXTREME EROSION AND EARTHQUAKE DAMAGE.

I now remembered Mom and Aunt Jackie talking a while back, on the boat dock, about the earthquake damage to caves out here and how some tourists had died in a cave-in. To the right of the sign was a pile of construction equipment—mostly metal pipes and lumber underneath some clear tarps, though I saw the handles of a pile of shovels and axes, too. I could see the entry to the cave was a small tunnel that had been bolstered by metal boards and a few pipes, as if to hold up the tunnel ceiling. On the right side of the cave was a scaffolding structure, with boards and pipes bracing the cave and in one place going directly through the cave wall. This cave was probably under repair. "Perfect hideout," I said, darting into the cave.

"But, Zan, it's not safe!" Sage lingered in the doorway instead of following me in, peering down the four-foot entryway tunnel I'd just passed through. "It could collapse. It really happens around here."

"Then hopefully Lazar and Vasil will pay attention to the sign. For now, it's our safest hideout. Now hurry! Before they see you!"

Sage looked behind her, then ran inside to join me.

It was a few degrees cooler inside, and dim, with light coming in only through the mouth to the cave and a couple of holes near the cone-shaped top. I touched the rough wall, which was made of the same soft volcanic material we'd found in the cave city. My throat burned, and I longed for water. But there was none to be seen, except—almost cruelly—a drawing on the cave wall that showed the sea.

That wasn't the only fresco inside the cave. Other drawings

showed people in colorful robes, only their faces were all rubbed out, which gave me the shivers all over again.

Sage followed my gaze. "I learned in my art history class at the international school that Islam traditionally prohibits showing human faces in art," she said. "These caves would have been occupied at some point by Christians. This one might even have been a small church. But later, people came and erased the faces."

Stolen faces. Was no art safe in this country? I thought of what Uncle Berk had said, how when art or artifacts are stolen, everyone loses. And I made myself another promise. If I got out of this place alive, I would never steal again. I was sure that other people I didn't know had paid in some way for my crimes. And my family had paid a lot.

Crack. Crack.

"Bullet!" Sage hissed, her eyes wide. "Oh, crap. They must have seen us come in. Get away from the entrance! Hit the floor!"

We retreated to the walls opposite the entryway and crouched down low, covering our heads with our arms.

Crack, crack, crack. This time, bullets whizzed right by the entrance to the cave and echoed off the surrounding rocks. When I dared to open my eyes, I saw, just outside the doorway, a red haze from the dust the exploding bullets had stirred up outside.

"Oh my God. What are we going to do?" Sage squeaked when the volley of gunfire was over. "There's only one doorway. If we walk out, they'll shoot us! And if we stay in here, they'll shoot us! We're cornered!"

"They're trying to scare us," I said. The ringing in my ears was so bad, my own voice sounded far away to me. "They don't want a mess on their hands. Lazar has cleaner ways of offing people. Like pushing them over cliffs and making it look like an accident."

"It's different this time," Sage insisted. "We know too much about his business, and about the Karun Treasure urn. He's at the end of his rope. And we're in the middle of nowhere. Who's going to see any mess he leaves behind?"

I shook my head. "It's precisely *because* he's so desperate that he needs to avoid a mess," I said. "You're the one who told me he never shoots at close range. He can't risk a murder investigation so close to his headquarters, with everything that's been going on. He can't shoot us and leave our bodies for someone else to find, let alone a trail of blood that might lead to him. He knows my dad would stop at nothing, and use every connection he has, until he found whoever killed us. To bury his secrets, Lazar needs to bury us so we'll never be found. That's why he tried to seal us up in the cave city."

"Why don't they just come in here and haul us back to the cave city, then?" Sage demanded after another volley of bullets was fired.

Dust rained down the cave walls as the bullets hit the exterior walls. I recalled the warning sign outside.

"No need," I said. "We're right inside a spectacular accident that's just waiting to happen. If we stay here, this thing will conveniently collapse and bury us, except maybe for the entryway. They're not trying to scare us out. They're trying to bring this cave down. On us."

Sage's hands flew to her mouth and she stifled her cry.

"We have to get out," I added.

"What, through the door? Right into their clutches?" said Sage.

"No." My eyes traveled up. Up and up and up an imaginary top rope, to the narrowing top of the cave, about forty feet high. To the only way out that would let us avoid walking right into gunfire. I pointed. "There."

42

Light leaked in through the small carved-out windows way up at the top of the wall. If we could find enough holds in the rough wall, we might make it nearly up to the ceiling, which narrowed at the top, like a cone. Then we could climb up and out one of those small holes, and down the other end of the rock formation, on the opposite side of the entrance to the cave.

I stood up and felt the wall for rock features that might hold our weight, testing out a couple. Some of the volcanic rock crumbled beneath my grip, but eventually I found a few holds.

"What are you doing?" Sage asked, joining me.

I quickly explained my plan. "Follow me up. Put your hands and feet exactly where I do."

Sage looked terrified. "I can't," she said, quaking. "I'm afraid of heights, remember? And I don't know about these walls." She pointed to a wide, spreading crack that ran diagonally around the perimeter of the cave walls, and a spiderweb of cracks and fissures radiating from the doorway. "I'm really worried about the warning sign. Some tourists were buried alive in a cave city a few months ago when they went into a restricted area and started looking for tunnels. Just the pressure of their feet on some weak spots brought the whole structure down on them."

I stared at her. "If this cave's stood for hundreds or thousands of years, it's going to have to stand for ten more minutes. And I do know you hate heights. But you also hate Lazar."

Another round of shots rang out. This time some of the bullets whizzed into the cave. One lodged itself in the ankle of one of the painted figures on the wall, right between Sage and me. We both flattened ourselves against the wall, as if we were frescoes, too. Frescoes with faces twisted in terror.

"At least try to climb," I said when the bullets had stopped. "The higher up we get, the less likely we'll get hit by a stray bullet. And if you can make it halfway up the wall, I bet you can get to the top."

Grim-faced, she looked upward. She wiped her hands on her dress and blew on them. "Okay. Let's do this thing."

My heart was pounding. I tried to take deep breaths and calm myself as I stared at the hole near the ceiling. We had zero climbing gear. And Sage was a novice climber.

I started my ascent. I'd never climbed barefoot before. But suddenly I understood why some outdoor climbers ditched their shoes. I could feel for footholds more quickly without a rubber sole in the way, and use my toes to help grip the rock features.

Sage followed close behind, breathing hard.

We were free soloing now, as I'd started to do back in Fethiye. Soon we were even higher than I'd gotten on the cliff wall back there. And fortunately the bullets had stopped ricocheting around the cave walls inside and out.

"I have no idea how to do this!" Sage cried.

"You're doing great!" I assured her. "Stand on your feet. Pull up with your hands. Don't make your forearms do all the work. Make most of the moves come from the pushing up and your core strength." The voices of my climbing instructors echoed in my head, coaching me, urging me on, and I told Sage every piece of advice I'd ever heard. "Trust your feet!" I called down to her more than once. Every so often I looked down to make sure she was behind me. Once, a hold that looked like solid rock turned out to be only volcanic material. It disintegrated beneath me, sending a cloud of powder into Sage's face. I hung from my handholds, my feet scrambling for something to ground them while Sage spat out dust.

Suddenly we heard a series of loud thuds, and the whole cave seemed to shake.

"They're hitting the walls with something from outside!" Sage cried.

"The metal pipes," I said, remembering the pile of construction equipment outside the mouth of the cave. "Could that really take this cave down?"

"If they hit loose spots, maybe," Sage panted. "If they find just the right spots, it could happen."

"Keep climbing!"

My heart felt like it was going to burst. My throat screamed for water. We climbed at a steady pace, onward and upward.

Our destination, that hole big enough for us to crawl through at the top, was just above me now. But the texture of the cave wall had changed. Except for more spiderweb cracks, it was smooth, and curved upward. There were no natural features to grab hold of. I'd been in a chimney at the climbing gym before, where I'd learned to spread my body between two faces at an angle. I could almost do that here, but my foot scrambled for purchase on the opposite wall, slipping off every time. Volcanic dust snowed down. I had no idea how to swing up to that window.

I'd screwed up and made everything worse. "Zan?" Sage called up. "We're close, right?" The banging of the pipes against the cave walls was relentless. Then we heard a sharper metallic sound. An ax blade striking wood.

"Oh, no," said Sage. "They're hacking at the scaffolding."

A chunk of rock material broke off near the doorway and fell to the floor with a clatter.

"We're so close," I said. "But we're out of holds."

"Isn't there anything we could do to make more?" she asked. "This volcanic stuff can be carved into, you know. That's how people made their cave homes, back in the day."

"I'd need some kind of tool," I said. "Got anything sharp in your pockets?"

"No."

I looked down at Sage's head and saw that her scarf had fallen off. Her long curls were clipped back from her forehead, held by two large barrettes. "Hey," I said. "Let go with one hand, and take off one of your barrettes. Then pass it up to me."

"I'm scared," she said, her voice quaking. "I don't want to let go."

"Don't think about it. Just do it," I begged her. "Nice and slow. There you go," I said, as she slowly released one hand and removed a barrette.

She handed it up to me. I reached down with one hand as far as I could. There were still about five inches between us. I couldn't quite get it.

"Damn!" she cried out as she dropped the barrette. We both watched it slide to the bottom of the cave and lie there among the bullet casings.

"We have to try again," I said.

She ripped out her remaining barrette, then pushed herself up one more foothold to raise herself a few inches higher.

"You're awesome, Sage! You can do it!"

My fingertips grazed the barrette, then grabbed it. Now I had a tool. I got busy scraping at the wall. We were just four moves away from the window. Removing some of the loose volcanic tuff exposed hard rock beneath, which allowed me to create surfaces that stuck out enough for us to grab. In a few minutes I had two new handholds. I inched up higher and exposed more rock to make two footholds. At the very top, it was narrow enough for me to reach out with one foot and one leg to the opposite wall, for balance. Then I reached for the base of the window hole and pulled myself up.

I'd done it! I was out!

The other side of the cave was steep, at a sharp forty-five-degree angle, and a three-foot drop would land us on the top of a narrow mesa below it. It should be even easier than jumping from Aunt Jackie's rooftop to Nazif's. But first I had to get Sage out. I lay on my stomach against the side of the cave, reached in through the window, and helped pull her through. She crouched in the window hole for a minute while I dropped to the top of the mesa, and then she followed me. We stood there a moment, panting and dazed, while little avalanches of pebbles and volcanic tuff skittered down beneath our feet. Our skin and the ripped remains of our clothes were covered in reddish dust.

"There they are," Sage breathed, pointing below. "Lazar and Vasil. They stopped hitting the cave. What are they doing?"

"Arguing, I think," I said. We watched as the two men exchanged a volley of angry words with each other. They dropped the heavy pipes they were carrying. Then Vasil turned to pick up an ax from the pile of construction equipment near the mouth of the cave. Lazar hurried after him.

Sage and I exchanged a look. "They don't know we made it out," she said.

"They'll figure it out soon enough," I said. "Look, they're going into the entryway. Maybe they're going to give up on bringing the cave down, and knock us out and drag us back to the cave city after all."

We heard the rhythmic, metallic sound of an ax on wood again. "The wooden support beams in the entryway," said Sage. "I bet they're going to try to take it down that way. Destabilize the structure from the inside scaffolding. They probably think we're still hiding in the cave behind a rock or something."

I dropped to my knees and started crawling, fast, along the

narrow mesa top, away from the cave. "Don't try to stand. It's like a balance beam, and you'll fall thirty feet if this stuff gives way. Let's get as far from the cave as we can and look for a safe place to slide down this mesa."

"Okay," Sage said, following my lead.

I looked at the landscape for any sign of life. In all directions, it still looked as if we were on another planet. The red rocks and fairy chimneys gave way to pink and then white terrain, folds of smooth hills and valleys like I'd seen on the Voyager Balloons brochure. Occasional scrubby bushes and parched-looking trees poked up here and there.

Then I saw a gray road, snaking through the hills in the distance. A steady stream of cars, trucks, and buses drove along it. Traffic had never been such a welcome sight.

"Look! We can get help!" I exclaimed, almost crying with relief.

In that moment, a loud rumbling made us both stop in our tracks. We turned to look behind us, as the cave we'd just escaped from—the cave containing Lazar and Vasil—crumbled.

All was quiet then, except for the startled cry of a bird that flapped away and left a cloud of red dust in its wake. Then there was only an eerie quiet. Not one cry for help, not one groan.

"I think it killed them," Sage said at last.

"We don't know for sure," I said. "Come on. We have to keep going."

We crawled to the opposite end of the mesa, then sat and slid down a steep slope. When we hit the ground, coughing and gasping from the dust that had risen up, we started running in the direction of the road, with every bit of energy we had left. But suddenly my legs crumpled beneath me. Sage flopped down by my side.

"Guess the road's a little farther than I thought," I said. My own voice sounded far away.

Sage looked at me closely. "You don't look so good."

"I don't feel so good." Everything seemed gray, as if it were going to rain any minute, even though the sun seared my skin.

Sage dragged me under an overhanging rock that offered up some shade, as my legs seemed to have completely stopped working. "I'm going all the way to the road to find help. You rest."

"Don't leave me," I murmured, my eyelids fluttering.

"I have to. Stay there," she commanded. "And don't fall asleep. You might have heatstroke." She smoothed back my hair. "I'll be back as fast as I can, with help. I promise. You just saved our lives back there. I promise, I won't let you down."

She might have said more, but my ears began to buzz and ring. Then she was gone, and the landscape around me erased itself. And then there was nothing, nothing at all.

43

I was amazed to discover I hadn't died.

When I came to, I was in a dim room that smelled of disinfectant. I panicked, groping around me, expecting to feel dirt under my hands, expecting to be back in a dark, dank cave.

Then I heard beeping sounds. From machines. Machines that I was hooked up to. I gasped. Blinked. Looked around. I was in a hospital!

There was a woman leaning over me. Mom! I blinked again. Two figures merged and separated, blurring at the edges. Dad? Was Dad here, too? I suddenly wished that both my parents were with me, together. I forced my eyes open with all my strength. The two figures separated, and one of them came into full focus. Not my dad. It was Inspector Lale.

"You're awake!" Mom exclaimed. "Oh, thank goodness!" She leaned over and hugged me. "My God," she murmured into my hair. "Never, never, never, never do I want us to go through something like that again."

"Me neither," I said, hugging her back. Hard. "Where—where am I?"

"You're in a hospital, in the town of Ürgüp, Cappadocia."

said Inspector Lale, since Mom seemed too overwhelmed to speak. She pulled away at last to sit in a chair by my bed, and held my hand in hers, tears rolling down her cheeks. "You've been treated for severe dehydration and heatstroke," continued Inspector Lale, then went on to explain what had happened.

After Sage left me, she ran until she reached a main road. Two mountain bikers passed by, and she flagged them down and told them there was an emergency. The cyclists, a Turkish couple on their honeymoon, said they'd heard gunfire, and had already called the police. Terrified, they were cutting their ride short and getting out of Zelve. But they detoured and followed Sage back to where she'd left me. Sage was frantic because I'd passed out. The mountain bikers called for an ambulance.

"Meanwhile, Sage used their phone to call your aunt's hotel," Inspector Lale went on. "We'd already assumed you'd been abducted by Ron and Judy Clarkson. Nazif told us everything as soon as it was clear you'd gone missing, when your mother couldn't find you in your room."

"He did? He—Nazif told you? About the urn and everything?"

"Everything," said Inspector Lale, smiling at me. "It's a good thing you confided in him. He was able to give us a great many leads, including turning us on to the Clarksons, who had disappeared as well. He told us he had seen them at a Lycian Society meeting that took place in your aunt's hotel, and that they were the only Americans there. When he saw them watching the beginning of the puppet show, he realized that he knew who they were and he tried to get you a note. He asked one of the caterers to deliver it, to warn you about them. But I'm guessing you didn't get it."

"I didn't," I said. "I wish I had. I wouldn't have gone looking for the urn, then. I would have come right to you."

"I wish you *had* come right to me," she said, a flash of disapproval crossing her face. "But what's done is done. And you've been extremely brave under the circumstances. And, it turns out, extremely helpful."

"Where's Sage? Is she okay?"

"Sage is also being treated for dehydration, in the room next door. She's doing just fine."

I could hear voices murmuring from the other side of the thin wall that separated our rooms.

"Who's she talking to?" I wondered aloud.

"One of my sergeants from the Istanbul police, and some officials from the local precinct," said the inspector. "I've finally persuaded them to take this case seriously and follow all of my commands."

"Are they going to put her in jail?" I asked, suddenly fearful for her. It didn't seem fair. Yes, she'd worked for a smuggling ring, and overstayed her visa, and lied to just about everyone. But she'd also started telling the truth. And she'd gotten pulled into this mess by circumstances beyond her control, and gotten in over her head, unable to navigate the murky waters of real, human relationships as easily as she could swim.

"That remains to be seen," Inspector Lale admitted. "It is possible some leniency will be granted in return for her cooperation. She seems quite willing to talk to us and help us prosecute Lazar and other members of his ring. And she should be especially helpful in identifying some of the objects they're removing in the raid."

"The raid?"

"Sage was able to tell us where the entrance to the cave city was, and Zelve national park rangers helped police find it," she said. "They've found a lot of objects already. So even though the urn's been lost, there's a great deal of recovery."

"And Lazar and Vasil? They're dead, right?" I asked. "We saw them run into a cave and then it collapsed. They'd been shooting at us. Did that bring the cave down?"

"We found them both alive, in the rubble, though they were pretty banged up," said Inspector Lale. "Vasil was conscious, with broken bones. Lazar was pinned under rock, unconscious.

They're in custody now. It's possible the bullets they fired and the other damage they caused to the exterior walls and the scaffolding accelerated the cave-in. But that cave was badly damaged from an earthquake last year. Restoration efforts on it had only just begun. You girls are extremely lucky it didn't collapse when you were inside."

I struggled to sit up, but Mom put her hand on my forehead, smoothing my hair and urging me to settle back down. I melted into the pillows. "You should rest," she murmured. "We'll talk later. It's all okay."

Relief washed over me. I was safe. And we'd succeeded—we'd shut down the whole operation! Uncle Berk's death would be looked into again in light of all these new connections. It seemed like a happy ending.

Except. The Clarksons had made off with the urn. The Karun Treasure would remain incomplete, probably forever.

But that wasn't my problem. Or was it? Nazif's words from the other day came rushing back to me: *This smuggling situation, this is all of our problem. Lazar is stealing our history.*

I'd been a thief, but I wasn't one now. I'd forgiven myself for my shoplifting, even if I couldn't explain it, or excuse it. I had been wrong to steal. But if I could do one big thing to make up for all the dumb things I'd done, and all the worry I'd caused other people—especially my mom and dad—I could do it now, by not giving up on the last part of this problem.

"The Clarksons," I said. "They got the urn. And I think they have other stuff Lazar got for them, too. You have to stop them from leaving the country!"

"I spoke with the Clarksons in Istanbul," said Inspector Lale. "They seemed to be victims of the *Anilar* scam, the unregistered boat that was hijacked by criminals. I took down their contact information at that time, but they're not where they said they'd be staying. There is obviously more to their story than innocent tourists being scammed on a cruise. They were directly involved in your abduction. So believe me, I'm very interested in speaking further with them, if only I could find them."

"I bet they're still here in Cappadocia," I said. "And they're the ones who poisoned me and took the urn right out of my hands just before I passed out."

Inspector Lale gave me a long look. "I can take them in for questioning, if we find them, on the grounds of your accusation alone. And it will help that Nazif can testify he saw them at the Lycian Society meeting back in April. But you must be very, very certain about what you're saying."

"Of course she's sure," Mom snapped. "My daughter wouldn't make up something like that."

"I'm sure Judy gave me a drink of laced juice. And I saw Ron's shoes at the party, right before I passed out," I said. "They're the same brand my dad wears. I'm positive he took the urn from me. Also, Lazar said they were on the private plane with Sage and me, while we were drugged. They came out here to pick up the rest of their order. Lazar's like their personal shopper."

"I'll put out an alert at the local airports right away, in case they try to leave," said Inspector Lale, taking out her phone.

"Voyager Balloons," I said. "Call them, too. The Clarksons booked a balloon ride with them. It's supposed to launch tomorrow at six in the morning."

"I don't know if they'll have the leisure time for a balloon excursion if they're holding on to hot goods and they know Lazar was taken down in a raid," said Mom.

"Every lead is worth following," said Inspector Lale. "Even if they don't take the balloon ride, they may have given the company some contact information. I'll give them a call." Already she was dialing numbers as she left the room, her heels clicking on the tiled floor.

"*Now* you can relax," Mom said, pushing me gently back into the pillows. "It's all out of your hands, officially."

I managed a smile. But I knew there would be no relaxing for me unless the Clarksons were captured and the urn was recovered once and for all.

"Do you want anything?" Mom asked. "Or do you want to try to sleep some more?"

I swallowed hard. I knew what I wanted. A connection to both my parents right now, even if we couldn't all be together. "A phone," I said softly. "I want to call Dad."

44

In the late afternoon, when Sage and I had recovered enough to be discharged, Inspector Lale borrowed a car from the local police precinct and drove us, and Mom, to a hotel run by Aunt Jackie and Uncle Berk's friends in a nearby village. She told us that she'd reached Voyager Balloons, who'd said the Clarksons had called to cancel their ride.

"They're on the run, then," I said.

"They won't get far," said Inspector Lale. "They can't cross a border without getting apprehended."

"I don't know." I couldn't shake the feeling that the Clarksons might have some devious way to get out of the country with all their illicit goods. "Anyway, even if you catch them, they might have shipped the urn somewhere, or hidden it again. And without that urn, I feel like we failed Uncle Berk." I leaned my head against the window, in the backseat I shared with Sage.

"We didn't," said Inspector Lale. "There'll be an investigation into his death. This is exactly what your aunt wanted to happen. Lazar and Vasil are going to be in prison for a long, long time."

"But the urn is gone for good," I said.

Inspector Lale shook her head. "Not necessarily. We have enough on the Clarksons to get them extradited, if we can locate them. But what's most important, Zan, is that your Uncle Berk would be so glad that you did everything you could to prevent this crime." She hesitated, then continued. "You see, your uncle was deeply concerned about our country's vanishing history. We were working together, these past two years."

Mom frowned. "I thought you worked together a decade ago."

"We did, at the museum," said Inspector Lale. "But more recently, he approached me asking if I had any job leads. I had just started working for the national police, and I told him I had an unusual one. It didn't pay, and it involved some secrecy, but it was for a very good cause. When we worked together at the archaeology museum, we were secretly writing a catalogue of items in the storage facility, which were at great risk of theft because no one really knew about everything that was there. I asked him if he would continue this work, going into smaller museums and mosques to catalogue their storage collections, too. So many of these places don't even know what they have, and they have more than they can ever display. This information would help me to identify stolen or confiscated items that might surface, and it would help to make these smaller institutions less vulnerable to theft."

I nodded, recalling the spreadsheets I'd seen on my uncle's office computer, and the stack of printouts he'd had in an envelope with Inspector Lale's name on it. Those documents must have been part of their project. Uncle Berk and the inspector had been like underground warriors, trying to preserve Turkey's heritage from within.

"I thought *everything* in museums had to be catalogued anyway," said Sage.

"It should be," said Inspector Lale. "But that's not always the case. Museums and mosques often have more art objects than they can handle. Smuggled artifacts that get confiscated are sometimes given to museums by the police stations, which simply have no room to store them. Or items are given to them when more treasures are unearthed by construction work in cities, or even by earthquakes. It's a massive project to document these hidden treasures, but we made it our mission. And we told no one, outside a trusted circle of professionals and police officers, thinking that discretion would be to our advantage. Berk's data can prove that certain stolen items came from particular storerooms."

"But Berk went to those secret Lycian Society meetings," said Mom, scratching her head. "And he was given the urn at that meeting. He'd been hiding it in his office, passing it off as a fake. Doesn't that make him a thief, too? Or at least an accomplice to crime?"

"I understand your concern," said Inspector Lale. "But I assure you, the urn was housed in his office temporarily, with my full knowledge. He kept it there, with the replicas he used for his lectures, in case anyone broke into his office and went looking around. All the while he was working undercover for me, and we were creating a plan to get the urn into the hands of museum officials. This was going on just days before he died."

"So he was working for the good guys all along?" I asked, relief flooding over me.

"He *was* one of the good guys," Inspector Lale said. "I authorized him to work for Lazar as my undercover agent. He did small jobs for Lazar first, to gain his trust. He certified some smaller antiquities as replicas to facilitate their transport, and worked his way up in Lazar's business as a freelancer in that way. Ultimately, the goal was for him to expose Lazar's operation, as well as the Lycian Society's secret group of illicit collectors. But when Berk saw the seahorse urn, he immediately knew it was a long-lost item from the Karun Treasure that scholars have been seeking. It was a groundbreaking discovery for archaeology scholarship, and for Turkey. He couldn't let this precious item slip away into the black market, and suddenly the mission was not so easy. We knew we had to expose Lazar with the Karun Treasure urn."

"But where did Lazar get the urn in the first place?" asked Mom.

"From a villager who was one of the original looters of the tomb," said the inspector. "The villager had kept this one item, believing it was too beautiful to part with, and that he was meant to care for it. And so it remained in his family for decades, in his little village. But so many bad things happened to this man over the years. All his children died. His wife died. His businesses failed."

"The Karun Treasure curse," I whispered. "Maybe it's true."

"Maybe. So this man, who by then was quite old, finally decided to sell it," Inspector Lale continued. "And he knew Lazar and his group because they frequented his village, coming by and shaking artifacts out of villagers' homes, persuading them to sell. The irony is that the day after giving the urn to Lazar, the old man died. So he cannot even be a witness in a trial."

"Or maybe it's not ironic," Sage said darkly. "Maybe Lazar needed to off him to keep the history of the artifact obscured."

"That was my fear," Inspector Lale admitted. "I was concerned about that, and I wanted Berk to stop his work. It was getting too dangerous; we risked angering Lazar. But Berk insisted on seeing it through." She sighed, then continued. "On the appointed day, Berk gave Lazar the documents. And a fake urn that we had specially made. We had undercover officers ready to arrest Lazar. But we needed the real artifact to remain hidden."

"That's what we were planning, too, at the hotel party, only with the real one!" I said.

"Those kinds of reveals can work," said Inspector Lale. "And the reveal that Berk and I planned was a good idea, in theory. But the problem was that Lazar was smarter than we'd given him credit for. And he didn't fall for the fake, even though we got the best artisan we could find to create it. He fled the meeting place before the Istanbul police could get him and contacted Berk later. He was furious with Berk for trying to trick him. He said that if Berk didn't bring him the real urn, his wife would be killed."

Aunt Jackie! Tears burned my eyes. Aunt Jackie—and my unborn cousin—could have been two more casualties of this mess, had it played out differently. "So how did Lazar lure my uncle to Cappadocia?" I managed to ask.

"Lazar told him to drive out to his headquarters, and to bring the urn. Berk felt he had to do it. He told your aunt he had a tour guide interview because he wanted to protect her. He didn't want her to be questioned and have to lie. I strongly advised him not to travel. I insisted on sending backup for him. He refused the offer—he was sure Lazar would be suspicious if he showed up with an entourage. So he went, alone, and I assumed he'd given Lazar the real urn. But when I heard he died on a hike, I suspected he'd veered from the plan." She paused, then said, "And you know the ending."

Mom raised an eyebrow. "You suspected foul play and you didn't immediately arrest Lazar?"

"I needed evidence," said Inspector Lale. "And more importantly, I needed Lazar. He's slippery, and has many disguises and accomplices. I've worked on little else since Berk died. Now, thanks to the work of Zan, Sage, and Nazif these past few days, I believe I can do one last favor for my old friend, and make sure that justice is served. Berk left our mission intact. He protected me, and our secret project, until the very end. I owe him so much for that. It's a debt I might never fully repay."

I managed a smile. It was so good to hear my uncle was not a bad person after all. Even though he must have taken some money from Lazar, an advance, to pay for the IVF treatments. But however this baby had come into being, our family was going to grow. That would be my uncle's real legacy in this world.

45

Aunt Jackie's friends, a nice middle-aged couple named Can and Fatma Ozden, insisted we stay in their cave hotel for free for the next several days. Sage and I would be required to answer questions for the local police starting the following day, questions about the underground cave and what had happened out on the mesa with Lazar and Vasil. Then we could return to Istanbul and expect to answer even more questions. What was left of our vacation, if you could call it that, was shaping up to be a grand tour of police stations.

Pretty much the last place I wanted to be was in a cave hotel. I was so over caves. But I was pleasantly surprised when Inspector Lale pulled off the highway and threaded through a tiny village that seemed to have been sculpted out of white sand and rock. Pink and red rosebushes dotted the roadside. Women in floral shirts, wide trousers, and white headscarves worked in a field. Several men sat in a shaded plaza playing backgammon. We passed goats and chickens and children playing, finally pulling up to a bluff with outcroppings and ledges, and dotted with windows and doors. Once again, we were in another Turkey.

We came through a gate and into a garden cooled off by lush trees. An oasis. Happy tourists were lounging in chairs, reading books, or chatting quietly. And the room that Sage and I got to share was beautiful. The windows offered a sweeping view of the hills and mesas, which the setting sun was casting in gold. The beds were comfortable, and a tiny rounded door led into a bathroom with a spa-like shower and two fluffy white bathrobes.

I was still wearing Aunt Jackie's now-shredded evening gown, and Sage was still in her friend's outfit, which hadn't held up any better. "They might not be quite your size, but I hope these will do," said Mom, gesturing to two outfits laid out on the beds. Cargo pants, flip-flops, and T-shirts that read *Cappadocia ROCKS!* "I got them at a gift shop near the hospital," Mom explained. "Inspector Lale and I flew out here so fast when we got Sage's phone call, I had no time to pack a bag."

Sage sank onto one of the beds and let out a long breath. "Inspector Lale is amazing," she said. "I can't believe they're not making me stay in prison during all my questioning. I was sure I'd be arrested on the spot."

"I felt the same way when she got us out of the police station in Dalaman," I said. "I think she understands that some situations are complicated."

"I could still end up in prison, though," Sage said, biting her nail. "They're questioning Riza. I know he got arrested. I didn't do that much smuggling for Lazar, and I really just dealt with the smaller items, but Riza might say anything to try to save himself."

"You're out for now, though," I said. "Enjoy your freedom. What do you want to do?"

She thought a moment. "Dinner," she said. "Under the stars. Because if I do end up in a jail cell, that's one of the things I'll miss most." She smiled a sad smile at me. "That and my friends. Like you."

◇◇◇◇◇

By early evening, Sage and I were freshly showered and changed, wearing our identical cargo pants and *Cappadocia ROCKS!* T-shirts. Inspector Lale was staying in Ürgüp, close to the police station, and would be having dinner with her colleagues there. Fatma and Can led us and Mom to specially set-up tables on an outdoor terrace atop the cave, apart from the other guests, sensing we needed some quiet time to talk among ourselves and process all that had happened.

"I don't even know where to begin," Mom said with a sigh, as Fatma brought out our salads. "There's so much to talk about still. I have a lot of questions for you girls. I'm just exhausted from the day."

"I'll ask you a question, then," I said. "When did you realize I was gone?"

"Not long after I checked in on you in your room. Orhan told me he thought he saw you and another girl hanging out."

"That'd be me," said Sage, waving her hand.

"Naturally I was curious," said Mom. "And yes, Sage, the thought occurred to me that you might have come looking for Zan. As soon as Nazif's puppet show ended, I went to check on you, Zanny, since you didn't look well. I just couldn't shake the thought you'd been drinking, and maybe your friend Sage had resurfaced."

"But I wasn't partying," I said. "I'd been poisoned."

"I know that now," Mom said, her eyes glistening. "I can't even comprehend what would make a person poison a child. I'm angrier about that than anything else. But I need to know how you got dragged into all this in the first place. There's a lot you've been keeping from me on this trip, isn't there?"

I hesitated, then nodded and looked down.

"I know I haven't been very available to listen," Mom said, more softly. "I've focused too much on my own problems. But I'm ready to hear you now."

So with Sage's help, over a five-course meal, I told Mom everything. Starting from day one of the Blue Voyage and including one detail I'd held back from Mom and Inspector Lale this entire time: our midnight swim to the *Anilar,* where we'd met the Clarksons, and where I'd first encountered Lazar and Vasil. Even after Fatma brought us dessert—Turkish coffee and rice pudding—we were still talking, pausing only briefly when the call to prayer was chanted from the village mosque. It didn't feel right to me to talk over it. I wasn't sure what I believed in, but I felt a faith in something that I hadn't felt before I came to Turkey. Maybe it was faith in myself.

And for the first time, Mom actually listened, without interrupting, or questioning, or challenging. She just took it all in.

When we were done, with our story and our food, she let out a long sigh.

"We were all frantic, of course, when I came to our room and there was no sign of you," said Mom. "The party broke up immediately. It turned into a search-and-rescue event. Everyone started combing the place. Even Aunt Jackie—I couldn't restrain her."

"What about Milton and Maeve?" I asked, thinking with a pang of the Lobsters, my fake grandparents on this trip. I felt so confused about them, now that I knew they'd held on to the artifact. "Did they ever explain why the urn was in their luggage?"

"Maeve was hysterical," said Mom. "Seriously. We had to give her two glasses of wine to calm her down. She insisted she wasn't a thief. She said she glimpsed the urn in the bushes during the search efforts, and convinced Milton to go and get it. Then she didn't know how to return it to Jackie. The longer she kept it in her cabin on the boat, admiring it, the more awkward she felt about giving it back. Milton kept trying to convince her to do it, so she said she planned to leave it for Aunt Jackie with an apology note before they left the hotel."

"Does she know we did her a big favor by stealing it back?" I asked. "If she'd tried to take it back to Australia, they would have found it at customs."

"She knows now," said Mom. "And she's happy to have it off her hands. She's horribly embarrassed about the whole thing, and she just wants you back safe and sound, Zan. Maybe you'll even get to see her while we're out here. They're flying to Cappadocia this evening. Guess who won the Voyager Balloons raffle!"

I laughed. "Milton must be furious. He had to buy an airplane ticket out here! Are the others coming too?"

"No, they're moving on for different tours. But you should have seen everyone's faces when I told them that you were alive—and with Sage, and that you'd led investigators to the hive of the biggest smuggling network in Turkey. They all went crazy, cheering and clapping."

I smiled. "And Nazif?"

"Oh, he cheered louder than any of them," she said, with a knowing look. "He looked pretty shaken up while you were missing."

I smiled to myself, thinking of how great it would be to talk to Nazif again, to sit close to him on the rooftop. I squeezed my hands together beneath the table, remembering the press of his palms against mine. I could almost conjure up the tingling sensation I'd felt in the stairwell before he gave me the room keys.

"Now, can we all get some rest?" said Mom, pushing her chair back from the table. "We have an appointment tomorrow at the police station in Ürgüp, and I'm sure it won't be a short one."

We walked back to our rooms. Sage and I were sharing a room right next to Mom's. Outside her door, Mom and I hugged.

"I'm sorry," I said. "I should have told you what was going on from the beginning."

"I'm sorry, too," she said. "I probably didn't seem like a very good listener, did I?"

I shrugged.

"I was so busy trying to repair my relationship with my

sister, and stewing over the past, I didn't pause to see what was right in front of me." Mom squeezed my shoulders. "We're still family, you know. You. Me. Aunt Jackie. Your cousin on the way."

"I know that now," I said, smiling. A cousin on the way. I couldn't wait.

When we got inside the room, I changed and lay down on the comfortable bed, under the soft white sheets. I had more space and safety than I'd had in over a week, but I still couldn't sleep. The Clarksons were probably on the run. The urn was still missing.

Eventually a song reached my ears, some kind of music coming from the village. It sounded both festive and mournful, and made me think of gypsies. I could hear what sounded like a clarinet against the wail of strings and the steady tap of drums. A woman's voice slowly rose up in song, riding on those instruments, curling and drifting like smoke. I let the song carry me away, too, into a restless sleep.

◇◇◇◇◇

I woke with a start before dawn. I'd barely slept. I checked my watch in the dim light of the room. It was five in the morning.

Dawn was coming. And a new realization. I reached over to the other bed and shook Sage's arm.

"Hey!" I said. "Wake up."

"I am awake," she said. "What's up?"

"Remember the Clarksons were going to do that balloon tour? With Voyager Balloons?"

"Yeah."

"It's today. It launches in an hour."

"How do you know?"

"I know their brochure by heart. I had to make a sign for our raffle prize, remember? And this is the day the Clarksons planned to go. Ron was griping about the early launch time."

"But Inspector Lale said she called Voyager Balloons and was told the Clarksons cancelled," said Sage.

"Maybe they officially cancelled," I said. "But they must have known Lazar got caught. They probably had to wipe their name off any reservation. It doesn't mean they won't actually go on the ride, though. It seemed really important to Judy. All that stuff about a 'once-in-a-lifetime trip.'"

"Zan, the Clarksons are on the run. They're not going to do a balloon excursion."

I sighed impatiently. "I don't think the balloon ride is really a romantic adventure. I think it's a business venture. And I think it's a one-way trip."

Sage stared at me.

Seeing I had her, I continued. "I think it's a way to get the illegal stuff they bought out of the country. Where they won't get searched at passport control or stopped at a border. They're no strangers to paying for private services. What if they quietly paid a pilot to go off course, into Bulgaria or some other country?"

"Maybe," said Sage, sitting up. "Maybe they're even selling these things to some other buyer. They're art dealers, after all. Zan, I think you should call Inspector Lale."

I picked up the phone by my bedside and dialed Inspector Lale's mobile number, which I had managed to memorize after having called it so often.

She answered on the fifth ring, just as I was about to hang up.

"Sorry to wake you," I apologized. "But I have an idea about the Clarksons."

"You didn't wake me up, Zan, don't worry," said Inspector Lale. I heard cars in the background. "What's on your mind?"

"I think the Clarksons might be doing the Voyager Balloons ride after all. Maybe even under a fake name, or maybe paying someone to keep their names off the passenger lists." I quickly explained the rest of my theory. "Can you drive to Voyager

Balloons right now and see if they're there? I think the launch site isn't too far from where you're staying."

"That won't be necessary," she said. "You see, the Clarksons won't be there. I'm almost at the Kayseri Airport. We got a phone tip last night that they bought two airplane tickets to California. We're planning to intercept them at the gate."

"That's great. But—"

"So you can go back to sleep and not worry now. We're closing in on them. I'll call you a little later and let you know everything that happened. I promise."

I hung up the phone and stared at the wall, thinking hard. Something seemed off.

"What's up?" Sage asked.

"She said she got a phone tip that the Clarksons are heading to the Kayseri Airport, so she's on her way there now."

"Excellent!" said Sage. "Isn't it? You don't look so thrilled."

"It just seems too easy," I said. "I don't trust that tip. Messages aren't always right. Remember, I got two from you that somebody else had written."

I yanked off my pajamas and put on yesterday's clothes.

"What are you doing? Where are you going?"

"Voyager Balloons," I said. "I bet this whole airplane ticket thing is one enormous diversion. I still think my theory holds."

"Wait. What are you going to do there? Stop a balloon from taking off?"

"That's exactly what I plan to do," I said. "At least stall them, until the police can come. And I think we can catch Ron and Judy by surprise. After all, they believe we're dead, right? Last they heard we were brought to Lazar's cave and sealed up somewhere inside it. We're not in the news yet. I think we should just go to Voyager Balloons and rock their world."

Sage got up and dressed quickly too. "But how?" she asked. "We don't even know what town it's in."

"Didn't I tell you I know that brochure by heart?" I said.

"I had to reproduce the map by hand for the raffle sign. The launch site is just a couple of miles away on the main road. If we hurry, we can get there just in time."

Sage flinched as she put on her shoes. "I'll try. But I'm pretty banged up from the rock climbing yesterday."

I knew what she meant. My muscles ached. My skin was raw in places, and my feet were blistered. But I had to put all of that out of my mind. We had to get to the launch site, and with no car, and no driver, we had only our feet to carry us there.

As we slipped out of our room and tiptoed past Mom's room next door, I felt a stab of guilt. I'd snuck back into my house at this hour many times in the past; I just hoped Mom would understand, when this was all over, that I'd done it for a good reason now. I paused by her door, considering waking her up to join us. I hesitated, then tapped on it softly. Then louder. But she didn't answer.

"Zan, there's no time. We have to go without her," said Sage. I cast one last glance at Mom's door, hoping she would forgive me for this one last deception.

46

As the sky turned from pink to gold, we walked down the main highway, as quickly as was possible in the flip-flops Mom had bought us. My feet were soon coated in white dust.

At a sign that read VOYAGER BALLOONS, we veered onto a long dirt road that threaded through scrub brush and mesas. Chalky dust rose up in a cloud around us. We ran up a hill, and saw the launching area spread out at our feet. It was crowded with Voyager Balloons vans, and giant fans inflating hot-air balloons—about twenty of them, I guessed.

"Let's go," I said, and Sage and I hurried down the other side of the hill. Employees wearing blue windbreakers that read VOYAGER BALLOONS on the back rushed around setting things up. The balloons and the baskets lay on their sides, making me think of beached jellyfish, huge swaths of colorful material lying on the chalky ground, rustling in the soft breeze.

"Name for the reservation?" said a man, coming up to us with a clipboard.

"Hotel Mavi Konak," I said confidently.

He looked at the clipboard.

"I'm sure we're on there," I said. "We won the raffle?"

"Ah. Yes." He looked down at his clipboard and frowned. "But these passengers have already checked in."

"Those are my grandparents," I said. "We're flying together. We just came in separate cars."

I held my breath, waiting for the man to accuse me of lying or tell me to get lost.

The man scribbled a note on the clipboard and then pointed with his pen to a red-and-white-striped balloon. "Balloon number twelve. Launch is soon. You are just in time."

We hurried over to the Lobsters' balloon, as all the inflating balloons around us bobbed and rippled and swelled. Giant fans swept cold air into them. There was heat, too, as fuel jets pumped flames. Pilots tested the equipment.

We pushed through billowing balloon fabric until we stumbled out into the air again and found ourselves looking right at balloon number twelve, which was almost entirely inflated now. The Lobsters were standing beside it, looking excited for their ride.

Then, as the fabric of the balloon rippled, I caught sight of another couple. Judy was backing away. Judy and Ron. Judy was pulling Ron by the arm toward another balloon, looking as though she did not want to be noticed by the Lobsters.

"That's them!" cried Sage, pointing. "Let's go!"

"Wait a second." I pulled her behind an inflating yellow balloon so we wouldn't be visible. "Let's see what they're up to first."

Peering around the yellow balloon, I saw that the Clarksons were lugging five medium-sized bags with them, and a square box, as they hurried toward another balloon some distance away.

"Do you think those bags and the box are filled with stolen artifacts?" asked Sage, following my gaze. "Could the seahorse urn be in one of them?"

"Maybe," I replied. Where would *those* things end up if we let them get out of the country? Lost to Turkey. Lost to history.

Ron got into the wicker basket on a blue-and-white balloon. Judy started handing him the bags. He took them gently and set them down inside the basket. When she handed him the box, the lid fell off. The intense rays of the morning sun caught something inside, making it glint.

I nudged Sage. "I think that's the urn! Look how fast Judy's putting the lid back on. We have to call Inspector Lale!"

"On what phone?" Sage displayed empty hands. "Anyway, she'll never get here in time. Their balloon is more than half-way full. They'll be in the air in a few moments."

Already some of the other balloons at the launch site were filled and slowly rising up.

Then Judy took a teal Longchamp tote bag out of another bag, unfolded it, placed the box inside it, and zipped it up. She handed the bag to Ron.

I sucked in my breath sharply. "A bag switch," I guessed, "in case anyone saw the urn in a different bag. And so many women have those tote bags, probably no one would look twice at it."

After the basket was loaded with their bags and packages, a pilot got into the wicker basket with Ron and tested some of the jets. I watched the flames shoot up. "I wonder how far these things can travel, anyway?" I said.

"Far enough with a little extra boost, I bet." Sage pointed to another employee, who was now fastening extra fuel cylinders to the outside of the basket.

At that moment, Judy turned around as she got into the basket. The balloon was almost completely inflated. As she did, a wind caught the yellow balloon we were hiding behind, and moved it enough for us to be seen.

Judy gaped at us. Then she elbowed Ron, who turned and looked at us, too, shock registering on his face.

"Now or never," I said. "Let's go find out what they're traveling with."

We sprinted past the Lobsters' balloon and waved at them, smiling at their astonished faces as we moved on to the Clarksons' balloon.

"Nice day for ballooning," I called out to the Clarksons.

"Nice day to *be alive,*" Sage added with a wicked grin.

Ron muttered something to Judy, which we couldn't hear because of the roar of the fans and fuel tanks all around us.

"I don't think you girls belong here," Judy called out to us.

"Oh, we do," I said, pointing at the Lobsters, who now noticed the Clarksons and looked shocked to see us all together. "Milton and Maeve won the hotel's raffle. We thought we'd join them. Unless you'd like some company?"

"Looks like you have plenty of room for us," said Sage. She stepped up to the basket and looked inside. "Wow. You've sure got a lot of luggage for a day trip."

"Step back," said the pilot, his voice sharp. "This is a private flight."

"Really?" I challenged him. "This is one of those baskets that holds up to sixteen people. You're really going to take it up with just two? And these bags?"

"I am calling security," said the pilot, taking a cell phone from his pocket.

"Good! Do that!" said Sage. "Tell them who these people really are! Tell them—"

"Run along, girls," Judy interrupted, her face clouding over. "You're just in the way."

"Are you really going to treat us so rudely? With Milton and Maeve over there watching?" Sage gestured to the Lobsters, who were squinting in our direction. "I'm sure they heard all about the poisoning and the abduction."

I turned toward Milton and Maeve's balloon. "Call the police!" I shouted, pointing to the Clarksons.

Milton cupped his ear, not quite hearing me. I swore under my breath and pantomimed dialing a phone, hoping he'd get the idea.

"We just want one thing," I said, turning back to the Clarksons. "Give us the urn."

"I don't know what you're talking about," said Judy.

As the balloon inflated behind the Clarksons, my emotions fired up, full-on. I didn't like being talked to like that by yet another person I'd trusted. *"You're* the real reason my uncle, Berk Yilmaz, is dead," I said. "His life's work was all about recovering artifacts that Turkey was losing. I'm going to finish his job. Give me back the urn."

Suddenly, two security guards were on either side of Sage and me. One grabbed Sage. The other lunged for me. I dodged his grasp.

Oh my God. This was all going wrong! We were going to get kicked out of here, and the Clarksons were going to escape with their loot!

Now their balloon was nearly full, and the basket was tipping upward, straining at the tethers that kept it anchored.

The other security guard held my arm and tried to steer me away. "Please, you have to help us!" I cried out. "We're trying to stop a crime. These people are stealing ancient artifacts. They're robbing your country. You can't let this balloon fly!"

"We must ask you to leave the launch area at once," said the grim-faced security guard. "You are not authorized to be here."

"Call the Ürgüp police station," said Sage. "Tell them Ron and Judy Clarkson are here!"

The balloon basket slowly started to rise, as did the other balloons all around us. A ground crew started untying the ropes that anchored the Clarksons' balloon.

"Bye, now!" Judy called down to me as the security guards marched us away.

Rage boiled inside me. Berk couldn't be dead while the Clarksons escaped with the urn. My uncle's work, his life, could not be for nothing.

In a twist maneuver I sometimes used on a rock wall to reach for a distant handhold, I yanked free of the security guard's grasp and ran. I jumped up and grabbed for a handle on the bottom of the Clarksons' basket. Then I clambered over the side and into the basket, and we rose into the air.

47

"Get down!" shouted the pilot.

I grabbed the side of the basket tighter, refusing to go anywhere.

"We're not that high up yet. You can go back over the side and jump down safely," Ron urged me. He almost sounded like the kind father figure I'd met on the *Gulet Anilar.* He even held out a hand as if to help me. But I knew better.

"Oh, *now* you're concerned about my safety?" I said, glaring at him. "After poisoning me? That's so considerate of you."

"That was my wife's idea," said Ron. "Really, I think you should get down now, while you still can."

"Don't pin this all on me, Ron," snapped Judy. "We agreed this was the only way."

I looked over the edge of the basket. Everyone was getting smaller; I couldn't even see Sage anymore. Then the balloon began to drift over the hills and mesas, rising above the landscape I couldn't possibly appreciate now.

I dropped down to the floor of the basket and grabbed one of the weekender bags, the one that was covering up the teal Longchamp bag. The bag was heavy, as if it were full of rocks, and hard. "I'm guessing this isn't clothes," I said.

Judy shoved me aside. "These are our personal belongings." She made a grab for the bag, but I held fast to the handles.

"The police will catch up with you eventually," I said. "There was a raid at Lazar's headquarters. You know, the headquarters in the cave city, where Sage and I were sealed up and left for dead? After you poisoned us?"

Judy gave me a long look. I met her gaze. This time I didn't see kindness in her eyes, but dark intentions, laced with fear. She took a deep breath. "You have no idea how much is at stake here," she said. "How much Ron and I have gone through to get these items. To save them. And you know something? I never fail. I have no intention of failing now."

"And your little scheme of getting someone to call the police won't help," Ron added, the warmth in his voice now completely gone. "We have no record. We're upstanding American citizens. And we won't be caught with anything because these artifacts will be safely transferred to their next destination. Now hand over the bag."

I coiled the straps around my wrists and backed away, out of Ron's reach. Judy grabbed for the bag, and I dodged her too, grateful for the huge size of the basket that allowed for this complicated dance while I tried to figure out what to do next. "So how long do you plan to hide out with this stolen stuff in Bulgaria?" I asked.

Ron and Judy looked at each other, then burst into laughter.

"Oh my goodness. You think we're flying out of the country in a hot-air balloon?" said Judy. "To *Bulgaria*?"

Ron roared with laughter, and even the pilot smirked.

"That's very fanciful," said Judy. "Very imaginative thinking. Bulgaria is a nearby country, but not anywhere near here. Don't they teach geography in school these days? No. We're going to a drop point. We have a client of our own who's expecting these."

"A nice gentleman from Dubai," Ron added. "We made

a better deal. We drop, the client collects, we get our money wired, we're gone, and—"

Judy kicked at his shin, and he pressed his lips together.

"So then where does this balloon end up?" I asked, looking down at the fairy chimneys and the mesas for signs of the chase vehicles that typically followed balloon rides. I couldn't see it, so maybe they hadn't left yet. All the balloons were drifting in the same direction, blown by the soft wind, but our pilot kept working the burners, catching air currents and climbing higher.

Judy smirked. "Oh, we'll get to the drop area with the others, but we'll take our sweet time. After we transfer the goods, we'll land, and the police will surely be interested in knowing why you illegally boarded our balloon, violating all safety regulations, let alone not paying for the ride. Especially since you're a bit of a celebrity yourself, *Alexandra Glazer*," she added, giving me a meaningful look.

I felt dizzy, and not from the swaying basket. She knew who I was. A quick Google search had no doubt revealed all my family dirt, and now she would use it against me.

But I didn't care if the media portrayed me in a negative light. My world had been reduced to the size of this wicker basket, and I was inches away from the Karun Treasure urn. I just had to get it before the drop. But get it and do what with it?

"So your buyer is waiting for you down there?" I asked, scanning the landscape again. Could I jump into a tree? But the landscape was practically lunar—there were barely any trees.

"Actually, our buyer's associates," said Ron. "They work with our friendly pilot here."

The pilot tipped his cap at me and grinned, not kindly.

"I adore this balloon company," said Judy. "They really are the best. Great service. Except they're a bit lax on security. Maybe we should offload you, too. What do you think, Ron?"

"Probably not necessary," said Ron. "The police can do their job when we return."

"Oh, you big baby," said Judy. "You just don't want to do any dirty work, do you." She rolled her eyes at the pilot. "You see what I have to put up with?"

"Why don't you just give up the urn," I said. "And maybe whatever else you bought, too. You can do something great for this country by keeping all these things here."

Judy snorted. "When Turkey gets its act together and has enough museums and decent security, we'll be more than happy to give everything back—for a fee, of course. But until then, we're traveling in a country that doesn't preserve its history. We work with clients who will appreciate these objects. And if we happen to make some money from that, how can we be faulted?"

I scanned the sky around us. Most of the other balloons from our launch were ahead of us, though a few were still nearby, making splashes of color against the stark landscape. We were now slightly lower than all the others, however, and losing altitude rapidly.

I looked down again, then realized the balloon was now approaching a high mesa with a narrow, flat top. We'd be passing over it in just a minute, I guessed, and we were close enough that if I climbed out of the basket, I could drop down. Close enough so I could heave the Longchamp tote with the urn inside it over the side of the basket. It wasn't such a big drop, so hopefully nothing would break.

While the pilot adjusted the jets on the fuel tanks, I dropped the weekender bag onto the floor of the basket. Ron and Judy both lunged for it. As they did, I took a duffel bag from the luggage pile and tossed it over the side. The handles on the Longchamp tote were plainly visible now, and the corners of the box inside could be viewed through the fabric. I grabbed that bag and held on tight.

"Ron!" squawked Judy. "Stop her!"

Ron grabbed me by the arm, but I squirmed out of his grasp and hurled the tote out of the basket. It landed right on the edge of the mesa. Now both Ron and Judy gripped my arms, trying to bring me down to the floor, while the pilot worked the jets furiously to raise the balloon. I wrenched free of their grasp once again and leaped to the other end of the basket, where I flung one leg over the side. And jumped.

I hit the ground, hard, just barely making it to the top of the mesa. My hands scrabbled at dirt and rocks to keep from going over the side. I was a few yards away from the first duffel bag I'd thrown out of the basket. I ran to it and tore it open. Inside were plastic bags filled with jewelry and old coins. No wonder it had been so heavy! I scanned the top of the mesa for the Longchamp bag, and spotted it about ten feet away, lying on its side in the shadow of a boulder. I ran to it and unzipped it. I forced the square box out. I tore off the lid.

Inside was the urn, its seahorse handles and acorn lid intact. And though I'm sure their mouths had always curled up at the ends, I swear the seahorses seemed to be smiling. I looked up at the brilliant blue sky, dotted with balloons, including the one with the Clarksons that the wind was now pushing away. I put the urn back in the bag, sat on the edge of the mesa, and slid down the slope. Already I could hear sirens wailing in the distance, the most welcome sound to my ears.

48

We spent another week recovering at the cave hotel, as the questions at the police station were suddenly more complicated. Mom sucked it up and called Dad, and he helped get Sage a good lawyer through the embassy in Turkey. It looked like potential charges against her for her involvement with the smuggling ring would be dropped, and she'd be sent back to Oregon, not to prison. After all, Sage had convinced the Voyager Balloons security staff to call Inspector Lale. She'd done so in time for the police to chase the Clarksons' balloon and intercept it when it finally ran out of fuel. She'd cooperated fully with the police investigation. And we'd both worked to bring down the masterminds behind Turkey's biggest antiquities smuggling ring.

No surprise, I was in the news again, thanks to the video that a balloon passenger had recorded of my scuffle with the Clarksons and my leap out of the basket onto the mesa. The video was shared everywhere. I even got emails from some of my former friends, wanting to know all the details. I didn't write back right away. It was nice to have the attention again, but I'd have to take a little time to sort out whom I actually wanted in my life. And I realized I'd come full circle, from the Athleta incident to something that people said was "heroic." I had to admit it felt pretty good, even though I hadn't set out to be heroic. My uncle had done most of the work before me. I'd just finished the job.

And this time, I was in the news in Turkish! It was kind of funny to see my face on TV and in newspapers alongside headlines I couldn't read. Mom didn't let me do interviews, but I was glad that the story got out as a counterweight to the old stuff I'd done. In Cappadocia, and back in Istanbul a week later, people looked at me in the street, recognizing me from the news. With my unmistakable white blotches on my face and arms, I'm sure it wasn't hard to pick me out of a crowd. I didn't try to hide myself, either.

We were all relieved that the Clarksons were out of the picture for good. Ron and Judy were being detained in a Turkish prison, pending numerous charges. As far as I know, they're still there now, and their art gallery in Carmel and a shadowy online art business they ran were completely shut down. Their various homes were raided, too, and more suspicious objects from their international shopping sprees were discovered and returned to their countries of origin.

As for the seahorse urn that had caused all this trouble? It was reunited with the other Karun Treasure objects, in a museum. There it would be seen and marveled at by visitors for years to come. Maybe not as many as would see it at the Met, but still, it would be seen, in broad daylight, and not in the shadowy world of black-market transactions. Already, journalists and scholars from all over the world were descending on Turkey to see it for themselves, and to learn about its spotted history.

Everything looked brighter now, except for the fact that Sage and I wouldn't see each other for a long time.

"I wish I could hang out in Istanbul with you just for fun," Sage said, as we sat out on the top of the cave hotel beneath the stars, on our last night there together.

"You don't have to stay there, you know. Back in Oregon, I mean," I said. "You're the real passionate nomad. You can go anywhere."

"I'm broke," she reminded me. "I have to go live with my uncle again, like I did when I was finishing high school. I'll probably have to get some job in a 'shoppe.'"

"So do that. It's not so bad. Work, save money, and then travel again," I said. "It's what you're good at. Oregon? That's just a rest stop. You have places to go."

She gazed up at the stars. "You're right," she said. "Hey, maybe when you're out of high school, I'll have money saved up and we can go somewhere again, be traveling companions!"

"I'd like that." I smiled. "Let's totally do that. Remember, the beckoning counts."

She smiled back. "Not the clicking latch behind you."

◇◇◇◇◇

The evening Mom and I got back to the Mavi Konak Hotel, after a week of interrogation in Cappadocia, Aunt Jackie greeted us with huge hugs. Her bump—the home of my unborn cousin— was slightly more visible now, and the gray shadows under her eyes were gone. "You look better," I said.

"You do," Mom agreed. "Radiant!"

"I'm off bed rest," she said. "For now. I still have to take it easy, but I can walk around more. My last blood tests came out great. My hormones are in balance. Things look good." She paused for a moment, then said, "I started cleaning out Berk's office today. Now that the detectives are gone and have taken what papers and files they want. And you know what? It felt good. I've only made a dent, but I think I can keep going. I don't feel him in there anymore. He's with me, but not in there. It's just a room now. And it'll make a great nursery when it's painted and furnished. Thanks to Zan." She grinned at me.

"Thanks to all of us," I corrected. "I'm glad the reward money will pay for the renovations and let you keep the hotel in business." Reward money from Interpol had been paid to me for the information leading to Lazar's arrest. I'd given most of it to Aunt Jackie. But I'd given some to Sage, too, since I couldn't have done all this without her, and I knew she was worried about money. Finances were something I'd never had to worry about too much, and now I realized how lucky I was.

Mom slung her arm around Aunt Jackie's shoulders. "I'm proud of you," she said. "It's hard letting stuff go. I know. But it does get easier. I could help decorate. . . ."

"Please do," said Aunt Jackie. "I'd love your opinion on the paint samples. And you can remodel the Harem Suite, if you like. That will be set aside for you and Zan any time you come visit."

Mustafa came up and greeted us warmly, kissing us on both cheeks. "I am glad you are back safe and sound," he said to me. "You gave us all a big fright."

All. I looked around. "Is Nazif working today?" I asked, trying to sound casual.

"Not today," said Mustafa. "He is beginning an art class." He shrugged, with a helpless gesture. "Cartooning."

"Really? That's awesome!" I exclaimed, even though something inside me sank. I wanted to see him so badly. Not only see him, but touch him, kiss him. Was it possible? Wasn't that about where we'd left off in our story, before I'd been poisoned and kidnapped?

"It's an animation workshop, Mustafa," Aunt Jackie corrected. "Computer animation."

"Yes." Mustafa smiled wryly. "Computer animation," he repeated, almost dutifully.

"Mustafa doesn't like to admit it, but he had a change of heart after seeing Nazif's show at the party," Aunt Jackie said, winking at me. "The downside, of course, is we're missing a bellboy two days a week. But this hotel has made it through a lot of changes. We'll soldier on without him. By the way," she added when the front-desk phone rang and Mustafa went to answer it, "he was asking about you."

"Mustafa?"

"Nazif, silly. Every single day. Demanding updates and wondering how you were holding up."

I nodded, emotions swelling inside me. We'd emailed each other a few times while I was in Cappadocia, but with only one terminal in the cave hotel, and all the time I had to spend talking to police and lawyers, our exchanges had been brief.

"I'll let him know you're back," she said with a knowing smile.

Orhan, whom Aunt Jackie had hired as a full-time cook, came out of the kitchen with heaping plates of food. After dinner with Mom, Aunt Jackie, and Orhan, I went to my room and unpacked. In my suitcase, my hand brushed the fancy journal my dad had given me.

Suddenly, for some reason, it called out to me. I grabbed the other gift from Dad, the astronaut pen, and ran up to the rooftop.

◇◇◇◇◇

The roof was full of construction equipment and lumber. The temporary fence from the party was down, and the new, sturdier fence would be put up soon. But even though the roof was full of fence supplies, it still felt like an oasis of peace to me. I settled myself on the white couch, between the geranium pots, and watched the sun set over the Sea of Marmara, turning the water gold. Then I turned to face the Blue Mosque, whose minarets lit up the indigo sky. I switched on a string of paper lanterns hanging over the trellis, left over from the party, and opened the journal to page one. All those empty pages! I could easily fill them with the story of everything that had happened to me. I could record my adventures, like

Freya Stark had. And like my dad had asked me to do. I could tell my side of the story, in my own way. When I was ready, that's what I would do.

But we had two weeks left in Istanbul. There was a lot more to explore here, and maybe there were some happier stories to fill up some of these pages.

And after Istanbul? I had more mountains to climb: Hard conversations with my dad. Getting to know Victoria Windham. Finding new friends, maybe at Burlington Boulders, maybe at school. I could try to put the past behind me and start a new chapter. I'd been so mad at my ex-friends for being fakes, but maybe I'd been a little fake myself, always covering myself up and never revealing who I really was.

The past few months I'd spent so much time building monuments to my own disappointment. But I didn't have to do that anymore. My parents' story was not my own. I could make different choices. I could get busy leading my own life instead of just reacting to theirs. Civilizations end, but new ones rise up in their place. Now I had a foundation to build upon. I trusted my own strength.

I set the tip of my pen on the cream paper of the journal's first page and started writing down my thoughts. Soon they became a manifesto. In the dwindling light, I pressed down hard on the pen, etching all my promises to myself, carving them into the paper. My own mottos, for my own new era. I filled four pages without once looking up, not even when my hand began to ache.

Until a light winked on, over on Nazif's rooftop.

I set down my pen and turned my head.

Nazif's white screen was strung up in the grape arbor again, light shining behind it. Suddenly the glorious bird shadow soared across the screen. Then it circled back and cocked its head, almost quizzically. It seemed to be looking at me.

The boy shadow puppet came out to join it. It ran from side to side as if looking for something, while the bird tried to get the boy's attention. The bird poked the boy with its beak, and gestured toward me with its unfurling wing, as if letting the boy know that I was there watching.

The boy shadow jumped for joy. He spun around, beckoning with his arm. *Come.*

I stood up, and the puppets vanished. My heart sank. I didn't want the show to end. It didn't feel like the end of the story.

Then Nazif stepped out from behind the screen.

I smiled and waved.

He grinned and waved back. Then he put the puppets down and beckoned to me, with his own hand. "Zan! Come over!" he called out.

I ran and took a flying leap across the short distance between our roofs.

Author's Note

In *Blue Voyage,* Zan is obsessed with authenticity. Not only is she trying to figure out whether the people in her life are authentic, she's also trying to determine whether the artifacts she encounters are the real deal.

As a fiction writer interested in historical accuracy, I had to grapple with similar issues. I started with the facts. The following situations you read about in *Blue Voyage* are true.

Fact: Antiquities trafficking in Turkey happens. Unscrupulous buyers and sellers seek opportunities to profit from the shards of past civilizations. In fact, Turkey is often called a "plunderer's paradise" because of its layers of ancient civilizations.

Fact: Forgeries can be created and sold to unsuspecting buyers on the black market; fake artifacts can be used to conceal real artifacts in transit; fake provenances (histories) can be written to accompany real antiquities in order to get them past customs officials.

Fact: Turkey's archaeological museums are bursting with artifacts confiscated from smugglers, and the number of confiscated artifacts grows every year. In 2011, 68,000 artifacts were seized from smuggling rings. According to the law, the nearest museum must take responsibility for items confiscated by police. These museums then face the burden of storing, cataloguing, or displaying the items. Security problems at museums mean these artifacts continue to be vulnerable to theft, and so the cycle of looting and loss continues.

Fact: Many antiquities were looted long ago and smuggled

to Western countries, where they were absorbed into museums or private collections. Turkey is currently involved in a massive effort to repatriate its looted antiquities and restore its cultural heritage.

Fact: The Karun Treasure (also known as the Lydian Hoard) actually exists, and many do believe it is cursed. The three hundred and sixty-three artifacts that make up the bulk of the hoard were discovered in New York's Metropolitan Museum of Art. They are currently housed in the Uşak Museum of Archaeology. A Turkish journalist named Özgen Acar tracked down the illegally purchased Karun Treasure items in the basement of the Met, and helped arrange for their return to Turkey in 1993. A couple of the returned items, however—including the golden seahorse brooch—were subsequently stolen from the Uşak Museum and replaced with fakes. The museum director was arrested and found guilty of selling the golden brooch and other artifacts to pay off gambling debts. He blamed his actions on the curse of the Karun Treasure. At the time of this writing, the real items have been discovered in Germany, but their return to Turkey has yet to be arranged. (You can read more about this fascinating real-life detective story in a book called *Loot* by Sharon Waxman.)

Because some of the artifacts I wanted to write about are still under investigation, involved in ongoing legal action, or being relocated soon, I decided to take some fictional liberty. I was intrigued by some accounts I read suggesting some Karun Treasure items had surfaced in other parts of the world and more might still be at large. So I invented an artifact for Zan to encounter. The seahorse-handled urn does not actually exist, but its design is closely based on the seahorse brooch—also known as "the gold hippocampus." That 2,500-year-old solid-gold brooch features a mythical winged horse with the tail of a fish and dangling golden acorns. I also found inspiration in another real-life Karun Treasure item: a jug with an elaborately carved handle featuring a person and two rams. I found room for invention in the fact that we may never know how many of the original Karun Treasure items were stolen and smuggled out of the country, or where they ultimately ended up. Ancient artifacts in transit often appear and disappear on the black market, so I imagined a missing Karun Treasure urn could be one of them.

In inventing an urn for this story, I suppose I created my own kind of fake. But the issues behind the urn are unfortunately all too real. Should ancient artifacts and art objects always be kept in their country of origin? Is it better for ancient objects to be seen by many people, even if that means they are not displayed where they were found? Who has the right to own history? And when pieces of that history get stolen, what price do all of us pay?

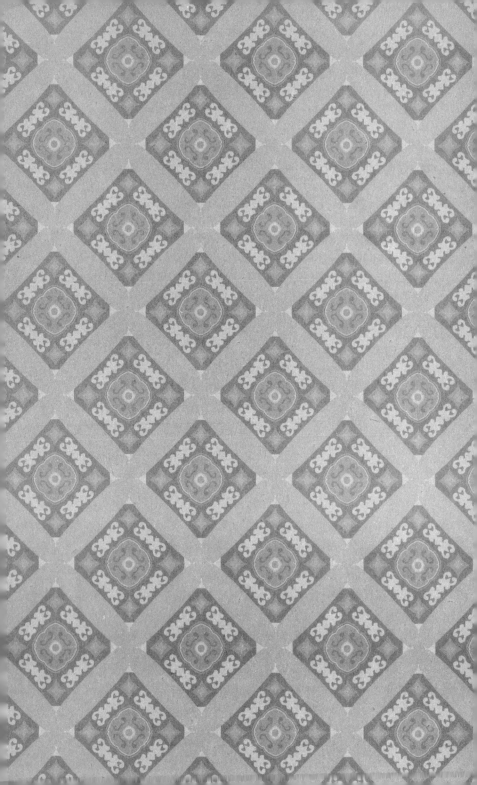

Acknowledgments

I am deeply grateful to the following people who helped me at various stages of writing and publishing *Blue Voyage*:

I would like to thank my agent, Kirby Kim, for always being so supportive of my work and for understanding the kinds of stories I love to tell.

Enormous thanks to my editor at Viking, Leila Sales. We've now journeyed through three books together, and with each project I find myself more in awe of her attention to detail, her impeccable logic, her creative thinking, and her patience. Not to mention her good humor and unwavering confidence, even as I tore my hair out over thorny plot points. I couldn't ask for a better companion to help me navigate these travel mysteries, especially *Blue Voyage*.

I would like to thank Ken Wright, Tara Shanahan, and the whole crew at Viking Children's/Penguin Young Readers Group. Thank you for your enthusiasm and support. I feel very grateful to have the world's best production editor, Janet Pascal. Janet followed my research tracks through everything from Turkish expressions to musical instruments to antiquities trafficking, and I deeply appreciate the time she has spent in checking for accuracy, not to mention pointing out my blind spots. Thanks to Diana Joao for her meticulous attention to every sentence, word, and punctuation mark. And many thanks to Kate Renner for another exciting cover design, an invitation to adventure!

I have deep gratitude for my longstanding writing group: Erin Cashman, Eileen Donovan Kranz, Patrick Gabridge,

Vincent Gregory, Ted Rooney, Deborah Vlock, Rob Vlock, and Julie Wu. These people read huge chunks of this book, sometimes on short notice, and always gave me their honest appraisal. Thank you also to Kerri Majors and Elisa Ludwig, who helped me to get early versions of this book into some kind of recognizable shape. Thanks to Catey Miller, who read a later stage draft and offered her keen insights.

An enormous thank-you goes to my dear friend and critique partner Erin Cashman. (Okay, Erin, this is the whole entire paragraph I promised you!) I have lost track of how many manuscript versions, chapters, and scenes Erin has read, often on short notice. While juggling parenthood demands, other work demands, and the writing of this book, I had days when I worried I could not go on in the story. Knowing that Erin was expecting pages, and getting her words of encouragement and her laser-sharp critiques, often kept me going. I'm so grateful for the gift of her precious time and her sharp critiquing skills.

A number of other people gave of their time and expertise to help me. Among them, I must thank Ilgin Korugan for reading the manuscript to check the accuracy of Turkish language and culture; any mistakes are entirely my own. I thank friends Can Erbil and Susannah Madan-Erbil for additional help with Turkish culture questions. My adventurous brother-in-law, Jay Underwood, assisted with my rock climbing scenes, helping me to understand the lexicon and the mindset of a climber. I also must credit Jay with introducing me to this fascinating sport, which in turn inspired much of Zan's character. Thanks to Shannan at Airial Balloon Company in Snohomish, Washington, for fielding random questions about hot-air balloons (and for not reporting me to authorities when I asked how I might bring one down).

They say that sometimes our characters lead us into unexpected places. For me, it was the dermatologist's office. I am grateful to Dr. Fern Wirth for answering questions about vitiligo and teenagers—and for saving my life by catching an early-stage melanoma. I am grateful for the happy outcome, and would urge everyone to check their moles, or have them looked at professionally.

Finally, thanks to my ever-supportive parents and my entire extended family. Heartfelt thanks to my husband, Jim, and my son, Gabriel, who have managed to be so patient with me when I journey into books. Thank you for your enduring love and support, and for being my peaceful harbor.